THE IGNORANCE
OF BLOOD

Books by Robert Wilson

The Hidden Assassins
The Silent and the Damned
The Blind Man of Seville
The Company of Strangers
A Small Death in Lisbon
A Darkening Stain
Blood Is Dirt
The Big Killing
Instruments of Darkness
The Ignorance of Blood

The
IGNORANCE
of BLOOD

Robert Wilson

MARINER BOOKS
HOUGHTON MIFFLIN HARCOURT
Boston   New York

First Mariner Books edition 2010

www.hmhbooks.com

First published in 2009 by HarperCollins Publishers

Library of Congress Cataloging-in-Publication Data
Wilson, Robert, date.
The ignorance of blood / Robert Wilson.
p. cm.
ISBN 978-0-15-101245-9
1. Falcon, Javier (Fictitious character) — Fiction. 2. Detectives —
Spain — Seville — Fiction. 3. Mafia — Russia (Federation) — Fiction.
4. Seville (Spain) — Fiction. I. Title.
PR6073.I474I35 2009
823'.914 — dc22   2009003669

ISBN 978-0-547-33587-2 (pbk.)

Printed in the United States of America

DOM 10 9 8 7 6 5 4 3 2 1

For Jane

Acknowledgments

This is the last book in the Javier Falcón Seville quartet and I would like to take the opportunity to thank the people of Seville for being so understanding at having all this fictional mayhem created in the streets of their beautiful and, comparatively, tranquil city.

My friends in Seville, Mick Lawson and José Manuel Blanco, have, as always, been great sources of information, tremendous support and brilliant hosts. They have now been relieved of duty for the former, but I hope not the latter. As for the middle, writers always need support.

Thanks to Nick Ricketts for giving me much needed remunerative work when I was a struggling writer and his advice on the marine section of this story.

My thanks to the brilliant Mr Ravi Pillai and his assistant, Dr Hassan Katash, whose surgical skills have kept the Robert Wilson show on the road. Also thanks to my friend and fellow crime writer, Paul Johnston, for all his support.

Finally, it seems ridiculous to say thank you to Jane because my gratitude is now so long, wide and profound as to make those two little words seem paltry. She has been a tower of strength in my hours of need, a pillar of wisdom when my brain has failed, and a beacon of light to give me hope for the future. What more could a writer ask for? Just that I wish she'd write the books as well.

Love is the master key that opens
the gates of happiness, of hatred,
of jealousy, and, most easily of
all, the gate of fear.

—Oliver Wendell Holmes

The ice-cold vodka slipped down Vasili Lukyanov's throat as the traffic thundered past the lay-by on the new motorway from Algeciras to Jerez de la Frontera. The heat had started the sweat beading in his dark hair as he stood by the open boot of the Range Rover Sport. He was waiting for it to get dark, didn't want to do this last stretch into Seville in daylight. He drank, smoked, ate, and thought about his last night with Rita, the whole escapade making him silently, but grossly, oral. My God, she knew how to do it to him. He felt bad leaving her behind. He'd trained her to perfection.

The blood thumped hard in his throat as he looked down on the solid block of Samsonite luggage, jammed up against the open cool box with its chilled champagne and bottles of vodka set in blocks of ice. He tore another chunk off his bocadillo, enjoying the rip of the ham between his teeth, chugged the icy vodka. Another carnal scene from his last night with Rita came to him. Her violoncello waist, the caramel of her skin as soft as toffee in his kneading fingers. A chunk of the bread roll suddenly clogged his throat. He gasped, his eyes came out on stalks. He struggled and finally

1

coughed. A clod of masticated bread and ham shot out over the Range Rover's roof. Steady, he thought. Don't want to choke now. Die in a lay-by with the trucks rumbling past and your future all before you.

Pepe Navajas had just finished loading the steel rods, the twenty bags of cement, and the wooden planking for making reinforced concrete pillars, which he'd stacked alongside some plumbing equipment, sanitaryware, floor and wall tiles. He was going to build an extension for his daughter and son-in-law who'd just taken delivery of twins and needed more space in their small house in Sanlúcar de Barrameda. They also had no money. So Pepe was buying everything on the cheap and, because his son-in-law was useless, he was doing the work for them over the weekends.

Pepe parked the heavily laden truck outside a restaurant in Dos Hermanas, a few kilometres before the start of the motorway heading south to Jerez de la Frontera. He'd had a beer or two with the guys from the building supplies depot. Now he was going to have an early dinner and wait for dusk. He kidded himself that the Guardia Civil didn't notice so much between dusk and night and only stopped cars later on, when people were more likely to be drunk.

Vasili turned on his mobile phone for the first time that day at just after 11 p.m. He had resisted the temptation until he was through the tollgate on the last stretch of motorway to Seville because he knew what was coming. It had been a while since he'd spent a whole day on his own and he was bursting to talk. The first call came through in a matter of seconds and, as expected, it was from Alexei, his old fellow at arms.

'Are you alone, Vasya?' asked Alexei.

'Yes,' said Vasili, his lips thick and mouth slow from the vodka.

'I don't want you to get upset,' said Alexei, 'make a mistake while you're driving.'

'Have you called to upset me?' asked Vasili.

'Try this,' said Alexei. 'Leonid's back from Moscow.'

Silence.

'Did you hear that, Vasya? I'm not breaking up, am I? Leonid Revnik is in Marbella.'

'He wasn't supposed to be back until next week.'

'He came back early.'

Vasili opened the window a crack and sniffed the warm night air. It was pitch black, flat fields on either side. Only tail lights in the distance. Nothing coming the other way.

'What did Leonid have to say?' he asked.

'He wanted to know where you were. I told him you'd be at the club, but they'd just come from there,' said Alexei. 'They'd found your office locked and Kostya on the floor unconscious.'

'Are *you* on your own at the moment, Alyosha?' asked Vasili, suspicious.

'Leonid already knows you've crossed over to Yuri Donstov.'

'So what is this? A warning?'

'It's me finding out that Leonid's not lying,' said Alexei.

Silence.

'Something's gone missing from your office,' said Alexei. 'He told me that, too.'

Vasili closed the window. Sighed.

'I'm sorry, Alyosha.'

'Rita took a heavy beating for you. I haven't seen her, but Leonid had that animal with him – you know, the one that even the Moldovan girls won't go with.'

Vasili hit the steering wheel five times. The horn blared into the night.

'Steady, Vasya.'

'I'm sorry, Alyosha,' said Vasili. 'I'm fucking sorry. What more can I say?'

'Well, that's something.'

'It wasn't supposed to happen like this. Leonid wasn't supposed to be back until next week. I was going to talk to Yuri, get permission to bring you in. You were going to be part of it. You know that. I just had to . . .'

'That's just the point, Vasya: I *didn't* know that.'

'I couldn't tell you. You're too close, Alyosha,' said Vasili. 'Yuri made an offer that Leonid wouldn't have given me in a million years.'

'But without *me*. You didn't want *me* protecting your back and . . . what the fuck does it matter anyway?' said Alexei, trailing off. 'What was that, Vasya?'

'Nothing.'

'I heard it. You're crying.'

Silence.

'Well, thank fuck for that,' said Alexei. 'At least you're fucking sad, Vasya.'

Pepe was on the road, a little later than planned, with a few more drinks inside him than he'd intended, all because of the football: Sevilla FC winning a UEFA cup game in Athens. He'd got caught up in the post-match euphoria, eaten dinner with wine and brandy. Now he had the music on full blast and was singing along with his favourite flamenco singer, El Camarón de la Isla. What a voice. It was making him tearful.

Perhaps he was driving a little too quickly, but there wasn't much traffic and the lanes of the motorway seemed as wide and well lit as an airport runway. The music drowned out the rattling of the steel rods. He was happy, bouncing up and down on his springy seat, looking forward to seeing his daughter and the babies. His cheeks were wet with emotion.

And it was at that moment, at the very peak of his happiness, that the tyre beneath him blew. It was a noise loud enough to penetrate the cab. A muffled thump like distant

4

heavy ordnance, followed by the crack and rip of the tyre peeling off the rim and slapping around the wheel arch. His stomach sank with the cab as it listed to the left. In the break in the music he heard the pieces of tyre smacking down the side of the truck, metal screeching on the tarmac. His head-lights, which had been locked steady between the lanes, slewed across the straight white flashes, and although everything was slowing down so that no detail escaped his wide-open eyes, some deep instinct was telling him that he was going danger-ously fast, in a cab with a very heavy load behind it.

Fear sliced through his innards but the alcohol in his veins only gave him the presence of mind to grip the steering wheel, which had powers of its own. El Camarón started up again just before Pepe's truck smashed into the barrier of the central reservation. Only with that abrupt halt did he realize the full extent of his forward momentum as he was catapulted through windscreen glass into the warm night air. Over the agonized voice of El Camarón he heard a noise that was the last thing his befuddled brain managed to compute. Steel rods, now loose, taking off like a battery of launched spears into a tunnel of approaching light.

And the reason Vasili was crying was that he'd just under-gone that extraordinary human facility for compressing a life into a compact emotional experience. Seven times in six years of service in Afghanistan Alexei had protected his back. And now, having survived all those years fighting the Pashtoons, Alexei was going to get shot in the back of the head by one of his own in a forest on the Costa del Sol, for no other reason than that he was Vasili Lukyanov's best fucking friend.

'Tell Leonid –' he started, and stopped when he sensed something flashing towards him, a strange agitation in the air. 'What the fuck . . .?'

The steel rods, their tail ends quivering with expectation, entered the cone of light, as if attracted to him at its apex.

They hit with explosive force.

Tyres smeared their rubber on to the dark road, thumped against an unseen obstruction and the Range Rover took off into the abysmal black of the fields beyond. There was a momentary silence.

'Vasya?'

1

Falcón's house, Calle Bailén, Seville – Friday, 15th September 2006,
03.00 hrs

The phone trembled under the warm breath of the brutal night.

'*Diga,*' said Falcón, who was sitting up in bed with a file from one of the hundreds concerning the 6th June Seville bombing resting on his knees.

'You're awake, Javier,' said his boss, Comisario Elvira.

'I do my best thinking at this time in the morning,' said Falcón.

'I thought most people our age just worried about debt and death.'

'I have no debts . . . not financial ones anyway.'

'Somebody has just woken me up to talk about death . . . about *a* death,' said Elvira.

'And why were you called, rather than me?'

'At some time before eleven thirty-five, which was when it was reported, there was a car accident at kilometre thirty-eight on the northbound motorway from Jerez to Seville. In fact, on both sides of the motorway, but the deaths have occurred on the northbound side. I'm told it's very nasty and I need you to go out there.'

'Something that the Guardia Civil can't handle?' said Falcón, glancing at his clock. 'They've taken their time.'

'It's complicated. They originally thought there was just one vehicle, a truck, which had crashed into the central reservation barriers and shed its load. It took them a while to realize there was another vehicle, beyond some pine trees down a bank on the other side of the motorway.'

'Still no reason to involve the Homicide squad.'

'The driver of the northbound vehicle has been identified as Vasili Lukyanov, a Russian national. When they finally got round to looking in the boot of his car they discovered a suitcase had split open and there was a lot of money . . . I mean a hell of a lot of money. I understand we're talking about millions of euros, Javier. So, I want a full forensic examination of the vehicle and, although it's clearly an accident, I want you to investigate it as if it was a murder. There could be implications for other investigations going on around the country. And, most important, I want that money fully accounted for and made safe. I'll get a security van sent up there as soon as I can raise someone.'

'I assume we're talking about a Russian mafia gang member,' said Falcón.

'We are. I've already spoken to the Organized Crime Intelligence Centre. They've confirmed it. Area of expertise – prostitution. Area of operation – Costa del Sol. And I've contacted Inspector Jefe Casado – you remember him? The guy from the GRECO, the Organized Crime Response Squad in the Costa del Sol.'

'The one who gave us a presentation back in July about setting up a GRECO in Seville to handle the mafia activity here,' said Falcón. 'And nothing's happened.'

'There's been a delay.'

'Why can't he handle this?'

'That's the delay, he's in Marbella running about twenty

investigations down there,' said Elvira. 'And anyway, he hasn't started work on the situation in Seville yet.'

'He'll know more than we do *and* he'll have the intelligence on Lukyanov's Costa del Sol activity.'

'Exactly, which is why he's sending us one of his own men, Vicente Cortés, who'll bring someone from the Organized Crime Intelligence Centre with him.'

'Well, I'm awake, so I might as well go,' said Falcón, and hung up.

Shaving was the usual morning trial, facing the full prosecution of his stubbled face. Same old story with a few more lines. The mind engraving its doubts and fears. They'd all told him that the ultimate solution to the Seville bombing was not expected of him. He knew it himself. He'd looked at the other inspector jefes who did their ugly work in the world of violence and left it in the office. But that was not for him, not this time. He ran a hand over his short-cropped hair. The life-changing events of the last five years had turned the salt and pepper to steel grey and he didn't dye it, unlike the other inspector jefes. The light and the remnants of his summer tan brought out the amber in his brown eyes. He grimaced as the razor made lanes through the foam.

Dressed in a navy blue polo shirt and chinos, he left the bedroom, rested his hands on the railing around the gallery and leaned out. No visible stars. He looked down on to the central patio of the massive eighteenth-century house he'd inherited from his disgraced father, the artist, Francisco Falcón. The pillars and arches were roughly sketched in by a solitary light whose sulphurous glow lit the bronze boy tiptoeing across the fountain and brought up the far recesses behind the pillars of the colonnade, where a plant, dried to a rustling husk, still lurked in a corner. He must throw that out, he thought for the hundredth time. He'd asked his housekeeper, Encarnación, to get it done months ago, but

9

she had her strange attachments: her mobile Virgins, her Stations of the Cross, that wretched plant.

Toast with olive oil. A small, strong coffee. He got into his car with the caffeine sharpening his reactions. He drove through the stifling, uneasy city, which still seemed to be panting from the uproar of the day, its tarmac ruptured into thick biscuit, cobbles piled on pavements, roads ploughed up to reveal vital inner workings, machinery poised to strike. Every street, it seemed, was fenced off and taped, bollarded to kingdom come. The air reeked of Roman dust uncaked from subterranean ruins. How could anybody settle down in this tumult of reconstruction? But, of course, everything had its purpose. This was nothing to do with the bombing of a few months ago but the mayoral elections which were to take place in early 2007. So the population had to feel the torment of the incumbent's beneficence.

It was fast work getting out of the city at this time in the morning, still dark, four hours to go before sunrise. He was across the river and out on the ring road in minutes, flying down the motorway towards Jerez de la Frontera inside a quarter of an hour. It wasn't long before he saw the lights: the surgical halogen, the queasy blue, the unnerving red, the slow, revolving, sickly yellow. He pulled up on the hard shoulder behind a huge tow truck. Disembodied luminous jackets floated in the dark. There was hardly any traffic. He crossed the motorway and entered the noise of the generator powering the lights that brutally illuminated the scene. There were three Nissan 4x4s in the white and green of the Guardia Civil, two motorbikes, a red fire engine, a Day-Glo green ambulance, another smaller tow truck, halogen lighting up on stalks, wiring all around, a spray of glass diamonds from the crashed truck's windscreen swept on to the hard shoulder.

The firemen had their cutting tools ready, but were waiting for the law men to show. As Falcón arrived more cars pulled up on the other side. He introduced himself, as did the duty judge, the forensics, Jorge and Felipe, and the médico forense. The Guardia Civil talked them through the accident.

'The Range Rover was driving from Jerez to Seville in the fast lane at an estimated speed of 140 kilometres per hour. The truck was travelling from Seville to Jerez in the near-side lane when the front left tyre burst. The truck swerved across to the fast lane and hit the barriers of the central reservation at approximately 110 kilometres per hour. The impact sent the driver through the windscreen, dislodged a load of steel rods, wooden planking and metal tubing, which shot over the cab roof and flew into the fast lane of the oncoming traffic. The driver of the truck cleared the central reservation and the fast lane and came to rest by the crash barrier on the hard shoulder. The Range Rover was hit by two steel rods thirty metres beyond where the truck had hit the barriers. The first went through the windscreen, speared the driver through the chest and continued through the front seat, the rear seat and the floor of the vehicle, missing the fuel tank by millimetres. The second rod went through the rear window and into the boot. This rod seems to have ripped open the suitcase, exposing the money. The driver of the Range Rover died on impact, lost control of the vehicle, which must have hit some of the truck's shed load, giving the car sufficient lift so that it cleared the crash barriers, smashed through the pine trees and disappeared down the bank, into the fields.

'If that steel rod hit him with a combined velocity of 250 kilometres per hour,' said the médico forense, 'I'd be surprised if there was anything left of him.'

'What *is* left is not a pretty sight,' said the Guardia Civil.

'I'll take a look,' said the médico forense, 'then you can start cutting him out of there.'

Felipe and Jorge completed their initial inspection of the

scene and took their photographs. They joined Falcón while the médico forense finished his work.

'What the fuck are *we* doing here?' asked Felipe, yawning wider than a dog. 'It's not murder.'

'He's Russian mafia and there's a lot of money here,' said Falcón. 'Any evidence we gather might be usable in a future conviction. Fingerprints on the money and suitcase, mobile phone, address book; there might be a laptop in there . . .'

'There's a briefcase on the back seat, which wasn't touched by the steel rods,' said the Guardia Civil. 'And there's a cool box in the boot. We haven't opened either of them.'

'This is why we need an Organized Crime Response Squad in Seville,' said Jorge.

'We're running this for the moment. They're sending someone up from the Costa del Sol GRECO and an intelligence guy from CICO,' said Falcón. 'Let's take a look at this money. Elvira called me on the way to say he's got Prosegur to send a van out.'

The Guardia Civil opened the boot. There was suddenly a crowd.

'*Joder,*' said one of the motorbike cops.

The visible money was in used notes and bound in packs of €100- and €50-denomination notes. Some of the packs had burst open on impact from the steel rod, but there was no loose money outside the vehicle.

'Let's have some room around here,' said Falcón. 'Glove up. Only the forensics and I will touch this money. Jorge, bring a couple of bin liners over, one for each denomination.'

They counted out the packs of money, avid eyes looking on. At the bottom of the suitcase were several layers of €200-denomination notes and below them two layers of €500 notes. Jorge went to get two more bin liners. Falcón made his calculations.

'Not counting this loose money, we're looking at seven million, six hundred and fifty thousand euros.'

'That's got to be drug money,' said the Guardia Civil.

'More likely people-trafficking and prostitution,' said Falcón, who was calling Comisario Elvira.

As he gave his report the Prosegur van pulled up in front of the last Nissan 4x4. Two helmeted guys lifted a metal trunk out of the back. Falcón hung up. Felipe had taped up the packs of money into tight black blocks and was marking up the bin liners with white stick-on labels. They put the four blocks into the trunk, which was locked with two keys, one given to Falcón, who signed for it.

The money moved off. The scene relaxed.

Falcón lifted out the cool box, opened it. Krug champagne and melting blocks of ice around bottles of Stolichnaya.

'I suppose eight million euros would merit a bit of a celebration,' said the Guardia Civil. 'We could have all retired on that lot.'

While one of the fire brigade teams winched the steel rods out of the car, the other reached through the window, cut away the air bag and started on the door frames with an oxyacetylene torch. Vasili Lukyanov's body was taken out in pieces and laid on an opened body bag on a stretcher. His arms, shoulders and head were intact, as were his legs, hips and lower torso. The rest had vaporized. His face was deeply furrowed with red streaks where the windscreen glass had shredded the skin. His left eye had exploded, part of his scalp was missing and his right ear was a mangled flap of gristle. He grinned horribly with lips partially torn away and some teeth ripped from their gums. His lap was stained dark with his blood. His shoes were brand new, the soles hardly scuffed.

A young fireman vomited into the oleanders by the side of the road. The paramedics tucked Lukyanov into the body bag and zipped it up.

'Poor fucker,' said Felipe, bagging the suitcase. 'Eight million in the boot and you get speared by a flying steel rod.'

'You're more likely to win the lottery,' said Jorge, taking a look at the briefcase's combination lock, trying to open it, unsuccessfully, and then bagging it. 'Should have bought a ticket and stayed at home.'

'Here we go,' said Felipe, who'd just opened the glove compartment. 'One nine-millimetre Glock and a spare clip for our friendly Russian comrade.'

He sorted through the car papers and insurance documents, while Jorge worked through a selection of motorway receipts.

'Something to brighten up his day,' said Jorge, shaking a plastic sachet of white powder which had fallen out of the receipts.

'And something to dull someone else's day,' said Felipe, pulling out a cosh from under the seat. 'There's blood and hair still stuck to it.'

'He's got GPS.'

'Anyone got the keys?' asked Felipe, over his shoulder.

The Guardia Civil handed him the keys, they turned on the electrics. Felipe played with the GPS.

'He was coming from Estepona, heading for Calle Garlopa in Seville Este.'

'That narrows it down to a few thousand apartments,' said Falcón.

'At least it didn't say Town Hall, Plaza Nueva, Seville,' said Jorge.

Everybody laughed and went quiet, as if it might not be so far from the truth.

Another hour and they'd been through the rest of the car. They crossed over the motorway with the evidence bags, loaded them into the back of their van and drove off. Falcón oversaw the loading of the Range Rover on to the breakdown truck.

First light creaked open at the hinge of the world as he walked back up to where the truck had hit the barrier, whose galvanized metal ballooned. The truck had been pulled away and was now on the hard shoulder, front jacked up behind the tow truck. He called Elvira to tell him that the Prosegur van had left and to make sure someone was at the Jefatura to receive the money. The forensics still needed to go over it before it could be sent to the bank.

'What else?' asked Elvira.

'A locked briefcase, a handgun, a bloody cosh, Krug champagne, vodka and a few grams of coke,' said Falcón. 'A violent party animal was Vasili Lukyanov.'

'Animal is the word,' said Elvira. 'He was arrested back in June on suspicion of rape of a sixteen-year-old girl from Málaga.'

'And he got off?'

'The charges were dropped on him and another brute called Nikita Sokolov and, having seen the photos of the girl, it's nothing short of a miracle,' said Elvira. 'But then I called Málaga and it seems that the girl and her parents have moved into a brand-new, four-bedroomed house in a development outside Nerja and her father has just opened a restaurant in the town . . . which is where his daughter now works. This new world makes me feel old, Javier.'

'There are a lot of well-fed people out there who are still hungry,' said Falcón. 'You should have seen the reaction to all that money in the back of the Russian's car.'

'You got it all, though, didn't you?'

'Who knows if a few packs were lifted before I arrived?'

'I'll call you when Vicente Cortés gets here and we'll have a meeting in my office,' said Elvira. 'Maybe you should go home and get some sleep.'

They came for Alexei just before dawn and couldn't raise him. One of them had to scramble down the side of the small villa and get into the garden over a low wall. He broke the lock on the sliding window, let himself in and opened the front door for his friend, who took out his Stechkin APS handgun, which he'd hung on to since leaving the KGB back in the early 1990s.

They went upstairs. He was in the bedroom, wound up in a sheet on the floor with an empty bottle of whisky next to him, dead to the world. They kicked him awake. He came to, moaning.

They stuck him in the shower and turned on the water, cold. Alexei grunted as if they were still kicking him. The muscles trembled under his tattoos. They kept the water trained on him for a couple of minutes and let him out. He shaved with the two men in the mirror and took some aspirin, swilled down with tap water. They walked him into the bedroom and watched him while he got dressed in his Sunday best. The ex-KGB man sat on the bed with his Stechkin APS dangling between his knees.

They went downstairs and out into the heat. The sun was just up, the sea was blue, there was barely any movement, just birds. They got into the car and drove down the hill.

Ten minutes later they were in the club, sitting in Vasili Lukyanov's office, but with Leonid Revnik behind the desk smoking an H. Upmann Coronas Junior cigar. He had short grey hair, cut *en brosse* with a sharp widow's peak, big shoulders and chest under a very expensive white shirt from Jermyn Street.

'Did you speak to him last night?' asked Revnik.

'To Vasili? Yes, I got through eventually,' said Alexei.

'Where was he?'

'On the road to Seville. I don't know where.'

'What did he have to say?' asked Revnik.

'That Yuri Donstov had made him an offer that you wouldn't have given him in a million years.'

'He's right there,' said Revnik. 'What else?'

Alexei shrugged. Revnik glanced up. A hard fist clubbed

16

Alexei in the side of the head, knocked him and the chair over.

'What else?' said Revnik.

They hefted Alexei and the chair back to vertical. A lump was already up on the side of his face.

'"What the fuck,"' said Alexei. 'He had an accident.'

That had Revnik's attention.

'Tell me.'

'We were talking and he suddenly said: "What the fuck is this . . ." then BANG! and the sound of tyres screeching, a thump, a crash and then it all went dead.'

Revnik hit the desk.

'Why the fuck didn't you tell us that last night?'

'I was drunk. I passed out.'

'You know what that means?' said Revnik to no one in particular, but pointing across the room. 'It means that what was in there is now in the hands of the police.'

They looked at the empty safe.

'Take him away,' said Revnik.

They took him back out to the car, drove up into the hills. The smell of pine was very strong after the cool of the night. They walked him into the trees and the ex-KGB man finally got to use his Stechkin APS.

2

The sun had been up for twenty-five minutes over the flat fields of the fertile flood plain of the Guadalquivir river. It was close to 30°C when Falcón drove back into the city at 8.30 a.m. At home he lay on his bed fully clothed in the air-con and tried to get some sleep. It was hopeless. He drank another coffee before heading into the office.

The short drive took him down by the river, past the spearhead railings and gates to the Maestranza bullring, whose whitewashed façade, smooth and brilliant as the icing of a cake, had its porthole windows and dark red doors and shutters piped with ochre. The high phoenix palms near the Toro de Oro sagged against the already bleached sky and as he crossed the San Telmo bridge the slow water was almost green and had no autumnal sparkle.

The emptiness of the Plaza de Cuba and the shopping streets leading off it was a reminder that it was still a summer heat beating down on the bludgeoned city. Sevillanos had returned from their August holidays to find their new vitality sapped by suffocating apartments, drained by power cuts and the old city centre crammed with hot, unbreathable air.

18

The end-of-summer storms, which scrubbed the cobbles clean, hosed down the grateful trees, rinsed the uninspired atmosphere and brought colour back to the faded sky, had not arrived. With no respite since May, ladies' fans no longer opened with the customary snap and their wrists trembled with a fluttering palsy at the thought of another month of endless palpitations.

Nobody in the office at 10.15 a.m. The paperwork from the 6th June Seville bombing still stacked knee-high around his desk. The court case against the two remaining suspects was going to take months, possibly years, to construct and there was no guarantee of success. The wall chart pinned up opposite Falcón's desk with all its names and links said it all – there was a gap in what the media were calling the Catholic Conspiracy, or rather, not so much a gap as a dead end.

Every time he sat at his desk the same five facts presented themselves to him:

1) Although the two suspects they had in custody had been successfully linked to the two ringleaders of the plot – all four were right-wing and staunch Catholics, hence the name of the conspiracy – neither of them had **any** idea who'd planted the bomb, which on 6th June had destroyed an apartment building and a nearby pre-school in a residential area of Seville.

2) The ringleaders themselves, Lucrecio Arenas and César Benito, had been murdered before they could be arrested. The former had been shot just as he was about to dive into his swimming pool in Marbella and the latter had had his throat so brutally chopped with the blade of a hand that he'd choked to death in his hotel room in Madrid.

3) Over the last three months a plethora of agencies, at the behest of the board of directors, had gone through the

19

offices of the Banco Omni in Madrid, where Lucrecio Arenas had been the Chief Executive Officer. They'd interviewed all his old colleagues and business contacts, searched his properties and grilled his family, but had found nothing.

4) They'd also gone through the Horizonte Group's building in Barcelona where César Benito had been an architect and board director of the construction division. They'd searched his apartments, houses in the Costa del Sol and studio, and interviewed everybody he'd ever known and likewise found nothing.

5) They had tried to gain access to the I4IT (Europe) building in Madrid. This company was the European arm of an American-based investment group run by two born-again Christians from Cleveland, Ohio. They were the ultimate owners of Horizonte and, through a team of highly paid lawyers, had successfully blocked all investigations, arguing that the police had no right to enter their offices.

Every time Falcón threw himself into his chair he faced that chart and the hard brick wall behind it.

The world had moved on, as it always did, even after New York, Madrid and London, but Falcón had to mark time, wandering aimlessly in the maze of passages that the conspiracy had become. As always, he was haunted by the promise he'd made to the people of Seville in a live broadcast on 10th June: that he would find the perpetrators of the Seville bombing, even if it took him the rest of his career. That was what he faced, although he would never admit it to Comisario Elvira, when he woke up alone in the dark. He had penetrated the conspiracy, gained access to the dark castle, but it had rewarded him with nothing. Now he was reduced to hoping for 'the secret door' or 'the hidden passage' which would take him to what he could *not* see.

What he had noticed was that the one person, over these

three long months, who was never far from his thoughts was the disgraced judge, Esteban Calderón, and, by association, the judge's girlfriend, a Cuban wood sculptor called Marisa Moreno.

'Inspector Jefe?'

Falcón looked up from the dark pit of his mind to find the wide-open face of one of his best young detectives, the ex-nun, Cristina Ferrera. There was nothing very particular about Cristina that made her attractive – the small nose, the big smile, the short, straight, dull blonde hair didn't do it. But what she had on the inside – a big heart, unshakeable moral beliefs and an extraordinary empathy – had a way of appearing on the outside. And it was that which Falcón had found so appealing during their first interview for the job she now held.

'I thought you were in here,' she said, 'but you didn't answer. Up early?'

'A colourful Russian got killed by a flying steel rod on the motorway,' said Falcón. 'Have you got anything for me?'

'Two weeks ago you asked me to look into the life of Juez Calderón's girlfriend, Marisa Moreno, to see if there was any dirt attached,' said Ferrera.

'And here I am, by remarkable coincidence, thinking about that very person,' said Falcón. 'Go on.'

'Don't get too excited.'

'I can tell from your face,' said Falcón, drifting back to the wall chart, 'that whatever it is, it's not much to show for two weeks' work.'

'Not solid work, and you know what it's like here in Seville: things take time,' said Ferrera. 'You already know she has no criminal record.'

'So what *did* you find?' asked Falcón, catching a different tone in her voice.

'After getting people to do a lot of rooting around in the local police archives, I've come up with a reference.'

'A *reference*?'

'She reported a missing person. Her sister, Margarita, back in May 1998.'

'Eight years ago?' said Falcón, looking up at the ceiling. 'Is that interesting?'

'That's the only thing I could find,' said Ferrera, shrugging. 'Margarita was seventeen and had already left school. The local police did nothing except check up on her about a month later and Marisa reported that she'd been found. Apparently, the girl had left home with a boyfriend that Marisa didn't know about. They'd gone to Madrid until their money ran out and then hitched back. That's it. End of story.'

'Well, if nothing else, it gives me an excuse to go and see Marisa Moreno,' said Falcón. 'Is that all?'

'Did you see this message from the prison governor? Your meeting with Esteban Calderón is confirmed for one o'clock this afternoon.'

'Perfect.'

Ferrera left and Falcón was once again alone in his head with Marisa Moreno and Esteban Calderón. There was an obvious reason why Calderón was never far from his thoughts: the brilliant but arrogant instructing judge of the 6th June bombing had been found, days after the explosion, at an absolutely crucial moment of their investigation, trying to dispose of his prosecutor wife in the Guadalquivir river. Calderón's wife, Inés, was Javier Falcón's ex-wife. As the Homicide chief, Falcón had been called to the scene. When they'd opened the shroud around the body and he'd found himself looking down into Inés's beautiful but inanimate features he'd fainted. Given the circumstances, the investigation into Inés's murder had been handed over to an outsider, Inspector Jefe Luis Zorrita from Madrid. In an interview with Marisa Moreno, Zorrita had discovered that, on the night of the murder, Calderón had left her, taken a cab home and let himself into his double-locked apartment. Zorrita had drawn together an extraordinary array of lurid detail involving domestic and sexual abuse, and extracted a confession from a stunned Calderón, who had been subsequently charged. Since then Falcón had spoken to the judge only once, in a police cell, shortly after the event. Now he was nervous, not because he feared a resurgence of the earlier emotions, but because, after all his file reading, he was hoping he'd found the smallest chink into the heart of the conspiracy.

The internal phone rang. Comisario Elvira told Falcón that Vicente Cortés from the Costa del Sol GRECO had arrived. Falcón checked with the forensics, who'd so far only found fingerprints that matched those of Vasili Lukyanov. They were about to start work on the money, but they needed Falcón for the key. He went down to the evidence room.

'When you're done, tell me and I'll put the money in the safe until we can get it transferred to the bank,' said Falcón. 'What about the briefcase?'

'The most interesting things in there were twenty-odd disks,' said Jorge. 'We played one. It looked like hidden-camera footage of guys having sex with young women, snorting cocaine, some S&M stuff, that kind of thing.'

'You haven't transferred it to a computer, have you?'

'No, just played it on a DVD player.'

'Where are the disks now?'

'On top of the safe there.'

Falcón locked them inside, took the lift up to Comisario Elvira's office where he was introduced to Vicente Cortés from the Organized Crime Response Squad, and Martín Díaz from the Organized Crime Intelligence Centre, CICO. Both men were young, in their mid-thirties. Cortés was a trained accountant who, from the way his shoulders and biceps strained against the material of his white shirt, looked as if he'd been put through a few assault courses since he'd graduated from number-crunching. He had brown hair swept back, green eyes and a mouth that was permanently on the brink of a sneer. Díaz was a computer specialist and a linguist with Russian and Arabic up his sleeve. He wore a suit which he probably had to have made especially for him, being close to two metres tall. He played basketball to professional standard. He was dark-haired with brown eyes and a slight stoop, probably earned by trying to listen to his wife, half a metre shorter than him. This was the reality of catching organized criminals – accountants and computer whizzes, rather than special forces and weapons-trained cops.

Falcón delivered his report to the three men. Elvira, with his dark, laser-parted hair, kept straightening the files on his desk and fingering the neat and perfect knot of his blue tie. He was conservative, conventional and played everything by the book, with one eye on his job and the other on his boss, the Jefe Superior, Andrés Lobo.

'Vasili Lukyanov ran a number of *puti clubs* on the Costa del Sol and some of the main roads around Granada,' said Cortés. 'People-trafficking, sexual slavery and prostitution were his main –'

'Sexual slavery?' asked Falcón.

'Nowadays you can rent a girl for any amount of time you like. She'll do everything, from housework to full sex. When you get bored of her, you hand her back and get another one. She costs fifteen hundred euros per week,' said Cortés. 'The girls are traded in markets. They may come from Moldova, Albania, or even Nigeria, but they're sold and resold as much as ten times before they get here. Normal price is around three thousand euros, depending on looks. By the time the girl arrives in Spain she may have accumulated sales of thirty thousand – which she has to pay off. I know it's illogical, but that's only to you and me, not to people like Vasili Lukyanov.'

'We found some cocaine in his car. Is that a sideline or . . .?'

'He's recently moved into cocaine distribution. Or rather, his gang leader has struck a deal for product coming in from Galicia and they've now come to some form of agreement with the Colombians with regard to their operations on the Costa del Sol.'

'So where is Lukyanov in the hierarchy?' asked Elvira.

Cortés nodded to Díaz.

'Difficult question, and we're wondering about the significance of finding him in a car bound for Seville with nearly eight million euros,' said Díaz. 'He's important. The Russians make huge profits from the sex trade, more than they make from drugs at the moment. The hierarchy has been a problem in the last year since we had Operation Wasp in 2005 and the Georgian boss of the Russian mafia here in Spain fled to Dubai.'

'Dubai?' asked Elvira.

'That's where you go nowadays if you're a criminal, a terrorist, an arms trader, a money-launderer . . .'

'Or a builder,' finished Cortés. 'It's the Costa del Sol of the Middle East.'

'Did that leave a power vacuum here in Spain?' asked Falcón.

'No, his position was taken over by Leonid Revnik, who was sent from Moscow to take control. It was not a popular move with the mafia soldiers on the ground, mainly because his first act was to execute two leading mafia "directors" from one of the Moscow brigades who had encroached on his turf,' said Díaz.

'They were both found bound, gagged and shot in the back of the head in the Sierra Bermeja, ten kilometres north of Estepona,' said Cortés.

'We think that it was some old feud, dating back to the 1990s in Moscow, but what it did was create nervousness among the soldiers. They found they were having to run their business *and* look out for revenge attacks. There have been four "disappearances" so far this year. We're not used to this level of violence. All the other mafia groups – the Turks and Italians, who run the heroin trade; the Colombians and the Galicians, who control cocaine; the Moroccans, who traffic people and hashish – none of them practise the sort of spectacular violence they use in their own countries because they see Spain as a safe haven. They followed our old, long-standing friends the Arab arms dealers, who run their global businesses from the Costa del Sol. To all of them it's just a massive laundromat to clean their money, which means they don't want to draw attention to themselves. The Russians, on the other hand, don't seem to give a damn.'

'Any idea why Vasili Lukyanov would be heading for Seville with eight million euros in his boot?' asked Elvira.

'I don't know. I'm not up to date on what's happening in Seville. It's possible that CICO in Madrid have some intelligence on what's been going on here. I've put in a request,' said Díaz. 'It wouldn't surprise me if there was a rival group opening up here. Leonid Revnik is fifty-two and old school. I think he'd be suspicious of someone like Vasili Lukyanov, who didn't come up through the Russian prison system but was an Afghan war veteran who bought his way in *and* works with women, which Revnik probably considers inferior, despite its profitability.'

'How profitable?' asked Elvira.

'We have four hundred thousand prostitutes here in Spain and they generate eighteen billion euros' worth of business,' said Díaz. 'We are the biggest users of prostitutes and cocaine of any country in Europe.'

'So you think Leonid Revnik despised Vasili Lukyanov, who would then have been open to offers for his expertise in a very profitable business?' said Falcón.

'Could be,' said Díaz. 'Revnik has been away in Moscow.

We were expecting him back next week, but he returned early. Maybe he heard Lukyanov was making a move. I can tell you one thing for sure: Lukyanov wouldn't be going it alone. He'd need protection; but whose support he's getting, I don't know.'

'And the eight million?' asked Elvira, still not satisfied.

'That's a sort of entry fee. It forces Lukyanov to burn his bridges,' said Cortés. 'Once he's stolen that sort of money he's never going to be able to go back to Revnik.'

'The disks in the briefcase I mentioned in my initial report,' said Falcón. 'Hidden-camera stuff, older men with young girls . . .'

'It's how the Russians get things done. They corrupt whoever they come into contact with,' said Cortés. 'We might be about to find out how our town planners, councillors, mayors and even senior policemen spent their summer holidays.'

Comisario Elvira ran his hand over his perfectly combed hair.

3

Seville Prison, Alcalá de Guadaira – Friday, 15th September 2006, 13.05 hrs

Through the reinforced glass pane of the door, Falcón watched Calderón, who was hunched over the table, smoking, staring into the tin-foil ashtray, waiting for him. The judge, who'd been young for his position, looked older. He had lost his gilded, moisturized sheen. His skin was dull and he'd lost weight where there was none to lose, making him look haggard. His hair had never been luxuriant, but was now definitely thinning to baldness. His ears seemed to have got longer, the lobes fleshier, as if from some unconscious tugging while musing on the entanglements of his mind. It settled Falcón to see the judge so reduced; it would have been intolerable had the wife-beater been his usual arrogant self. Falcón opened the door for the guard, who held a tray of coffee, and followed him in. Calderón instantly reanimated himself into an approximation of the supremely confident man he had once been.

'To what, or to whom, do I owe this pleasure?' asked Calderón, standing up, sweeping his arm across the sparsely furnished room. 'Privacy, coffee, an old friend... these unimaginable luxuries.'

'I'd have come before now,' said Falcón, sitting down, 'but, as you've probably realized, I've been busy.'

Calderón took a long, careful look at him and lit another cigarette, the third of his second pack of the day. The guard set down the tray and left the room.

'And what could possibly make you want to come and see the murderer of your ex-wife?'

'*Alleged* murderer of *your* wife.'

'Is that significant, or are you just being accurate?'

'This last week is the first time I've had since June to think and... do some reading,' said Falcón.

'Well, I hope it was a good novel and not the transcript of my interview with my Grand Inquisitor, Inspector Jefe Luis Zorrita,' said Calderón. 'That, as my lawyer will tell you, was not my finest hour.'

'I've read that quite a few times and I've also gone over Zorrita's interview with Marisa Moreno,' said Falcón. 'She's been to see you a number of times, hasn't she?'

'Unfortunately,' said Calderón, nodding, 'they've not been conjugal visits. We talk.'

'About what?'

'We were never very good at talking,' said Calderón, drawing hard on his cigarette. 'We had that other language.'

'I was just thinking that maybe since you've been in here you might have developed some other communication skills.'

'I have, but not particularly with Marisa.'

'So why does she come to see you?'

'Duty? Guilt? I don't know. Ask her.'

'Guilt?'

'I think there might be a few things she regrets telling Zorrita about,' said Calderón.

'Like what?'

'I don't want to talk about it,' said Calderón. 'Not with you.'

'Things like that little joke you had with Marisa about the "bourgeois solution" to costly divorce: . . . murder your wife.'

'Fuck knows how that bastard Zorrita squeezed that out of her.'

'Maybe he didn't have to squeeze too hard,' said Falcón calmly.

Calderón's cigarette stopped on the way to his mouth.

'What else do you think she regretted talking to Zorrita about?' asked Falcón.

'She covered for me. She said I left her apartment later than I did. She thought she was doing me a favour, but Zorrita had all the timings from the cab company. It was a stupid thing to have done. It counted against me. Made me look as if I needed help, especially taken in conjunction with the cops finding me on the banks of the Guadalquivir river trying to dispose of Inés's body,' said Calderón, who stopped, frowned and did some concentrated smoking. 'What the fuck are you doing here, Javier? What's this all about?'

'I'm trying to help you,' said Falcón.

'Are you now?' said Calderón. 'And why would you want to help the *alleged* murderer of your ex-wife? I realize that you and Inés weren't particularly close any more, but . . . still . . .'

'You told me you were innocent. You've said so from the very beginning.'

'Well, Inspector Jefe Javier Falcón, you're the expert on the murderer's constant state of denial,' said Calderón.

'I am,' said Falcón. 'And I'm not going to pretend to you that my investigation into what happened on that night doesn't have ulterior motives.'

'All right,' said Calderón, sitting back, paradoxically satisfied by this revelation. 'I didn't think you wanted to save my ass . . . especially if you've read that transcript as many times as you said.'

'There's some very ugly stuff in there, I can't deny that, Esteban.'

'Nor can I,' said Calderón. 'I wouldn't mind turning back the clock on my whole relationship with Inés.'

'I have some questions relating to the transcript,' said Falcón, heading off a possible descent into self-pity. 'I understand that the first time you hit Inés was when she discovered the naked photographs of Marisa on your digital camera.'

'She was trying to download them on to her computer,' said Calderón, leaping to his own defence. 'I didn't know what her intentions were. I mean, it's one thing to *find* them, but it seemed to me that she was going to make *use* of them in some way.'

'I'm sure Inés knew you very well, by then,' said Falcón. 'So why did you leave the camera hanging around? What were you thinking of, taking shots of your naked lover?'

'*I* didn't take them, Marisa did . . . while I was asleep. She was nice about it, though. She told me she'd left some "presents" on the camera,' said Calderón. 'And I didn't leave the camera hanging around. Inés went through my pockets.'

'And what were you doing with the camera in the first place?'

'I took some shots of a lawyers' dinner I'd attended earlier in the evening,' said Calderón. 'My alibi, if Inés found the camera.'

'Which you knew she would.'

Calderón nodded, smoked, searched his memory; something he did a lot these days.

'I'd overslept at Marisa's,' he said. 'It was six o'clock in the morning and, you know, I wasn't as collected as I would have been normally. Inés appeared to be asleep. She wasn't. When I dropped off, she got up and found the shots.'

'And that was the first time you hit her,' said Falcón. 'Have you thought about that since you've been in here?'

'Are you going to be my shrink as well, Javier?'

Falcón showed him an empty pair of hands.

'If you didn't take the shots of Marisa and the only reason you had the camera with you was to provide yourself with an alibi for Inés, how come it was at hand for your lover to take photos of herself naked?'

Calderón stared into the wall for some time until he gradually started chopping the air with his cigarette fingers.

'She told me she went through my jacket pockets. She said: "I come from a bourgeois family; I kick against it, but I know all the tricks,"' said Calderón. 'They all go through your pockets. That's what women do, Javier. It's part of their training. They're very exigent on details.'

'Did she volunteer that information?'

'No, I asked her.'

'Any reason?'

'I don't know,' said Calderón. 'I think I was hunting for my shoes. I was nervous about getting back to my apartment and having a confrontation with Inés. I'd never stayed out all night before. I suppose Marisa's behaviour just struck me as a bit odd.'

'Any thoughts about it now?'

'It's the sort of thing a wife would do . . . not a lover,' said Calderón, crushing out the cigarette in the tin-foil ashtray. 'It's what Inés did when I got home.'

'You're smoking a lot, Esteban.'

'There's nothing else to do, and it calms my nerves.'

'Maybe you should think of an alternative method of calming your nerves.'

Calderón looked up, suspicious.

'You can keep trying, Javier, but I'm not going to lie down on your couch.'

'What about somebody else's couch?' said Falcón, flicking

over a page in his notebook. 'Another question about the transcript . . .'

Calderón lit a cigarette, belligerently. He inhaled deeply without taking his eyes off Falcón and blew the smoke out the side of his mouth.

'Go on,' he said. 'I'm listening.'

'Why do you think Marisa told Inspector Jefe Zorrita that she'd met Inés?'

'Zorrita said that dealing with liars was like dealing with children. Marisa tried to lie about it but he broke her down.'

'Zorrita is a dictaphone man, not a note-taker. I've listened to the recording of the interview with Marisa,' said Falcón. 'If there was one bit of evidence you didn't want in Zorrita's hands it was the fact of Marisa and Inés having met before, and especially the circumstances of that meeting.'

'Probably,' said Calderón, not that interested in something he didn't regard as a development.

'Zorrita found a witness to that meeting in the Murillo Gardens on 6th June. It wasn't too difficult because, apparently, it was quite a showdown between the two women. The witness said they went at each other like a couple of whores competing for the same patch.'

'Doesn't sound like that witness hung around in very nice places.'

They smiled at each other with no humour.

'According to this witness, Marisa had the last word,' said Falcón, flicking through his notebook. 'She said something along the lines of: "Just remember, Inés, that when he's beating you it's because he's been fucking me so beautifully all night that he can't bear to see your disappointed little face in the morning." Is that what Marisa told *you*? Because she didn't happen to mention that to Zorrita.'

'What's your point?'

'First of all, how did Marisa find out that you'd been

beating Inés? She didn't have a bruised face. Did you tell her?'

'No.'

'Maybe one of the ugly lessons she learnt in her early life in Havana was how to spot an abused woman.'

'Your *point*, Javier?' said Calderón, with courtroom lawyer's steel.

'Marisa gave Zorrita the impression that Inés had the upper hand. She mentioned Inés's phrase several times: "*La puta con el puro.*"' The whore with the cigar.

'That's what *she* told me,' said Calderón, listening hard now.

'Zorrita thought Marisa had told him all that because she was still furious at being shamed by Inés in public, but clearly she wasn't. Marisa crushed Inés. The witness said that Inés went off like "the village cur". So what was Marisa's purpose in telling Zorrita about that meeting?'

'You think it was calculated,' said Calderón.

'I listened to the tape. Zorrita only had to prod her a couple of times to get the story out of her. And the story, her version of it, was crucial in redoubling your motive to beat Inés and perhaps take it too far and kill her. Now that would be a story that you'd want to keep out of the investigating officer's mind at all costs.'

Calderón was smoking so intently that he was making himself dizzy with the nicotine rush.

'My final question to do with the transcript,' said Falcón. 'Inspector Jefe Zorrita came to see me some hours after he'd interviewed you. I asked if you'd broken down and confessed, and his answer was: sort of. He admitted that when you refused a lawyer – God knows what you were thinking of at that moment, Esteban – it meant that he could be more brutal with you in the interview. That, combined with the horror of the autopsy revelations, seemed to create doubt in your mind and, Zorrita reckoned, it was then that you believed that you *could* have done it.'

'I was very confused,' said Calderón. 'My hubris was in refusing the lawyer. *I* was a lawyer. *I* could handle myself.'

'When Zorrita asked you to describe what happened when you went back to your apartment that night, he said you rendered the events in the form of a film script.'

'I don't remember that.'

'You used the third person singular. You were describing something you'd seen . . . as if you were out of your body, or behind a camera. It was clear you were in some kind of trance. Didn't your lawyer mention any of this?'

'Maybe he was too embarrassed.'

'There seems to be some confusion about what you saw when you came into the apartment,' said Falcón.

'My lawyer and I have talked about *that*.'

'In your film script version, you describe yourself as "annoyed", because you didn't want to see Inés.'

'I didn't want a confrontation. I wasn't angry, as I had been when Marisa told me about meeting Inés in the Murillo Gardens. I was pretty much asleep on my feet. Those were long days. All the work, followed by media engagements in the evening.'

Falcón flipped over another page of his notebook.

'What interested me was when you said: "He stumbled into the bedroom, collapsed on to the bed and passed out immediately. He was aware only of pain. He lashed out wildly with his foot. He woke up with no idea where he was." What was all that about?'

'Is that a direct quote?'

'Yes,' said Falcón, putting the dictaphone on the table and pressing 'play'.

Calderón listened, transfixed, as the smoke crawled up the valleys of his fingers.

'Is that me?'

35

Falcón played it again.

'It doesn't seem *that* important.'

'I think Marisa put a cigarette lighter to your foot,' said Falcón.

Calderón leapt to his feet as if he'd been spiked from underneath.

'My foot was sore for days,' he said, with sudden recall. 'I had a blister.'

'Why would Marisa put a cigarette lighter to your foot?'

'To wake me up. I was dead to the world.'

'There are more charming ways to wake your lover up than burning his foot with a cigarette lighter,' said Falcón. 'I think that she *had* to wake you up because the timing of your departure from her apartment was crucial.'

Calderón sank back into his chair, lit another cigarette and stared up into the light coming in through the high, barred window. He blinked as his eyes filled and he bit down on his bottom lip.

'You're helping me,' said Calderón. 'The irony's not lost on me, Javier.'

'You need different help to what I can give you,' said Falcón. 'Now, let's just go back to my original point from the transcript. Just one more thing about that night. The two versions you gave Zorrita about how you found Inés in the apartment.'

Calderón's brain snapped back into some pre-rehearsed groove and Falcón held up his hand.

'I'm not interested in the version you and your lawyer have prepared for court,' said Falcón. 'Remember, none of this is about *your* case. What I'm trying to do *might* help you, but the design is not to get *you* off the hook, it's for me to find my way in.'

'To what?'

'The conspiracy. Who planted that small Goma 2 Eco bomb in the basement mosque, which exploded on the 6th of

June, detonating the hundred kilos of hexogen stored there, bringing down the apartment building and destroying the pre-school?'

'Javier Falcón keeps his promise to the people of Seville,' said Calderón, grunting.

'Nobody's forgotten that . . . least of all me.'

Calderón leaned across the table, looked up through the pupils of Falcón's eyes into the top of his cranium.

'Do I detect something of an obsession going on here?' he said. 'Personal crusades, Javier, are not advisable in police work. Every old people's home in Spain probably has a retired detective gaping from the windows, his mind still twisted around a missing girl, or a poor, bludgeoned boy. Don't go there. Nobody expects it of you.'

'People remind me of it all the time in the Jefatura and in the Palacio de Justicia,' said Falcón. 'And what's more, I expect it of myself.'

'See you in the loony bin, Javier. Save me a place by the window,' said Calderón, sitting back, inspecting the conical ember of his cigarette.

'We're not going to end up in the loony bin,' said Falcón.

'You're pretty keen to get me down on some shrink's couch,' said Calderón, dredging for lost confidence. 'And you know what I say? Fuck off, you and anybody else. Mind your own madness. You especially, Javier. It's been less than five years since your "complete breakdown" – wasn't that what they called it? – and I can see you've been working hard. God knows how many times you went through the files on the bombing before you started combing Zorrita's reports, looking for the flaws in my case. You should get out more, Javier. Have you fucked that Consuelo yet?'

'Let's get back to what happened at around 4 a.m. on Thursday 8th June in your apartment in Calle San Vicente,' said Falcón, tapping his notebook. 'In one version you came

37

in to see Inés standing at the sink and you were "so happy to see her", and yet in the other version you were "annoyed", there was some sort of hiatus, you woke up lying in the corridor and when you went back to the kitchen you found Inés dead on the floor.'

Calderón swallowed hard as he replayed that night in the darkness of his mind. He had done it so many times, more times than even the most obsessive director would have edited, and re-edited, a scene from a movie. It now played in short sequences, but in reverse. From that moment of intense guilt when, trapped in the patrolman's torch beam, he'd been discovered trying to throw Inés into the river, to that blissful, pre-lapsarian state when he'd got out of the cab, helped by the driver, and walked up the stairs to his apartment, with no other intention than to get into bed as quickly as possible. And that was the point he always seized on: he knew at *that* moment he did not have murder on his mind.

'There was no intent,' he said, out loud.

'Start from the beginning, Esteban.'

'Look, Javier, I've tried it every which way: forwards, backwards and inside out, but however hard I try there's always a gap,' said Calderón, lighting another cigarette from the stub of the last one. 'The cab driver opened the apartment door for me, two turns of the key. He left me there. I went into the apartment. I saw the light from the kitchen. I remember being annoyed – and I repeat, "annoyed", not angry or murderous. I was just irritated that I might have to explain myself when all I wanted to do was crash out. So I remember that emotion very clearly, then nothing until I woke up on the floor in the corridor beyond the kitchen.'

'What do you think about Zorrita's theory, that people have blank moments about terrible things they have done?'

'I've come across it professionally. I don't doubt it. I've searched every corner of my mind . . .'

'So what was this about seeing Inés alive and being so happy?'

'My lawyer tells me that Freud had a term for that: "wish fulfilment", he called it,' said Calderón. 'You want something to be true so badly that your mind invents it for you. I did not want Inés to be dead on the floor. We were not happy together, but I did not want her dead. I wanted her to be alive so badly that my mind substituted the reality with my most fervent wish. Both versions came out in the turmoil of that first interview with Zorrita.'

'You know that this is the crux of your case,' said Falcón. 'The flaws I've found are small. Marisa going through your pockets, getting the upper hand in the shouting match with Inés in the Murillo Gardens and burning your foot to wake you up. These things amount to nothing when put against your recorded statement, in which you say that you entered the double-locked apartment alone, saw Inés alive, blacked out and then found her dead. Your inner turmoil and all that wish-fulfilment crap is no match for those powerful facts.'

More concentrated smoking from Calderón. He scratched at his thinning hair and his left eye twitched.

'And why do you think Marisa is the key?'

'The worst possible thing that could have happened at that moment in our investigation into the bombing was to have our instructing judge, and our strongest performer in front of the media, arrested for the murder of his wife,' said Falcón. 'Losing you pretty well derailed the whole process. If your disgrace was planned, then Marisa was crucial to its execution.'

'I'll speak to her,' said Calderón, nodding, his face hardening.

'You won't,' said Falcón. 'We've stopped her visits. You're too desperate, Esteban. I don't want you to give anything away. What you've got to do is unlock your mind and see if you can find any detail that might help me. And it might be advisable to get a professional in to do that for you.'

'Ah!' said Calderón, getting it finally. 'The shrink.'

4

Leonid Revnik was still sitting at Vasili Lukyanov's desk in the club, but this time he was waiting for news from Viktor Belenki, his second-in-command. When Revnik had taken control of the Costa del Sol after the police had mounted Operation Wasp in 2005, he'd got Belenki to run the construction businesses through which they laundered most of the proceeds of their drugs and prostitution trade. Belenki had just the right veneer of the good-looking, successful businessman and he spoke fluent Spanish, too. The veneer, though, was only an expensive suit thick, as Viktor Belenki was a violent brute with access to a rage so incandescent that even Revnik's most psychopathic henchmen were afraid of him. Belenki could also be very friendly and extremely generous, especially if you jumped when he told you to. This meant that he had developed good contacts in the Guardia Civil, some of whom had thick wads of Belenki's euros hidden in their garages. Leonid Revnik was hoping that Belenki could tell him where the money and disks that Lukyanov had stolen from the *puti club* safe had ended up.

He was on his third cigar of the day. The empty safe was still gaping. The air-con was on the blink and he was uncomfortably hot. The mobile on the desk rang.

'Viktor,' said Revnik.

'It's taken some time to get this information because it's out of the normal area of my guy's jurisdiction,' said Belenki. 'The Guardia Civil who went to the scene of the accident came from a town outside Seville called Utrera. When they found the money they called the police headquarters in Seville and, because it was clear that this wasn't just any old guy who'd died in a car accident, they went to the top for instructions: Comisario Elvira.'

'Shit,' said Revnik.

'And he put it in the hands of Inspector Jefe Javier Falcón. Remember him?'

'Everybody remembers him from the bombing in June,' said Revnik. 'So where's it all gone?'

'It's in the Jefatura in Seville.'

'Have we still got somebody in there?'

'That's how I know where everything is.'

'Right, so how do we get it out?'

'You can say goodbye to the money,' said Belenki. 'Once the forensics have been over it, they'll stick it in the bank – unless you want to hold up a Prosegur van.'

'I don't give a fuck about the money. I mean, I do, but . . . you're right. The disks, they're a different matter,' said Revnik. 'What can we get on Falcón?'

'You're not going to be able to buy him, that's for sure.'

'So what else?'

'There's always the woman,' said Belenki. 'Consuelo Jiménez.'

'Ah, yes, the woman,' said Revnik.

At the traffic lights Falcón searched his eyes in the rear-view mirror, trying to find the evidence of obsession Calderón had seen there. He didn't really need to look at the tell-tale blackberry smudges; he knew from the slight gaucherie in his left hand, and that feeling of wearing someone else's right leg, that what was cradled in his mind was beginning to have physical manifestations.

Work had sat on Falcón's shoulders like an overweight, badly packed rucksack, and it never slipped off, not even at night. In the mornings he opened an eye, his face crushed hard into the pillow after snatching an hour's lethal sleep, to feel his bones creaking in his skeleton. The week's holiday he'd taken at the end of August, when he'd joined his friend Yacoub Diouri and his family on the beach at Essaouira in Morocco, had worn off on his first day back in the office.

Horns blared behind him. He pulled away from the traffic lights. He came into the old city through the Puerta Osario. He parked badly near the San Marcos church and walked down Calle Bustos Tavera to the tunnelled passageway that led from the street into a courtyard of workshops where Marisa Moreno had her studio. His footsteps sounded loud on the large cobbles of the dark tunnel. He broke out into the fierce light in the courtyard, squinted against it to take in the dilapidated buildings, the grass growing up through old rear axles and expired fridges. He walked up a metal stairway to a doorway above a small warehouse. Foot shuffling and dull thuds came from inside. He knocked.

'Who is it?'

'Police.'

'*Momentito.*'

The door was opened by a tall, slim mulatto woman with an unusually long neck, who had wood chips stuck to her face and in her coppery hair, which was tied back. She wore a cobalt-blue gown under which she was naked apart from some bikini briefs. Sweat pimpled across her forehead, over the undulation of her nose and trickled down the visible bones of her chest. She was breathing heavily.

'Marisa Moreno?' he said, holding up his police ID. 'I am Inspector Jefe Javier Falcón.'

'I've already told Inspector Jefe Luis Zorrita everything I know a couple of hundred times,' she said. 'I've got nothing to add.'

'I've come to talk to you about your sister.'

'My *sister*?' she said, and Falcón did not miss the momentary fear that froze her features.

'You have a sister called Margarita.'

'I know my own sister's name.'

Falcón paused, hoping that Marisa might feel the need to fill the moment with more information. She stared him out.

'You reported her missing in 1998, when she was two months short of her seventeenth birthday.'

'Come in,' she said. 'Don't touch anything.'

The studio's floor was patched with rough concrete where the clay tiles had come up. The air smelled of bare timber, turps and oils. There were chippings everywhere and a pile of sawdust in the corner. A meat hook large enough to take a full carcass hung from the tie rod which spanned the room. Suspended from its sharp hook was an electric chain saw, its flex thrown over the bar. Three dark and polished statues stood beneath the oily, sawdust-encrusted tool, one with its head missing. Falcón made for the space around the piece. The headless statue was that of a young woman, with breasts high on her chest, perfect orbs. The faces of the men flanking her had nothing in them. Their eyes were blank. The musculature of their bodies had something of the savagery of an existence in the wild about them. Their genitals were outsized and, despite being flaccid, seemed sinister, as if they were spent from a recent rape.

Marisa watched him as he took the piece in, waiting for the banality of his comments. She had yet to meet the white man who could resist a little critique, and her warriors with their prize penises drew plenty of lewd admiration. What she registered in Falcón's face was not even a raised eyebrow, but a brief revulsion as he looked down the bodies.

'So what happened to Margarita?' he asked, switching to Marisa. 'You reported her missing on 25th May 1998, and when the police came to check with you a month later you said she'd turned up again about a week after she'd disappeared.'

'That was how much they cared,' she said, reaching for a small half-smoked cigar which she relit. 'They took down her details and I never heard from them again. They wouldn't take my calls, and when I went round to the station they just dismissed me, said she was with some boyfriend or other. If you're pretty and mulatto like her they just think you're some kind of fucking machine. I'm sure they did nothing.'

'She *did* go to Madrid with a boyfriend, though, didn't she?'

'They were pretty pleased about that when I told them.'

'Where were your parents in all this?' asked Falcón. 'Margarita was still a kid.'

'Dead. You see, they probably didn't put *that* in the report. My father died up north in Gijón in 1995. My mother died here in Seville in 1998 and two months later Margarita went missing. She was upset. That was why I was worried.'

'Your father was Cuban?'

'We came over here in 1992. It was a bad time in Cuba; Russian aid had dried up after the Berlin Wall came down in 1989. There's a large Cuban community in Gijón, so that's where we settled.'

'How did your parents meet?'

'My father had a club in Gijón. My mother was a flamenco dancer from Seville. She'd come up to perform at the annual Semana Negra fair. My father was a good salsa dancer and there's such a thing as Cuban flamenco, so they taught each other things and my mother made the mistake that a lot of other women made.'

'So obviously she wasn't your natural mother?'

'No, we don't know what happened to her. She was Cuban of Spanish descent, white and political. She disappeared soon after my sister was born in 1981.'

'You were seven years old.'

'It's not something I think about very much,' said Marisa. 'Things like that could happen in Cuba. My father never talked about it.'

'So who looked after you?'

'My father had girlfriends. Some were interested in us . . . others weren't.'

'What did your father do in Cuba?'

'He was somebody in the government. An official on the Sugar Board. Export,' said Marisa. 'I thought you wanted to talk about my sister, and I'm beginning to wonder why.'

'I like to get people's family situation sorted out in my mind,' said Falcón. 'It doesn't sound like you had a normal life.'

'We didn't, until my stepmother came along. She was a good woman. The caring type. She really looked after us. For the first time in our lives we were loved. She even looked after my father when he was dying.'

'How was that?'

'Lung cancer. Too many cigars,' she said, waving **the** smoking stub in her hand. 'He only married her after his diagnosis.'

Marisa blew a plume of smoke out into the rafters of the wooden roof. She felt she had to keep this thing going. Do one long stint with this new inspector jefe and then maybe he'd leave her alone.

'What did you do after your father died?' asked Falcón.

'We moved down here. My mother couldn't stand the north. All that rain.'

'What about *her* family?'

'Her parents were dead. She had a brother in Málaga, but

he didn't like black people very much. He didn't come to her wedding.'

'How did your mother die?'

'Heart attack,' said Marisa, eyes shining at the memory of it.

'Were you living here at the time?'

'I was in Los Angeles.'

'I'm sorry,' said Falcón. 'That must have been hard. She wasn't very old.'

'Fifty-one.'

'Did you see her before she died?'

'Is that any of your business?' she said, turning away, looking for an ashtray.

This cop was getting under her skin.

'My mother died when I was five,' said Falcón. 'It doesn't matter whether you're five or fifty-five, it's not something you ever get over.'

Marisa turned back slowly; she'd never heard a Sevillano, let alone a cop, talk like this. Falcón was frowning at **the** floor.

'So you came back from Los Angeles and you've been here ever since?' he said.

'I stayed for a year,' said Marisa. 'I thought I should **look** after my sister.'

'And what happened?'

'She left again. But she was eighteen this **time so . . .'**

'And you haven't seen or heard from her since?'

There was a long silence in which Marisa's mind seemed to float off out of the room and Falcón thought for the first time that he was getting somewhere.

'Señora Moreno?' said Falcón.

'I haven't heard from her . . . no.'

'Are you worried about her?'

She shrugged and for some reason Falcón didn't think he was going to believe what he heard next.

47

'We weren't very close, which was why she left the first time without telling me.'

'Is that right?' said Falcón, locking eyes with her across the studio. 'So what did you do when she left the second time?'

'I finished the course I was doing at the Bellas Artes, rented out my mother's apartment, which my sister and I had inherited . . .'

'Is that where you live now, in Calle Hiniesta?'

'And I went to Africa,' she said, nodding. 'Mali, Niger, Nigeria, Cameroon, the Congo, until it got too dangerous and then I went to Mozambique.'

'What about the Touaregs . . . didn't you spend some time with them?'

Silence, as she registered that he'd heard that from someone else.

'If you know all this, Inspector Jefe, why are you asking me?'

'I know it, but hearing it from you arranges the furniture.'

'I let you in here to talk about my sister.'

'Who you're not close to.'

'You seem to have expanded your interests since you started using up my work time.'

'And then there was New York . . .?'

She grunted. Puffed on the cigar to get it going again.

'You've been talking to Esteban, haven't you?'

'How do you know?'

'I lied to him about New York,' she said. 'I saw a movie about an artist starring Nick Nolte, and I assumed the role of his assistant. I've never been to New York.'

'Did you lie to him about anything else?'

'Probably. I had an image to live up to.'

'An image?'

'That's how most of the men I've spent any time with see women.'

'You described Esteban Calderón as your lover to Inspector Jefe Zorrita.'

'He was then . . . still is, kind of, although prison doesn't help,' she said. 'I'm sorry he killed his wife. He was always so controlled, you know, still passionate in the way Sevillanos are, but a lawyer, too, and with a lawyer's mentality.'

'So you think he did it?'

'What I think doesn't matter. It's what Inspector Jefe Zorrita thinks that matters,' she said, and something clicked in her mind. 'That's it, I've got it now. It was *your* ex-wife that Esteban murdered. That's interesting.'

'Is it?'

'I don't know what you're doing here,' she said, puffing on her cigar, appraising him anew.

'Was your sister with a boyfriend when she left the second time?'

'There was always a man involved with Margarita.'

'Pretty girl?'

'That . . . and the other thing.'

'Sex?'

'Not exactly,' said Marisa, who went over to a small plans chest, opened a drawer and slapped a sheaf of photos down on the top. She was going to let him in, or rather let him think that she was opening up. 'Take a look. I took these three weeks before her eighteenth birthday.'

Falcón flicked through the shots. A sadness lodged itself in his chest. It wasn't sex, despite the provocative nudity. Even when she was lying back, legs splayed, she had an innocence about her. An innocence that itched to be desecrated in the eyes of men. That was why Marisa had taken the shots and only Marisa could have taken them. Even in the most pornographic of poses Margarita never lost her childlike purity, whereas the viewer, or the voyeur, felt the beast rise up on its hind legs and dance on its furry hooves.

'For a Sevillano, you don't say very much, Inspector Jefe.'

'Nothing to add,' he said, giving up on the shots halfway through, feeling the woman's intention and not flattered by it. 'They do their work.'

'You're the first person to see those.'

'I'd like a shot of Margarita with some clothes on,' he said, 'so that we can begin to look for her.'

'She's not lost any more,' said Marisa. 'She doesn't need to be found.'

'I'm sure you'd like to hear from her, though, wouldn't you?'

Another shrug from Marisa, something very uneasy about her. She handed over a head-and-shoulders shot of her sister.

'You used to go through Esteban's pockets,' said Falcón, taking the photo. 'Why did you do that? I mean, you're an artist, I can see that from the quality of this work. So you're curious, but not for the sort of crap you find in a man's pockets.'

'My stepmother did the same thing when my father came back at seven in the morning. She hated herself for it but couldn't help it. She had to know, even though she already knew.'

'That doesn't explain anything,' said Falcón. 'I could understand Inés wanting to go through his pockets, but you? What were you looking for? You knew he was married, and not very happily. What else was there?'

'My mother came from a very conservative Sevillana family. You can see the type in her brother. And she got involved with a black man when she was forty-five years old and he repaid her by fucking everything that passed beneath his nose. Her bourgeois instinct –'

'Hers, not yours. She wasn't your natural mother.'

'We adored her.'

'That's your only explanation?'

'You amaze me, Inspector Jefe.'

'Keys?' he said, cutting in on her digression, eyebrows raised.

'What?'

'You were after his keys.'

'That's why you amaze me,' said Marisa, puffing on her chewed-over cigar butt, spitting out flakes of tobacco. 'Zorrita told me, triumphantly no less, that he had a rock-solid case against Esteban for the murder of his wife, your ex, and here you are, trying to chip away at it for some reason that I don't quite understand.'

'Did you get a key made to his apartment and have a good look around for yourself, or make a duplicate for somebody else so that they could?'

'Look, Inspector Jefe, one time I found he had condoms which he never wore when he was with me,' said Marisa. 'Once a woman finds something like that, she keeps checking to see if there are any fewer.'

'I've spoken to the governor. We're stopping your prison visits.'

'Why?'

'I'd have thought that would be a relief.'

'Think what you like.'

Falcón nodded. Something caught his eye under the table. He knelt down and rolled it back towards him. It was a stained and polished wooden head. He inspected it under the light. Margarita's smooth unsophisticated face looked back at him, eyes closed. He ran a thumb over the jagged edge of her neck where the chain saw had bitten into the wood.

'What happened here?' asked Falcón.

'A change of artistic vision,' she said.

Falcón went to the door, feeling that the first phase of his work was done. He handed her the head.

'Too perfect?' he asked. 'Or not the point?'

Marisa listened to his feet on the metal stairway and looked down at the carved features of her sister's face. She ran her fingers over the eyelids, nose and mouth. Her arm, bearing the full weight of the head, trembled. She put it down, found her mobile on the work bench and made a call.

The cop made her nervous, but she was also surprised to find that she did not dislike him. And there were very few men that Marisa liked, not many of them were white, and none of them were policemen.

Leonid Revnik hadn't moved. He'd cleared his henchmen out of the room and they'd got a technician in to fix the air-con. He was taking a drink from the half-bottle of vodka that was still left in Vasili Lukyanov's freezer. Viktor Belenki hadn't called him back. He had to remind himself to relax because he kept coming out of his thoughts to find his biceps tight in his shirt and his pectorals clenched. The land-line phone on the desk rang. He looked at it suspiciously; nobody used these things any more. He picked it up, spoke in Russian without thinking. A woman's voice answered in the same language and asked to speak to Vasili Lukyanov.

'Who is this?' he asked, hearing a strange accent.

'My name is Marisa Moreno. I've tried calling Vasili on his mobile but there's no answer. This is the only other number he gave me.'

The Cuban woman. Rita's sister.

'Vasili isn't here. Maybe I can help; I'm his boss,' said Revnik. 'If you want to leave a message, I'll make sure he gets it.'

'He told me I should call him if I had any trouble.'

'And what's happened?' asked Revnik.

'A homicide cop called Inspector Jefe Javier Falcón came round to my workshop and started asking questions about my sister, Margarita.'

That name, Falcón, again.

'What did he want with her?'

52

'He said he was going to find her.'

'And what did you say?'

'I told him she didn't need to be found.'

'That's good,' said Revnik. 'Have you spoken to anybody else about this?'

'I left a message on Nikita's phone.'

'Sokolov?' he asked, barely able to control his rage at having to pronounce another traitor's name.

'Yes.'

'You did the right thing,' said Revnik. 'We'll handle it. Don't worry.'

5

There were two people in the world for whom Falcón would drop everything. One was Consuelo Jiménez and the other was Yacoub Diouri. Ever since he'd tracked down Yacoub four years ago he'd become the younger brother Falcón had never had. Because of Yacoub's own complicated past he'd had a special understanding of the complexities of the family horrors that had led to Falcón's complete mental breakdown back in 2001. In gradually revealing themselves to each other, Yacoub had become synonymous with the reassertion of sanity in Falcón's mind. Now, in the wake of the Seville bombing, he was even more than a friend and brother. He had become Falcón's spy. The Spanish intelligence agency, the CNI, in their sudden, desperate need for agents in the Arab countries nearest their borders, had researched the special relationship between Falcón and Yacoub Diouri. Having seen other Western intelligence agencies fail in their bid to recruit Yacoub, they'd used Falcón to bring him into their fold.

It was for this reason that, when Falcón received a text from Yacoub Diouri as he stood in the courtyard outside Marisa's studio, he went immediately in search of a public telephone. They hadn't spoken since the short break in Essaouira last month. Their only communication had been on 'business', via the intelligence service's encrypted website. The CNI had insisted on zero physical contact with Yacoub since he'd successfully penetrated the radical Moroccan Islamic Combatant Group, the GICM, in the days after the Seville bombing. It was this group which had been storing a hundred kilos of the high explosive, hexogen, in the basement mosque in a residential quarter of Seville. Yacoub had found out how that hexogen was going to be used, and in doing so the CNI were concerned that his cover had been blown. There had been some tense days in Paris when they thought that their new agent might be assassinated. Their fears had been groundless. Yacoub returned to Rabat, but the CNI were still so nervous that the only contact they'd allowed was on Falcón's August holiday, which had been arranged in April, two months before the recruitment of Yacoub Diouri.

It took him a while to find a public phone. Falcón understood from the text, which they'd arranged between themselves in Essaouira, that this was to be a private conversation and he should not to use his home phone or mobile to make the call.

'I'm in Madrid,' said Yacoub, with a quiver in his voice.

'You sound nervous.'

'We have to meet.'

'When?'

'Now . . . as soon as possible. I couldn't warn you before because . . . well, you know why.'

'I'm not sure how I'm going to be able to get away at such short notice.'

'I'm not asking you to do this for no reason at all, Javier. It's complicated and important. It's the most important thing that's happened so far.'

'Is this business?'

'It's business *and* it's personal.'

Falcón had something else 'personal' going on tonight. He was supposed to be having dinner with Consuelo, just the two of them. Another assignation in the gradual process of their coming together.

'Are you talking about tonight?' asked Falcón.

'Earlier.'

'It sounds like you want me to catch the next possible train.'

'That would be good,' said Yacoub. 'It's *that* important.'

'I'll have to work up a plausible reason for . . .'

'You're in the middle of an international investigation. There must be a hundred reasons for you to come to Madrid. Call me when you know which train you're on. I'll let you know where I'm going to be. And, Javier . . . don't tell anyone that you're coming to see *me*.'

It was strange how, even after all this time, there were still certain moments which demanded an immediate cigarette. He drove to the Santa Justa station, got caught in traffic and called Inspector Jefe Luis Zorrita, said he needed to talk to him about Marisa Moreno's evidence. Did he have some time this evening? Zorrita was surprised; the case was locked off. Falcón said he had other things to discuss as well. They arranged to meet as close to 7 p.m. as possible.

A thought came to him as he replayed Yacoub's conversation. He wondered if this 'business *and* personal' problem was related to Yacoub's homosexuality. Although Yacoub was a happily married man with two children, he had this other secret life which, to the radical Islamic GICM, would be unacceptable.

The traffic opened up. Falcón moved on, put a call through to his second-in-command, Inspector José Luis Ramírez, whose usual stolid pugnacity had given way to a mixture of anger and excitement after viewing the disks they'd found in Vasili Lukyanov's briefcase.

'You won't believe this shit,' he said. 'A councillor with two girls at the same time. A town planner giving it to a teenager in the ass. A building inspector snorting cocaine off a black girl's tits. And that's the mild stuff. This will crack the Costa del Sol wide open, if it gets out.'

'Don't let it. You know the rules. Only one computer in our department —'

'Relax, Javier. It's all under control.'

'I'm not coming back in today,' said Falcón. 'Am I going to see you tomorrow?'

'Elvira's out. It's quiet here. I'll be here in the morning and I'll stay if you want me to, but I'd rather not.'

'Let's see how it goes,' said Falcón. 'I hope you can have a nice weekend.'

'Hold on a sec, the GRECO guy, Vicente Cortés, was in here earlier looking for you. He wanted to tell you that he's had a report about a Russian who was found up in the hills behind San Pedro de Alcántara, with a nine-millimetre bullet in the back of his head. Alexei Somebody. A big friend of the guy you found on the motorway with a steel rod through his heart. Mean anything?'

'More to Cortés than to me,' said Falcón, and hung up.

At the Santa Justa station, Falcón found that the next AVE to Madrid was at 16.30, which would put him there just in time for his meeting with Inspector Jefe Zorrita. He called Yacoub on a phone in the station, trying to work out when he could get back to Seville and whether it would still be possible to make it to Consuelo's for dinner. Wanting that. Needing that. Even though progress was slow.

'See Zorrita,' said Yacoub. 'I'll let you know where to go afterwards.'

Falcón ate something unmemorable, drank a beer, sunk a *café solo* and boarded the train. He wanted to sleep but there was too much brain interference. A woman sitting opposite him was talking to her daughter on her mobile. She was getting remarried and her daughter wasn't happy about it. Complicated lives, getting more complicated by the minute.

The prison governor called to say that Esteban Calderón had put in a request to see a psychologist.

The train slashed through the brown, parched plains of northern Andalucía.

Where had the rain gone?

'He won't see the prison psychologist,' said the governor. 'He talks about this woman you know, but he can't remember her name.'

'Alicia Aguado,' said Falcón.

'You're not the investigating officer in Señor Calderón's case, are you?'

'No, but I'm seeing the officer who is this evening. I'll make sure he contacts you.'

He hung up. The woman opposite had finished speaking to her daughter. She spun the mobile on the table with a long, painted nail. She looked up. The sort of woman who always knows when she's under observation. Dangerous, save-my-life eyes, thought Falcón. The daughter was right to be concerned.

Up since before three and still not even lethargic. He closed his eyes to the dangerous ones opposite, but never reached below that confused state on the edge of oblivion. Now that he was worried he might not see her this evening, Consuelo surfaced in his mind. They'd first met five years ago when she'd been the prime suspect in the murder of her husband, the restaurateur Raúl Jiménez. A year later they'd met again and had a fling. Falcón had been hurt when she broke it off, but, as he'd recently discovered, Consuelo had had her own problems, which had sent her to the consulting rooms of the blind clinical psychologist, Alicia Aguado. Now, for the last three months, they'd been trying again. He could tell she was happier. She was easing him into her life gradually: only seeing him at weekends and quite often in family situations, with her sister and the

58

children. He didn't mind that. His work had been punishing. Consuelo, too, was expanding the restaurant business left to her by Raúl Jiménez. Falcón enjoyed the feeling of belonging that he got from sitting at her family table. He wouldn't have minded more sex, but the food was always good, and in their moments alone they were getting on.

Thoughts of Consuelo always seemed to involve Yacoub. The two were inextricably linked in his mind. The one had led to the other. Falcón and Consuelo had first been drawn together by their fascination with the fate of Raúl Jiménez's youngest son from his first marriage, Arturo, who'd vanished in the mid 1960s never to be seen again. The boy had been kidnapped by a Moroccan businessman as an act of revenge against Raúl Jiménez, who had impregnated the businessman's twelve-year-old daughter and then fled back to Spain. After his brief affair with Consuelo, Falcón had set out to find Arturo, hoping that this would bring her back to him. It hadn't worked, but the reward had been to discover that Arturo had been brought up as one of the Moroccan businessman's sons and had even been given his family name to become Yacoub Diouri.

Their strange pasts: Falcón, who had been raised in Spain by Francisco Falcón only to find that his real father was a Moroccan artist, and Yacoub, born a Spaniard, forsaken by his father Raúl Jiménez, to be raised by his Moroccan abductor in Rabat, had been the bizarre foundation of their powerful friendship. And for the first time, perhaps as a result of his exhausted state, Falcón found his mildly confused mind reflecting, within the emotional compression of these unusual events, on what had happened to the child of the twelve-year-old daughter who'd been impregnated by Raúl Jiménez. He must ask Yacoub.

His mobile vibrating against his chest brought him back with a start to the dusty fields flashing past. It was his police mobile and he took the call without checking the name on the screen.

'Listen, Inspector Jefe Javier Falcón. Keep your nose out of things that don't concern you.'

'Who is this?'

'You heard.'

The line went dead. He checked the number. Withheld. He folded the phone away. The woman opposite was looking at him again. Across the aisle they were watching him, too. Paranoia, that horribly infectious disease, closed in. The voice on the mobile. Had there been an accent? How had they got his police number? Something a little more uncomfortable than satisfaction eased between his shoulder blades as he realized that, in putting pressure on Marisa Moreno, he must be on the right track. He'd been dredging his mind for something to talk about to Inspector Jefe Zorrita. He didn't want to annoy him with a bunch of hairline cracks in his cast-iron case. Now things were firming up in his mind.

The train eased into the Atocha station. Falcón hadn't arrived in Madrid on the AVE for some years and as he came into the main concourse he was distracted by the continuing memorial to the victims of the 11 March 2004 bombings. He was standing there, looking at the flowers and candles, when the woman from the train appeared by his side. This was too much, he thought.

'Forgive me, now I know it must be you,' she said. 'You are Javier Falcón, aren't you? May I shake your hand and tell you how much I admire you for what you said on the television, about catching the perpetrators of the Seville bomb. Now I've seen you in the flesh, I know you won't let us down.'

He held out his hand, almost in a trance, thanked her. She smiled and brushed past him and in that moment he found that his other hand now contained a piece of folded paper. He wasn't sure who'd put it there, but he was sensible enough not to look at it. He left the station, picked up a cab to the Jefatura. The folded note gave an address just off the Plaza de la Paja in the Latina district and instructions to enter via the garage.

Inspector Jefe Luis Zorrita welcomed him into his office. He was wearing a dark blue suit, a red tie and a white shirt in a way that hinted that minus the tie was about as informal as he ever got. He had his black hair combed back in rails to reveal a forehead with three lines drawn to a focal point above the bridge of his nose. It struck Falcón that there was no mistaking him for anything other than a cop. His hardness had been added in layers; the lacquer of experience. A meeting of the eyes, a handshake, dispelled any possibility that this person was a civil servant or businessman. He had seen it all, heard it all, and his whole family structure and belief system had kept him powerfully sane.

'You look tired, Javier,' he said, falling back into his chair. 'It never stops, does it?'

They looked out of the window at the bright, sunlit world that kept them so fully employed. Falcón's eyes shifted back to the desk where there was a photo of Zorrita with his wife and three children.

'I didn't want to do this over the phone,' said Falcón. 'I have enormous respect for the work you did last June under very difficult circumstances . . .'

'What have you found?' asked Zorrita, cutting through the preliminaries, interested to hear what he could possibly have missed.

'As yet . . . nothing.'

Zorrita sat back, hands clasped over his flat, hard stomach. Not so concerned now that he knew he wasn't going to have to confront a failing on his part.

'My interest in this case is not to get a wife-beater and suspected murderer off the hook,' said Falcón.

'That man is a *cabrón*,' said Zorrita with profound distaste from behind his family photograph. 'A nasty, arrogant . . . *cabrón*.'

61

'He's beginning to recognize that himself,' said Falcón.

'I'll believe that when I see it,' said Zorrita, who was a man incapable of complications in his love life, because there'd only ever been one woman in it.

'The prison governor just called me to say that he's volunteered to see a shrink.'

'No amount of talking, no amount of disentangling the shit that went on between him and his parents, no amount of "light" shed on "feelings", will take away the fact that he beat that poor woman and then killed her and, if he's given half a chance, like all those other weak brutes, he'll do it again.'

'This isn't what I've come to talk to you about today,' said Falcón, seeing that this was something that stoked Zorrita up. 'Would you mind if I laid out the basic problem I've got? Some of it you'll know, but other parts of it will be news to you.'

'Go ahead,' said Zorrita, still simmering.

'As you know, the destruction of the pre-school and apartment block by the Seville bomb of 6th June, three months ago, came about as a result of the detonation, by a smaller device, of approximately one hundred kilos of hexogen. This high explosive was being stored by a logistics cell of the Moroccan terrorist group, the GICM, in the basement mosque of the building. The smaller device was comprised of Goma 2 Eco, the same explosive used in the 11th March bombings here in Madrid back in 2004. Prior to the explosion, the mosque was cased by two men masquerading as council inspectors, who, we believe, inserted some device in the fuse box, which blew and caused a power failure. These men have not been found, nor have the electricians who were brought in to repair the fuse box, restore power and do some other work, during which we believe they planted the Goma 2 Eco device in the false ceiling of the mosque.

'The idea of the so-called Catholic conspiracy was to use this outrage to blame Islamic extremists, to make it look as if they had a plan to return Andalucía to the Muslim fold. The conspirators wanted to turn public opinion in favour of a small right-wing party called Fuerza Andalucía, who, in becoming the new partner of the ruling Partido Popular, would put the conspirators in control of the Andalucían state parliament. It didn't work and the alleged masterminds of the plot – César Benito, a board director of Horizonte, and Lucrecio Arenas, the ex-CEO of Banco Omni, who were Horizonte's bankers – were executed a few days after the bombing.'

'What about the Islamic calling cards left near their bodies?' asked Zorrita.

'Nobody thinks that those killings were carried out by any radical Islamist group,' said Falcón. 'It's believed they were terminated by their co-conspirators.'

'Who are, as yet, unknown.'

'We're coming to that.'

'What about the company that owned Horizonte?' said Zorrita, squinting at the evening sunlight coming in through the window. 'The media tried to make something of them – a couple of American Christian fundamentalists.'

'I4IT own Horizonte. It's an American investment group run by two born-again Christians, called Cortland Fallenbach and Morgan Havilland. They are so far removed from this situation as to be completely untouchable and, for legal reasons, we have as yet been unable to gain access to I4IT's European offices here in Madrid.'

'And presumably the lives of the Catholic Kings, as the media now calls César Benito and Lucrecio Arenas, have been taken apart.'

'That has been, and still is, a time-consuming business. The CNI's banking and accounting department are working their way into the offshore world. Benito and Arenas were what are known in that world as Hen-Wees – High Net Worth Individuals. Their assets are hidden behind nominee directors and shareholders and unregistered offshore trusts.

It will be pure luck if somebody manages to find something in the next six months that we can act upon.'

'So you're blocked,' said Zorrita. 'And the whole of Spain knows what Javier Falcón is after.'

'I think I only want what any police officer in my position would want,' said Falcón, leaning forward in his chair. 'To catch the people responsible for casing that mosque and planting the Goma 2 Eco device, along with the bosses who ordered them to do it.'

Zorrita held up his hand to calm Falcón down, nodded his agreement.

'You're not getting anything from the suspects in your custody and the two ringleaders have been "executed",' said Zorrita. 'So where else have you got to go?'

'I've decided to take a long look at the violence,' said Falcón. 'Where do a bunch of conspirators, sophisticated men like Lucrecio Arenas and César Benito, access that sort of violence?'

'As you say, every news channel and paper, apart from the ABC, are calling this the Catholic Conspiracy. What with the national obsession with Opus Dei, the PR campaign by the Church to counteract all this has been unprecedented,' said Zorrita. 'Do Opus Dei have an Improvised Explosive Device division?'

The two men smiled at each other.

'What we *do* know from our suspects in custody and other inquiries is that Arenas's motivation was *not* his Catholic beliefs,' said Falcón. 'The Hen-Wee spoke from his heart.'

'And César Benito was in construction,' said Zorrita.

'Where there's always large amounts of black money, which can be hidden away in the offshore world.'

'But you're not getting anywhere by following the money,' said Zorrita.

'Only that there's undoubtedly money-laundering involved and that both men were well set up in property in the Costa del Sol.'

'The Russian mafia,' said Zorrita. 'I know it's a knee-jerk reaction when you hear the words "money-laundering" and "Costa del Sol" in the same sentence, but after the recent Marbella town council scandal . . .'

Falcón nodded.

'And you think they're going to be easier to penetrate than the offshore world?' said Zorrita.

'Let's just take a look at the violence,' said Falcón, holding up a finger. 'In that period around the 6th June bombing there were five expressions of violence. The first was the murder of Tateb Hassani, who was vital to the conspiracy for his drafting in Arabic script of the extremists' plans for taking over Andalucía. He was found on the Seville dump, poisoned and mutilated, on the morning of the explosion. Murdered because a) he knew too much, b) he would always be a vulnerable point to the conspiracy and c) it got everybody's hands dirty. The second expression of violence was the bomb itself which, as I said, was designed to point the finger at Muslim extremism whilst increasing the prestige of Fuerza Andalucía, making them the preferred partners of the ruling Partido Popular.'

'The third, presumably, was Esteban Calderón's murder of his wife,' said Zorrita, 'which derailed the investigation into the Seville bombing.'

'And four and five were the executions of Lucrecio Arenas and César Benito,' said Falcón. 'They had to be killed once we'd caught the other half of the conspiracy, because there were direct links between them. It would only be a matter of time before Arenas and Benito gave up the bombers they had employed.'

'So there's a clear motive in every case.'

'Except Calderón,' said Falcón.

'He was beating her, that was clear, and he's never denied it,' said Zorrita. 'If he didn't kill her, then why didn't he just call the police when he discovered her dead body in their apartment? Why did he try to dispose of her body in the river?'

'He made a serious error of judgement.'

'You're telling me.'

'Another angle,' said Falcón. 'What was the worst thing that could have happened to our investigation of the Seville bombing?'

'I agree, losing Calderón at that stage was a disaster for you.'

'He was at the top of his game,' said Falcón. 'Giving good direction. Keeping the media away from my squad, the counter-terrorism guys and the CNI. If you were at the zenith of your career, would you choose that moment to murder your wife?'

'He chose that moment to start abusing her.'

'And that was important.'

'Why?'

'Because I think that when Marisa Moreno saw Inés in the Murillo Gardens she noticed somehow that she was being abused,' said Falcón. 'I've just been speaking to her, getting her family background. Her natural mother "disappeared" in Cuba. Her attitude to her dead father was not exactly respectful. He was, like Calderón, an inveterate womanizer. She had more time for her Sevillana stepmother than she did for him.'

'This isn't going to stand up anywhere near a court, Javier.'

'I know; all I'm trying to do here is find weaknesses. The only killing about which there's a very slight doubt in my mind is that of Inés.'

'But not in *my* mind, Javier.'

'Two hours after I'd been to see Marisa this afternoon I got an anonymous phone call telling me to keep my nose out of things that were not my concern.'

'It wasn't from me,' said Zorrita, deadpan.

They laughed.

'What else did Marisa tell you?' asked Zorrita. 'You must have something more than that.'

'I decided to go to see Marisa to ram a stick in the wasps' nest, to see what happened,' said Falcón. 'The only thing I had to go on was something one of my officers found while trying to dig up some dirt on her.'

'Marisa had no criminal record, I know that,' said Zorrita.

'The only thing my officer found was that Marisa had reported her sister missing.'

'When?'

'Eight years ago.'

'You really are clutching at straws, Javier.'

Falcón was tempted to tell Zorrita about Marisa's wood carving, but another glance at the family photo on the desktop persuaded him otherwise. He felt weak in front of Zorrita's steadiness, but still resisted the temptation to point up all the other little flaws he'd found.

'Marisa is no fool,' said Falcón. 'If you despised your womanizing father, would you be drawn to an incorrigible womanizer yourself?'

'I doubt it would be the first time it had happened,' said Zorrita, still feeling as solid as a rock.

'Her sister went missing again, but this time she was over eighteen.'

'So Marisa didn't go to the police.'

'Her sister is the only family Marisa's got. Father, mother and stepmother are dead. Would you just shrug your shoulders if your sister ran off again?'

'If I didn't care, yes,' said Zorrita.

'She cares,' said Falcón.

'You've still got a long way to go with this, Javier.'

'I know,' said Falcón. 'I just wanted to ask you if you'd mind me digging around.'

'Dig away, Javier. The way you're going, you'll come out in Buenos Aires.'

6

The early-evening sun was still bright, but low in the sky so it was already dark in the cavernous Madrid streets. Falcón was sitting in the back of a patrol car, which Zorrita had arranged for him. He felt foolish as they left the Jefatura and he lay down across the back seat. The driver saw him out of the corner of his eye. Falcon told him to keep looking straight ahead.

The driver dropped him off at the Ópera metro station and Falcón took the one-stop ride to La Latina. He checked the other occupants of the metro carriage. He was still smarting at Zorrita's scorn for his theory on Marisa Moreno. Was all this getting out of control in his mind? Everything looked dangerously plausible at three in the morning, but laughable by ten. And did he really have to be this careful about his assignation with Yacoub? Were there actually people on every street corner looking out for him? Once your mind had been proven unstable there was always a doubt, and not just to outsiders.

A car went into the garage of the apartment block on Calle Alfonso VI and Falcón ducked in behind it as the door was closing. He walked down into the dark, took the lift up to the third floor, stepped out into an empty landing, rang the buzzer and waited. He sensed the eyeball on the other side of the peep-hole. The door clicked open. Yacoub beckoned him in. They went through the customary pleasantries; Falcón asked after Yacoub's wife, Yousra, and his two children, Abdullah and Leila. There was nodding and thanks, but Yacoub was strangely subdued.

A full ashtray was the centrepiece of the living room, with a smoking, filterless cigarette on its edge. The curtains were drawn. A single lamp in the corner half-lit the room. Yacoub was wearing faded jeans and a white shirt untucked. He was barefoot and he'd shaved his long hair off to a short stubble, which he kept dusting with the palm of his hand as if he'd only just had it done. His head now matched his beard. His eyes seemed deeper set and darker, as if some wariness had put him in retreat to a safer place. He sat on the sofa with the ashtray at his side and smoked enthusiastically, with lips that twitched more than Falcón remembered.

'I made some tea,' he said. 'You're all right with tea, aren't you?'

'You always ask me that,' said Falcón, throwing off his jacket, rolling up his shirt sleeves. 'You know I'm fine with tea.'

'Sorry about the heat,' said Yacoub. 'I don't want to turn on the air-con. I shouldn't be here. I'm hiding.'

'Who from?'

'Everybody. My people. Your people. The world,' he said, and, as an afterthought, 'Maybe myself, too.'

He poured the tea, stood up, paced around the room to bring his nerves back under control.

'So, nobody knows about this meeting,' said Falcón, encouraging Yacoub to open up.

'This is just you and me,' said Yacoub. 'The only man I can trust. The only one I can talk to. The only one I can rely on not to use what has happened against me.'

'You're nervous. I can see that.'

'Nervous,' he said, nodding. 'That's why I like you, Javier. You keep me calm. I'm not just nervous. I'm paranoid. I'm totally fucking paranoid.'

These last words were accompanied by a ferocious sideways slash of the air in front of him. Falcón tried to remember whether he'd ever heard Yacoub swear.

Yacoub then launched himself into a long rant about the lengths to which he'd had to go in order to arrive unseen in this apartment.

'You *were* careful, weren't you, Javier?' he said at the end of it all.

Falcón reciprocated with his own procedure, which seemed to have a mildly calming influence on Yacoub, who listened and gnawed at a hangnail. Then he lit another cigarette, sipped his tea, which was too hot, sat down on the sofa, and stood up again.

'The last time you got like this was after those four days in Paris,' said Falcón. 'But you were OK. You were taken back into the fold.'

'My cover's not blown,' said Yacoub, quickly. 'No, there's no problem with that. It's just that they've found the perfect way to keep me . . . close.'

'Keep you close?' said Falcón. 'You mean in the sense of not straying? Does that mean they suspect you?'

'Suspect is too strong a word,' said Yacoub, tucking his hand under his armpit and chopping the air with his cigarette. 'They like me. They need me. But they are naturally unsure of me. It's the part of my brain that isn't Moroccan that makes them nervous.'

'We're Andalucíans, Yacoub, same people, same Berber genetic marker,' said Falcón.

'The problem for them is that they can't rely on me to think in a certain way. I'm not consistently Moroccan,' said Yacoub. 'And that makes them uneasy.'

Falcón waited. If he'd been with another European he'd have asked the question: 'Is this something to do with you being gay?' But he had the same problem that the radical Islamist group, the GICM, had with Yacoub, but the other way round; Falcón couldn't rely on him to think like a European. His mentality for argument was more Moroccan. Direct questioning didn't work.

'Before Friday noon prayers last week, Abdullah, my son, came to see me,' said Yacoub. 'I was alone in my study. He closed the door and came to the edge of my desk. He said: "I am going to tell you something that will make you very happy and very proud." I was confused. The boy is only eighteen. I didn't remember any talk of a girl and, anyway, this would not be the way for that sort of thing to happen. I stood up as if I was about to hear important news. He came over to my side of the desk and told me that he had become a mujahideen and embraced me as a fellow warrior.'

'The GICM have *recruited* him?' said Falcón, cannoning out of his armchair.

Yacoub nodded, drew on the cigarette, took the smoke deep into his lungs and then held open his arms in a gesture of total helplessness.

'Directly after the Friday noon prayers, he left to continue his training.'

'Continue?'

'Exactly that,' said Yacoub. 'The boy's been lying to me. He's taken four weekends away in the last two months. I thought he was going to see his friends in Casablanca, but he's been out in the country on military-training exercises.'

'How was he recruited?'

Yacoub shrugged, shook his head. Falcón doubted that he was going to hear the precise truth.

'He's been working with me at the factory, just temporarily before he goes to university at the end of the month. We go to a mosque in Salé. There are . . . elements there. I thought he was steering clear of them . . . clearly, he wasn't.'

'Have you spoken to anyone about this?'

'You are the first outsider.'

'What about in the GICM?'

'The military commander is not there at the moment. Even when he is, he's not easy to get to see. I've only conveyed my gratitude via an intermediary.'

'Your gratitude?'

'What was I supposed to do? I *should* be happy and proud,' he said, and sank back down on to the sofa, buried his face in his hands and sobbed twice.

'And you assume that this has been done to keep you "close", to control you, to make them feel less uneasy about you.'

'Nobody but the maddest radical would want their son to become a mujahideen . . . potentially a suicide bomber. All this talk you hear on TV in France or England about honour and paradise and seventy-two virgins, it's just . . . it's just bull-shit. You might find that sort of thinking in Gaza, or Iraq, or Afghanistan, but you won't find it in Rabat – not in my circle.'

'Let's think this through,' said Falcón. 'What are they trying to achieve through this manoeuvre? If it's to keep you close, then . . .'

'They want to infiltrate my household,' said Yacoub. And then, touching his temple: 'They want to infiltrate my mind.'

'They're not convinced that they can control you, so they set about controlling all those around you?'

'Their whole reason for being interested in me is that they know that I can live "convincingly" in both worlds: Islamic and secular, East and West. It doesn't mean they like it. They didn't like the fact that my sixteen-year-old daughter, Leila, was wearing a swimsuit on the beach.'

'They were watching you on the beach?'

'When we were on holiday in Essaouira, they were watching us, Javier,' said Yacoub. 'Abdullah has stopped

72

playing his music, which I thought a blessing at first, but now I'm desperate for him to be normal. And, can you believe this, he reads the Qur'an. He doesn't play computer games any more. I had a look at the history on his browser . . . it's all Islamic websites, Palestinian politics – Hamas versus Fatah, the Muslim Brotherhood . . .'

'Where is *this* influence coming from?'

Another shrug.

Does he know? Why isn't he telling me? thought Falcón. Is it someone close to him? Someone in his extended family? When Yacoub had been recruited, he'd said he'd never give up a family member.

'They find their way in,' said Yacoub. 'And you know, until Abdullah came to me with his news last Friday, I didn't think these developments were such a bad thing. It's good for teenagers to have something serious in their lives, something other than violent video games and hip-hop . . . but mujahideen?'

'I know it's difficult for you to be calm about this,' said Falcón. 'But there's no immediate danger if, as you say, they're trying to keep *you* close. We have time.'

'They've taken my boy away from me,' said Yacoub, who shaded his eyes and sobbed again, before coming back at Falcón, angry. 'He's in one of their camps. That's 24/7. When they're not running over hills and assault courses, they're doing weapons training and bomb-making. And when that's all over, they're plugged into radical Islam. I have no idea what is going to come back to me, but I'm sure it won't be the Abdullah I knew. It will be *their* Abdullah. And then how will I live? Looking over my shoulder at my own son?'

The enormity of Yacoub's predicament hit Falcón hard. Three months ago he'd asked Yacoub to make what should have been a personal step towards embracing radical Islam. He had been stunned at the rapidity with which Yacoub had been taken deep inside the GICM organization. It could only mean that he had something that they wanted. And now the GICM were protecting themselves and it meant enclosing not just Yacoub but his whole family as well. And, worse still, there was no way out. Radical Islam was not something you changed your mind about. Once admitted to the close fraternity and their secrets there was no walking away. They wouldn't let you. It wasn't so different – and Falcón couldn't believe he was thinking this – to being part of a mafia family.

'You don't have to say anything, Javier. There's nothing to say,' said Yacoub. 'I just needed to tell someone and you're the only person I've got.'

'You don't want me to talk to Pablo at the CNI about this?'

'Pablo? What happened to Juan?' said Yacoub. 'Juan was the old, experienced guy.'

'Juan was given early retirement last week,' said Falcón. 'He'd blown it over Madrid and their assessment of his work in the Seville bombing wasn't so good either. Pablo's good. Forty-two years old. Very experienced in North Africa. Totally committed.'

'No, Javier, you must not tell anyone,' said Yacoub, the flat of his hand taking on the threat of a chopping blade. 'If you do they will only use it. That is how these intelligence people think: He's vulnerable, let's use it. *You* won't use it. I know that. And that's why you always have to be there between me and them. You are, and will be, the only one who truly understands my situation.'

Something like a cramp started up in Falcón's guts. This was different to the dead weight of his responsibility in this matter. That was just a few more rocks in the already unwieldy rucksack. This was the knot of fear making itself felt. Now he was being forced into the unique position of having to decide whether Yacoub was reliable or not. Given the choice between his son, Abdullah, and the anonymous face of the Spanish intelligence agency, there would be no doubt who Yacoub would choose. He'd said it from the very beginning and the CNI had accepted those terms.

'What can I do to make your situation any easier?' asked Falcón.

'You're a good friend, Javier. The only true friend I've got,' said Yacoub. 'You will be the one to help me with the plan to save my son.'

'I doubt he could walk away from being a mujahideen very easily, especially after he's been to one of their camps.'

'I think the only way would be for him to be arrested on his way to a mission,' said Yacoub.

'Those would be extraordinary circumstances,' said Falcón. 'For the GICM to let you know what was being planned . . . unless you were directly involved.'

'There you have it, Javier,' said Yacoub. 'It would also depend very much on whether my survival is considered critical.'

Falcón and Yacoub looked at each other for some time, smoke steadily rising from Yacoub's fingers and dissipating over his shaven head.

'What?' asked Yacoub.

'I can't believe you said those words.'

'We were naïve, Javier. We have absurdly idealistic minds. It was no accident that you were chosen to recruit me. All these agencies have people specifically employed to size you up, to perceive whether you have the necessary strengths and weaknesses for the work required of you. And I'm not talking about whether you're a good manager of people or handle stress well, but whether, under the right circumstances, you could torture a man to get the necessary information or . . .'

'Or be ingenuous enough to be completely malleable, or perhaps, utterly predictable?' said Falcón.

'The CNI saw in you a need. They knew your history. They knew that you no longer viewed the world in the blinkered way that most people see it, that you demanded a different perspective. They fed it to you. You fed it to me.

We didn't know the sort of people we were dealing with. Possibly we imagined that they might be like ourselves, and we could enter their world beneath the surface of everyday life and change things. And what happens? We meet completely ruthless minds who beat us into corners and force us to behave – or else.'

Falcón looked around the darkened room. Their situation – meeting in an anonymous Madrid apartment to discuss unseen dramatic developments – was so far removed from real life that he was suddenly desperate for the surface; but like the diver surrounded by sharks, who still needed to decompress, he had to hold the line, not panic.

'You envisage a situation where you will give us information about an imminent attack, which will enable us to intercept Abdullah's group and arrest him, but . . .'

'It will irrevocably undermine my position in the GICM and I will be immediately executed.'

'No,' said Falcón.

'Yes,' said Yacoub. 'It's the only way.'

'But you realize all that will happen is that Abdullah will end up in jail, where he will gravitate to the radical elements which exist in Spanish prisons, and he will come out even more zealous than he went in. Having done his time he will be welcomed back into the group, and all you will have achieved is your own death,' said Falcón. 'You have to let me draw on some experience in this matter. Pablo and others in the CNI must have come across this type of situation before. They will have ideas on how to handle it.'

'You're my friend,' said Yacoub. 'I'm in this because of you. By that I mean I wanted to do this and you were the only one I could trust. I don't want you to start talking to others. As soon as you do that, *I* lose control and they start to run the situation; and believe me, they will look after their own interests, not mine. Before you know it, we'll be in a hall of mirrors, not knowing which way to turn. And this is my *son*, Javier. I can't allow him to be sucked in, manipulated, turned into a piece of the game, a fanatic's mass murderer, who will imagine in his adolescent mind that in killing and maiming . . .'

'Yacoub, you're letting this get out of control in *your* mind.'

'This is my Moroccan side,' he said, leaping to his feet and pacing around the room, scratching at childhood scars on his head which had been laid bare by the severity of his haircut. 'I get very emotional. I can't seem to calm myself down, or rather, I can calm down. I do calm down. And you know how I do it?'

Falcón waited for him to come back into his line of sight, but Yacoub leaned over the back of the armchair, his face so close the tobacco breath was sharp in Falcón's nostrils. 'I imagine Abdullah safe . . . away from all this . . . this madness. I imagine myself under a funeral shroud and able to see the sun coming through the cotton, the breeze playing over the material, and I am at peace for the first time in my life.'

'Try an alternative vision, Yacoub. Don't be so fatalistic. Imagine yourself at home with Abdullah, his wife and your grandchildren on your lap. Try achieving that instead of your death and his incarceration.'

'I would, if it wasn't such an absurd dream, an impossible ideal, Javier,' said Yacoub. 'The boy is already a part of their organization. He has no thoughts for girls, wives, children. Normal life has become a miserable existence to him. He despises his carefree childhood. He mourns the lost hours spent on his Gameboy. His whole adolescence is a tragedy of unconsciousness to him now. There's no question of bringing him back. The irony of it all is that, in joining himself to this new world, he has, to me, become a lost soul. He wanders a world of death, destruction and martyrdom. While my stomach heaves at the thought of a market in Baghdad with two hundred dead women and children, the whole area a blackened, smoking charnel house, Abdullah smiles beatifically at the imagined grace of the martyr who has committed this godless atrocity.'

'So you've seen him again since he went to this training camp a week ago?' asked Falcón, confused at how Yacoub could have known all this.

'The purpose of admitting me to the GICM in the first place was primarily to make one of their international attacks possible,' said Yacoub inconsequentially, buying himself some time. 'This means, as you know, I have unprecedented access to the military wing of the GICM. As soon as Abdullah told me his news, it was arranged for me to be shown his training camp. I spent some time there. We had a couple of evenings together in which I was able to see the profound change wrought in his young mind.'

'But you didn't manage to see the commander of the military wing?'

'No, as I told you, he wasn't there,' said Yacoub, turning his back on Falcón to stare at the drawn curtains. 'I had to convey my gratitude for this honour through one of his officers.'

Was that how it happened? thought Falcón as he joined Yacoub by the window. They embraced and he caught sight of his own confused face over Yacoub's shoulder in the only mirror in the room.

'My friend,' said Yacoub, his hot breath on Falcón's neck. 'You know me so well.'

Do I? thought Falcón. Do I?

7

If on the train journey from Seville to Madrid he'd been slightly feverish with paranoia, then the ride back saw a serious multiplication of the uncertainty parasites in his bloodstream. The darkness rushing past outside meant that all he could see was his disconcerted visage reflected back to him and, with the movement of the train, it seemed to tremble like his vacillating mind.

Not only had Yacoub forbidden him to talk to any of the intelligence officers from the CNI, but he had also already set in motion a plan for extracting Abdullah from the ranks of the GICM. Yacoub had begged the senior officers in the military wing to ask their commander to send his son on a mission as soon as possible, with the condition that he be responsible for its planning, logistics and execution.

'Why did you do that?' asked Falcón. 'The one thing we need in this situation is time.'

'More important than time, at this stage,' Yacoub said, 'is to show them how honoured I am that my son has been chosen. Delay would have meant that suspicion would have

79

come down heavily on me and I would have been excluded from my son's future. This was the only way for me to keep my foot in the door.'

The high command were thinking about it. Yacoub had told Falcón that the following morning he would be flying back to Rabat, where he expected to be told of their decision. None of this was exactly calming, but it wasn't the cause of Falcón's paranoia. That had started with those cramps of fear in his gut. He'd tried to ignore them, like the man with acute appendicitis who'd convinced himself it was just wind, but they'd made him very apprehensive. One moment he was sitting in front of a man who'd become his closest friend, with whom he shared a level of intimacy he'd only ever experienced with the man he'd believed to be his father – Francisco Falcón. And the next there was a person he no longer completely trusted. Doubt had been interposed. That last embrace in front of the closed curtains had been an attempt to reinforce the relationship, but it was as if some impenetrable barrier, like a Kevlar skin, had come between them.

Perhaps that had been the fatal flaw; the only other time he'd experienced this level of intimacy, it had been based on lies and fraudulence: his father had tricked the five-year-old Javier into becoming the agent of his own mother's death. But how could it have been so quick with Yacoub? Suspicion had ripped through him. But why? He replayed the meeting in minute detail, almost frame by frame, to extract every nuance.

The haircut was part of it, or had it become part of it? Was that retrospective suspicion? Yacoub had always liked to keep his luxuriant hair long. Maybe he was just getting into role. In fact, before the haircut was the apartment. He hadn't asked him about it. Whose was it? He'd have to find that out. He called an old detective friend from his Madrid days who was in a bar on his way home. Falcón gave him the address, told him to keep it to himself. He wanted the owner's identity and background and he was to speak to Falcón only, no messages left in the office.

'I'm not even going to ask,' said his friend, who told him he'd probably have to wait until Monday now.

Headlights wavered in the blackness of the countryside and swung away. Someone across the aisle was studying him. He got up, walked down the train to the bar, ordered a beer. What else? He took out his notebook, jotted down his thoughts. Trust. Yacoub had kept on at Falcón about how much he trusted him: 'The only man I can trust . . . You always have to be between me and them . . .' That was where the cramps had started and when he'd first questioned Yacoub's reliability. 'You're a good friend. The only true friend I've got.' It was that line which had allowed the ugliest thought to enter his head: Is he using me? Falcón rewound to a question he'd asked: 'So where's this influence coming from?' The shrug. Had someone got to Yacoub? He knew the GICM didn't like his relationship with the inspector jefe. Were they breaking it up, and using young Abdullah to do it?

The notes streamed out of his pen. The swearing. The plan. There was no plan, but Yacoub wanted him involved. Why? 'You're my friend. I'm in this because of you.' He'd qualified that blame immediately, but there was no doubt that he wanted Falcón to feel culpable. Then there was Yacoub's vision of his own death. Had he overdone the self-pity? Finally, there was the slip. Was it a slip to reveal that he'd seen Abdullah since he'd gone to the training camp? Yacoub was under pressure. The stress of it created emotional extremes and mistakes were made.

He closed the notebook, took a swig of beer. He breathed back a sense of disequilibrium that he couldn't put his finger on. How do you describe that feeling when it occurs to you that your brother might be exploiting you? There was no

81

word for it. It couldn't be that it was so rare that they hadn't bothered to invent it. People were always exploited *and* betrayed by those closest to them. But what was the word for the feeling of the victim? The Americans have a good word: suckered. Because the feeling was one of being drained, having the marrow sucked out.

He took out his mobile, and it wasn't just for the usual banal exchange that was played out in trains all over the world; he needed to hear the sound of a voice that he believed in and who believed in him. He called Consuelo. Darío, her youngest boy, the eight-year-old, picked up the phone.

'*Hola*, Darío, how's it going?' he said.

'Javi-i-i,' screamed Darío. 'Mamá, mamá, it's Javi.'

'Bring the phone to the kitchen,' said Consuelo.

'Are you good, Darío?' asked Falcón.

'I'm good, Javi. Why aren't you here? You *should* be here. Mamá's been waiting and waiting . . .'

'Bring that phone here, Darío!'

He heard the boy sprinting down the corridor. The phone changed hands.

'I don't want you thinking I'm sitting around here like some lovesick teenager,' said Consuelo. 'Darío's been desperate for you to get here.'

'I'm on the AVE and running late.'

'He won't go to bed until you arrive, and we're going shopping tomorrow. New football boots.'

'I've got to see someone in town before I come out to your place,' said Falcón. 'It's going to be after midnight before I get to you.'

'Maybe we should have dinner out,' said Consuelo. 'That's a better idea. I really want him to go to bed now. I'll take him next door. He's in love with their sixteen-year-old daughter. Let's do that, Javier.'

'Tell him I'll have a kick around with him in the garden tomorrow morning.'

A hesitation.

'You think you're getting lucky tonight?' she said quietly, teasing.

They hadn't discussed his staying over. It was part of the new coming together. No assumptions.

'I've been praying for luck,' he said. 'Has Our Lady been good to me?'

Another hesitation.

'I'll tell Darío,' she said. 'But once you've made a promise like that, you've got to be prepared for him to jump on your head at eight in the morning.'

'Where shall we meet?'

She said she'd arrange everything. All he had to do was meet her in the Bar La Eslava on the Plaza San Lorenzo and they'd take it from there.

Calm restored. He nearly felt like a family man. Consuelo's two older boys, Ricardo and Matías, hadn't been so interested in him. They were fourteen and twelve. But Darío was still keen on the idea of a dad. The boy had brought him closer to Consuelo. She could see that Darío liked him and, although she would never say it, Darío was her favourite. He also distracted them from the seriousness of what they were trying to do, made them feel more casual, less anxious.

And with that thought, sleep finally claimed him.

He woke up sitting in the carriage in the Santa Justa station, with people shuffling out of the train. It was just after 11.30. He left the station, drove to Calle Hiniesta. Falcón wanted to have Marisa sleeping uneasily with the knowledge that after their chat this afternoon he'd taken an anonymous threatening phone call and that he wasn't scared by it.

As he parked at the back of the Santa Isabel church he saw that the light was on in her penthouse apartment, the plants were lit up on her roof terrace. He pressed her buzzer.

'I'm coming down,' she said.

'This is Inspector Jefe Javier Falcón,' he said.

'What are *you* doing here?' she said, annoyed. 'I'm on my way out.'

'We can discuss this in the street, if that's what you want.'

She buzzed the door open. He took the small lift up to her floor. Marisa let him in, closing down her mobile, nervous, as if she'd just asked her date to delay his arrival unless he wanted to meet the police.

'Going somewhere special?' asked Falcón, taking in her long, tight turquoise dress, her coppery hair down to her shoulders, the gold earrings, the twenty-odd gold and silver bangles on her arm, an expensive scent.

'A gallery opening and then dinner.'

She closed the door behind him. Her hands were uneasy at her sides. The bangles rattled. She didn't ask him to sit down.

'I thought we had a long talk this afternoon,' she said. 'You took up an hour of my work-time and now you've moved in on my relaxation . . .'

'I had a call from a friend of yours this afternoon.'

'A friend of mine?'

'He told me to keep my nose out of your business.'

Her lips opened. No sound came out.

'It was a couple of hours after we talked,' said Falcón. 'I was on my way up to Madrid to see another friend of yours.'

'I don't know anyone in Madrid.'

'Inspector Jefe Luis Zorrita?'

'There's the confusion,' said Marisa, dredging up some boldness. 'He's no friend of mine.'

'He's as interested as I am in your story,' said Falcón. 'He's told me I can dig away to my heart's content.'

'What are you *talking* about?' she said, her brow puckering with fury. 'Story? What story?'

'We all have stories,' said Falcón. 'We all have versions of these stories to suit every occasion. We've got one version

84

of your story, which has put Esteban Calderón in prison. Now we're going to find the real version, and it'll be interesting to see where that puts *you*.'

Even with the armour of her beauty, her lithe sexuality encased in the aquamarine sheath, he could see that he'd got under her skin. The fever had started. The uncertainty behind the big, brown eyes. His work was done. Now it was time to get out.

'Tell your friends,' said Falcón, making powerful eye contact as he walked past her to the door, 'that I'll be waiting for their next call.'

'What friends?' she said to the back of his head. 'I don't *have* any friends.'

On his way out of the apartment he looked back at her, standing alone in the middle of the room. He believed her. And for some reason he couldn't help but pity her, too.

Back in his car he wanted to hang on to see who turned up to take her out. Then he saw her on the roof terrace, looking down at him with the mobile to her ear. He didn't want to keep Consuelo waiting. He pulled away, drove back home where he had a quick shower to try to wash off all that police work. He changed his clothes and ten minutes later he was on his way to the Plaza San Lorenzo. The cab dropped him off in the square, which was full of people ambling about in the warm night under the high trees, with the impressive terracotta brick façade of the church of Jesús del Gran Poder behind. His police mobile vibrated in his pocket. He took the call without thinking, resigned to his fate.

'Listen,' said the voice. 'You'll realize when you've gone too far with this because something will happen. And when it does, you will know that you are to blame. You will recognize it. But there'll be no discussion and no negotiation because, Inspector Jefe Javier Falcón, you will never hear from us again.'

Dead. No number. He wrote the words he'd heard in a notebook he always carried with him. Having just seen Marisa he'd expected that call, but now that it had come he did not feel strengthened by it. Its psychology had unnerved him. That was the calculation of the voice, but his anticipation of it should have protected him. It hadn't. Like a probing question from the blind psychologist, Alicia Aguado, the voice had lifted the lid on something and, despite not knowing its precise nature, he dreaded it coming to the surface.

The Bar La Eslava was packed. Consuelo was standing outside, smoking and sipping a glass of manzanilla. Sevillanos were not known for respecting other people's personal space, but they'd made an exception for Consuelo. Her charisma seemed to create a forcefield. Her short blonde hair stood out under the street lights. She made the simple wild pink mini-dress she was wearing look even more expensive than it was and her high heels made her slim, strong legs look even longer. Falcón was glad he'd taken the time to shower and change. He walked through the crowd towards her and she didn't see him until he was on her.

They kissed. He tasted her peachy lipstick, put his hands around her slim waist, felt her contours fitting into his. He inhaled her smell, felt the sharp prick of her diamond-stud earring in his cheek as his lips found her neck.

'Are you all right?' she said, running a hand up the back of his head so that electricity earthed through his heels.

'More than all right now,' he said, as her hands travelled the outline of his shoulders and his blood went live. Her thigh slipped between his legs. His stomach leapt, cock stirred, perfume shunted into his head and he became human for the first time that day.

They parted, feeling the eyes of the people around them.

'I'll get a beer,' he said.

'I've booked us a table across the road,' she said.

The bar was heaving and noisier than the trading floor of a metal exchange. He fought his way in. He knew the owner, who was serving. A guy he didn't immediately recognize grabbed him around the shoulders. *'Hola, Javier. Que tal?'* The owner handed him a beer, refused payment. Two women kissed him on his way through. He was sure he knew one of them. He squeezed back out into the street.

'I didn't know you were going to Madrid today,' said Consuelo.

She knew Yacoub, but not that he was Falcón's spy.

'I had a meeting with another cop about all that stuff in June,' said Falcón, keeping it vague, but still stumbling around in the memory of his meeting with Yacoub, Marisa, that second phone call.

'You were looking as if you'd had a hard day.'

He took out his mobile, turned it off.

'That helps,' he said, sipping his beer. 'How about you?'

'I had some interesting conversations with a couple of estate agents and I had a session with Alicia.'

'How's that going?'

'I'm nearly sane,' she said, smiling, blue eyes widening hysterically. 'Only another year to go.'

They laughed.

'I saw Esteban Calderón today.'

'I'm not as nuts as he is,' said Consuelo.

'The prison governor called me on the way up to Madrid to say he'd put in a request to see Alicia.'

'I don't know if even she could sort out *his* madness,' said Consuelo.

'That was the first time I'd seen him since it happened,' said Falcón. 'He didn't look good.'

'If what he's got in his mind has started to come out in his face, he should be looking terrible,' she said.

'Are you moving?' he asked.

'Moving?'

'The estate agents,' said Falcón. 'You're not bored of Santa Clara already?'

'My business expansion plans.'

'Seville not big enough for all your ideas?'

'Maybe not, but how about Madrid or Valencia? What do you think?'

'Will you still talk to me when you've been photographed by *Hola*?' he said. 'Consuelo Jiménez in her glorious home, surrounded by her beautiful children.'

'And my lover . . . the cop?' she said, looking at him sadly. 'I might have to let you go unless you learn how to sail a yacht.'

That was the first time she'd called him her lover and she knew it. He finished his beer, took her empty glass and put them on a ledge. She took his arm and they walked across the square to the restaurant.

They knew her in the restaurant, which despite its Arabic name had a neo-classical feel to it – all pillars and marble and strong white nappery, with no such thing as a round plate. The chef came out to greet her and two glasses of cava, on the house, arrived at their table. There was a lull in the restaurant hubbub as the other diners looked at them, recognized their faces from distant scandalous news stories; moments later they were forgotten and the cacophony resumed. Consuelo ordered for both of them. He liked it when she took over. They drank the cava. He wished they were at home and he could lean over and kiss her throat. They talked about the future, which was a good sign.

The starter arrived. Three tapas on an oblong plate: a tiny filo pastry money bag containing soft goat's cheese, a crisp toast of duck liver set in sticky sweet quince jam, and a shot-glass of white garlic and almond soup with an orb of melon ice cream floating at the top and flakes of wind-dried tuna nestling in the bottom. Each one went off in his mouth like a firecracker.

'*This* is oral sex,' said Consuelo.

Plates were removed with their empty flutes. A bottle of 2004 Pesquera from the Ribeiro del Duero was opened, decanted and glasses filled with the dark red wine. They talked about the impossibility of going back to live in Madrid after the lotus life of Seville.

She'd ordered him duck breast, which was presented in a fan with a mound of couscous. Consuelo had the sea bass with crisp silver skin in a delicate white sauce. He felt her calf rub against his and they decided to forgo the dessert and get a taxi instead.

They practically lay down in the back and he kissed her neck as the street lights flashed overhead and the young people outside made their moves from the bars to the clubs. The lights were still on at her neighbour's house and the daughter let them in. Falcón lifted Darío from the bed. He was fast asleep.

As they walked across to Consuelo's house the boy came awake.

'*Hola*, Javi,' he said sleepily and thumped his blond head into Falcón's chest and left it there, as if he was listening to his heart. The trust nearly broke Falcón apart. They went upstairs where he poured the boy into his bed. Darío's eyelids fluttered against the weight of sleep.

'Football tomorrow,' he murmured. 'You promised.'

'Penalty shoot-out,' said Falcón, pulling up the bedclothes, kissing him on the forehead.

'Goodnight, Javi.'

Falcón stood at the door while Consuelo knelt and kissed her son goodnight, stroked his head; he felt the complicated pang of being a parent, or of never having been one.

They went downstairs. She poured a whisky for Falcón, made herself a gin and tonic. He could see her properly now for the first time that night. Those slim, muscular legs, a subtle line running down her calf. He found himself wanting to kiss the backs of her knees.

There had been a difference in her touch tonight. It wasn't as if they hadn't made love since they'd got back together after the Seville bombing. She hadn't been restrained in that department, although, what with the summer holiday and the kids being around, there hadn't been much opportunity. The first time they'd got together, a couple of years ago, it had been different. They'd both been a little wild then after a long drought. This time they'd been feeling their way around each other tentatively. They needed reassurance that this was the right thing to be doing. But tonight he'd felt a difference. She was letting him in. Maybe it was Alicia, her psychologist, telling her she should let herself go, not just physically this time, but emotionally, too.

'What's going on in there?' asked Consuelo.

'Nothing.'

'All men say that when they're thinking dirty thoughts.'

'I was thinking how magnificent that meal was.'

'Then they lie to you.'

'How is it that you always know what I'm thinking?'

'Because you are completely in my thrall,' she said.

'You really want to know what I was thinking?'

'Only if it's about me.'

'I was controlling a powerful desire to kiss the back of your knees.'

A slow smile crept across her face as a thrill streaked down the back of her thighs.

'I like a *bit* of patience in a man,' she said, sipping her drink, the ice cubes rolling and tickling the glass.

'The trick of the patient man is to recognize boredom before it sets in.'

She stifled a fake yawn.

'*Joder*,' he said, getting to his feet.

They kissed and ran upstairs, leaving their drinks quaking on the table.

She stepped out of her pink dress and a small pair of

90

knickers. It was all she had to do. He wrenched at his hands caught in the cuffs of his shirt, kicked off his shoes. She sat on the edge of the bed with her hands on her knees, tanned all over except a small white triangle. After some ferocious moments with his clothes he was naked, went over to her, stood between her legs. She stroked him, looking up at his agony. Her lips were moist, still with the vestiges of the peachy lipstick that matched her fingernails. She reached up from his thighs, over his abdomen, to his chest. Her hands slipped round his back and she dug her nails into his skin. As he felt her mouth on him, her nails clawed their way down to his buttocks. He was hanging on to his patience by the skin of his teeth.

She fell back on to the bed, rolled on to her front, looked over her shoulder at him and pointed at the backs of her knees. His thighs shivered as he knelt on the bed. He kissed her Achilles tendon, her calf, the back of one knee, then the other. He worked his way up her hamstrings, which trembled under his lips. She raised her buttocks to him, reached behind her for him, patience out of the question now. They shunted together, his hands full of her. She gripped the sheets in her fists. And all the hell of the day just fell away from them.

They lay where they'd collapsed, still joined, the room lit only by the glow of street light coming in through the blinds.

'You're different tonight,' said Falcón, stroking her stomach, kissing her between the shoulder blades, welded to her by their sweat.

'I *feel* different.'

'It was like two years ago.'

She stared into the dark, her vision still green at the edges, as if recovering from an intense light.

'Something happened?' he asked.

'I'm ready,' she said.

'Why now?'

He felt her shrug under his hands.

'Maybe it's because my children are leaving me,' she said.

'Darío still needs you.'

'And his Javi,' she said. 'He loves you. I can tell.'

'And I love him,' said Falcón. 'And I love you, too.'

'What did you say?'

'I said, I love you, too . . . always have done.'

She took his hand from her stomach, kissed the fingers and pressed it between her breasts. She'd heard those words before from men, but this was the first time she'd got close to believing them.

8

Morning began with football. Falcón in goal. He had a spring in his legs so that he had to remind himself not to save everything. He let Darío send him the wrong way a few times and watched on his knees as the boy ran around the garden with his Sevilla FC shirt over his head, flying. Consuelo looked out from the sitting room in her dressing gown. She was in a strange mood, as if last night's admissions had made her cautious. She knew she loved Javier, especially when she saw his mock dismay as another of Darío's penalties rifled past him and sizzled down the back of the nylon net. There was something boyish about her cop and it made her ache as much as seeing her own son lying on his back, arms open to receive the embraces of his imaginary fellow players. She knocked on the window as if checking the scene for reality and they came in for breakfast.

Falcón sat in the front of the cab on the way back to his house and chatted cheerfully with the driver about Sevilla FC's chances in the UEFA cup. He knew it all from Darío.

He picked up his car. The morning traffic on the other side of the Plaza de Cuba, screwed up by the ongoing metro construction, today posed no problems for him. He felt completely mended. Obsession had been cleared from his mind. A crescendo of the fullness of life expanded his chest. His paranoia seemed absurd. Decisions were easy. He knew now that he was going to have to talk to Pablo of the CNI about Yacoub's situation. That was something he wasn't going to attempt to manage on his own. It had come to him with clarity and accompanied by the words of Mark Flowers, the CIA agent, who doubled as a 'Communications Officer', attached to the US Consulate in Seville: 'Don't try to understand the whole picture ... there's nobody in the world who does.' Just realizing the thinness of the slice of the world he saw was enough to persuade him that he needed another point of view.

Nobody from the Homicide squad was in yet. He closed the door to his office and picked up the phone with the scrambled line, which would connect him directly to Pablo in the CNI's offices in Madrid. It was a Saturday and early but Pablo was the new section head since Juan had left and Falcón knew he'd be there. It took half an hour to talk Pablo through what had happened in the apartment in La Latina yesterday afternoon and another fifteen minutes for Pablo to ask all his questions, the last of which was:

'Where did he say he was going and when?'

'Rabat. This morning. The GICM high command were going to give him their decision.'

Long silence.

'Are you still there, Pablo?'

'I'm still here,' he said. 'I'm wondering if there's anything that needs to be done immediately.'

'What do you mean?'

'Yacoub is not in Rabat.'

'He's flying there from Madrid this morning.'

'That's the interesting thing,' said Pablo. 'He flew into Heathrow last night. It might not mean anything. It might just be an omission on his part, but we still haven't found a flight into Casablanca with his name on the manifest.'

Falcón felt that metallic coldness in his stomach again.

'This is the problem I had yesterday,' he said. 'I think I'm losing him.'

'Trust is a strange thing in this game,' said Pablo. 'It's more fluid than in the real world. You can't expect someone who's constantly dissimulating to be as reliable as yourself. Look what happens to married people when they have affairs. The first few lies are OK. Then, as time goes on and the subterfuge builds, the lying becomes an all-consuming activity. Yacoub is now having to pretend to be someone else almost twenty-four hours a day. The GICM have racked up the pressure by invading his domestic situation, which means that Yacoub now has one less rock to stand on to remind himself of who he really is.'

'And I'm his last remaining rock.'

'Without you, he's in danger of losing that vital sense of self,' said Pablo. 'Part of your job is to shore him up. Let him know that you are dependable, that you can be trusted in *every* situation.'

'He told me not to talk to you,' said Falcón. 'He was obsessed with losing control to others. He's trying to control me and yet he's putting himself beyond my control. I'm not sure where I stand any more. All I know is that it will be below his son, Abdullah.'

'You have to rebuild that trust. He must feel that it's you and him against the GICM. You have to anchor him,' said Pablo. 'I'm going to get more information on what he's doing.'

'Whatever you do now will expose me. He'll know that I've talked to you.'

'This fluidity of trust is a two-way thing,' said Pablo.

'He hasn't gone straight to Rabat as he told you. You've come to me for some advice on how to proceed. Nobody's been hurt. Just leave it with me for a while. Don't go anywhere else for advice, especially not to that "friend" of yours, Mark Flowers.'

He hung up. Pablo didn't like Falcón's relationship with Mark Flowers, which had started four years ago when Falcón had earned the CIA agent's respect during one of his investigations. Since that time they'd exchanged information, Falcón letting him know what was happening in his police work and Flowers helping out with specialist knowledge and FBI contacts. Cristina Ferrera knocked and came into Falcón's office as he put the phone down.

'What's happening?' he asked.

'We've gone through all the disks in the Russian's briefcase and we've singled out sixty-four individuals, fifty-five men and nine women. All of them have been caught on camera with their pants down, using drugs, receiving money and/or "presents".'

'And how are you getting on with identifying these people?'

'Vicente Cortés from GRECO and Martín Díaz from CICO have managed to identify all of the mafia guys and all but three of the so-called "victims" in the footage.'

'What are we talking about?'

'The usual local council people: mayors, town planners, building inspectors, health and safety, utilities, some local businessmen and estate agents, Guardia Civil. Cortés and Díaz weren't surprised by any of it . . . not even the child sex footage or the women with big black guys.'

'You look around at all these people you're supposed to be protecting,' said Falcón, eyes drifting to the window, 'and you find they're in it up to their necks.'

'I've isolated a still from one bit of footage that I want you to look at. You'll have to come next door to see it because Inspector Ramírez is making sure everything is confined to one computer. We don't even want the stills on a LAN in case they find their way out to our "friends" in the press.'

Falcón followed her out. Ferrera's fingers rapped the keys as she sat at the desk. An image came up on the screen of two people: a man kneeling behind a woman whose bottom was raised, face and shoulders on the bed. The girl was looking directly into the camera. Ferrera tapped the screen.

'I'm absolutely certain,' she said, 'that this woman is Marisa Moreno's sister. I even went back to the police station and found the picture which had been supplied by Marisa to her "missing" file. She's only seventeen in the old shot but . . . what do you think?'

Ferrera's photo was of a girl with her hair unplaited, Afro style. The eyes were innocent and wide, her mouth closed tight with bee-stung lips. The woman on the screen was in her mid-twenties, which would have been Margarita Moreno's age now. Her hair was plaited, which wasn't the only difference. The eyes weren't innocent any more but glazed, unfocused, out of it.

Falcón held the photo Marisa had given him yesterday up to the screen. Margarita's hair was plaited in the shot.

'You're right, Cristina. Good work,' he said. 'Now we're getting to it, Marisa, aren't we?'

'Getting to what?' asked Ferrera.

'Another version of Marisa's story,' said Falcón. 'The reason why she was having an affair with Esteban Calderón, why that affair included more than just sexual duties, and, perhaps, why Inés was murdered in her own home.'

'Marisa is in with the Russians?'

'I've been to see her twice and each time I've had a threatening phone call within hours of our meetings,' said Falcón. 'Has the man in this shot been identified?'

'Not yet.'

97

'Tell Cortés and Díaz that, out of the three, this is the first shot that they have to work on. This guy will tell us where Margarita is being held,' said Falcón. 'Now let's go back to Marisa.'

'Both of us?'

'She doesn't like men,' said Falcón. 'I want you involved with her.'

On the way to Calle Hiniesta Cristina Ferrera called Inspector José Luis Ramírez and Vicente Cortés. The shot was accessible on Ramírez's computer in padlocked files to which only he and Ferrera had the password.

Marisa was not at home. They walked to her atelier on Calle Bustos Tavera. Marisa answered the door in a scarlet silk dressing gown open to reveal bikini briefs. She held a hammer and a wood chisel in one hand, a chewed cigar stub in the other.

'You *again*,' she said, making eye contact with Falcón, before dropping her gaze to Ferrera. 'Who is this?'

'I can perfectly understand why you don't like men now, Marisa,' said Falcón. 'So I've brought another member of my squad to talk to you. This is Detective Cristina Ferrera.'

'*Encantada*,' said Marisa, and turned her back on them.

She put the hammer and chisel down on the work bench, tied up her dressing gown, sat on a high stool and lit the cigar stub. Resistant was a mild description of her attitude.

'Now?' she asked. 'Why can you understand it *now*, Inspector Jefe?'

'Because we've just found your sister,' said Falcón.

The line was intended to shock and it did. In the intense silence after its delivery Falcón saw pain, fear and horror flash across Marisa's beautiful features.

'I distinctly remember telling you that my sister was not lost,' said Marisa, summoning all the self-control she could muster.

Ferrera stepped forward and gave her the printout of the

still image taken from Vasili Lukyanov's disks. Marisa looked down at it, pursed her lips. Her face was impassive as she reconnected with Falcón.

'What is this?'

'This was in the possession of a known Russian gangster who died in a motorway accident yesterday morning,' said Falcón. 'Maybe you knew him, too: Vasili Lukyanov.'

'How is this relevant to me?' asked Marisa, that name thudding into her with the force of a slaughterer's bolt. 'If my sister, who I haven't seen for six or seven years, has chosen to take up prostitution . . .'

'*Chosen* to take up prostitution?' said Ferrera, unable to contain herself. 'Of the four hundred thousand prostitutes operating in Spain, barely five per cent have *chosen* their profession. And I don't think any of *them* are working for the Russian mafia.'

'Look, Marisa, we're not here to take you down,' said Falcón. 'We know you've been coerced. And we know who's been doing the coercing. We're here to relieve your situation. To get you out of it, and your sister.'

'I'm not sure what this situation is that you're talking about,' said Marisa, not ready yet, needing to keep it going while she weighed things up in her mind.

'What was the deal? Did they say they'd let Margarita go if you started up an affair with Esteban?' asked Falcón. 'If you fed them information, told them he was beating his wife, got them a key to his apartment . . .'

'I don't know what you're talking about,' said Marisa. 'Esteban and I are lovers. I go to see him every week in prison – or at least I did, until you stopped my visits.'

'So they haven't let Margarita go yet,' said Ferrera. 'Is that right?'

'Is what right?' said Marisa, turning on Ferrera, feeling that she could loose off some of her fierceness at her. 'What . . .?'

'That you've got to keep up the after-sales service,' said Falcón. 'But how long for, Marisa? How long do you think they'll keep you dangling? A month? A year? Maybe for ever?'

As he said this he wondered whether he was the right man for this job. Maybe he was too personally involved. This woman's responsibility for Inés's death was perhaps making him too brutal, giving her nowhere to turn. But he had to show the full weight of his knowledge, make her face the gravity of her circumstances, before showing her that he was the softer option. This, he thought, might not be achievable in a single visit.

'Esteban and I are very close,' said Marisa, setting off on another round of fabrication. 'It might not look it from the outside. You might think I've been using him in some way. That he was somehow my ticket to a better life. But I'm not . . .'

'I've heard all this before, Marisa,' said Falcón. 'Maybe I *should* let you see Esteban again.'

'Now that you've poisoned his mind against me, Inspector Jefe?' she said, getting to her feet, going on the attack with that cigar stub. 'Now that you've told him that he might not have to face twenty years in jail because you reckon you can shift the blame on to some black trash he was fucking. Is that it, Inspector Jefe?'

'I'm not the one who's put you in your situation.'

'What fucking situation?' she screeched. 'You keep talking about it, but I don't know what it is.'

'Your position between the gangsters holding your sister and the police investigating the Seville bombing,' said Falcón calmly.

'We're already close to finding where Margarita is being held,' said Ferrera, which snapped Marisa's head round in her direction.

'The man in the photo,' said Falcón. 'He'll talk. And if

you talk to us, Marisa, nothing will happen until Margarita is safe.'

Marisa looked at the printout. Still not ready. Needing more time to make up her mind, not sure who or what was going to be more dangerous for her sister. Ferrera and Falcón exchanged a look. Ferrera gave her a card with her fixed line and mobile numbers. They made for the door.

'Talk to us, Marisa,' said Ferrera. 'I would, if I was you.'

'Why? Why would you?' said Marisa.

'Because we are not in the business of killing defenceless women in their homes, planting bombs, bribing local government officials and forcing girls into prostitution,' said Falcón.

They went down the steps from her atelier and into the broiling heat of the courtyard. They stood for a moment in the cool of the tunnel leading to Calle Bustos Tavera.

'We were that close,' said Ferrera, holding up her thumb and forefinger pressed together.

'I don't know,' said Falcón. 'Fear does strange things to people. It can bring them to the brink of the only possible next logical step, and then they veer off into the night because some perceived threat appears to be nearer and uglier.'

'She just needs time,' said Ferrera.

'Time is the problem, because she's alone,' said Falcón. 'Under those circumstances, the person who's going to kill you seems more powerful than the one who's holding out a helping hand. That's why I want you involved with her. I want you to make her feel as if she's not facing this on her own.'

'Let's find Margarita then,' said Ferrera. 'If we can get her safe, Marisa will follow.'

Back at the Jefatura Inspector José Luis Ramírez was hovering over Vicente Cortés and Martín Díaz, arms folded, biceps bulging under his red polo shirt. His brow was furrowed with fury, the mahogany colour of his skin and his dark swept-back hair making him look even more thunderous. They were looking at the footage from the disks taken from Vasili Lukyanov's briefcase. The sight of young girls being defiled always made Ramírez uncomfortable. He didn't even like seeing his own teenage daughter hand in hand with her boyfriend, even though his wife had assured him she was still innocent.

Cortés and Díaz had found a better angle of the face of the man having sex with Margarita. His features had been isolated from the footage, blown up and sent out to every police station in Andalucía, the Guardia Civil and CICO in Madrid.

'Why just Andalucía?' asked Falcón.

'All of the sixty-one men and women we've already identified come from towns on the coast between Algeciras and Almería.'

'Maybe the reason you can't identify these three men is that they're outsiders,' said Falcón. 'I think you should at least send these shots to Madrid and Barcelona and have somebody take them round to the chambers of commerce. This is a break. If we can locate the girl and make her safe, we have a chance of getting Marisa Moreno to talk. And she's possibly the only person left who's associated with anybody who had a part in the Seville bombing.'

The phone rang in his office, the scrambled line to the CNI. Falcón asked Ramírez to email the close-up shot of the unidentified male to his computer.

'I spoke to MI5 about Yacoub,' said Pablo. 'Of course they knew about him coming in on that flight, but they've lost him.'

'Lost him? What do you mean?'

'They followed him. He took the metro into London. They lost him at Russell Square.'

'So Yacoub realized he was being tailed and lost them,

which means he now knows, or will assume, that I've talked.'

'Not necessarily. It's not the first time the British have taken an interest in Yacoub. What it does mean is that he didn't want them to know what he was doing,' said Pablo. 'We've now seen that his name has appeared on a manifest on a flight from London to Málaga tomorrow evening.'

'What does any of this mean?'

'It might mean that we have a rogue agent on our hands. On the other hand, it might just be that he is having to behave in a certain way because of pressure from the GICM,' said Pablo. 'What we have to do now is find out in whose interests he's working.'

'How are you going to do that?'

'Through you. But we're still thinking about it,' said Pablo. 'There's something else. An unidentified male has turned up in Yacoub's house in Rabat. He seems to be family, but the Moroccans haven't been able to place him yet and they don't want to go in there and spoil our show.'

'Can't they check his papers when he comes out of the house?'

'If he came out, they would, but he doesn't,' said Pablo. 'There's a shot of him on our website. Take a look. You might know him from that holiday you took with Yacoub down in Essaouira. By the way, you haven't communicated with Yacoub through the CNI website for three weeks.'

'He hasn't communicated with me.'

'But before that you were in regular contact.'

'Given his domestic situation, he's got to be more careful now.'

'That's what we're thinking here,' said Pablo. 'Anything else?'

'I'm working on a potential breakthrough in the Seville bombing. We've come across some disks in the possession of a known Russian mafioso showing men having sex with prostitutes,' said Falcón. 'You remember the two ringleaders of the conspiracy: Lucrecio Arenas and César Benito?'

'Benito was an architect for the Horizonte Group and Arenas was the CEO of their bankers, Banco Omni,' said Pablo.

'That's right. We never managed to find anything in either company that linked them to the conspiracy, but we're equally sure they weren't motivated by their Catholic beliefs,' said Falcón. 'I've isolated a male from the disks we found in the Russian mafioso's possession. Our two Organized Crime specialists from the Costa del Sol have been able to identify more than sixty people from these disks, but *not* this guy, and it occurs to me he may be an outsider.'

'And you think this may link the Russian mafia to Horizonte and Banco Omni?'

'It might do, if this guy happens to be in the hierarchy of either company or of Horizonte's holding company, an American-based investment group called I4IT,' said Falcón. 'The problem is that I know from my earlier investigations into these two companies how camera-shy their personnel are, and that you probably have access to . . . certain files that I don't. He might even be a foreigner.'

'You want me to see if I can match him?' said Pablo. 'For you, Javier, anything.'

They hung up. Falcón emailed the facial close-up of the male having sex with Margarita to the CNI website and, while there, checked the photo of the guy staying at Yacoub's house, but didn't recognize him.

'Send me those shots of the other two guys you haven't been able to identify from the Russian's disks,' Falcón shouted through to Vicente Cortés in the adjoining office.

The three faces came up on his screen. He inspected them carefully. Ramírez came in and stood by the window.

'This guy – "Unidentified B". He doesn't look Spanish to me,' said Falcón.

'No,' said Ramírez flatly, looking over his shoulder.

'The other two could be Spanish or Hispanic,' said Falcón, 'but this guy looks American.'

'American?' said Cortés, appearing at the door. 'How can you tell he's American from a grainy shot like that?'

'He doesn't look like a man whose face is burdened by centuries of history,' said Falcón. 'He has the innocence of someone who's spent his life embracing the future.'

'Even if he is fucking a teenager in the ass,' said Ramírez grimly.

'You can tell all that from this shot?' said Cortés, leaning over Falcón's desk.

'Look at his hair,' said Falcón. 'We don't have hair like that any more in Europe. That's what I would call American corporate hair. It's very conservative.'

'You should see the full clip. It doesn't even move during sex,' said Ramírez, looking out of the window. 'By the time he'd finished with that poor kid he should have had hair like a wrestler's, and yet . . . maybe it's a rug?'

'Possibly.'

The phone with the scrambled line to the CNI rang.

Ramírez took Cortés by the arm, led him out. Ferrera leaned in and closed the door.

'We want you to go to London,' said Pablo.

'I can't.'

'We've already spoken to Comisario Elvira.'

'I've just told you, things are breaking here. I feel as if I'm finally getting inside. I can't leave now,' said Falcón. 'And if I go to London, Yacoub will know I've spoken to you. He'll see it as a breach of trust.'

'You're going to see the British counter-terrorism squad, SO15, in New Scotland Yard. A guy called Douglas Hamilton. He will brief you. When you make contact with Yacoub you'll tell him why you're in London, which is to find out what the fuck he is doing losing an MI5 tail. That is not the kind of behaviour we expect from one of our "untrained" agents,' said Pablo. 'You understand me, Javier? And look, you'll be away from your desk for the rest of today only. We've got you on to a scheduled flight in an hour's time and we'll make sure you get an early-evening flight back.'

'All right,' said Falcón. 'I'm sending you another two shots of men from the Russian's disks who we can't identify. One of them I'm sure is an American.'

'Don't talk to your friend Flowers about any of this.'

'Are you going to say that every time I say the word "American"?'

'Mark Flowers is a very experienced operative. He has an instinct for when things are happening. I'd be very surprised if you didn't hear from him by the end of the day.'

'So what *is* happening?'

'Did you take a look at the mystery man who appeared in Yacoub's house?' asked Pablo, ignoring the question.

'Never seen him before,' said Falcón.

They hung up. Falcón stared grimly at the phone, not wanting any of this other, even more complicated, stuff. He called for Ferrera.

'I'm going to be out until this evening,' he said. 'I want you to go back to Marisa and work on her. Do everything you can to get her into your confidence. She has to tell us who is putting pressure on her.'

He sat back, tried to breathe down the stress, closed his eyes, thought about Consuelo's goodbye kiss. Everything had been in that kiss. The full complexity of a woman joining her life to his. Then he thought about football in the garden with Darío and remembered the boy's instinctive trust of him the night before, his head on Falcón's chest. The boy had done something for him, brought back memories of his own trust in his mother; those goodnight kisses in Tangier. It bound him to Darío in a way that made him feel both strong and vulnerable. He opened his eyes, placed his hands

106

on the desk, squared his shoulders and, as he raised himself to go to the airport, he suddenly realized what was happening. The process of Javier Falcón becoming a parent had begun, and that was what was different in Consuelo: she'd decided to let him all the way into her life.

'You *again*,' said Marisa, seeing Cristina Ferrera through the door, open a crack. 'I don't know what the matter is with you people. Half Seville could be robbed and raped, and you'd still come knocking at my door.'

'That would be because it's my job to investigate murder,' said Ferrera, 'rather than anything else.'

Marisa looked her up and down. Her eyes were glazed. Maybe she was drunk or stoned.

'Specially selected,' said Marisa.

'For what?' asked Ferrera, sweat gathering under her eyes.

'Come in,' said Marisa, voice suddenly bored, walking away from the door.

She was wearing bikini briefs only. She picked up a cigar stub, lit it, leaned against the work bench and blew out smoke.

'Sweet and virginal,' she said.

'I used to be a nun,' said Ferrera. 'Maybe that's got something to do with it.'

Marisa snorted laughter, which came out on a long plume of smoke from her nose.

'You've got to be kidding.'

Ferrera stared her down, saw the half-bottle of Havana Club and a can of Coke behind her.

'I'll put on a top,' said Marisa, found a T-shirt, fought her way into it.

'Your boss . . .' she said, and losing her way she rubbished the air with her cigar stub. 'Whatever his name is. He's a clever guy, that one. You don't see many cops like him. You don't see many Sevillanos like him. A clever guy. He's sent you here on your own. He's thinking all the time. He comes in here, looks at my pieces ... doesn't say a word. Thinking. Thinking. And he works things out. And that's why you're here, isn't it? The ex-nun. Everything is calculated.'

'I wasn't a great nun,' said Ferrera, cutting through the drunken babble.

'No? Why not? You look perfect,' said Marisa. 'I bet you only get guys you like coming after you.'

'What's that supposed to mean?'

'I get all sorts of people coming after me,' she said, to herself. 'Tell me why things didn't work out for you as a nun.'

'I was raped by a couple of guys in Cádiz one night,' said Ferrera, matter of fact. 'I was on my way to see my boyfriend. That's it. That's all you need to know. It wasn't working out for me as a nun. I had weaknesses.'

Marisa spat out some tobacco from the ragged end of her cigar stub.

'Even that's calculated,' she said nastily.

'The only thing that the Inspector Jefe has calculated is that you don't like men very much, so he sent me ... a woman.'

'An ex-nun who's been raped.'

'He didn't expect me to tell you that.'

'So why did you?'

'To show you that I'm not the sweet, virginal little woman you think you see,' said Ferrera. 'I've suffered ... maybe not as much, or as continuously, as Margarita is suffering, but enough to know what it's like to be a piece of meat.'

'Drink?' asked Marisa, as if Ferrera's words had signalled something.

'No, thanks,' said Ferrera.

Marisa poured herself a hefty measure of rum and topped it off with Coke.

'Take a seat,' she said, pointing at a cheap, low stool. 'You look hot.'

Ferrera sat in the smell of her soap and deodorant mixed with sweat.

'Do you always drink while you work?' she asked.

'Never,' said Marisa, relighting her cigar stub.

'So you're not working?'

'I'd work if people didn't keep interrupting me.'

'Other people?' asked Ferrera. 'Apart from us?'

Marisa nodded. Drank some more.

'It's not just that he thinks I hate men . . .' she said, pointing at Ferrera with her cigar stub. 'And I don't hate men. How can I hate them? Only men can satisfy me. I only fuck with men, so how can I hate them? You? Do you only fuck with men? After what those guys did to you?'

'So what else is it?' asked Ferrera, feeling Marisa's drunken mind swerving away from her.

'He thinks I killed her,' said Marisa. 'The Inspector Jefe thinks I killed his wife. I mean *his* ex-wife, Esteban's wife.'

'He doesn't think that.'

'Did you know her?'

'Inés?' asked Ferrera, shaking her head.

'I don't know why your Inspector Jefe married that one,' said Marisa, pointing to her head, blowing her brains out. 'There was nothing inside.'

'We all make mistakes,' said Ferrera, some of her own and their consequences flashing through her mind.

'She *was* right for Esteban,' said Marisa. 'Absolutely right.'

'Why do you say that?'

'Another empty vessel,' said Marisa, knocking on the side of her work bench. 'A hollow man.'

'So why did you like Esteban?'

'It's more to do with why did Esteban like *me*,' said Marisa. 'I was just there. He came after *me*. It didn't matter what *I* thought. That's what Sevillano guys are like. They come after you. They don't need any encouragement.'

'And Cuban guys are different?'

'They seem to know when you're not right for them. They see who you are.'

'But you didn't turn Esteban down.'

'I tell you, Esteban is not my kind of guy,' said Marisa, and her face struggled against the alcohol into a sneer.

'So what happened?'

'He pursued me.'

'You look as if you're old enough to be able to tell a guy that his interest is going to get him nowhere.'

'Unless . . .' Marisa said, holding up her finger.

Some tinny Cuban music started up in the back of the workshop. Marisa staggered off amongst the clutter and picked up her mobile phone. Ferrera gritted her teeth, the moment lost again. Marisa retreated into the darkness and listened intently without saying a word. After some long, silent minutes she dropped the phone and skittered away from it as if she'd suddenly realized it was emitting poison into her ear.

9

Consuelo was having trouble getting Darío out of the house and into the car. She was on the phone, talking to the estate agent in Madrid who'd found her 'the perfect property' in the Lavapiés district of the city. He was selling it hard because he was pushing something that was 'off brief'. Darío was on the computer, playing his favourite soccer game. He was impervious to her occasional shouts to turn the damn thing off, and he only complied when she appeared over his shoulder to wrestle the mouse from his hand.

The electricity demands at the airport were such that the air-conditioning was not working at its optimum level. Looking out on to the taxiways where the aircraft unpeeled their tyres from the searing tarmac, Falcón held his jacket slung over his shoulder and put in a call to the only person he wanted to talk to.

'I'm stuck in traffic,' said Consuelo. 'Darío, will you please just sit down. This is Javi.'

'*Hola*, Javi,' shouted Darío.

'We're on our way to the Nervión Plaza. The only place in the world where we're allowed to buy football boots. You know, the pilgrimage to Sevilla FC.'

'I'm going to be out of town again today,' said Falcón, 'but I want to see you tonight.'

'Do you want to see Javi tonight?'

'Ye-e-es!' roared Darío.

'I think that sounds as if it would be acceptable.'

'I love you,' said Falcón, trying that out again, seeing if she would react this time.

'What was that?'

'You heard.'

'The line's breaking up.'

'I love you, Consuelo,' he said, and it made him feel young and foolish.

She laughed.

'Let's go!' roared Darío.

'Traffic's moving,' she said. '*Hasta pronto.*'

The phone clicked off. He was disappointed. He'd wanted to hear it from her lips, but she wasn't quite ready for that yet, admitting to love in front of her youngest son. He put his hands up on the glass, stared out into the wavering heat and felt a great sense of longing in his chest.

How the hell would you fall in love if you were blind? thought Consuelo, phone in her lap, traffic at a standstill again. Smell would be important. Not the quality of a man's aftershave, although that in itself would tell you something, but rather his . . . musk. Nothing sharp or rancid and not soapy or fragrant, but not too manly either. Voice, too, would have powerful effects. You wouldn't want to listen to somebody whiny or booming, nothing guttural or sibilant. Then there was touch: the feel of a man's hand. No limpness, pudginess, nor clamminess. Dry and strong, but not crushing. Delicate, but not effeminate. Electric, but not furtive. And then there were the lips. The crucial mouth. How his lips fitted on to yours. Just the right amount of give. Not hard, unyielding, nor soft and mushy. Kissing blind would tell you everything. Is that why we close our eyes?

'Mamá?' said Darío.

Consuelo wasn't listening. She was too engrossed in her imagination, thinking how well Javier scored on smell, voice and touch. She'd never believed, after her marriage to Raúl Jiménez, that she would ever think these foolish things again.

'Mamá?'

'What, Darío?'

'You're not listening to me.'

'I am, sweetie, it's just that Mamá's thinking, too.'

'Mamá?'

'Yes.'

'You missed the turning.'

She squeezed his knee so that he yelped and made the complicated series of turns to get back to the Nervión Plaza parking.

'Mamá?' said Darío, as they descended into the underground car park, ground to a halt in the queue to go in.

'What is it, darling?' said Consuelo, feeling that the first three inquiring 'Mamá's' had been a prelude to some big, burning question, dying to be asked.

'Do you still love me now that Javi is with us?'

She looked at him, big eyes beseeching her, felt her insides collapse. How do we know these things? Even at eight years old he can tell something important might be swerving away from him. She stroked his head and cheek.

'But you're my little man,' she said. 'The most important one in the world.'

Darío smiled, that small confrontation with sadness instantly forgotten. He pushed his fists between his knees

113

and hunched his shoulders up to his ears as his world fell back into place.

The driver of the black Jaguar didn't say a word. The car sped along the M4 motorway into London. Falcón was cold, underdressed for the season, and he was feeling a Spaniard's uneasiness for silence in company, until he remembered his father, Francisco, telling him that the English liked to talk about the weather. But as he looked out on to the dull, grey, flat landscape overhung by dull, grey, pendulous clouds, he could find nothing to say about it. Couldn't imagine what anybody would find to say about it. He put his face close to the window to help him perceive what a local person might see in such unmitigated dullness and thought it might be what you couldn't see.

'When did you last see the sun shine?' he asked, in perfect English, his breath fogging the glass.

'Sorry, mate,' said the driver, 'don't speak Spanish. Go to Mallorca every year for my holidays, but still don't speak a word.'

Falcón checked him for irony but could tell, even from the back of the man's head and his quick glance at the rear-view, that he was totally good-natured.

'It's not our strong point either,' said Falcón. 'Languages.'

The driver whipped round in his seat as if to check he still had the same passenger.

'Oh, right,' he said. 'Yeah, no. You're pretty good. Where d'you learn to speak English like that?'

'English lessons,' said Falcón.

'Well, that's cheating, innit?' said the driver, and they both laughed, although Falcón wasn't quite sure why.

The traffic seized up as they came into the city. The driver turned off the Cromwell Road; twenty minutes later they went past the famous revolving sign of New Scotland Yard.

Falcón introduced himself at reception, handed over his

ID and police card. He went through security and was met at the lifts by a uniformed officer. They went up to the fifth floor. Douglas Hamilton met him off the lift, took him into a meeting room where there was another man in his late thirties.

'This is Rodney from MI5,' said Hamilton. 'Take a seat. Flight OK?'

'Not your sort of temperature, eh, Javier?' said Rodney, releasing Falcón's ice-cold hand.

Finally, the weather, thought Falcón.

'Pablo forgot to tell me it was already winter here,' he said.

'This is *our* bloody summer,' said Hamilton.

'You ever been to the Irish bar in Seville, down by the cathedral?' asked Rodney.

'Only if someone was murdered there,' said Falcón.

They laughed. The room relaxed. They were going to understand each other.

'You run Yacoub Diouri,' said Rodney, 'but you're a police officer.'

'Yacoub is a friend of mine. He said he would supply information to the CNI only on condition that I was his main contact.'

'How long have you known him?'

'Four years,' said Falcón. 'We first met in September 2002.'

'And when was the last time you saw him before yesterday?'

'We spent some time on holiday together in August.'

'And his son, Abdullah, was with you?'

'It was a family holiday.'

'And how did Abdullah appear to you then?'

'As I would have expected the son of a wealthy member of the Moroccan elite,' said Falcón.

'Spoilt brat?' asked Hamilton.

'Not exactly. He didn't behave any differently to a Spanish

boy of his age. He was very attached to his computer, bored by the beach, but he's a good kid.'

'Was he devout?'

'No more than the rest of the family, who take their religion very seriously. As far as I know, he wasn't leaving dinner early to go and study the Qur'an, but then Yacoub said his browser was full of "Islamic" sites, so maybe that's what he was doing.'

'Did he drink?' asked Rodney. 'Alcohol?'

'Yes,' said Falcón, feeling the strange weight of this question. 'Yacoub, Abdullah and I would share a bottle of wine at dinner.'

'Just one bottle between three?' said Rodney, whose top button was undone and the knot of his tie off centre.

There was a grunt of laughter from Hamilton.

'If I hadn't been there they wouldn't have drunk alcohol,' said Falcón. 'It was just to make me comfortable as their guest.'

'Has Abdullah ever joined Yacoub on any of his business trips to the UK?' asked Hamilton.

'I think so. I seem to remember Yacoub talking about taking Abdullah to the Tate Modern to see the Edward Hopper exhibition. That was before I recruited Yacoub.'

'Did you know that Abdullah was in London now?'

'No. In fact yesterday Yacoub told me he was in a training camp for GICM mujahideen back in Morocco. He also told me that he himself was returning to Rabat . . .'

'Pablo briefed us,' said Rodney, nodding.

'Have you found him yet?' asked Falcón, and Rodney glared. 'Pablo said you'd lost Yacoub, or rather Yacoub had lost your . . .'

'We picked him up again about an hour ago,' said Rodney. 'It was just him. Abdullah stayed in the hotel. It's not the first time he's lost one of our tails, you know that.'

'Do you follow him every time he comes to London?'

'We do now,' said Hamilton. 'Since the first time he lost a tail, back in July.'

'July?' said Falcón, amazed. 'That was only a month after I recruited him.'

'That's the question,' said Rodney, shifting in his seat, pulling his tie back to centre. 'How was an amateur able to take *us* to the cleaners so easily?'

'Take you to the cleaners?' said Falcón, puzzled.

'Fool us,' said Hamilton, clarifying.

'How could a fucking jeans manufacturer from Rabat take on MI5 and make us look stupid?' said Rodney.

'And the answer is . . .?' said Hamilton, not wanting Rodney's testiness to get a foothold.

'He's been very well trained,' said Rodney. 'And we don't believe he learnt that in a month.'

'If he did, it was auto-didactic,' said Falcón.

'You what?' said Rodney.

'Self-taught,' said Hamilton.

'Sorry, my English. Sometimes only the Spanish word comes to me,' said Falcón. 'Didn't you . . . or was it MI6, try to recruit Yacoub before me? And I heard the Americans had a go, too.'

'So?' asked Rodney.

'So you vetted him, didn't you?' asked Falcón.

'MI6 said there was nothing unusual,' said Rodney. 'Apart from him being a shirt-lifter. But no fucking PhD from spy school, if that's what you mean.'

'Shirt-lifter?' said Falcón.

'It's nothing,' said Hamilton.

'*Maricón*,' said Rodney, fixing him with a look.

'So what's going on?' asked Falcón, giving Rodney's aggression a quick sideways glance.

'We were hoping you'd be able to tell *us*,' said Hamilton, pushing over a piece of paper. 'These are the five separate occasions where we've lost him.'

Falcón looked down the list of dates, times and places. Holland Park, Hampstead Heath, Battersea Park, Clapham Common and Russell Square. Twice in July, once in August and twice in September. Never less than three hours, except this last time.

'So you lost him in these places, but where did he reappear?'

'We pick him up when he's on his way back to the hotel,' said Hamilton.

'Brown's?'

'Always.'

'And after your briefing to Pablo on what had happened between you and Yacoub in Madrid yesterday, we wouldn't mind knowing what he's been up to,' said Rodney. 'You're his controller and he's lying to you. He's not working with us, but he's supposed to be on our side. If he's operating in his own interests, that's one thing. If he's been turned, then, obviously, that's another.'

'We've already got thirty-two separate possible terror groups under some sort of surveillance here in the UK,' said Hamilton. 'Seventeen of them are in London. That's nearly two thousand people we're watching nationwide. Obviously we've had to step things up since 7/7 last year, which means we're stretched. We're having to recruit at the same pace as the terrorists.'

'So we can do without your shit on our doorstep,' said Rodney. 'To put it politely.'

'Are any of these groups you're watching connected to any of the GICM cells in the rest of Europe, or Morocco?' asked Falcón.

'Let's put it this way,' said Rodney, 'we haven't been able to match any known GICM players with any of the UK groups. But that's not to say it hasn't happened. The French are telling us there's already a live GICM cell here.'

'And how do they know that?' asked Falcón.

'They picked up a Moroccan kid on a drugs bust in Alès,

118

in southern France, who gave up some stuff on a group in Marseille in exchange for no jail. This Marseille cell were providing safe houses and documentation. The DSG went in there and beat out some good intelligence. The Moroccan kid was found dead in the river Gard a week later, with his feet beaten to a pulp and his throat slit. So the French reckoned they'd hit gold,' said Rodney, who recalled something else. 'And the Germans told us they saw Yacoub meeting a devout Turkish businessman at a trade fair in Berlin at the beginning of this month.'

'What sort of businessman?' asked Falcón. 'There's plenty of cotton in Turkey, and Yacoub's a clothing manufacturer.'

'That's why we weren't too concerned,' said Rodney. 'The Turk is a cotton manufacturer from Denizli. It's just that when we couple that with other information we find it's begging more questions.'

'What "other information"?'

'Where does the Turk's money go?' asked Rodney.

'Wealthy, devout Muslims regard it as part of their duty to the community . . .'

Rodney gave him the yapping hand.

'You know how it is in Turkey, with this battle between the secular and the religious,' said Rodney. 'We could understand it if the Turk's money was being put into a local school, but it's finding its way to Istanbul and political coffers there. And they're not secular coffers.'

'All right,' said Falcón, holding up his hands. 'So what you're looking for from me is some clarification of Yacoub's behaviour over the last few months.'

'Don't get us wrong,' said Hamilton, running his tie between his fingers. 'We're very grateful to Yacoub. His observations back in June on the four-wheel-drive plot were invaluable. MI6 were nowhere on that mission. But the point was that *then* he was on your territory, now he's on *ours*, and we're not taking any chances.'

119

'*We* don't think it was a coincidence that he turned down MI6 and the Yanks,' said Rodney, and Douglas Hamilton gave him a hard stare.

'And what do you mean by that?' asked Falcón.

'Time for a smoke,' said Rodney, who got up and left.

The sports shop, Décimas, on the first floor of the Nervión Plaza shopping centre, was full of kids and parents. Everybody with the same idea. The assistants were worked off their feet. Darío knew what he wanted. Black Pumas. Consuelo cornered a salesgirl and got her working on the project. Her mobile rang. Ricardo, her eldest boy, was asking, or rather telling her, that he was going down to Matalascañas on the coast for the afternoon. She told him to be back for the family dinner with Javier. She'd reached the shop entrance by the time she hung up. Two men looked in past her shoulders, then directly at her, one after the other. They raised their eyebrows, shrugged and walked off towards the escalators.

Back to Darío. He had the boots on. They were too small. Too small already? His feet growing by the month. The girl went back to the store room, got waylaid by a couple who would not take the brush-off. Consuelo's mobile rang again. The estate agent from Madrid. Working hard on a Saturday, trying to impress her. The signal was weak in the shop, started to break up. The salesgirl came back with the next size up. Immediately got snagged by somebody else. Consuelo got the boots on to Darío's feet. He trotted around the shop. Smiled. They were perfect. The girl came back, boxed them up and took them to the cash desk. Three people waiting to pay. The mobile went off again. She left Darío at the desk, walked out of the shop, went to the window overlooking the big open-air plaza in the middle of the shopping centre, the football stadium with Sevilla FC's coat of arms loomed to the left. She kept an eye on the progress of the queue from the main concourse. Two minutes. Cut off again. Went back into the shop. Tapped the desk with her credit card while Darío turned the box round in his hands. Couldn't wait to get back home, try them on, put a few past Javi this evening . . . if he got back before dark.

Consuelo's turn to pay. Rammed the receipt in her bag. Out of the shop. Grabbed Darío's hand, down the escalator. Mobile went off again. There'd be no signal in the garage, so she went outside into the plaza in front of the football stadium. The signal was good. She talked real estate and walked up the ramp towards the ticket office of the stadium. Darío got bored. Wandered off. Consuelo paced around aimlessly, making her points, stamping her heel. A group of kids streamed past her. Darío saw the Sevilla Futbol Club shop under the stadium and went in. She lit a cigarette, sucked in the smoke, turned to find Darío. Turned again. Did a 360. No Darío. Saw the Sevilla FC shop. Knew he'd have been unable to resist. She walked over to it. Finished the call, folded away her mobile. Had a good look around. A lot of space and too many people. She went into the shop. Darío wasn't there.

Despite some reassurances from Douglas Hamilton, Falcón was still feeling the weight of Rodney's accusation when the man came back into the room with three mugs of coffee.

'I put sugar in yours. I hope that was OK,' said Rodney.

'It sounds to me,' said Falcón, still smarting, 'that you think that we, or rather the CNI, have been set up. You reckon I'm just a channel for information that the GICM wants you to know . . . that, in fact, we're being disinformed by our own agent. Is that right?'

'We have to remain open to all possibilities,' said Rodney, staring him out over the rim of his steaming mug. 'Pablo told us you'd lost confidence in Yacoub.'

'I don't know whether I'd go that far,' said Falcón, finding himself irrationally defending his friend, because he was thinking that he probably *would* go that far and it made him sick to his stomach.

'All we can do is act on our uncertainties,' said Rodney. 'You meet him and we'll judge for ourselves.'

'You want to listen in?'

Rodney opened his hands as if nothing could be more obvious.

'I can't have you listening in,' said Falcón.

'You're on *our* territory,' said Rodney firmly.

'When I go in there I'll be talking to him as his friend, not his spymaster.'

'So how were you talking to him when you were in Madrid yesterday?'

'That was business,' said Falcón. 'He was under too much pressure to be able to talk to me openly.'

'And that was why he lied to you,' said Rodney. 'Why should it be any different if you go in there as Javier, his close personal friend?'

'In his culture, in business, a certain amount of flexibility with the truth is permissible. Combine that with the paranoia induced by the new uncertainty of his situation, after what he'd just found out about his son, and his evasiveness becomes understandable,' said Falcón. 'If I establish a different level of intimacy with him from the start and he still lies to me, then I know we are lost. And I can't do that if I'm wired up to you.'

'You won't even notice it,' said Rodney.

Falcón stared him out.

The two Englishmen looked at each other in a complex communication that left Falcón thinking that they would be doing exactly what they wanted, regardless.

Rodney nodded as if to give way. Falcón didn't like his look; the man had a sort of unearned confidence about him that was not appealing.

*   *   *

The ugliness of the Nervión Plaza shopping centre became more apparent the harder Consuelo looked for her son in its grey brutality. She thought it must have been designed by an East German before the Wall came down. She stood in the empty space at its heart, which was frequented by sprinting children and dazed adults. Above it there was a jazzy, modern awning which cast geometric patterned shade on the area, making it even more difficult to make out the children's faces. She could only assume that he had gone into the shop, got bored and been drawn to the animation here. There were a lot of ways in and out: the shopping mall, where they'd just been to buy his boots, the street, the stadium and the access to the cinema complex.

Consuelo walked around this area four or five times, darting down various alleyways to check for Darío, but always coming back to the centre in the hope of finding her blond boy clasping his cardboard box of football boots. As she did this, she called his brothers Ricardo and Matías, and told them they had to come to the Nervión Plaza immediately to help look for him. There was some protest, especially from Ricardo, who was already on his way to the coast.

Twenty minutes later they were all in Nervión Plaza. Consuelo's sister had brought Matías, and the family Ricardo had been with had joined in the search. The father went straight to the first security guard he could find and got them to involve the local police. Announcements were made. Car parks were searched. Toilets investigated. Every shop was visited. The kids' films showing at the cinemas were all halted for ten minutes while they checked the audiences. The search was extended out into the streets and around the stadium. Local radio was contacted.

Only after everybody's reassurances had stopped working and Consuelo had retraced her steps a hundred times and she'd ransacked her mind for the final image of the last moment that she could picture Darío, standing in that area in the godforsaken heart of the Nervión Plaza with the box of football boots in his arms, did her paralysed brain think to call Javier. His mobile was switched off.

Ramírez was still in front of the computer screen when Consuelo's call came through.

'Javier's not here . . .' he started.

'Where is he?' she asked. 'His mobiles are switched off, both personal and police.'

'He's not in Seville today.'

'But where is he, José Luis? I *need* to speak to him. It's urgent.'

'We can't say any more than that, Consuelo.'

'Can you get a message to him?'

'Not even that at the moment.'

'I can't believe this,' she said. 'What's he doing that's so . . . so fucking important?'

'I can't say.'

'Can you get a message to him as soon as he's back in touch?'

'Of course.'

'Tell him that my youngest son, Darío, has . . . has . . .'

'Has what, Consuelo?'

Consuelo fought against the word in her throat, the word that she had not permitted to enter her consciousness, the word that had lurked low in some hideous dark corner of her stomach, where all mothers cordon off their worst fears, but which was now sickeningly illuminated.

'He's disappeared.'

10

The receptionist at Brown's, an exclusive hotel consisting of eleven Georgian houses joined together in the heart of Mayfair, had an appraising eye, which was discernible only to those who did not meet his exacting standards. Falcón thought him polite, but did not realize how restrained this politeness was until someone, instantly recognizable but whose name escaped, appeared behind Falcón's shoulder. *That* was politeness, or maybe a caricature of it. Whatever, Falcón was made to wait for no other reason than it was evident, from his lightweight suit in autumn, that he did not belong.

The call was eventually made to Yacoub's room. Falcón, who'd already given his name twice, was asked to repeat it as if he might be a purveyor of game birds to back entrances. There was a lengthy silence while the receptionist listened. Then Falcón experienced the fully-fledged form of British hotel politeness.

Yacoub embraced him in the corridor outside his room. He put a finger to his lips, beckoned him in and shut the door. From the state of the room it was clear that Abdullah was staying there as well, but was not present. Still with his finger to his lips, he indicated that Falcón should undress. He went into the bathroom, shook out a towel and laid it on the bed. Falcón stripped to his underpants. Yacoub indicated that they had to come off as well.

They went into the bathroom. Yacoub didn't turn on the light. He ran the taps, shut the door. He minutely searched Falcón's ears and scalp and then made him take a shower and wash his hair. He fetched a packet of cigarettes from the bedroom and sat back on the bidet while Falcón dried himself off.

'Can't be too careful these days,' said Yacoub. 'They have devices the size of a nail paring.'

'Good to know you still trust me.'

'You've no idea how careful I have to be.'

'I don't know what's happening any more, Yacoub. One moment I'm swimming happily in the shallows, the next I'm off the continental shelf. I've got no idea who is with me or against me.'

'Let's talk about trust first,' said Yacoub, stone-faced. 'You spoke to Pablo.'

'You told me Abdullah was in a training camp back in Morocco.'

'You *spoke* to Pablo,' said Yacoub, pointing an accusing finger at Falcón's bare chest. 'That's why you're out of your depth. We've lost control of the situation. *They*, now, control it. The CNI, MI5 and MI6 . . . probably the CIA, too. If you hadn't spoken to Pablo it would have been between us.'

'I don't have the experience in this game to let something like Abdullah's recruitment go without getting advice from Pablo,' said Falcón. 'I knew when I met you in Madrid that, at best, you were being economical with the truth. I thought *that* was a breach of trust. So I spoke to Pablo and he confirmed that you'd lied to me, Yacoub.'

'He's my son,' said Yacoub, lighting a cigarette. 'You will never understand that.'

'You gave me information, not so that *we* could control the situation, but so that *you* could,' said Falcón. 'I would always be in the dark because blood is thicker than water. You told me that from the beginning.'

'My only motivation is to protect him.'

'Well, he's *unprotected* now, isn't he?' said Falcón, leaning back against the cistern. 'You knew that it would eventually get back to me that you'd met up with Abdullah in London and that I would then know that you'd lied to me in Madrid. I spoke to Pablo and found out a bit earlier, that's all. What we have to do now is re-establish the trust. I can understand why you were in a state in Madrid. I can understand your wariness and your paranoia.'

'Can you?' said Yacoub, derisively. 'Before I got into this I thought *I* could imagine it, but I had no idea it would be like this. So you've got there without even experiencing it. Impressive, Javier.'

'We're talking now,' said Falcón, nodding at him. 'I'm happy. I can feel the old Yacoub.'

'The old Yacoub is long gone,' he said, and smoked.

'I don't think so,' said Falcón. 'But I've got to give the CNI some answers now. You knew it would come to this in the end. You can't lose MI5 five times over the last three months and not expect questions to be asked. You can't tell me that your son has been recruited to the GICM without giving any idea of his involvement. The intelligence agencies are looking at you and asking themselves: Who is Yacoub Diouri? What is his connection to that Turkish businessman from Denizli he met at the trade fair in Berlin? Has he been making contact with an active GICM cell in London that they've learnt about from the French? Who is the stranger living at his home in Rabat? And none of these questions has come about because I spoke to Pablo. It's happened because you've been behaving like a . . . maverick.'

'That is a perfect description of my situation,' said Yacoub. 'I'm in the goldfish bowl. Everybody is looking at me. I have nowhere to go, nowhere to hide. I am as suspicious to my "friends" at the CNI as I am to my "enemies" at the GICM. Are you surprised that I start to act alone, that I am not as transparent as you'd like?'

'You might be in the goldfish bowl, but you've still managed to hide,' said Falcón. 'Now I have to explain how an "untrained" agent of mine can lose the professionals of MI5 five times over the last three months on their *own* turf – the first time barely a month after your recruitment. They *know* you've been trained. And I know it wasn't done by the CNI. So who did it? If we're going to get help for Abdullah, we have to rely on these people. It's the military wing of the GICM who are going to arrange a mission on which your son might well be killed, not MI5 or the CNI.'

The water rushed out of the taps. Yacoub's head rocked back against the wall. He smoked and stared at the sky beyond the high window for some time.

'Look at me,' he said. 'Look at what I have become.'

'What do you want me to say, Yacoub?' said Falcón. 'I'm sorry? I'm sorry that we went into this not knowing . . .'

'Nobody knows,' said Yacoub viciously. 'Do you think these professional recruiters tell their "victims" what it's like? How many new agents do you think they'd get if they told them they'd be . . . vivisected, masterfully kept alive while all their structures are dismantled around them, until all that's left is a mind with blood running through it; seeing things, hearing things, remembering things, photographing things, reporting things.'

'I want to help you, Yacoub, but I can't if I don't know anything, if what you're telling me is only the partial truth.'

'And if I tell you, who will you tell? Who will *they* tell? There's no knowing where it will end. We'll become chess pieces in a three-dimensional game where the players are incapable of calculating the ramifications of each move until it's too late.'

'It's not just symbolic that I'm sitting here naked in your bathroom,' said Falcón. 'They wanted to wire me up. I told them it wouldn't be possible for me to talk to you if I knew they were listening in. With your precautions, we know they're not. This *is* between you and me. And I know I'm back with you. This is different to what it was like in Madrid. So let's talk. Let's get it out in the open and then decide who should be told what.'

Yacoub looked across at him. The dull light from the big grey outside turned one side of his head to pewter. His eyes shifted and glinted in the dark. Their scintillas of light were like needles into Falcón's mind. *Are you the right stuff?* they asked.

'The reason why the GICM accepted me so readily when I crossed to their side of the mosque was that they'd wanted to recruit me for the past nine months,' said Yacoub slowly. 'Despite my family history and connections to various "movements" in the past, they had not made any approaches, because there was nothing in *my* behaviour to indicate that I was of their mentality. As I said before, they were nervous of that half that wasn't Moroccan, and still are. But the reason that I was taken in and elevated so rapidly that, for instance, I met their military high command within days of crossing the line, was that they'd been watching me for a long time. I had something that they wanted.'

'But you had no idea *what* they wanted or that they knew that you had something they desired?'

'No. I was naïve. I thought it was *my* game,' said Yacoub, tapping his chest, then grunting a laugh. 'It was like going to meet your prospective wife in an arranged marriage,

129

expecting the demure virgin and discovering someone terrifyingly experienced.'

'And when did you find this out?' asked Falcón.

'When I came back from Paris that time.'

'In June?'

'They were vetting me. We all thought it was to do with *our* mission and the four-wheel drives filled with explosives going to London, but it was nothing of the sort. They were making sure I was clean, that I didn't contact anybody and that nobody came anywhere near me.'

'So what did they ask you when you came back to Rabat?'

'Are you ready for this, Javier?'

'What do you mean?'

'Once you know it, you're a part of it, you can't unlearn it,' said Yacoub. 'You'll find yourself not just with knowledge, but holding things in your power, precious things, like people's lives. My life. Abdullah's life.'

'The reason I'm here is so that you don't have to go through this alone,' said Falcón. 'We went into this together, naïve as we were, and I'm not going to desert you now. So tell me.'

'If I tell you, you'll be in *my* boat, and that means you won't be able to tell anybody; not your own people and certainly not the British or the Americans.'

'Let's hear what it is before we decide anything.'

'There's no "we'll see" about it, Javier,' said Yacoub. 'I'm as good as dead if anything I tell you goes out of this room. You'll just have to live with the knowledge. And they'll interrogate you, pump you for everything you've got.'

'Spit it out,' said Falcón.

Yacoub ran his hands over his head, prepared himself.

'A short introduction,' he said. 'As you know, the primary design of the GICM was not international operations but to bring about a change in the Moroccan government.'

'They want Islamic rule with Sharia law,' said Falcón.

'Exactly. And the situation in Morocco is no less complicated than that other country which butts up against Europe's eastern border: Turkey. There is a complex battle between the religious and secular in both countries and terrorism is used on both sides. The situation is a little different in Morocco, because we have a monarchy of the Alawite dynasty, which can trace its ancestry back to the Prophet's son-in-law. We also had a king, Mohammed V, who identified himself with the nationalist struggle for independence back in the 1950s and was exiled for it. So the king had both religious lineage and political credibility, which meant that after independence he wasn't pushed to institute parliamentary government.

'He died early and his son, Hassan II, the hard man, took over in 1961. He didn't believe in democracy. Leaders of political parties were exiled. A whole apparatus of secret police, informers and terror was installed. His was a despotic regime, but it did maintain a secular order. Mohammed VI took over in 1999 and there has been a general relaxation: human rights, power and freedom for women, political pluralism. The fundamentalists don't like these reforms, but with the security system more or less dismantled, they saw opportunities.'

'To get themselves organized for political disruption.'

'That's right, but they needed help. They needed money,' said Yacoub. 'Nothing much seemed to be happening until 9/11, but even by then important connections had been made to the people who would eventually become known to the world as al-Qaeda. Extremely devout Moroccan Muslims have been going to the Middle East for centuries, ostensibly to receive an education, but since the 1980s they started getting fired up by what was happening in Afghanistan.'

'So there were already the right people around in Morocco by 2001, who could plug themselves into the al-Qaeda network.'

'The GICM was like a little start-up company looking for help from a larger corporation. But if you want to make yourself attractive, you have to be able to bring something to the table, which is why they involved themselves in international operations. But it didn't happen just like that,' said Yacoub, snapping his fingers. 'It's taken the GICM years to get into this position, with people-smuggling routes in and out of Spain, networks of cells to facilitate surveillance of targets, logistics of material, ID card and passport forgery and bomb-making.'

'So, in trying to make themselves attractive prospects, they've become formidable players.'

'Now they wouldn't even have to ask al-Qaeda for money,' said Yacoub. 'They're involved in drug-running, bank-card fraud and internet scams, all of which they see, not as criminal, but as legitimate "attacks" on the West. All part of the jihad. So, like anybody who's become a power in their own right, they start to think of themselves differently. Success brings a change of focus. They start thinking globally. Why bother to overturn the monarch of some poor, far-flung kingdom when you could bring about the complete revolution? Return all lands from Pakistan to Morocco, and maybe even Andalucía, to Islamic government and law, as we were over a thousand years ago.'

'The jihadi's dream,' said Falcón. 'But how do you pull it off? So far they've had a limited impact by blowing up the World Trade Center, killing commuters in Madrid and London, but they're a long way from the dream.'

'And they've realized that,' said Yacoub. 'All Osama bin Laden did was put them on the map. He made them understand that they have power. Only then . . . after 2001, did the real thinking start.'

'So, go on, how are they going to pull this off?'

'You see, Javier, that's the fatal error of the West.'

'What?'

'You don't believe it's possible. You think it's some ridiculous, far-fetched notion of a bunch of towel-headed fanatics sitting in mud huts, making plans with sticks in the sand.'

'I don't underestimate the capabilities of these groups,' said Falcón. 'But what I do know is that the Arab world has never been able to show a united front.'

'The *leaders* of the Arab world,' said Yacoub. 'Those people who've become the lapdogs of the West, they can't show a united front with the disenfranchised Palestinians, the split Lebanese, the sinister Syrians, the undecided Turks, the occupied Iraqis, the impossible Iranians. But what about their populations with sixty per cent under the age of twenty-five, who have nothing but belief and a sense of injustice? The *people* are more ready than ever to show a united front.'

'All right,' said Falcón. 'But there's still a long way to go.'

'But there *is* a key,' said Yacoub. 'One Arab country holds the key to everything. Not only is it the richest, with fabulous reserves of the most desired commodity in the world, but it also holds the keys to the holiest sites in Islam.'

'Saudi Arabia,' said Falcón. 'Your theory about why the Americans invaded Iraq with such haste was to protect that monarchy, who are the guardians of their most valuable interest.'

'A very difficult relationship for most Muslims to understand,' said Yacoub. 'Why do the guardians of the holiest sites in Islam embrace the most despised infidel on the face of the earth, the one who upholds the rights of Zion in the heart of the land of the Prophet? Very tricky, Javier. Possibly more understandable if the Saudis used their wealth, power and influence to achieve justice for the most abject people of the Arab world, but they don't.'

'So nobody would cry if the House of Saud came to an ignominious end,' said Falcón. 'But how do you achieve it?'

'First of all, al-Qaeda might not be able to get rid of the Americans from Iraq, but they will keep them so fully occupied over such a long time that, when the moment comes and the Americans have to respond, they will be too weak or overstretched or lacking in will to do so.'

'And in the meantime . . .'

'There are more than six thousand members of the Saudi royal family,' said Yacoub. 'Their total wealth is greater than the GDP of many smaller nations. All those people with all that wealth make the royal family a political monster. Every point of view is represented by its members, from the utterly corrupt, drug-running friends of America, to the reclusive, ascetic, profoundly devout Wahabi fundamentalists. Some flaunt their wealth in tasteless displays of extravagance while others quietly channel funds into international terrorism.'

'So the GICM and other terrorist groups have realized that it could just be a question of tipping the balance in favour of the radical fundamentalists within the royal family.'

'Combined with the support of a disgruntled population, who will see more opportunities for equality in an Islamic state than they ever would from an old-fashioned monarchy . . .'

'And there you have the makings of a new world order,' said Falcón. 'But it's not something that will be pulled off easily. How are the GICM going to do it? And how do you fit in?'

'Persuasion, manoeuvring and, if necessary, assassination,' said Yacoub. 'One by one.'

'I imagine there's quite a considerable security apparatus attached to the House of Saud,' said Falcón uneasily.

'Very experienced. Very well trained,' said Yacoub, nodding, staring at his feet.

'Did they train you, Yacoub?'

He looked up at the wall above Falcón's head. The light in his pupils seemed to be coming from a long way off, like a traveller at night making slow progress over a moonless desert.

'This is where you decide, Javier,' he said. 'I wouldn't blame you if you went next door, put your clothes on, left the room and we never see each other again.'

'I don't want that,' said Falcón.

'Why not?' asked Yacoub, lowering his gaze to meet Falcón's eye, his curiosity genuine.

Falcón thought about this for some time, not because he was unsure, but because it suddenly struck him how valuable this relationship had become to him. His friendship with Yacoub had all the complexities of the ties of blood, but without there being any. And he also knew there was no greater bond than that between parent and child. This bizarre situation: sitting naked in Yacoub's hotel bathroom, with a world of trouble seemingly on the brink of fulmination, made him feel a terrible loneliness at the loss of his own parental relationships and the knowledge that he would always be secondary in the lives of others who were important to him.

'If there's any doubt . . .' said Yacoub.

'There's no doubt,' said Falcón. 'You're the only person who understands what I've been through. I'm close to my brother and sister, but they still see me as the old Javier. They've never grasped the extent of the change, or perhaps they don't want to deal with it. You know me in a way that nobody else does, and I'm not going to give that up lightly.'

'Then why do you look so desolate?' said Yacoub.

'Because I think I might be destined for the ultimate loneliness of never being the most important person in anybody's life.'

Yacoub nodded. He had no intention of lying to him.

'But there are times,' he said, 'when only a friend will do.'

Falcón said nothing. Yacoub knew the questions he had to answer and he was either going to do it, or not. He sighed, as if this was going to be an enormous relief.

'I've been in a relationship with . . . well, let's leave it as "a member of the Saudi royal family" for the moment,' said Yacoub. 'We can call him Faisal without fear of identification.'

'How long have you known him?'

'We first met in 2002 at the house of a friend in Marbella,' said Yacoub. 'We became friends. He does a lot of business in London. Whenever I had meetings or attended fashion shows we would always see each other.'

'Let's be clear about it, Yacoub,' said Falcón. 'Is he your lover?'

'Yes,' he said. 'When it became clear that this was serious and Faisal, being an important member of the family, was suitably paranoid, he had me vetted and then trained, so that I could get to see him without bringing the world to his door. His security detail is British trained. They've also actively helped me in the last few months when, because of my successes, MI5 have been a little more assiduous in tailing me.'

'So what does he know about you?' asked Falcón. 'If his security detail is helping you lose MI5, he must realize that you're not "normal".'

'We share a lot of beliefs. We know the world is not black and white. We spend a lot of time talking about the grey. It was Faisal, for instance, who told me why the Americans invaded Iraq, as if it had become a matter of extreme urgency. Quite a few of those six thousand members of the royal family live in a state of total paranoia and terror. The least bit of trouble and they're on their private jets and out of there.'

'Taking the details of their Swiss bank accounts with them.'

'Quite,' said Yacoub. 'He despises them. He and I both have an interest in what is happening beneath the surface. You'd like him. We talk about you.'

'Does that mean he's comfortable with your "spying" activities for the CNI?'

'It's to his advantage and, as you know, he tells me things, too.'

'Where does he stand on the integral line between "friends of America" and "Wahabi fundamentalist"?'

'He's both and yet neither.'

'So he's an important member of the royal family, who is in the balance,' said Falcón. 'The ideal target for the GICM. Someone they would like to see converted to their cause.'

'Not quite,' said Yacoub. 'You're forgetting that the radicals in the GICM *do* see everything in black and white. They don't like grey areas. They can't stomach a man who holds conflicting opinions. However devout Faisal might be – and he is very devout, more devout than I'll ever be – he is still a very loyal family member. However powerful the arguments are that any radical could put to him, he would never betray his king.'

'How did the GICM find out about your relationship with Faisal, and do they know its full extent?'

'They do know its full extent and we are unsure how they got that information,' said Yacoub. 'I overlapped with another lover. Faisal often travels with a large entourage and other family members. There are indiscretions. There are servants. However hard you try, you can't hermetically seal yourself off from the world. And something like the homosexuality of an important family member has a way of getting out. Salacious gossip can find a crack in any wall.'

'And this was what the GICM told you when you came back from Paris in June?'

Yacoub had his feet up on the rim of the bidet. His elbows propped against his knees, his forehead in his hands. He nodded.

'And is this why the GICM have recruited Abdullah?' asked Falcón. 'The only tie more powerful than a lover is that between father and son. This is how they keep you "close". But what exactly do they want?'

'Faisal can never be entirely and securely converted to the cause,' said Yacoub. 'They want him dead.'

11

'I'm not going to talk to anybody except Javier,' said Consuelo, not loudly, but with such an edge to her voice that all the men stood back from her, as if she'd just unsheathed a sword.

They were in the office of the director of the Nervión Plaza shopping centre, which looked out through thin slatted blinds on to the broad avenue of Calle Luis de Morales. It was cold in the room. The sun was blinding and fierce outside. White bars of intense light, spectrum edged, laddered the far wall, on which hung a copy of a Joan Miró painting. Consuelo knew that this painting was called *Dog Barking at the Moon* and, indeed, it consisted of a small, colourful dog, a scimitar of white moon and an unforgiving black background, broken only by what looked like a railway track going to oblivion. It turned her stomach to look at Miró's intention; to show tiny forms in vast empty spaces. Where was Darío now? Normally he was a large presence in a small space, but now she could only think of his defenceless tininess in the larger outside world.

The thought of him came in waves; one moment she was tough and assertive, commanding respect from all the men in the room, and the next she had her face in her trembling hands, hiding that vulnerability, pressing the tears back into her eyes.

'This is not Javier's kind of work,' said Ramírez, the only one who knew her well enough to raise any sort of objection.

'I know it's not, José Luis,' said Consuelo, looking up from the sofa. 'Thank God for that. But I can't . . . I don't want to talk to anyone else. He knows me. He can get everything he needs out of me. We don't have to start from scratch.'

'You should talk to the officers from the Crimes Against Children squad,' said Ramírez. 'The GRUME have enormous experience with missing children. And it's important that we establish the possibilities and probabilities of what may have happened here immediately. Is this a case of a child having wandered off or has he been abducted and, if so, what could be the motives of . . .?'

'Abducted?' said Consuelo, her neck lengthening by ten centimetres.

'Don't alarm yourself, Consuelo,' said Ramírez.

'I'm not alarming myself, José Luis. *You're* alarming me.'

'This is what the GRUME do. They look at the background. They judge probabilities. Have you made enemies in business?'

'Who hasn't?'

'Have you noticed anyone hanging around your home?'

She didn't answer. That made her think. What about that guy last June? The gypsy-looking guy who'd muttered obscenities at her in the street, then she'd seen him again in the Plaza del Pumarejo, not far from her restaurant. She'd thought he was going to rape her down a back street. He'd known her name. He'd known all sorts of things. That her husband was dead. And, yes, her sister, later, had referred to him as the 'new pool guy' when she'd been looking after the kids and had seen him hanging around the house.

'You're thinking, Consuelo.'

'I am.'

'Will you talk to the GRUME officers now?'

'All right, I'll talk to them. But as soon as Javier is available . . .'

'We're trying to get a message to him now,' said Ramírez, patting her on the shoulder with one of his huge, steadying mahogany hands. He felt for her. He had his own kids. The abyss had opened up in him before now and changed him.

They were angry with Falcón. Douglas Hamilton, who was on the brink of losing his usual calm, was jabbing him with irony. Rodney had already called him a cunt. Falcón knew from his English lessons that this was the worst thing you could say to someone in England, but to him, a Spaniard, the world's greatest insulters, it was water off a duck's back.

They were mildly irritated by the fact that the listening device they'd planted on him hadn't worked, but what was really incensing them was that Falcón wouldn't tell them anything juicy from his meeting with Yacoub.

'You can't tell us where he's been on the five occasions he's lost us. You can't tell us who trained him. You can't tell us why his son is with him in London . . .'

'That I don't know,' said Falcón, cutting in on the litany. 'He wouldn't tell me that.'

'Maybe we should just shoot the fucker anyway,' said Rodney.

'Who?' said Falcón.

Rodney shrugged as if it didn't matter.

'It won't come to that,' said Hamilton smoothly.

'He's in a very difficult position,' said Falcón.

'Oh, fuck right off,' said Rodney.

'Aren't we all?' said Hamilton. 'You're talking to people

140

with two thousand suspected terrorists under constant watch. Can't you at least throw us a bone, Javier?'

'I can tell you about the Turkish businessman from Denizli.'

'Fuck that,' said Rodney.

'We're listening,' said Hamilton.

'They've signed a contract for the supply of denim to his factory in Salé,' said Falcón. 'The first shipment was received . . .'

'Bugger off,' said Rodney. 'You know what he's doing and you're not fucking telling us. We don't give a shit about the Turkish tosser.'

'Maybe you knew that Yacoub and the Turk had a genuine business relationship,' said Falcón, 'and you were just using their mildly suspicious backgrounds to make them appear more threatening.'

'We know about the Turk,' said Hamilton, holding up a calming hand. 'What else *can* you tell us?'

'Yacoub knows of no active GICM cell currently operating in the UK,' said Falcón. 'This doesn't mean there isn't one, it just means he has never been asked to make contact with it, and he's never heard any reference to one in any of his discussions with the military wing of the GICM.'

'Brilliant,' said Rodney.

'Let's at least get something straight,' said Hamilton. 'Do you know what he's been up to when he's lost the MI5 tails?'

'Not exactly. All I do know is that it's a private matter . . .'

'Which requires top-level spy craft?'

'In order to stay private . . . yes,' said Falcón.

'All right,' said Hamilton. 'The person or group that he's met on these occasions, you're saying they're not an active GICM cell.'

'I can confirm that,' said Falcón. 'I can also confirm that they are in no way your enemies.'

'Then why the fuck can't you tell us who they are?' said Rodney, in a crescendo.

'Because you'll start to make assumptions,' said Falcón. 'I'll tell you one thing and you'll put it together with other, perhaps unrelated, bits of information about Yacoub. You'll build a picture. The wrong one. Then you'll act in your own interests and not those of my agent, and that will more than likely put Yacoub and his son in serious danger.'

'What's Yacoub's interest?' asked Hamilton.

'That everybody close to him gets out alive . . . and he doesn't necessarily include himself in that number.'

'Fuck me, now he's giving you the sacrificial lamb shit,' said Rodney.

'Why does he think that we wouldn't help him?' asked Hamilton.

'Yacoub turned down approaches from both MI6 and the CIA,' said Falcón, 'because he had very good reasons for thinking that they would quite quickly find him expendable.'

'Let's just take him out,' said Rodney, bored by it all. 'Then we won't have to worry about him any more.'

Falcón had been waiting for this moment. He needed to create a little scene and Rodney had just given him the opportunity. He took three steps across the room, lifted Rodney out of his chair and slammed him up against the door.

'You're talking about my friend,' said Falcón, through gritted teeth. 'My friend who has given vital information at considerable risk to himself, which prevented an attack on a landmark building in the heart of the City of London containing thousands of people. If you want to put yourself in the way of more information like that, then you'll have to be patient with him. Yacoub, unlike you, is not in the business of endangering people's lives.'

'All right,' said Hamilton, grabbing Falcón's tensed bicep. 'Let's calm things down.'

'Then get this trigger-happy imbecile out of my sight,' said Falcón.

Rodney grinned and Falcón realized that the man had been playing a part all along, getting under his skin, trying to lever him open.

Falcón, still simmering, allowed himself to be guided back to his chair.

'Just give us something to go on, Javier,' said Hamilton, 'that's all we ask.'

'All right,' said Falcón, who'd been prepared by Yacoub for this free gift. 'A number of agencies, including the CNI, have been concerned by the appearance of a stranger in Yacoub's household.'

'In Rabat?'

'That's where he lives, Rodney.'

'What the fuck's that to us?'

'Then that probably concludes our business,' said Falcón coldly, preparing to leave.

'Take no notice of him,' said Hamilton. 'Tell us about the stranger.'

'He's a family friend. His name is Mustafa Barakat. He runs a number of tourist shops in Fès, which was where he was born in 1959 and has lived his entire life.'

'What's he doing in Yacoub's house?'

'He's a guest. It's not the first time, although it is probably the first time since foreign and Moroccan agencies have taken an interest in Yacoub's life.'

'We'll check him out,' said Rodney, as if that was a threat.

'She'll talk to you now,' said Ramírez, addressing the two officers from the Crimes Against Children squad, GRUME, who were standing in the corridor outside the director's office.

'What's her problem?' asked the younger one.

'She's been investigated by the police before,' said Ramírez. 'That's how we know her. We suspected her – or rather, *I* suspected her – of murdering her husband, Raúl Jiménez.'

143

'And Falcón didn't?' asked Inspector Jefe Tirado, the older GRUME officer. 'Is that why she'll only talk to him?'

'They're close,' said Ramírez, and cut off that line of questioning with his hand.

'She didn't kill her husband, did she?' asked the younger officer, nervously.

'Just stick to the fucking point,' said Ramírez, ignoring him. 'Stay focused on her missing son, don't try to broaden things out too quickly. Concentrate on the immediate facts and then work back . . . slowly.'

'But that's not how we work,' said the young officer.

'I know. That's why I'm telling you,' said Ramírez. 'If you start rooting around in her private life, her business associates, her family album before you've gained her complete trust, then she'll clam up until Falcón gets here.'

'And when is that going to be?'

'I don't know. Maybe ten or eleven o'clock this evening.'

'I hear she lost sight of the boy when he went into the Sevilla Futbol Club shop,' said Tirado. 'You know they don't have CCTV out there. It's going to be hard going for us to establish whether he wandered off or was abducted. You got any feeling for what might have happened, José Luis?'

'I doubt the kid wandered off,' said Ramírez. 'You're going to find out that she's a complicated woman.'

'I don't even understand them when they're simple,' said the young officer, looking down the corridor.

Ramírez made a short mental appeal to the Holy Virgin. 'Stick to the facts. Broaden out slowly,' he repeated the mantra. 'We may have to wait for Falcón, anyway.'

'What does that mean?'

'It means Falcón's stirring a lot of pots at the same time and a fair few of them have shit at the bottom.'

They opened the door. Consuelo's voice barged out into the corridor.

'What do you mean, they *don't* have CCTV?' she asked.

'Why don't you have CCTV? In England I've heard they have CCTV everywhere ... even on roundabouts in the middle of nowhere.'

'This isn't England,' said the director, feeling sorry for her but having to tamp down his irritation, too, as he was having to repeat himself again and again because not much was sticking in her mind.

'But there must be *something*.'

'Good afternoon, Señora Jiménez, my name is Inspector Jefe Tirado,' said the senior GRUME officer, as he entered the room. 'We are from the Crimes Against Children squad. There *is*, of course, plenty we can do. We're going to check all the footage of every camera in the Nervión Plaza, and that includes the internal shops' CCTV. As you know, there are cameras in the central area, too, and it's possible that we will get sufficient angle on some of them to include the Sevilla FC stadium and shop. There are already officers conducting interviews with people in and around the shop and stadium. I expect that we will find out very quickly what has happened to your son, Darío.'

Consuelo stood up and shook the man's hand.

At 18.00 Falcón was on his way back to Heathrow. Douglas Hamilton had told him he'd make sure they held the flight, but Falcón wasn't sure the man liked him enough to actually do it. Despite the aggression from the two men, Falcón was relaxed. Yacoub had told him the truth. They were back on track and he didn't mind doing some blocking for him. There were still moments of panic when he thought about the ruthlessness of the GICM, but he calmed himself with the thought of Faisal's Saudi security detail.

He turned his mobile on without thinking. It exploded with messages and missed calls. He went into the inbox. Twelve messages from Consuelo. He leaned back in his seat. The Jaguar coasted along the raised section of the Great

West Road, past empty high-rise office space. He allowed some exhaustion to creep into his neck and back as he savoured the weight of the unread messages. He smiled to himself, thinking: Javier Falcón, the romantic. He'd never have believed it. He shrugged and opened the first message.

'Darío missing. Help.'

He clicked through all twelve messages hoping that this was just the first panicked text and that by number twelve he'd get 'Darío found. See you tonight.' Instead he pieced together the chain of events and the last message read: 'WHERE ARE YOU? I NEED YOU HERE.' It was timed 17.08. His insides felt hideously cold, as ugly thoughts stirred at the back of his mind.

Ramírez was still in the corridor outside the director's office waiting for news when he took Falcón's call. He gave him the update, told him that Consuelo was with the GRUME officers.

'I'm not going to get back until ten thirty tonight at the earliest,' said Falcón. 'Let me talk to her . . . in private.'

'Hold on a second, Javier.'

While listening to the extended muffled conversation at the other end, Falcón tried to think of consoling things to say to Consuelo, but he knew that no words of comfort ever worked in these situations.

'Cristina's found a couple living in an apartment block on Avenida de Eduardo Dato. They have a perfect view of the Sevilla FC stadium and the shop,' said Ramírez. 'They saw two people dressed in black jackets, black jeans and baseball caps with a small boy in between them, who was wearing a Sevilla FC scarf, but appeared to be struggling and not particularly happy. One of the adults was carrying a box. When they arrived at a car parked in front of the couple's block, one of the adults got in the back with the boy. The one carrying the box threw it on the ground, got in the driver's seat and drove off. They managed to see that it was a red Fiat Punto and had an old Seville number plate. Cristina's recovered the box, which contained a pair of football boots bought today from a shop called Décimas.'

'Take that news and the football boots in to Consuelo and the GRUME officers,' said Falcón, 'and let me speak to Cristina.'

Ferrera came on the line.

'Did you go and see Marisa?' asked Falcón.

'This morning, just after you left.'

'Every time I went to see Marisa I got a threatening phone call afterwards.'

'And you think they've taken their threat one step further.'

'I know they have,' said Falcón. 'I went to see Marisa late last night and I got a call just before I met Consuelo for dinner about ten minutes after midnight. The voice told me that something would happen and when it did I would know that it was my fault and I would recognize it. These people know me. They know my vulnerabilities. Whoever is coercing Marisa has kidnapped Darío. It's the next logical step.'

Falcón was talking to her in his usual measured way, but for the first time in four years working for him, she could hear a trembling at the edges of his voice that told her he was afraid. She knew he was close to the boy. He was always asking her questions about what her own son was like at eight years old; what he was interested in, what he liked to do. Her boss was learning how to be a father, and he'd just been thrown in the deep end.

'I'll go and see Marisa again,' she said.

'How was she the last time?'

'She was in a state. Drunk on rum. She was just opening up to me when she got a call. Then she fell to pieces, couldn't get rid of me quick enough.'

'Go and see her now, Cristina,' he said. 'As soon as possible. Get the pressure back on her. Tell her they've kidnapped a child. Work on her emotions. Make her . . . suffer. Do whatever you have to.'

'I'll do it. Don't worry,' she said. 'But what about the GRUME officers? Technically, it's their investigation. We're only involved because Consuelo called Ramírez when she was trying to find you.'

'We'd already started a line of inquiry with Marisa Moreno. She is a suspect in a conspiracy to murder case. GRUME will obviously have to be kept informed, but you are going to lose valuable time bringing them up to speed. So you go to see Marisa and I will explain our position to GRUME. Now let me speak to Consuelo while Ramírez is talking to GRUME about what you found out from that couple on Avenida de Eduardo Dato,' said Falcón. 'That was good, fast work, Cristina.'

Ferrera called Consuelo into the empty corridor, handed her the phone.

'Where *are* you?' she said, hugging the phone to her cheek.

'I can't tell you. It's not police business and I can't talk about it. All I can say is that I'm a flight away and I'm on the road to the airport. I'll be with you before midnight.'

'Cristina found witnesses who saw two people leading Darío away. I've seen the football boots. They're the ones I just bought for him,' she said, the emotion constricting her throat, having to squeeze the words past the barrier. 'They were leading Darío away, Javier.'

Consuelo was not prepared for this. Now that she was talking to him, all the powers that made her such a formidable person to deal with in business, that enabled her to run her complicated life, that made people sit up in the presence of her personality, deserted her. She found herself in the same state she'd been in with Alicia Aguado, holding her hand; the lost little girl, the troubled teenager, the adult gone awry, the mature woman on the edge of insanity.

Falcón, after that little logistical exchange, came to an unexpected halt in the face of his insurmountable guilt. All that cold, black hideousness that he'd felt on reading her messages rose in his chest. She was coming to *him* for help, for comfort, for solutions. And all he could think of was that he was the *cause* of her terrible predicament. He could feel her desperation, her need to melt into him, but, having wanted that more than anything else in his life this morning, he now found he was insoluble to her substance.

'This is what you have to do,' said Falcón, whose only recourse was to the professional in him. 'There's going to be CCTV footage of the two people . . .'

'The Nervión Plaza's CCTV doesn't go out that far.'

'Those two people will have had to come into the shopping centre to find you. They will have been looking at you for some time before they saw their opportunity. You have to look at all the available footage and find them. Then when you've found them you have to think where you've seen them before, because, Consuelo, those two people have been somewhere in your life. They might have been at the very periphery of it, but they have been there. Nobody can do what they've just done without any planning, without having watched you and Darío for some time.'

'But maybe somebody else did all that and these people just did the . . . the abducting.'

'That's possible, but at some stage those people will have had to see their target. You should talk to the school, take Inspector Jefe Tirado with you and talk to the teachers and other children, not just the ones in his class.'

'I need you here, Javier,' she said.

'And I'm going to be there, but in the meantime this is the most important moment. Remember that. The first hours are critical. You have to clear your mind of everything and concentrate only on what can help us find Darío.'

A deep breath from Consuelo.

'You're right,' she said.

149

'When you see those two people on the CCTV footage – and I promise you, they will be there – they might not be in their baseball caps, or they might be in reversible jackets, but they *will* be there, Consuelo. You *will* have seen them.'

'I've seen them,' she said.

'What do you mean?'

'I remember now. Two men. They looked straight at me when I was on the phone in Décimas, waiting to pay for the football boots. I noticed their look.'

'Think about them when you're looking at the CCTV footage. Ask the security people to play the footage from outside Décimas first and when you see those two men look at everything about them. The way they walk, their size, height, clothes, hands and feet, jewellery – anything that will give you a clue, that will jog your memory of where you have seen them before. That's all you do, Consuelo, think about that, answer the questions from Inspector Jefe Tirado and nothing else. I'll be back tonight and we'll find him.'

'Javier?'

'Yes.'

'I love you,' she said.

'You again,' said Marisa, face impassive, rubbery with alcohol, her eyes rheumy. 'Still haven't found anything better to do?'

She let the door fall back, revealed herself in bikini briefs again, a fat smouldering joint in her fingers. The smell of rum was strong, its sweetness mixed in with the hashish.

'Come in, little nun, come in. I'm not going to bite you.'

Marisa walked extravagantly to the work bench, swivelled and landed heavily on a stool. She swayed backwards and managed to sweep up a glass of Cuba libre and sipped it with distaste. It was warm and sticky. She licked her lips.

'What you looking at?' she asked, her face weak and evil by turns.

150

'You.'

Marisa posed with her legs spread, ran a finger under the waistband of her briefs.

'Fancy a bit of that?' she asked. 'Bet you had to do a bit of that in nun school, or whatever they call it.'

'Shut up, Marisa,' said Cristina. 'I'll make some coffee.'

'Your boss,' said Marisa, adopting a mock sexualized tone, 'the Inspector Jefe – he knows why he sent you here. He thinks I'm into that. Hates men, loves –'

Marisa stopped dead as Cristina lashed her across the face with her open palm. It knocked her off the stool. She dropped the joint, hunted for it among the wood shavings, replugged it into her mouth, got to her feet blinking, tears streaking her cheeks. Cristina made the coffee, forced her to drink water, got her into a T-shirt and a robe.

'No amount of alcohol or dope is going to stop you thinking about what you've got on your mind, Marisa.'

'How the fuck do you know what I've got on my mind?'

Cristina got up close, grabbed hold of Marisa's chin, made those lazy eyes pop open. She took the joint from her fingers, crushed it underfoot.

'Every time the Inspector Jefe has come to see you he's taken a threatening phone call afterwards from the same people holding Margarita,' she said. 'He got a call last night. They told him something bad was going to happen. And this morning the Inspector Jefe's partner is in the Nervión Plaza, and what happens, Marisa? Are you listening to me?'

She nodded, Cristina was hurting her.

'They kidnapped her son. Eight years old. They led him off, stuffed him in the back of a car,' said Cristina. 'So now, because you won't talk to us, an innocent child is suffering. And you know what these people are like, don't you, Marisa?'

Marisa jerked her head back, tore her chin out of Cristina's grip, paced the floor with her arms over her head, trying to close it all out.

'Eight-year-old little boy,' said Cristina. 'And you know what they said, Marisa? They said that we would never hear from them again. So, because you won't talk, the little boy's gone and we will never get him back. Not unless you —'

Marisa stamped her foot, clenched her fists, looked up to an unseen, uncaring God.

'That's the point, little nun,' she said. 'They'd do *anything*, these people. You know, they have guys who don't care one way or the other. A girl, a baby, an eight-year-old boy – it doesn't make any difference to them. And if I speak to you, if I say one word . . .'

'We can protect you. I can have a patrol car around here —'

'You can protect *me*,' said Marisa. 'You can put me in a concrete bunker for the rest of my life and that would give them pleasure because they would know that all I'd think about would be Margarita and the terrible things they would do to her. That is how these people operate. Why do you think they've got her anyway? An innocent teenager.'

'I'm listening, Marisa.'

'When my father died, he had a debt on his club in Gijón. My mother scraped together money from wherever she could to pay them. Then she got ill. They took Margarita to clear the debt,' said Marisa. 'But you see, we didn't really owe them money. They had my father's club. They had made money out of him all his life, even when he was on the Sugar Board in Cuba. But then they saw some helpless women and they invented a debt, an unrepayable debt. My sister will whore for them until she's finished. And when she's dried out and gaping from the drugs and the endless fucking, they'll kick her out on to the street and let her live in the gutter. To them, livestock has more value.'

12

He hadn't been able to respond. He'd waited for those words all this time and when they'd come he couldn't say them back. Why not? Because the words that had so comforted her and elicited those heavily guarded and locked-away sentiments had come from the office of Inspector Jefe Javier Falcón. He'd said those words to hundreds of people staring down the empty luge run that opened up when they learned that somebody close to them had been murdered. It had been taught to him by a retired Norwegian detective at the police academy back in the 1980s. When Per Aarvik had told them that the luge run was unavoidable for those closest to the victim, he'd had to start by describing what a luge run was. Its icy insanity sounded terrifying to a class of Spanish twenty-year-olds. And, as Per Aarvik said, everybody went through it, but if you wanted someone to be of use to you in your investigation you had to focus their mind, steady their nerve, point them in the right direction and, by the time you let them go, make them believe that you would be with them to the end. If you said it right, if you believed in it yourself, they would love you as they would close family.

Consuelo loved him for the course he'd done at the police academy. Per would have been proud.

Clear the mind. This is avoidance thinking. He could see what was happening to him. The stress of the flight had been terrible, even though, with the plane full, they'd had to put him in business class. He'd sipped a whisky and water, gnawed on his thumbnail and writhed deeper into his luxurious seat at the thought of Darío in the hands of strangers. She would know as soon as she looked into his face that he was guilty, that he was the cause of her most loved son's abduction.

If he told her she would not forgive him.

If he didn't tell her she would never forgive him.

There was only hope in the first course of action.

And he'd have to find the boy.

He called Cristina Ferrera as he trotted through the arrivals hall at Seville airport. It was 10.35 p.m., he'd lost an hour to the time difference. Ferrera had stayed with Marisa for two hours and the Cuban hadn't cracked. She'd walked her home, given her some aspirin and put her to bed. Marisa hadn't even been prepared to confirm that it was the Russians who'd taken her sister and who were putting her under such extreme pressure not to talk. She wouldn't admit to knowing Vasili Lukyanov. She wouldn't talk about the purpose of her relationship with Calderón. She'd never got drunk enough to forget her fear.

'You took her home,' said Falcón. 'That's good.'

'I think I'm all she's got.'

'What are you doing tonight?'

'I'm going to bed so that I can get up tomorrow to take the kids to the beach on the way down to Cádiz for lunch with my mother.'

'Of course you are.'

'And you?'

'I thought I'd do the first shift on a twenty-four-hour surveillance of Marisa Moreno.'

'For which you have no budget,' said Ferrera. 'What about Consuelo?'

'I don't think she'll want to see me for very long.'

'You're going to tell her?'

'The alternative is not an option.'

'I'll go and sit outside Marisa's apartment. Relieve me when you can.'

'What about the kids?'

'My neighbour's good for a few hours, but I'm not going to be able to get to Marisa's immediately,' she said. 'I haven't eaten.'

'As soon as you can.'

Falcón kept on the run to his car where he called Inspector Jefe Tirado from the Crimes Against Children squad. They'd already spoken at Heathrow. Tirado was on the road somewhere.

'I've just left Señora Jiménez,' he said. 'She's with her sister and her other two boys. She's remarkably calm. A doctor's been round to check her out – blood pressure, that kind of thing. She's fine. He's given her some sleeping pills and something for anxiety, which she says she won't take.'

'How's it going on your side?'

'The big news is that we've found them on CCTV.'

'Good footage?'

'Not bad, but not a lot of it. Señora Jiménez has it with her. She's looking at it.'

'Any more witnesses?'

'We haven't been able to add much more detail beyond what Cristina Ferrera found out this morning,' said Tirado. 'We have to hope that when they said they wouldn't make contact they were just adding a level of threat. It would be unusual if they didn't make demands eventually, but I reckon they'll make her sweat until Monday.'

'What about the press?'

'It was too late for the Sunday editions and I wanted to

155

hold back on the Monday papers, give Señora Jiménez some time to collect herself. It will be big news. We made some announcements on local radio so they're pushing for the story, and I've a feeling that Canal Sur are already sniffing around the Jefatura.'

'I'm going to mount some surveillance on Marisa Moreno.'

'Cristina Ferrera told me about her,' said Tirado. 'So you think the Russians will make contact?'

'Can you spare any manpower for the surveillance?'

'I thought you might ask me that,' he said. 'Look, Javier, you've got a good theory about why the boy was taken, but I can't give up on all other lines of inquiry just yet. If they'd made contact and we were in negotiations, then that would be different. But I've got to find this guy who assaulted her near the Plaza del Pumarejo and, according to her sister, appeared later at her house. I haven't started on her business associates and I haven't even looked at the enemies of Raúl Jiménez. And it is *his* son we're talking about. I never knew the guy, but I've heard he wasn't everybody's friend. You know what they say about revenge.'

Still close to 36°C at 11.00 p.m. Falcón pulled away from the airport with the faint smell of jet fuel coming through the air-con. It made him think of escape. His palms were sweaty. Yes, he wouldn't mind escaping now. He tried to think of things to say to Consuelo. Still nothing believable from the heart came to him. That thoroughfare seemed to be blocked off, barricaded with guilt.

Cars flashed past him on the motorway; he'd slowed to just sixty kilometres per hour, his reluctance for the next scene subconsciously finding its way to his foot. He crossed the ring road. The Barrio de Santa Clara was just there, an enclosed nest of wealth surrounded by industrial zones and the drug dens of Polígono San Pablo.

He parked. Rang the bell at the gate. The front door opened. A silhouette appeared. He walked into her arms like an impostor. Felt her warm breath on his fraudulent neck. Some wetness touched his cheating cheek. He held her. She clung to him tightly. He patted her back, because he'd been told that it reminded everyone of the comforting memory of their mother's beating heart from the womb.

'We have to talk,' said Falcón.

'Let's go upstairs,' she said. 'They're all in the living room.'

She'd set up a television in the bedroom. There was a dent at the foot of the bed where she'd been sitting, taking time out from other people and watching the CCTV footage.

'It hasn't been on the news yet, has it?' asked Falcón.

'Not yet. They've kept it out of the press, too, once we saw this,' she said, and pressed the remote.

Black and white. The same as the *noir* films that had drawn him to police work in the beginning. But this was grey and uninteresting, the camera static, at a dull angle from above. The flat glass of the sports goods shop was visible on one side. The tiled floor was matt, empty, and then suddenly full of two dark-haired men, one in a long-sleeved shirt, the other in a polo shirt, both carrying other clothing. They stopped, looked, and moved off away from the camera.

'What about the other angle?'

'That's coming.'

There they were again, but caps on now, heads down, jackets on, too, hands buried in pockets, moving away from the shop.

'They know what they're doing,' said Falcón.

'That's how they look in all the other footage,' said Consuelo. 'They only took their hats and jackets off to check us out in the shop.'

'What about footage from outside the stadium?'

'It's coming,' she said. 'It's all been laid down on this tape.'

'Anything from the people serving in the Sevilla Futbol Club shop?'

'Nothing. The shop was full and busy. They didn't even

157

see Darío,' said Consuelo. 'This is the confirmation of what Cristina found out from the couple in their apartment on Avenida de Eduardo Dato.'

It was over in a fraction of a second. Rewind. Play. Rewind. Play. Rewind. Freeze frame. Consuelo circled the three figures in the background of the screen.

'Darío is wearing a scarf. The guy on the right is carrying the football boots. They're the same men picked up by CCTV in the Nervión Plaza, jackets, baseball caps.'

'That's all they've got outside the shopping centre?'

He sat down with her on the end of the bed, leaned forward, elbows on knees, hands in prayer over his nose. She rewound the tape, played the footage again, hoping that his police brain would pick something out that she hadn't herself.

'Talk me through your shopping trip,' he said, turning off the television. 'I want to know every centimetre and second of what you did from the moment we finished that call I made to you from the airport this morning. Every detail, every minuscule, unimportant detail that stuck in your brain. Every phone call you made and received. You're never off that phone these days. The reception isn't always good in these shopping centres, you probably had to walk around. What did you see? I want you to talk without interruption.'

Falcón locked the bedroom door, turned the lights off, leaving just a bedside lamp glowing in the corner. He took out his notebook. Consuelo started with the heartbreaking moment that had lodged itself in her chest, when Darío had asked her: 'Do you still love me now that Javi is with us?' Falcón couldn't bear to look up. He nodded when he heard her reply. She looked out of the dark window, at their reflection with the lamp, almost a cosy scene. He let her talk. Only every so often did he break in to coax out more detail from her, just so that her brain didn't get lazy and glide over what appeared to be unimportant. He wanted the whole thing to play like a movie in her mind. He wanted to see what her camera saw. She took him through the moment she first saw the two men.

'Both Spanish. I'd say in their twenties. One thick set, conventional hair, side parted, eyebrows sliding off the side of his face, nose a little fat as if he might have broken it, clean shaven, good teeth. The other thin, long hair, two lines running down from his cheekbones to his jaw, forehead creased.'

'How did you see his forehead if he had long hair?'

'He wore it tucked behind his ears.'

'What shirt was he wearing?'

'He was in the long-sleeved shirt. Dark blue. He wore it untucked. The thick-set guy had a Lacoste shirt on. The little crocodile. Dark green.'

'Feet?'

'I can't see their feet.'

'In their hands?'

'The jackets. Yes, I remember thinking: Jackets, on a day like this? The car computer said it was 40°C when we went into the underground car park.'

'Colour?'

'Dark. I can't say more than that.'

He played the footage again. He watched it on his hands and knees, face close up to the screen. She sat behind him on the bed. He froze the frame just as the three figures came out of the shop.

'They'll work on that shot, get it sharp and publish it in the press,' he said. 'Then we'll interview all these people standing around . . .'

'But *who* are these guys?' she asked, joining him on her knees, tapping the screen.

They turned to each other and she saw it straight away in the light coming from the trembling image.

'You know something,' she said, blinking. 'What do you know, Javier?'

He couldn't bear to be so close to her. He got to his feet. She came up with him.

'You don't know these men, do you?' she asked. 'You can't know them. How can you know them?'

'I don't know them,' he said. 'But I do know that my work is responsible . . .'

'Your *work*. How can your *work* be responsible? *You* do your work. *You*, therefore, are responsible. How?' she asked.

He told her about his meetings with Marisa Moreno and why she was of interest to him. The finding of the disks in the dead Russian mafioso's briefcase. The intensifying of his interrogations of Marisa. The phone calls. The phone call he'd had just before he'd seen her last night.

'So these people are watching you,' she said. 'Which means they've been watching my house, me, my children . . .'

'That's possible.'

'You *knew* that,' she said and turned away from him to look out of the black window, the lamp and the two of them reflected back to her, but now transformed in her mind to a scene of gross betrayal.

'I've been threatened before,' he said. 'It's a classic scare tactic, a delaying tactic. It's done to slow me down. To distract.'

'Well, this is a major fucking distraction,' she said, turning on him. 'My son . . .'

She stopped, something else occurring to her.

'They did the same thing four years ago,' she said. 'I don't know how I could have forgotten that because . . . how *could* I forget that?'

She walked away from him and turned back, like a lawyer.

'It was one of the reasons I broke it off with you four years ago,' she said.

'The photograph.'

'The red cross on the photograph,' she said. 'The red marker pen that crossed out *my* family. People coming into *my* home, leaving the television on and crossing out *my* family. That was one of the reasons I couldn't carry on with you the last time. How am I supposed to live with that?'

'You shouldn't have to,' said Falcón.

'They were *Russians*, too,' she said, eyes fierce, mouth stretched tight across her teeth.

'They were, but a different group. The two men who sanctioned that are now dead.'

'Who killed them?' she asked, finding herself livid now, all logic gone, the stress of the day suddenly releasing itself into her veins, her heart thundering in her chest. 'Or doesn't it matter who killed who? People kill each other all the fucking time. That's who you deal with, Javier – killers. *They* are your meat and drink.'

'This isn't a good idea,' he said. 'I should go.'

She was on him in a flash, hitting him with both her fists high on his chest, knocking him back against the wall.

'You brought those people into my house the last time,' she said. 'And now, just as I've let you back into my . . . into everything . . . they're back.'

He grabbed her wrists. She tore them out of his hands, pummelled him about the head and shoulders until he managed to get hold of them again. He pulled her to him.

'The most important thing for *you* to understand, Consuelo,' he said, looking into her livid face, 'is that none of this is your fault.'

That turned something in her, switched something off. He didn't like it. The passion disappeared. Her blue eyes turned to ice. She pushed herself away from him, eased herself out of his slackening grip. Backed away into the centre of the room, folded her arms.

'I don't want to see you again,' she said. 'I don't want your world in mine ever again. You are responsible for Darío's abduction and I cannot forgive you. Even if you bring him back to me tomorrow you will never be forgiven for what you have done. I want you to leave and I don't want you ever to come back.'

She turned her back on him. He could see its tense muscularity under the light top and could find no words to soften it. And he realized what this was all about. She was punishing herself. She held *herself* completely responsible. She had taken her eye off Darío for the sake of some stupid phone call from an idiot estate agent trying to sell her something she didn't want, and *that* was why he'd been kidnapped. And no amount of his taking the blame on to himself was going to change that. He unlocked the door, left the room, went down the stairs and out into the suffocating night, full of the uneasy susurrating of the trees and the low, distant threat of the city grinding out its future.

Cristina Ferrera started at the appearance of Falcón in the frame of the driver's window.

'You told her,' she said, seeing it in his face.

He looked off down Calle Hiniesta and nodded.

'Then I'm glad I didn't call,' she said.

'What's happened?'

'Nothing. The light's on, but I'm not convinced she's there.'

She got out of the car. They looked up at the apartment. Light shone on to the roof terrace, illuminating the plant life growing around it.

'I got here around eleven thirty and I haven't seen anything move.'

'Have you looked at the studio?'

'It's in darkness.'

'Let's call her,' he said, and punched the number into his mobile. No answer.

'Ring the bell?' asked Ferrera.

They crossed the square in front of Santa Isabel, past the bars on Calle Vergara, which at 12.45 a.m. were now shut. Falcón pressed the buzzer. Ferrera stood back in the street.

'I can hear it buzzing,' she said.

'Nobody home.'

'Or too drunk . . . dead to the world.'

'You didn't leave the lights on when you took her back home and put her to bed?'

'No.'

'Saturday night?'

'She didn't look like she was going anywhere.'

'Let's take a look at the studio,' he said. 'When did you last check it?'

'About half an hour ago.'

They headed down Calle Bustos Tavera and found the arched entrance in profound darkness. They turned on their pen torches and went into the courtyard, where a hot breeze played lazily around the rusted remains of chassis and rejected white goods. Falcón led the way. A dog barked some way off. A torch beam picked up two small discs of reflected light. The cat didn't move until it felt too exposed, and then it turned and shrank away into the shadows. The metal steps up to the studio shook under their weight, the masked window had a crack in it he didn't remember. He reached the landing in front of the door, Ferrera, two steps below. Falcón pushed the door, which gave way. He put the pen torch in his mouth, took out a packet of latex gloves and put them on.

'This doesn't feel right,' he said.

13

Black and white again, in the torch beam, but this time the real *noir*. Liquid on the floor, black as an oil spill with a grey flotsam of wood shavings.. The work bench's pylon standing in welled crude. A sketch scratched across paper, a bleached square on the lake of tar. A foot, grainy, off-white, creased with grime. Stool on its side, chrome legs, the pitch lagoon sucking up to the silver. Pencils like a barge flotilla broken up in a harbour.

A foot?

His torch beam travelled back.

Is that carved from wood? The creases of toil and age meticulously etched.

Falcón leaned in, slapped the light switch. Two horror flashes, two mind gasps, the brain needing two attempts to transform the black and white to full Technicolor. Then solid, unwavering, penetrative, buzzing neon to show the full extent of the abattoir.

The blood had achieved terminal viscosity about half a metre from the door. It wasn't a carving. It was a human foot lying on its side, sole straining against the encroaching tide. Marisa's body was stretched out on the work bench. The caramel of her mulatto skin now the only part of the picture that was grey. Her handless arm hung down straight as a drainpipe to the pool of blood. She had no head. The only detail which distinguished the meat as human were the bikini briefs, which were soaked through. The monster which had perpetrated this butchery was propped up on some blocks of wood further along the work bench. The meat hook where it had hung, empty above it. The teeth of its chain were clogged with gore. Next to it stood the final horror. The carving of the two men on either side of the young girl, who now had a head. Eyes closed. Face slack. Coppery hair matted with blood. Marisa: part of her own work.

The smell wafted out to them. The metal of Marisa's blood. The cess of her guts. The sulphur of her incipient rot. And on the back of this foetor came her terror, wriggling like a live worm in the brain, touching all the atavistic points, twitching up the old fears of the unstoppable agony with only one possible exit. Falcón turned away with the slaughterhouse image burned into his mind. The sweat stood off his face in beads. The saliva thickened to an eggy slop in his mouth. He sucked in the black night air, thick as bitumen.

'Don't look,' he said.

Too late. Ferrera had already seen enough for her to lose another rasher of her faith. It had taken her off at the knees. She slumped on the stairs, holding on to the banister, panting under her thin cotton blouse, which now had the weight of a trench coat. The torch hung slack on a loop of cord from her wrist, its light wavered over the weeds and junk beneath them. She stared, mouth gaping, until the torch light was completely still and only then did she regain her footing in the world.

The sweat stung Falcón's eyes as he called the communications centre in the Jefatura and gave his report. He hung up, wiped his face with his hand and flung it out into the darkness. He lowered himself down on to the top step, reached out to Cristina Ferrera and squeezed her shoulder, as much to comfort himself that there were still good people in this world. She rested her face on his hand.

'We're all right,' she said.

'Are we?' said Falcón, because he was already thinking that the people who had done this were the same people who'd taken Darío.

The courtyard was frozen under the portable halogen. Falcón sat, listing to one side, on a broken chair. The suited forensics did their work, moving to and fro before him with their evidence bags and cases. Anibal Parrado, the instructing judge, stood by looking down on the bristle-cut head of the Inspector Jefe. He spoke to his secretary in a low murmur. Falcón's eyelids were heavy and his vision kept closing in on him. Ramírez came through the archway from Calle Bustos Tavera carrying a black plastic bin liner.

'We found this in some rubbish bins round the corner, just off Calle Gerona,' he said, 'which probably means that the forensics aren't going to find very much up there.'

Still with latex gloves on, he pulled out a white paper suit covered in dramatic slashes of blood, which had already dried to a reddish brown.

'Match the blood to Marisa's first,' said Falcón, on automatic. 'Then send them down to the lab . . . get what we can from the inside.'

'Go home, Javier,' said Ramírez. 'Get some sleep.'

'You're right,' he said. 'I need more than sleep.'

Ramírez called up a patrol car, stuck Falcón in the back, told the driver and his partner to see the Inspector Jefe all the way up to his bed.

Falcón woke momentarily, hanging like a drunkard between the two men's shoulders halfway up the stairs in his home. Then more oblivion. The only place to be.

Nikita Sokolov had arrived at eleven o'clock, told Marisa to get down to the street, said they were going for a little walk. She felt like hell. Not used to alcohol. Her stomach was sore and belching up Cuba libre, which filled the cavities of her face with the old sticky stink. She puked in the toilet, brushed her teeth. Slumped in the lift. Through the bars of the front door she saw his cigarette glowing from where he was leaning against the back wall of the church. Small, wide, dark, horribly muscular and hairy with very pale white skin. He revolted her. They avoided the drinkers outside the bars. He steered her by the elbow to the studio. She stumbled over the cobbles in the darkness of the archway, was nauseated by the shakiness of the metal stairway up to her studio. She unlocked the door, slapped on the light. Two flashes to bring her work to life. She sat on the stool, too weak to stand. He stood in the doorway, asked his questions. His polo shirt was stretched tight over the muscles in his chest and shoulders. Dark patches under his armpits. Hair sprouted from the open collar of his shirt. Colossal quadriceps shrugged under his trousers. She'd been told Nikita Sokolov was a weightlifter before he got into slapping girls around.

She told him about the visits from the police. The questions. The stuff about the little boy. What did they tell you about the little boy? He wanted to hear what they knew. Everything. She spoke. Her arms, with nothing in them, hung by her sides. She couldn't seem to satisfy him. She couldn't seem to find enough detail to make him believe her. He told her to strip. He went out on the landing to flick a cigarette into the courtyard. Pulling off her T-shirt, dropping her skirt left her exhausted. She was still wearing the bikini briefs. She could smell herself. It wasn't nice.

The sound of footsteps coming up the stairs. He blocked the doorway again and stepped quickly aside to let two men into the room. Panic seized her throat as she saw their white suits and hoods, their masked faces, blue latex gloves. He nodded to her from the doorway – or was it to them? She had nothing in her legs now. One of the men reached for the chain saw, unhooked it, checked its teeth and the chain oil. He knew the work. Her tongue rattled in her head, mouth dry as parchment. More questions about what she had told them. Her answers no more than the clucks of a chicken beaking around in the dust. More nodding from the doorway. The one with the chain saw unravelled the flex, plugged it in, flicked off the safety, ran the motor for a second. The noise went through to her spine, left her stomach quivering. The other paper suit came for her. Turned her. Stretched her arm out on the work bench, viced her head so that she had to watch. The chain a blur coming down on her thin wrist. Had she given any names? Nothing came out of her throat. She tried to shake her head. The chain trembled above her skin. She felt the arousal of the man holding her. She lost control of her bladder. No answer would save her now. She shut her eyes, wished she'd talked to the little nun.

Shoes off. Sweat in his shirt. Falcón came awake as if he'd been defibrillated back into the world. He hurt. All the mental anguish had found its way into his muscles and skeleton. Time? Just after midday. He showered. No clarity from the cascade, just vacillation between the two colossal problems which had landed on his shoulders in the last twenty-four hours. He dressed in fresh clothes. The patrolmen had taken the mobiles out of his pockets and turned them off so that he wouldn't be disturbed. He sat on the edge of the bed and played them over each other in his hand. Action for the day of rest? There was nothing to be done about Yacoub's situation. He'd entered into a pact. Silence was the only game. Breakfast. Think about how to find Darío. Resist the intrusion of all images of Marisa's terrible end.

Sitting at a table underneath the gallery was Pablo from the CNI. He had an empty coffee cup in front of him. Falcón had never seen him out of a suit. He looked younger, more approachable, in his dark green polo shirt and white chinos, although the scar running from his hairline to his left eyebrow demanded that he always be taken seriously. Out of his work clothes, Falcón could also see that the man was athletic, and that his body hadn't been sculpted out of vanity but by repeated physical demands.

'How did you get in?' asked Falcón, as they shook hands.

'The patrolman at the door,' said Pablo. 'It took a direct order from Comisario Elvira. You're under protection now, it seems.'

'From who?'

'The Russians, I'd have thought.'

'What do you know about the Russians?'

'After you asked me to look at those unidentified guys from the mafioso's disks we had a talk with our old friends at the Organized Crime Intelligence Centre in Madrid,' said Pablo.

'Another coffee?'

Pablo shook his head.

'I don't think you came all this way to talk to me about the Russians,' said Falcón, heading for the kitchen, setting the percolator on the stove, making toast.

'The Russians have given you a problem very close to your heart,' said Pablo. 'And that has an impact on *my* problem.'

'Tell me about the Russians.'

'Vasili Lukyanov was coming to Seville to join forces with a fellow Afghan war veteran called Yuri Donstov, who's set up a successful heroin-smuggling operation between Uzbekistan and Europe. He already understood the importance of reliable supply from his army service in Afghanistan. Then he had to find a retail outlet which wouldn't offend anyone back in Moscow. He chose Seville. It's thought that he lives in an apartment block in Seville Este, but some say he's holed up in the Polígono San Pablo. Since the head of the Russian mafia in Spain fled to Dubai after Operation Wasp in 2005, Yuri Donstov has begun to believe that he can control the whole of the Iberian Peninsula. Leonid Revnik doesn't see it like that. Vasili Lukyanov was being brought into Yuri Donstov's opera- tion to run prostitution in Seville. CICO think that Donstov has also secured the services of another gangster with expertise in casinos. Yuri Donstov, it seems, is gradually developing all the talent to run a successful criminal organ- ization, using Seville as a base rather than taking on Leonid Revnik on his own territory in the Costa del Sol.'

'How old is this Yuri Donstov?' said Falcón, pouring olive oil on to his toast.

'Born 1959. His nickname is the Monk, which he has tattooed on his back beneath two angel wings and a crucifix. He wears his head completely shaved and has a strong beard, although that description is based on his gulag mug shot. There is no recent photo of him. He doesn't drink, but he smokes upwards of sixty cigarettes a day. What else? He has only one kidney. The other was damaged in a shooting incident and had to be removed.'

'"The Monk"?'

'Yuri Donstov is a very religious man.'

'Why Seville Este or the Polígono San Pablo? They're hardly upmarket.'

'He despises luxury. A lot of the money he makes ends up going back to Russia to finance various monasteries and church-building programmes.'

'Vicente Cortés from the GRECO in the Costa del Sol didn't know about him,' said Falcón. 'Why not?'

'Seville is still not his area of expertise. Cortés is more concerned about Leonid Revnik and his right-hand man, Viktor Belenki, who runs all their construction companies.'

'How long have you had this information about Yuri Donstov?'

'Me? Since yesterday,' said Pablo. 'But these are all developments since the beginning of this year. Yuri Donstov is a very quiet man. Nothing flamboyant about him.'

'Any connection between him and Lucrecio Arenas from the Banco Omni?'

'Not yet,' said Pablo. 'We've found no concrete link between Yuri Donstov and the bombing of 6th June, nor with Leonid Revnik, for that matter.'

Falcón sipped his coffee, ate his toast.

'Now all we have is a further complication,' he said.

'You don't know whether it's Yuri Donstov or Leonid Revnik who's holding Darío,' said Pablo. 'They'll tell you soon enough.'

'They said they wouldn't. They said I'd never hear from them again,' said Falcón. 'And I don't like the lessons they've given me so far. Yesterday I had a potential witness to a murder conspiracy and a woman who loved me. Now I have a dead witness, a kidnapped boy and a woman who never wants to see me again.'

'The Russians will call,' said Pablo. 'They have to.'

'Did you have any luck identifying those men from Vasili Lukyanov's disks?' asked Falcón.

'As a matter of fact, we did,' said Pablo. 'They're businessmen. The one having sex with Marisa's sister is Juan Valverde. He's a Madrileño and the Chief Executive Officer of I4IT Europe. The one you spotted as an American is a consultant to I4IT, personally appointed by Cortland Fallenbach. His name is Charles Taggart. Two years ago he had to resign from his post as head of the fifth largest television church in America when some footage of him with three prostitutes appeared on the internet.'

'The fallen preacher,' said Falcón. 'An ideal recruit for the born-again Christian founders of I4IT.'

'The third man is Antonio Ramos. He is on the board of directors of the Horizonte Group. He is a civil engineer who was the late César Benito's right-hand man. Benito was the creative guy with the designs and presentation skills. Ramos got them built. He now heads up the whole construction arm of Horizonte.'

'Was he in it from the beginning?' asked Falcón. 'Didn't you go through Horizonte's offices and give them a clean bill of health?'

'*We* didn't, but the Barcelona police did, and they found nothing,' said Pablo. 'If Horizonte were in on the bombing conspiracy they kept it out of their offices.'

Falcón poured more coffee. Just as he seemed to be getting somewhere, the new information presented more complications.

'I know it doesn't help you make a clear-cut case,' said Pablo, 'but at least you've got it more or less confirmed by the footage on Vasili Lukyanov's disks that the Russians were somehow connected to the Banco Omni, Horizonte, I4IT conspiracy and provided the violence for the Seville bombing. Concentrate on that . . .'

'But which Russians?' said Falcón.

'The disks were found on Vasili Lukyanov, who stole them from Leonid Revnik.'

'But when was the footage of the men with the girls taken? Is there a date on it?'

'I don't know,' said Pablo. 'You've got the original disks in the Jefatura.'

'Was it before or after the Seville bombing?' asked Falcón. 'That could be significant. Were Yuri Donstov and Leonid Revnik ever together as part of the same group before Donstov broke away at, say, the time of Operation Wasp in 2005?'

'That's not how it was explained to me.'

'You have no recent photographs of Yuri Donstov, which probably means you don't know exactly what he's been doing,' said Falcón. 'Is it significant that Donstov was set up in Seville, where the bombing occurred? Who were Lucrecio Arenas and César Benito in bed with: Yuri Donstov or Leonid Revnik?'

'All right. You've made your point,' said Pablo. 'You'll have to leave it to the kidnappers. They will make their demands.'

'There's a further complication because of the defections from Revnik's group to Donstov's,' said Falcón. 'There are probably going to be members of each group who were responsible in some way for elements of the Seville bombing and wanted to keep Marisa quiet.'

'Leonid Revnik must be holding her sister. Margarita was having sex with the I4IT Europe boss, Juan Valverde, on Vasili Lukyanov's disk.'

'Right, so there would have been contact between Marisa and Leonid Revnik. But what about any defections to Yuri Donstov's group before Vasili Lukyanov?' said Falcón. 'We have no idea whether Lukyanov was the first. Given Marisa's terror and unwillingness to talk, it wouldn't surprise me if she had been taking heat from both sides.'

'Find Margarita?' said Pablo, shrugging.

Falcón checked him, detected a flagging interest in his problems.

'All right, you've helped me, Pablo,' said Falcón. 'You've given me enough to go on. So what do you really want to see me about?'

'The notes of your meeting with MI5 and SO15 were sent to me yesterday,' said Pablo. 'I'd already heard about the kidnapping, so I held off until today.'

'Very thoughtful of you,' said Falcón.

'I realize that you're pledging your support to Yacoub,

173

which is what I asked you to do. It's just that you're doing it blindly,' said Pablo. 'All you know is what he's told you: that the GICM have recruited his son.'

'Why would he lie about that?'

'You also know that Yacoub would never do anything that might result in a family member being harmed or arrested,' said Pablo. 'This may mean he'll want to put you off the scent. What *we* can do is prevent that, through corroboration of information and a broader view of the intelligence picture. But *you* have to get us started. You have to tell us what you know about Yacoub's actions or intentions.'

'But that would endanger Yacoub.'

'Just out of interest,' said Pablo, 'what did Yacoub tell you about the one piece of information he was prepared to give away: the identity of Mustafa Barakat?'

'No more than I told the British,' said Falcón. 'He's a family friend. He has a carpet business and tourist shops in Fès.'

'And this is what Yacoub told you to say?'

'It's the information he gave me.'

'You said he'd lived in Fès all his life.'

'A lot has happened, Pablo. I don't remember everything perfectly.'

'You probably don't know this, but before I came back to the CNI in Madrid I ran agents in the Maghreb for more than ten years. I'm part of an enormous North African intelligence community,' said Pablo. 'If you give me a name like Mustafa Barakat I have access to all my friends' archives as well as my own. I put that name straight across to my Moroccan colleagues, who don't just look at their files but, because they understand the complex nature of families in their country, they get down on the ground as well. They feed their informers into the termites' nest of the medina. That's a lot of manpower I can draw on.'

'And what did they find?'

'That there are very close ties between the Barakat and Diouri families. Since 1940 there have been thirty-six marriages between the families, which have produced one hundred and seventeen children. Sixty-four with the name Diouri and fifty-two with the name Barakat. Eight of those Barakats are called Mustafa. Two of them are interesting because they were both born in the late 1950s. The other six are either too old or too young to be the Barakat staying at Yacoub's house.

'Of those two remaining Mustafas, one went into the family carpet business during the seventies and never left Morocco, but the other had a much more interesting life. In 1979 he went to a madrassa, a religious school, in Jeddah for three years. From there he went to Pakistan, where nothing more was heard about him until he resurfaced in Morocco in 1991. The word on the street is that he spent quite a few of those years in Afghanistan. Now this is where there's a bit of confusion, because in 1992 Mustafa Barakat died in a car accident on a steep road up in the Rif mountains on his way back from Chefchaouen, where the family had opened a small hotel and tourist shop. It was sad because he'd only just settled back in his own country and . . .'

'Which Mustafa Barakat are we talking about?' asked Falcón.

'That's where it gets confusing. The interesting thing is, after the accident on the road from Chefchaouen, the other Mustafa Barakat still ran the family carpet business, tourist shops and hotels but, having never left the country before, he suddenly started an import/export business. He would fly to Pakistan to buy carpets. Since the Afghan war, all carpets in that area of Afghanistan, Tajikistan, Uzbekistan, even the eastern part of Iran, come to Pakistan and are exported as Pakistani carpets. These carpets, which he brought back from Pakistan, were then re-exported to countries like France, Germany, Holland and the UK.'

175

'You think there was a switch?'

'There are no post mortems performed out there in the Rif.'

'Presumably the Mustafa Barakat who'd gone to the madrassa in Jeddah had also made the pilgrimage to Mecca and was al-Hadji.'

'Mustafa Barakat, who'd only just started travelling in 1993, did the Haj that same year,' said Pablo. 'Detail is something we're good at in the intelligence service. So before you ask: no dental records.'

'Anything else that might help us identify which Mustafa Barakat we're dealing with?'

'It would be nice if the mujahideen kept army records and let us have a look at them. It would be better to have some DNA.'

A wave of paranoia swept through Falcón. He stared into Pablo's face, like a poker player looking for tells. Is this true? Is this just a construct to get me back on side? Why would Yacoub have given such a thing away, exposing a family member to such scrutiny?

'Don't cut yourself off from that level of intelligence,' said Pablo, 'without at least giving it a second thought.'

In the end Consuelo had taken the sleeping pills left by the doctor. She'd watched the clock work its way round to 6 a.m. with her mind unable to hold steady on any logical path. She was caught in triangular thinking, flitting between Darío, herself and Javier, but unable to concentrate on any one of them.

Even with her sister and her two other sons in the house she felt a terrible loneliness. In between the bouts of rage that periodically washed over her she reluctantly identified a need for the one person she'd banished from her sight for ever. Almost as soon as this came to her she was consumed by hatred for him. Then despair would crash in and she would sob at the thought of her little boy lost in the dark, terrified and alone. It was exhausting, emotionally draining, but the mind would not shut down and let her drift into sleep. So she took the pills. Three instead of two. She woke up at two in the afternoon with her head and mouth full of cotton wool, feeling as if she'd been embalmed.

The sleep had weakened her and she couldn't stand in the shower. She sat and let the water fall on her pitiful shoulders. She sobbed and raged all over again.

She drank water and her strength slowly returned. She dressed, went downstairs. Everybody looked at her. She read their faces. Victims were always the stars of their own dramas and the supporting cast had nothing to offer.

This was Sunday. Sitting with her arms folded, waiting for the phone to ring.

14

His name was Roque Barba but he was known to everybody in the run-down, dead-end *barrio* of Las Tres Mil Viviendas as El Pulmón, because he only had one lung. He'd lost the other one two months after his seventeenth birthday at a *corrida* in a small village in the east of Andalucía when he was still a *novillero*. He'd liked the look of his second bull of the afternoon and told the *picador* not to dig too deep with the lance because he wanted to show the crowd what he could do. It was right at the beginning of the *faena* and the bull still had his head up. El Pulmón had two problems: he wasn't quite tall enough and the bull had a little hook from right to left, which he hadn't seen. This meant that during the first pass the bull's horn, instead of flashing past his chest, caught him under the armpit, and the next thing he knew he was up in the air. There was no pain. No sound. Life slowed down. The crowd and the arena came to him in sickly waves as the bull's immensely powerful neck reared up and then shook him from side to side. Then he hit the deck, felt the sand grind into his face and heard his collar bone crack in his ear.

The bull's horn broke two ribs and cracked another two. It tore the lung apart and drove splinters of bone close to the heart. The surgeons removed the ragged lung that night. That was the end of his career as a *torero*. Not because he only had one lung; the other expanded to compensate. But he could no longer raise his left arm above shoulder height.

Now he sat on the fourth floor of one of the many brutalized tower blocks in Las Tres Mil Viviendas. There was a gun on the table, which he had just finished cleaning. He'd bought it last week. Until then he'd only ever used a blade. He still had the knife, which he carried in a spring-loaded mechanism attached to the underside of an ornately tooled leather wrist strap on his right forearm.

He'd bought the gun for two reasons. The high-quality product he'd started selling a few months ago had brought him a lot more clients, which meant that he was now handling more money on a regular basis. Only he knew about this – and, of course, his girlfriend Julia, who was asleep in the bedroom. But El Pulmón knew that people loved to talk, and in Las Tres Mil they loved to talk about the one commodity that was in short supply – money. Hence the gun. Although that wasn't the full story.

The gun wasn't needed to control any of his clients. They knew he had balls. Anybody who was prepared to get into a confined space with a half-ton bull was not lacking in that department. And he still had the reflexes. No, the gun had become necessary because, although he was now receiving high-quality product from the Russians, he hadn't stopped selling the gear that he was getting from the Italians. In fact, he'd started cutting the one with the other. So, not only was there the potential for trouble from outsiders interested in money, but there was also an element of unpredictability in his suppliers.

Now, when he handed over his €10,000 for the week, he

was never quite sure whether he was going to be given another package to sell or find himself hanging out of the window upside down, with a four-floor drop beneath him. It had already happened once. The weightlifter, the one called Nikita, had dropped by to remind him that his supply was exclusive and if he didn't like the arrangement they'd install their own dealer. Four floors to a concrete pavement had been Nikita's way of trying to make him see reason. He hadn't enjoyed the adrenaline rush.

Fucking Russians. This had never been a friendly business. Dealing in death was never going to be that. But the Italians spoke his language, and he didn't know how long the Russian product was going to last. So he was going to play this tricky game until things got a little clearer, and that's why he was tooled up.

His girlfriend sighed in her sleep. He shut the bedroom door and looked around the living room. He moved the table to a more central position between the window and the wall, on which hung an oblong mirror. With a screwdriver he put a five-centimetre screw in the centre of the table. He eased the safety off the gun and positioned it so that the trigger rested against the screw and the barrel pointed to the right of the mirror. He inserted another couple of screws to maintain the line of the barrel. He placed a copy of 6 *Toros* magazine over the handgun. He put a chair by the table which, when he sat on it, would leave his good right arm free and his poor left arm close to the gun. He sat and checked the view he got from the mirror. It gave him angles on the two corners of the room behind him. He dropped the blinds on the window, shut out the sunlight and the view of the busy Carretera de Su Eminencia. He didn't bother with any other chairs. The supplier, with his Cuban translator, never sat down. They did smoke, even though they knew he didn't like it. He was the drug dealer with one lung who didn't smoke, didn't drink and didn't do drugs. El Pulmón breathed in slowly, the way he'd always done to control his fear.

Ramírez was standing at the window in Falcón's office, looking out. Ferrera was at her computer.

'I've had the three mystery men in the Russian's disks identified,' said Falcón. 'The guy with Margarita is Juan Valverde, the boss of I4IT Europe in Madrid. The American is Charles Taggart, an ex-TV preacher, who's an I4IT consultant, reporting back to the owner, Cortland Fallenbach. The last guy is Antonio Ramos, who is an engineer and the new director of Horizonte's construction division. I want you to find out where those three men are, because I want to talk to them as soon as possible.'

Cristina Ferrera nodded. Falcón went through to join Ramírez in his office, gave him the intelligence he'd learned from Pablo about the renegade Russian gang set up by Yuri Donstov in Seville. Ramírez said he'd put detectives Serrano and Baena on a door-to-door, starting in Calle Garlopa in Seville Este, which was the address they'd found in the GPS of Vasili Lukyanov's Range Rover. They moved on to other matters.

'The blood on both those paper suits we found in the rubbish bins on Calle Feria has been confirmed as a perfect match to Marisa Moreno,' said Ramírez.

'Anything on the inside of them?' asked Falcón.

'Both the hoods contained hairs, and we've picked up some sweat patches from the suits,' said Ramírez. 'One of them even had a semen deposit.'

'Sweat patches? Semen? Was he naked underneath this suit?'

'Not if he stripped it off, walked round the corner to Calle Gerona and stuck it in the bin,' said Ramírez. 'But it *was* a hot night, maybe they had a car.'

'Gangsters driving around in their underpants?' said Falcón, making for the door.

'Where are you going?' asked Ramírez. 'You've only just got here.'

'To talk to Esteban Calderón.'

'The judge on the Marisa Moreno case is going to want to see us at some stage,' said Ramírez. 'It's the new guy: Anibal Parrado. He's all right. How's Consuelo holding up?'

'She's *not* all right,' said Falcón. '*We're* not all right.'

'So you told her about Marisa and the threatening phone calls.'

'And she remembered those Russians breaking into her house four years ago, putting a red cross over a family photograph.'

'I'm sorry,' said Ramírez. 'I wasn't thinking when I told you about the semen deposit. That's not a nice thing to know . . . I mean, given Darío's situation.'

'I *have* to know,' said Falcón. 'Give me a call when you get the full forensics. Let's get the DNA on the semen deposit to Vicente Cortés and Martín Díaz. They can see if it matches DNA on the GRECO and CICO databases from any Russians they've had in custody. And get everybody in the squad to remember that this is *all connected*: the Seville bombing, the murder of Inés, the cutting up of Marisa and the kidnapping of Darío.'

'The only problem,' said Ramírez, fingers exploding up into the air, 'is evidence.'

Today was delivery day, but he wasn't sure when the Russian was going to turn up. All he knew was that he had four hundred grams of Italian left, which wasn't going to satisfy those of his clients who were already coming out of their dens all twitchy and gabbling, with the first sweats and that clawing and gnawing in the blood. They'd be looking for his boys on the streets, the sign that the Russian product had arrived and that all would soon be well.

El Pulmón checked on Julia. Still asleep. Should he wake

her? Get her up and out before the guys came? He shrugged; it seemed a shame. Softly, he closed the door. She could sleep all day, that one. He had to keep an eye on her, though, make sure she wasn't sampling the product. He sat down. Breathed slowly, got the fear crouched down low in his stomach. He was always scared these days, what with the money getting bigger and these Russians being so unreadable.

Maybe he *should* wake Julia. Keep calm, just the nerves talking. Keep the fear. He knew he needed the fear, but it had to be where he wanted it. Low in the stomach, not all up his throat and over his head. He'd seen that with *novilleros* facing their first full-size bull. The fear that paralysed and got you killed.

The knock came at 12.45 p.m. First man in was the Cuban translator. Behind him was the weightlifter – head shaved with just a dusting of black showing through the white skin, nose slightly flattened, one cheekbone with a red scar. He was smaller than El Pulmón, but twice his width. His arms were very hairy and were covered in indiscernible tattoos. His legs moved as if he had animals up his trousers. El Pulmón led them into the room, felt their eyes searching his back, took his seat by the table. The Cuban stood to the left of the mirror. The weightlifter kept his back to the wall, moved to the right of the mirror and had a good, long look around with his dark, deep-set eyes. El Pulmón didn't like it. He knew now that the Russian was carrying a gun in the small of his back. He wished he'd woken Julia. He had the roll of money in his shirt, but he didn't take it out. He could feel some questions backed up against the wall over there.

'He wants to know if you're still buying from the Italians?' asked the Cuban.

'No, I told you I'd stopped.'

'Take a look,' said the Cuban, giving him a twist of silver foil.

El Pulmón opened it up, saw the white powder, knew that he was in trouble. He shrugged.

'Where did you get this?' he asked.

'We bought it from one of your clients,' said the Cuban. 'Paid eighty euros for it.'

'I don't know what the problem is.'

'It's our product cut with the Italian shit you told us you'd stopped moving.'

'I still have some Italian product left. I didn't want to just throw it away.'

'You buy from the Italians,' said the weightlifter, his first words in rough, accented Spanish.

'I didn't know you spoke Spanish,' said El Pulmón, taking the opportunity for a bit of distraction.

'He knows you're still buying from them,' said the Cuban.

'How does he know that?'

'One of your clients told us.'

'Which one?' asked El Pulmón. 'They're all junkies out there. They'll do and say anything for a fix.'

'The flamenco singer.'

'Carlos Puerta is hardly reliable,' said El Pulmón. 'He's been looking to fuck me up since his girlfriend moved in with me.'

'That's why we kept an eye on your place, to see the Italians for ourselves,' said the Cuban, who'd moved to the window and was peering through the blinds.

El Pulmón looked at the Russian and kept an eye on the Cuban through the mirror.

'We tell you the last time,' said the weightlifter.

The Cuban came away from the window. He had a large hunting knife in his hand. He went to grab El Pulmón by the hair. El Pulmón leaned forward and slapped the copy of *6 Toros*. The roar of the gunshot filled the room and El Pulmón's blade sprang into his hand. He kept low and swung round, driving the narrow length of steel into the Cuban's

184

left side. He heard nothing with the gunshot ringing in his ears, but he felt the Cuban's body stiffen. As he drove the blade in, he grabbed the Cuban's right wrist with the hunting knife in it and whirled the man round so that he ended up between El Pulmón and the weightlifter, who was now on the floor, lying on his back, arm extended, gun in hand. Another head-ringing bang inside the four hard walls of the apartment and the Cuban's rigid body leapt and jerked. El Pulmón forced him backwards on to another spine-rupturing explosion. He dropped his shoulder and shoved the Cuban at the Russian, who grunted under the weight and El Pulmón, still with his blade, was out of the door, down the stairs and on the other side of the garages before he remembered Julia, asleep in the bedroom.

There was a taxi waiting in the prison car park, engine running, air-con roaring, cabbie asleep, head thrown back, mouth open. As Falcón went up the path to the prison reception he took a call on his mobile from his old detective friend in Madrid, calling him about the apartment in La Latina where he'd met Yacoub.

'It's not privately owned,' he said. 'The whole block belongs to the Middle East European Investment Corporation, based in Dubai.'

'Was that apartment rented out to anyone?'

'It's one of three in the block that's empty.'

Falcón hung up, found Alicia with her serene white face, red lipstick under a jet-black bob, waiting patiently in the reception area. He greeted her. They kissed. She squeezed his shoulder, happy to hear his voice. He told her about her taxi.

'I've been sitting here for twenty minutes,' she said, annoyed. 'What's the matter with these people?'

'He's a taxi driver from Seville,' said Falcón. 'It's their nature.'

'How are you?' she asked.

'Complicated,' he said.

'That seems to be the default setting for people our age,' she said.

Falcón told her that Consuelo's youngest son had been abducted and the effect on their relationship. Alicia was shocked, said she'd call her straight away.

'She must be going crazy.'

'Don't speak to her on my behalf,' said Falcón.

'Of course not.'

He walked her to her cab, the heat cracked down on their heads. He opened the cab door for her, showed the cabbie his police card, pointed at his meter with a long hard stare. The cabbie zeroed it, pulled away.

When the guards first brought Calderón into the room made available to them by the prison governor, he looked so shattered Falcón thought he might send him straight back to his cell. The guards got him seated and left the room. Calderón ransacked his pockets for cigarettes, lit up, sucked in a huge drag, swayed in his chair.

'What brings you here, Javier?' he asked.

'Are you all right, Esteban? You look . . .'

'Bedraggled? Crazy? Fucked up?' said Calderón. 'Take your pick. I'm all of them. You know, I hadn't really understood it before, but there's nowhere to hide in psycho . . . you wouldn't call it therapy, exactly, would you? It's more like . . . extraction. Psycho-extraction. Yanking rotten memories from the brain.'

'I just saw Alicia in the car park.'

'She doesn't give much away, that one,' said Calderón. 'I reckon psychoanalysis is no different to poker, except that nobody knows what cards they have. Did she say anything interesting?'

'Nothing about you. She's very discreet. She didn't even

tell me why she was here,' said Falcón. 'Maybe you shouldn't look at it as extraction, Esteban. You can't extract memories, nor can you hide from them without consequences. You just illuminate them.'

'Thanks for that, Javier,' said Calderón, dismissively. 'I'll see if that makes it any less painful. Doctora Aguado asked me what I wanted from our sessions. I said I wanted to know if I'd killed Inés. It's interesting. She's no different to a lawyer making a case. She starts with a premise – Esteban Calderón hates women. Me – can you believe it? Then she starts wheedling the usual shit out of me about how I despise my stupid mother and how I fucked up a girlfriend who didn't like my poems.'

'Your poems?'

'I wanted to be a writer, Javier,' he said, holding up his hand. 'It's all a long time ago and I'm not going into it. What are you doing here?'

'We're getting somewhere on Inés's murder,' said Falcón. 'But we've also hit a brick wall.'

'Come on, Javier. Don't talk shit to me.'

'I've been working on Marisa.'

'That sounds like the wet-towel treatment.'

'It probably was something like that for her and she's been getting it from all sides,' said Falcón, and went on to tell him about finding the footage of Margarita, the threatening phone calls and the kidnapping of Darío.

'You keep your inner turmoil better hidden than I do, Javier.'

'Practice,' said Falcón. 'Anyway, I sent Cristina Ferrera to talk to Marisa, and while intoxicated she pretty well admitted that she'd been coerced to start a relationship with you.'

'By whom?'

'The people holding her sister. A Russian mafia group.'

Calderón smoked intensely, staring at the floor.

'What I need to know from you, Esteban, is how you met Marisa,' said Falcón. 'Who effected that introduction?'

187

Silence for a moment while Calderón leaned back in his chair, eyes narrowed.

'She's dead, isn't she?' he said. 'You've come to me because she can't tell you any more.'

'She was murdered last night,' said Falcón. 'I'm sorry, Esteban.'

Calderón leaned across the table, looking up into Falcón's head.

'What are you sorry about, Javier?' he asked, tapping his own chest. 'Are you sorry for me, because you think I loved her and she was just fucking me under orders?'

'I'm sorry because she was a woman in an impossible position, under immense strain, whose only thought was for the safety of her own sister,' said Falcón. 'That's why she didn't talk to us. A singular, but very compelling reason.'

That did something to Calderón's equilibrium. He even wobbled in his chair and had to anchor himself with his hands flat on the table. Emotion rose in his chest. And maybe it was because this conversation had come hard on the heels of his session with Alicia Aguado that he managed to see beyond his own self-interest and realize that sitting before him was a man with a completely different moral centre to his own.

'You've forgiven her, haven't you, Javier?' he said. 'You now know that Marisa was in some way involved in Inés's murder, and yet . . .'

'It would be very helpful if you could remember who introduced you to Marisa,' said Falcón.

'Does this mean,' said Calderón, blinking back the tears, 'that I *didn't* do it?'

'It means that Cristina Ferrera *thought* that Marisa, who was drunk at the time, had been coerced into consorting with you,' said Falcón. 'Marisa never admitted that it was the Russians who'd forced her. We have no signed statement and no recording of the conversation. There's no new evidence. We have, however, lost Marisa. Her words will never be heard. We have to go back to an earlier level of involvement, which means finding out how she met you. Were you introduced?'

Falcón could see quite clearly that Calderón did remember. He was staring at a point above Falcón's head and running his thumbnail up and down between his front teeth, weighing something up; and whatever it was it had weight.

'It was at a garden party at the Duchess of Alba's house,' said Calderón. 'Marisa was introduced to me by my cousin.'

'Your cousin?'

'That is the son of the Juez Decano de Sevilla,' said Calderón. 'Alejandro Spinola. He works in the mayor's office.'

15

On the way back from the prison, Falcón got the call.

'Two officers from the Narcotics squad in Las Tres Mil just called in a double murder in the apartment of a drug dealer called Roque Barba, also known as El Pulmón,' said the operator. 'A Cuban male called Miguel Estévez found in the living room, shot twice in the back and stabbed in the side, and a Spanish female, Julia Valdés, believed to be El Pulmón's girlfriend, found in the bedroom shot in the face.'

Falcón came off the motorway and on to the ring road. He took the exit before the golf club and joined the Carretera de Su Eminencia, a road he'd always thought ridiculously named, given that it enclosed one of the grimmest public housing projects in Seville.

In the 1960s and 70s the municipality had lured gypsies from the centre of town out to this development of residential blocks on the edge of civilization. Years of poverty, lack of community and self-respect had transformed a half-hearted attempt at social engineering into a neighbourhood of drugs, murder, theft and vandalism. This did not mean that the *barrio* was without soul. Some of the greatest flamenco voices came from here, and quite a few of them had done time in the prison he'd just come from. It was more that the soul was not evident from the bare, treeless landscape, the grimy concrete blocks, the cheap clothes hanging out to dry on metal bars over the windows and landings, the rubbish collecting in the basements and stair-wells, the graffiti and the air of complete desolation that told anyone who was in any doubt that these were forgotten people in a place that had fallen off the back of the town hall's mind.

The operator in the Jefatura hadn't bothered with an address. It was just a question of cruising around, looking for the crowd of people, the collection of police cars and the green day-glo ambulances, which he soon found at the foot of an eight-storey block. The patrolmen were nervous. Some of the people gathered around the metal security cage at the entrance of the block looked more desperate than the usual citizens of Las Tres Mil. Some of them were crouched low on the grassless earth, arms wrapped round their shins, holding on to themselves and shaking. The name of El Pulmón reached his ears. These were his clients, and they'd just lost their supply.

A patrolman told him to watch his step going up. There were blood drips circled in yellow on a number of steps going up to the fourth floor. The stink of rubbish followed him. No lift. The apartment was full of the usual crime-scene personnel. The bodies were still in position. Falcón shook hands with the médico forense and the instructing judge, Anibal Parrado. Sub-Inspector Emilio Pérez, with his dark good looks of a thirties matinée idol and total devo-tion to detail, was running the investigation. They talked Falcón through the scene.

'We're not sure of the sequence of events, but we're assuming that the gun found on the floor by the window was secured to the table by those screws. It has been fired only once and the blood spatter on the wall beneath the mirror would suggest that we're looking for a wounded man. There is no other firearm in the apartment. A hunting knife was found close to the Cuban's body, which had not been used. From the entry wounds, the ballistics guys think that the same gun that killed Miguel Estévez also killed Julia Valdés in the adjacent room. Obviously, given that two shots killed the victims, they were not killed by the gun found on the floor, which they think is of a different calibre anyway. They will confirm that when they get the bullets out of the two victims. An initial inspection of the gunshot wounds to Miguel Estévez suggests that he was shot by someone lying on the floor. The body seems to have fallen on to the shooter, which would suggest that someone was using him as a shield and pushed him back on to the killer. Judging by the blood drips on the threshold of the bedroom, it is believed that the girl was shot from there by the wounded man.'

Over the médico forense's shoulder Falcón could see the girl's ruined face. Her upper body was slumped against the wall, which was covered with blood and cerebral matter. Her neck was crooked over the low bed-head, while her left hand was flung out towards the window. Her other hand had come to rest between her splayed legs but, with the palm upwards, it indicated the awkwardness of sudden death rather than the demureness of a final modesty. She was naked, but with her right leg caught up in the twisted sheet. The cameo spoke of fear, panic, paralysis and, finally, violent death.

'The blood drips leave the apartment and go down the stairs to the pavement, where they disappear. We assume the shooter got into a car.'

'And the stab wound to Estévez?'

'The Narcs say that El Pulmón favoured a blade,' said Pérez. 'And it looks as if he's taken it with him.'

Falcón inspected the gun on the floor, the screws in the

table, the bullfight magazine on the floor in front of the mirror.

'There are clear prints on the gun,' said Jorge, appearing from under the table with his custom-made inspection glasses on.

'We've got El Pulmón's prints on file from previous drug arrests,' said Pérez.

'We have to assume that this gun did not belong to the Cuban, Miguel Estévez. Two men with guns are no match for a single man with a blade. Which means,' said Falcón, 'that this was the gun secured to the table and that El Pulmón was expecting trouble.'

'He must have bought that gun recently,' said one of the Narcs. 'He was always a knife man before. You know he was an ex-bullfighter?'

'Have you seen this guy before?' Falcón asked the Narc, pointing at Estévez.

'No, but things have been changing around here. The product is different to what it was last year. We still haven't been able to work out where the packages are coming from.'

'Have you come across any Russians?'

He shook his head.

'Were you the one who found the bodies?' asked Falcón.

'Me and my partner,' said the Narc.

'Any idea what time this happened?'

'The guy upstairs said he heard the first gunshot at about one o'clock,' said the Narc.

'Did he call in the shooting?'

'Nobody calls in a shooting in Las Tres Mil,' said the Narc.

'What were you doing here?' asked Falcón. 'Did somebody send you?'

'At a quarter past one we got a call from Inspector Jefe Tirado asking us to find a junkie called Carlos Puerta, who he wanted to question. If we found him, we were to call Tirado and he'd come down here.'

'Did you find him?'

'He's downstairs with my partner, waiting for the Inspector Jefe.'

'Tell me when Tirado gets here.'

Two of Falcón's young detectives, Serrano and Baena, appeared, ready to do some door-to-door.

'I want you and your partner to work with my two detectives here,' said Falcón to the Narcotics agent. 'I want some ideas about where we're going to find El Pulmón . . . before somebody else gets to him.'

Consuelo paced the long glass doors of her living room. The air-con was too chill to sit for long. A patrolman was slumped in the shade of the umbrella on the other side of the pool. She thought he might be sleeping under his mirrored sunglasses. His arm hung limply down by the side of his chair.

A sound technician who'd come in to set up some professional recording equipment, rather than the temporary stuff Inspector Jefe Tirado had left on Saturday evening, was sitting in the kitchen. He was talking to the family liaison officer. There was another patrolman at the front door. She'd told him to come in from the heat. He stared morosely out of the glass panel of the front door. She'd phoned her restaurant manager, told him to contact the estate agents she was currently dealing with to ask them not to call until further notice. She'd taken only one call, from Alicia Aguado. She'd yanked the wire out of her mobile, which was connected to the recording equipment, and taken the call upstairs in her bedroom.

Alicia wouldn't say it, but Consuelo knew that the only reason she could be calling was that she'd heard from Javier. The press and TV still had not been informed, and the radio stations, who'd been involved in the initial stages, had been asked to keep quiet for the moment. Inspector Jefe Tirado didn't want a media circus, or to have to deal with hoaxers, until there'd been contact from the kidnappers, or it became clear that there would be none.

Aguado's call had helped. Consuelo had started by venting her bile against Javier, and Aguado had heard her out to the bitter end before asking her what had actually happened. It was good for Consuelo to talk to someone who listened. It had calmed her down. She began to get some perspective on her anger. Blame and guilt were natural. Rage was inevitable. The call did not cure her of her animosity towards Falcón, or prevent her from replaying that moment when she'd lost sight of Darío over and over in her mind, but it had allowed some resolve to harden inside her. She felt stronger, less jittery. Her mood swings from despair to fury were not so violent. The tears still came, but with some warning.

After the call Consuelo had sent her other two sons away with her sister. She didn't want the boys caught up in such an oppressive and potentially volatile atmosphere, with everybody staring at the phone, willing it to ring. She didn't want them to see her hope and despair, the possible joy and the probable disappointment. Despite Alicia's call, she knew her emotions would be uncontrollable because she still felt exposed.

Upstairs she had a small study next to her bedroom – a chair, a desk, a laptop, nothing more. Alicia Aguado had encouraged her to pass the time writing her thoughts and feelings down, to get them out of herself where they could be seen. She closed the blinds and sat there in the dim light, tried to purge her brain of all the unimportant white noise. She booted up the computer and was automatically linked to the internet. She saw she had new mail. This address was different to the one in the restaurant and it was one only used by her family and close friends. There was one new message sent today at 14.00 entitled 'Darío'. Just seeing the name made her heart lift and her stomach cold. The sender was someone called Manolo Gordo. She knew no one of that name. Her hand trembled as she opened it.

If you want to see your son again call 655147982. Do not tell the police. Do not try to record the call. Use your mobile outside the house. Delete this email – it will not help you find your son.

She read it over and over. Not many people knew this email address, but her sons did. It gave her hope. An excitement gripped her. Contact had been made. She looked over her shoulder as if she should be hiding this from someone. She put the email in her 'spam' folder, closed down the computer and thought about how she was going to make this call.

'Inspector Jefe Tirado is waiting for you outside,' said Baena.

Falcón trotted down the stairs, being careful to avoid the yellow-circled blood drips. There was no shade outside and they had to stand in the stink of piss and rubbish in the stairwell.

'Who's this guy Carlos Puerta?' asked Falcón.

'He's the one who assaulted Señora Jiménez near the Plaza del Pumarejo back in June and was seen later snooping around her house by Señora Jiménez's sister,' said Tirado. 'I spent the morning tracking him down. His friends in the Plaza del Pumarejo told me he was a junkie, so I asked the Narcs to help me out.'

'Do you mind if I listen in?'

'No problem,' said Tirado, who beckoned to the Narc. 'He doesn't look much now, does he? But he's got a good voice. As soon as I saw him I recognized him. Five years ago he cut an album, made some money, got fucked up, failed an audition with Eva Hierbabuena to go to London. And this is the state he's in now.'

The officer pushed Carlos Puerta towards the apartment block. He shuffled forward with little, jittery steps like a comic actor. His shoulder-length hair had seen neither water nor brush for a good six weeks. It was book-thick, matted and coated in dust from the wrecked building where he'd been found. He had a problem with his left arm, which looked wasted, the hand swollen. His T-shirt had white stencilling, which had faded into the oblivion of the background material. Falcón could just make out that it was from the Flamenco Biennale of 2004.

'He was with a woman,' said Tirado. 'She was so emaciated the Narcs called an ambulance for her.'

Tirado introduced himself and Falcón. Puerta's lean, pockmarked face was a mass of tics. He begged for a cigarette. They found him one, sat him down on a couple of breezeblocks.

'You recognize this woman?' asked Tirado, holding a shot of Consuelo in front of his face.

Puerta peered from under black eyebrows angled sharply into his nose. An eyelid fluttered at the smoke trickling up his face. He shook his head.

'You know her name, Carlos.'

'I don't think so,' said Puerta, who touched his chest and wheezed a laugh. 'Not my type.'

'You also know where she lives.'

'All the people I know live in Las Tres Mil, and she doesn't look like any of them,' said Puerta. 'Not with those earrings, that necklace, that hair and make-up. If she appeared like that in my world, she'd get picked clean.'

'You met her in the Plaza del Pumarejo,' said Tirado. 'She runs a restaurant near there. You know it.'

'I don't eat in restaurants.'

'You also know about her husband, Raúl Jiménez. He was murdered.'

'I know a few people who've been killed. Some more

who've overdosed, but I can't remember their names. Did he run a record label?'

'We've got witnesses who said you assaulted Consuelo Jiménez one night last June in a street just off the Plaza del Pumarejo.'

'What sort of witnesses?' asked Puerta, dredging up some derision. 'If you're talking about those cretins in the Plaza, they'd tell you anything for a litre of Don Simón.'

'We've got another witness. Not a cretin. This woman's sister, who saw you snooping around Consuelo Jiménez's house in Santa Clara the day after you assaulted her,' said Tirado. 'If you can tell me what that was all about I won't take you down to the Jefatura and stick you in a cell until your last fix wears off.'

'I'm not sure what you mean,' he said, listening intently.

'Señora Jiménez doesn't want to press charges for the assault or for trespassing,' said Tirado. 'But if you've had anything to do with the abduction of her eight-year-old son . . .'

That got his full attention. His head started shaking, not in denial, but with some sort of heroin-induced tremor.

'I'm a junkie,' he said. 'So I recognize vulnerable people and I try to get money out of them. I knew that woman and her story. She's famous, been all over the news. I'd seen her around. I thought there was something unstable about her. Then she turned up in the Plaza del Pumarejo one night a bit dazed, possibly drunk, and I bummed some money off her.'

'What were you doing around her house the day after?'

'Looking for her again, see if I could get something more out of her,' said Puerta. 'That's what junkies are like. And I can tell you that I haven't seen her since.'

'Why didn't you keep after her?' asked Tirado.

'It's a long way out to Santa Clara and I found some money closer to home.'

Tirado and Falcón moved away from him to confer.

'I think he's telling the truth,' said Tirado. 'It fits with what I've heard from Señora Jiménez and her sister . . . more or less. She told me she was depressed at the time, and her sister said she started therapy soon after. And neither of them have seen him since. I'll get one of my guys to show his photo around Señora Jiménez's neighbours, just to make sure.'

'Do you mind if I talk to him now?' said Falcón. 'See what he knows about this killing upstairs?'

Tirado clapped him on the shoulder, went back to his car. Falcón found another cigarette and went back to Puerta, who smiled to reveal teeth with a brown scum line.

'Is El Pulmón your dealer?' asked Falcón, handing him the new cigarette.

'Yes, and my friend.'

'You know what happened up there?'

Puerta shook his head, pawed at a spasm in his cheek.

'Someone shot his girlfriend.'

'Julia?' said Puerta, who looked up with brilliant green eyes, gone weak as slime.

'Shot her in the face.'

Puerta seemed to have difficulty swallowing. The hand with the cigarette trembled to his mouth. He coughed. Smoke came out in rags. He hunched over, rested his forehead on his good hand and sobbed himself silent. Falcón patted him on the shoulder.

'Why don't you tell me what you saw,' he said, 'and then we can get the guy who shot Julia before he shoots your friend.'

'So now we're sure there's a Russian mafia ingredient,' said Anibal Parrado, the instructing judge, pacing the window in El Pulmón's apartment.

'But I've only got the word of a complete wreck of a junkie and not one bit of evidence,' said Falcón. 'Marisa

Moreno didn't even tell us that the Russians were holding her sister; we've only surmised that from finding the disk in the possession of Vasili Lukyanov. The Narcs have never seen this Cuban before, don't know about any Russian involvement. I've got nothing to give you that you could use in court – unless we find El Pulmón.'

'So where are you going now?'

'There's nothing more for me to do here,' said Falcón. 'Detectives Serrano and Baena are going to work with Narcotics to find El Pulmón. Sub-Inspector Pérez is going to run this investigation. Inspector Ramírez is looking after the Marisa Moreno murder. We should all meet up this evening and compare notes.'

'Where are you going now?'

'I'm looking for people who've had direct contact with the Russians,' said Falcón. 'Marisa Moreno is dead. It's going to take time to find El Pulmón. I've got one other candidate.'

Falcón sat in his car making calls, trying to find out where Alejandro Spinola would be at this time of the afternoon. He was in a press conference in the Andalucían parliament building. Falcón left Las Tres Mil, opted for the ring road rather than mess with the traffic through the centre.

Alejandro Spinola was as pretty as a man could get without slipping over the gender line. He liked to run his hand through his longish black hair with off-centre parting, and clench it in his fist at the back of his head. He had the athletic body of a professional tennis player gone slightly to seed. He wore a good suit with the cuffs of his white shirt shot beyond the sleeves and a light blue silk tie. He talked easily and kept the press amused while turning a gold ring on one of the fingers of his right hand. He didn't look like someone who had the intention of playing second fiddle to the mayor for the rest of his life. There was too much vanity streaming from every pore. He was a man who'd learnt not to blink in flash photography and tap-danced to the percussion of lens shutters.

The press were thick around Spinola, all looking for an off-the-record discussion. Falcón shouldered through them and showed Spinola his police ID card.

'Can't this wait?' he asked, careful not to use Falcón's rank in front of the political press corps.

'Probably not,' said Falcón.

Spinola took him by the arm and guided him out of the room, casting jokes and compliments as he went. They crossed the corridor; Spinola checked for an empty office, found one. He sat behind the desk, pulled out one of the side drawers and rested his expensive loafers on the edge. He sat back, comfortable, hands resting on his stomach, which proved to have its first gathering of middle-aged fat.

'What can I do for you, Inspector Jefe?' he asked, vaguely amused by it all.

'I want to talk to you about Marisa Moreno.'

'Esteban's girlfriend?' he said, frowning. 'I hardly know her.'

'But you met her first.'

'That's true. I met her at a gallery opening,' he said, nodding, looking out of the window. 'Over the past few years Esteban hasn't had much time for art. He used to go to openings all the time. He was always interested in paintings, literature, that kind of thing, much more so than me.'

'Then why did you go?'

'The people. A good art dealer can always bring together an interesting bunch of people. Collectors tend to have money and influence. And that's my job.'

'What *is* your job?'

'I work for the mayor.'

'That's what Esteban told me,' said Falcón. 'I'm sure you've got more to add?'

'I make sure the mayor is in touch with the right sort of

people to achieve his aims,' said Spinola. 'Things don't happen on their own, Inspector Jefe. Whether you're building a mosque in Los Bermejales or pedestrianizing the Avenida de la Constitución, or remodelling La Alameda or tunnelling a metro under the city, there are huge numbers of people to deal with. Angry residents, disgruntled religious groups, disappointed contractors, furious taxi drivers, to name but a few.'

'Presumably there are happy people as well.'

'Of course. My job is to help the mayor convert those unhappy people into . . . well, maybe not totally happy people, but at least quieter, more manageable people.'

'And how do you do that?'

'You must know my father, Inspector Jefe, he's a lawyer,' said Spinola. 'I never had the temperament for sitting down and learning lots of stuff from books, like Esteban did. But in my own way I'm like both of them. I'm a very persuasive guy.'

'So what happened with Marisa, then?' said Falcón, smiling.

'Oh, yes, right, exactly. What happened with Marisa . . .' said Spinola, giving him a delayed laugh. 'I met her at Galería Zoca. Do you know it? Just off the Alfalfa. She wasn't showing. She's not a big enough name for that place. But she's very nice to look at, no? So, José Manuel Domecq, the owner, always invites her to, you know, prettify the usual assembly of toads and trout with their crocodile-skin handbags and wallets bulging with cash. I already knew everybody there, so I didn't have to work very hard, and we all went out to dinner and Marisa and I sat together and, you know, Inspector Jefe, we got along. We got along very well.'

'Did you sleep with her?'

Spinola initially narrowed his eyes, as if preparing to take affront, but in the end decided on a lightness of touch. He laughed, a little exaggeratedly.

'*No, no, no, que no*, Inspector Jefe. It wasn't like that.'

'I see,' said Falcón. 'Forgive my misunderstanding.'

'No. We exchanged numbers and I called her the following week to invite her to the garden party at the Duchess of Alba's house. It's an annual affair and I thought it would be . . . exotic to turn up with a beautiful black girl on my arm.'

As Spinola's eyes travelled from the window back across the room, they stopped for a beat to check how things were going down with Falcón, then carried on to the door. For a persuasive man, Spinola was weak on eye contact.

'So, how did your introduction of Marisa to your cousin come about?'

'Well, it wasn't so much an introduction as Esteban arriving on my shoulder within seconds of my arrival and introducing *himself* to Marisa.'

'I think you might have misremembered something.'

'I don't think so. I can see it now. Esteban cutting her away from me while I got drawn into the crowd. He hogged her the whole evening.'

'I think that's doubtful,' said Falcón, 'because Esteban was married to Inés and, at that point in their relationship, he was not in the habit of brazenly displaying his inclination for infidelity, especially in front of his and her parents and, of course, your father, the Juez Decano de Sevilla, who was his employer.'

A pause for thought. Some rearrangement of the details. Falcón could hear the brain furniture scraping around in Spinola's head. Then the mayor's fixer suddenly shrugged and threw his hand up in the air.

'These are just details, Inspector Jefe,' he said. 'Think of how many parties I go to, how many social situations I find myself in. How am I supposed to remember the finer points of every meeting and introduction?'

'Because, as you've just told me,' said Falcón, 'it's your job. Your job is to know what makes people tick. What they like and dislike. And people in social situations don't wear their needs and intentions on the outside, especially, I imagine, when you're around and they're very conscious of the impression they want to make on the mayor's office. Yes, I would have thought that, under those circumstances, it would all be in the detail. And your reading of that detail is what makes you so successful.'

Finally, the eye contact, very level and sustained. A mixture of respect and fear. Spinola now thinking: What does this man know?

'How does Esteban remember it?' he asked, in order to avoid another lie and to give himself a chance of building a different point of view on the rock of truth.

'He remembers you pulling him out of a family group. You were on your own at the time. You told him that he must meet this wonderful sculptress that you'd found at an opening the previous week. He says you took him into the house, to a room with some magnificent paintings where you'd left Marisa to wait alone. He remembers you introducing her and the next thing he knows *you* are no longer in the room. Does that refresh your memory?'

It did. Spinola's eyes drifted above Falcón's head as he tried to massage the facts he'd just heard into something perfectly comprehensible.

'How old are you, Señor Spinola?'

'Thirty-four,' he said.

'You're not married?'

'No.'

'Perhaps you could explain why you, a single man, would effect an introduction to a very attractive woman, also single, to your married cousin?'

Something like relief passed over Spinola's face and Falcón realized a strategy had occurred to him.

'I'm sorry to say this, Inspector Jefe, but Marisa would not be the first woman I'd ever introduced to my cousin.'

'What does that mean exactly?'

'It means what I've just said. I've introduced single women to Esteban before and he's had affairs with . . . some of them.'

'I was wondering if you meant that you had an arrangement, like some sort of informal pimping service,' said Falcón mildly, but with calculated aggression.

'I resent that, Inspector Jefe.'

'Then clarify the understanding you had with your cousin for me.'

'I'm younger than him. I'm not married. I meet young, available women . . .'

'But *what* is the understanding? Has anything ever been said between the two of you about what you're doing?'

'As you said yourself, Inspector Jefe, my job is to know what people like.'

'In that case, what was *your* purpose, Señor Spinola?'

'My purpose, Inspector Jefe, is to build up favours in all walks of life, so that in my own, or the mayor's, crucial moments I can call on people for support,' said Spinola. 'Local politics is only pretty on the surface, and the surface is very important. Nobody ever *asks* for a bribe. Nobody ever *asks* for a nice young chick to blow him under his desk. *I* have to know, and then I have to make it look as if I didn't, so that we can still look at each other at the next party.'

Spinola had taken the first round by a whisker. Falcón stood up. He went to the door, reached for the handle. Spinola lifted his feet off the drawer, shoved it in.

'You might not have heard, Señor Spinola,' said Falcón. 'Marisa Moreno was murdered last night. They used her own chain saw on her. Cut off her hand. Cut off her foot. Cut off her head.'

The small triumph disappeared from Spinola's face and what was left behind was not sorrow or horror but a very live kind of fear.

16

Consuelo had found an old mobile phone, but with a flat battery, which she was now recharging. She reckoned half an hour would give her enough juice. Voices reached her from downstairs. She was nervous about making the call in the house. If something happened and she had an emotional reaction, they would hear her and that might affect Darío's safety.

The patrolman at the front door did not move as she passed him. She saw that his head was resting on the wall. He was asleep. In the kitchen, the sound man and the family liaison officer were having one of those endless Sevillano conversations about everything that had ever happened to them and their families. Consuelo made some coffee, served them and took her own into the living room. She watched the second patrolman sitting by the pool. He was slumped in his chair. It was 40°C out there. He, too, must be asleep. Time leaked by until she could bear it no longer.

Back upstairs. The phone had recharged enough. She entered the phone number from the email into the memory, not sure, in her emotional state, that she could rely on her brain to remember it. She called the service provider and set up a pay-as-you-go account for twenty-five euros. She changed into some flat pumps, slipped back downstairs, past the first patrolman, past the kitchen and out through the sliding doors. She walked the length of the pool. The patrolman didn't move. At the bottom of the garden there was a rough break in the hedge where a gate led to the adjoining property. It was rusted and had never been opened as far as she knew. She vaulted over it and found herself at the back of her neighbour's pool house.

She called the number. It rang interminably. She breathed back her fear, apprehension and rampant agitation, but when the answer came it was still like cold steel in the stomach.

'*Diga*.'

Nothing came out of her paralysed throat.

'*Diga!*'

'My name is Consuelo Jiménez and I've been told to call this number. You're holding my −'

'*Momentito.*'

There was muffled talk. The phone changed hands.

'Listen to me, Señora Jiménez,' said a new voice. 'Do you understand why we have taken your son?'

'I'm not sure who you are.'

'But do you understand why your son has been **taken** from you?'

Put like that she nearly broke down.

'No, I don't,' she said.

'Your friend, Javier Falcón, the inspector −'

'He is *not* my friend,' she said, blurting it.

'That's a pity.'

She wasn't sure why he should have said that: **sad** because they'd split up, or a shame because he could be useful?

'You need friends at a time like this,' said the voice.

'Why do I need *him*?' she asked. '*He* is the cause of all this.'

'It's good that you understand that much.'

'But I don't understand why *you* have taken *my son* because of *his* investigations.'

'He was warned.'

'But why *my* son?'

'I am in no doubt that you are a good person, Señora Jiménez, but even you, in your business, must understand the nature of pressure.'

'The nature of pressure,' she said, her mind blank.

'Direct pressure is always met with resistance. However, *indirect* pressure is a much more complicated business.'

Silence, until Consuelo realized that her response was required.

'And you want me to apply . . . some indirect pressure. Is that it?'

'There was a car accident on the motorway between Jerez and Seville a few days ago in which a Russian named Vasili Lukyanov was killed,' said the voice. 'Inspector Jefe Falcón was put in charge of this accident because there was a lot of money in the boot – eight million two hundred thousand euros – and a number of disks, which contain footage of men and women in compromising situations. We would like the money and the disks returned to us. If you are successful in persuading Inspector Jefe Falcón to act for you, then no harm will come to your son. He will be released, you have my word on that. If, however, you decide to involve other agencies, or your old friend calls on other resources, then your son will still come back to you, Señora Jiménez, but piece by piece.'

The line went dead. Consuelo vomited a horrible bilious liquid that burned her throat and nostrils. She wheeled around under the big, white sky and fell back against the pool house, panting, sweat streaming down her face and neck. She wiped her nose, coughed, sniffed. Blurted out some more tears and frustration. Remembered the patrolman by the pool. Pulled herself together. She got back into her own garden. Slipped into the house. Up the stairs. She stripped and stood under the shower. The first solid thought to form in her mind was: had she just done something very stupid?

'Where are you?' asked Falcón.

'I'm with Inspector Ramírez at the Jefatura,' said Cristina Ferrera. 'We're typing up the report on Marisa Moreno.'

'Did you get anything apart from the paper suits?'

'A witness. A twenty-three-year-old woman saw three men in Calle Bustos Tavera, but she's a bit hazy about the time. She thought it was around midnight, which probably sounds about right. She was going home early, felt sick in a club on La Alameda.'

'Did she get a good look?'

'She lost her nerve, didn't like the . . . not so much the look of them, because she couldn't see much down there at night. It's unlit. But she didn't like the feel of the situation. She made a detour to avoid them.'

'Height, weight, frame?'

'Two guys about the same height, one eight-five to one ninety metres, who looked around the hundred-kilo mark. The third guy was very short and stocky. She said he was noticeably wide and muscular. Thick neck. She thought he might have been a bodybuilder. One of the taller guys was carrying a full bin liner. The other thing was that, although she couldn't see their features, she knew they weren't Spanish. Something to do with their head shape.'

'The description of that last guy is very interesting,' said Falcón. 'That squares with a witness description I've got to the double killing in Las Tres Mil.'

'We picked that up on the police radio.'

'Tell Ramírez that the two bodies in the drug dealer's apartment in Las Tres Mil are connected to what he's doing.

Anibal Parrado is the instructing judge for both cases. We'll all meet within the Edificio de los Juzgados this evening, time to be arranged. What about those three businessmen's names I gave you to check out?'

'Juan Valverde is in Madrid right now and Antonio Ramos is in Barcelona, but where they're *going* to be is a different matter. Their personal assistants have been told not to give out that kind of information,' said Ferrera. 'So I lifted all their data from their ID files and sent it to a friend of mine in the Comisaría General de Información, who works in counter terrorism. They've got access to airlines, trains, private jets, and can find out if these people are moving around at all in the next few days . . . assuming they've made bookings. They'll check out the American consultant, Charles Taggart, too. I got his data from the visa office. I couldn't find out where he is at the moment. He's not directly employed by I4IT Europe. All I can say is that he wasn't in their office in Madrid, nor in Horizonte's Barcelona office.'

'I didn't really mean for you to go into that kind of detail,' said Falcón. 'We need to talk to those men face to face. I just didn't want to go to Madrid and find they were in Frankfurt.'

'I thought it was more sinister than that,' said Ferrera. 'Still, my friend will get all the information and you can use it against them if they start getting difficult. Inspector Ramírez wants a word.'

'Just to warn you, Javier,' said Ramírez, 'Comisario Elvira has been on the phone asking where you are. And I've just seen your friend and mine, the Jefe Superior Andrés Lobo; after giving me one of those "fuck off" salutes of his, *he* also wanted to know where you were.'

'Why don't they just call me?'

'In my experience, they never do that when they're going to give you a kicking,' said Ramírez. 'Upset anyone recently?'

'Have you heard of a guy called Alejandro Spinola?'

'That smarmy fucker.'

'So you've met him?'

Pause.

'No,' said Ramírez, as if that was obvious. 'I just know a smarmy fucker when I see one. And I know he works in the mayor's office and he's the Juez Decano's son . . . so I don't call him a tosser to his face.'

'He introduced Marisa to Esteban Calderón.'

'Aha!' said Ramírez, as if the whole case had fallen open into his lap. 'What the fuck does that mean?'

'We had a very interesting little fencing match,' said Falcón. 'He's a bit of a maestro. I'm beginning to think it might mean that the June 6th conspiracy is still alive and moving on another front, or that perhaps it was attempting to develop two spheres of influence – parliament *and* the mayor's office.'

'And they blew it with trying to control the regional politics so now they're trying to infiltrate the mayor's office?' said Ramírez. 'Don't you think you might be reading too much into very little, Javier?'

'I can smell something on Spinola,' said Falcón. 'That guy is an operator and he's ambitious. I get the impression that in his family circle Esteban Calderón has been held up as the paragon of intelligence and capability. And Alejandro has spent his life trying to prove himself equal. He didn't have the brains to become a lawyer, but he's got other qualities.'

'And he's used them to fuck up his cousin?'

'It wouldn't surprise me.'

'Hold on a sec,' said Ramírez. 'Cristina has just told me you've been given the summons. Elvira *does* want to see you, and it seems to be pressing.'

'And that in itself is a symptom,' said Falcón. 'The forces are gathering. Tell the Comisario I'll be there as soon as I can.'

* * *

211

Consuelo sat in a T-shirt and pants, hair wet, face lit by the computer screen. She had been stupid and impetuous; now she was going to slow down, consider her next move more carefully than her first. She had written down the dialogue from the phone call, as best she could remember it, on the computer. She read it over, made adjustments each time her memory flung up another half-remembered phrase.

The work had a dampening effect on her hysteria. After her shower, she'd got dressed with the notion that she would call Javier, go straight out to meet him and confront him with the latest development. Only when she reached for the phone did she realize that this was what was expected of her. She'd stripped off, just in case the impetuosity struck again, and sat down to start doing some serious thinking.

She began by answering the kidnapper's question: Why had Darío been taken? Because they didn't like the intrusion of Javier's investigations. In kidnapping Darío they knew that she would call directly on Javier's position and experience in criminal investigations. Perhaps they had expected that Javier would not give her the reason behind Darío's kidnap and would become directly involved in trying to find the boy. This would divert Javier's attention from his investigation that so concerned them. But Javier had insisted on the Crimes Against Children squad being involved in the kidnapping, which meant that the Russians' application of indirect pressure had not had the desired effect. Now she was being used as their agent to draw Javier into Darío's predicament. They wanted her to use her considerable influence with Javier, who would be feeling profoundly guilty, to induce him to corrupt himself by stealing back their money and the disks from the Jefatura. Their strict condition, that there should be no involvement of other agencies and resources or it would result in harm to Darío, might mean they had informers in the Jefatura.

If Javier was caught stealing evidence he would be immediately suspended from duty, and that would be a good
result for the Russians.

This was the first logical chain of thought she'd managed
since Darío had been snatched. It gave her strength, she felt
her brain tightening around the problem.

So far I've done exactly what you expected me to do, she
thought. You've sweated me for forty-eight hours until I
was so desperate I'd do anything you asked. Now it's my
turn to show you what sort of an opponent you've decided
to take on.

Comisarios Lobo and Elvira, Falcón's bosses. The odd couple.
The Beast and the Accountant. The former, with his thin
dark lips in a cumin complexion, looked as irritated as if he
had sand in his teeth, while the latter restored even greater
order to his already well-organized desk.

'What cases are you working on at the moment, Javier?'
asked Elvira mildly, while Lobo stared on, leaning slightly
forward as if it would take only the slightest provocation to
make him violent.

'The murder of Marisa Moreno is my primary concern,
as I believe it's linked to the two murders in Las Tres Mil.'

'You were seen recently in Madrid, where you spoke to
Inspector Jefe Luis Zorrita about "digging around" in Esteban
Calderón's case,' said Elvira. 'Which, as you know, comes
up for trial here in Seville at the end of the month.'

'What's all that about, Javier?' asked Lobo, unable to
restrain himself any longer.

'Politeness.'

'Politeness?' said Lobo. 'What the fuck has politeness got
to do with anything?'

'I was telling Inspector Jefe Zorrita that I was going to look
at Marisa Moreno. I'd read the case notes and listened to the
Calderón interview, and there were some anomalies which

merited attention. I was informing him because it might have an impact on his case, which as you've just . . .'

'And after the meeting with Zorrita, where did you go?' asked Elvira. 'The driver of the patrol car said you "hid" in the back seat.'

'I had some CNI business which I'm not able to discuss with you.'

'You are, and have been, under a great deal of strain,' said Elvira, wanting to move things along to the conclusion he already had in mind.

'We have an agreement with the CNI about your second-ment to their duties,' said Lobo, who wanted to run this meeting without Elvira.

'If you do, I don't know what it is.'

'The essential element is that your work for them must not have a deleterious effect on your duties as the Inspector Jefe del Grupo de Homicidios,' said Elvira. 'If it does, then we have to decide where your resource would be better concentrated, so that you can be relieved of some of that pressure.'

'The CNI have made inquiries as to the work stress you're under here,' said Lobo.

'Have they? You mean Pablo has spoken to you?'

'Higher than Pablo,' said Lobo.

'As your commanding officer,' said Elvira, 'I am in posses-sion of your career records, where it is clearly documented that you suffered a serious nervous breakdown in April 2001 and did not return to full duties until the summer of 2002.'

'Which was four years ago and I think you'll agree that, not only were the circumstances extremely unusual, but also that I've made a full recovery to the point of success-fully conducting one of the most complex and demanding investigations in the history of the Seville Jefatura, that of the Seville bombing three months ago,' said Falcón. 'And, I might add, at the same time I made some very delicate interventions for the CNI, which resulted in the prevention of a major terrorist attack in London.'

'We also understand that your partner, Consuelo Jiménez, has seen her youngest child kidnapped two days ago,' said Elvira.

'Which reminds me: you can take the police guard off my house in Calle Bailén. I don't need protection,' said Falcón.

'It was a temporary measure,' said Elvira.

'Don't tell me, Javier, that all this isn't enough stress for even such a man as yourself to bear,' said Lobo. 'We all know the promise you made to the people of Seville on TV last June and, whilst we don't know the ins and outs of the CNI work, *they* have made inquiries to *us* about your mental reliability. Added to that, three murders for your department to investigate and the kidnapping of Darío Jiménez . . .'

'And what if I tell you that it's all connected?' said Falcón.

'The intelligence work as well?' asked Elvira.

'That is an inevitable development from the situation that occurred back in June,' said Falcón. 'Pressure is being applied in the most inventive way possible to get someone to do what is against their nature. I am responsible for that person being in that position. I cannot desert him.'

'But what has it got to do with what is happening here in Seville?' asked Lobo.

'I'm not sure, other than that the same situation exists here: pressure is being applied to all sorts of people to get them to perform,' said Falcón. 'And I include this meeting.'

Lobo and Elvira looked at each other and then at Falcón.

'This meeting?' said Lobo, with the threat level in his voice close to red.

'You're just transferring to me what's been applied to you,' said Falcón.

'If you mean by that that the CNI have been in touch with us . . .'

'Not just the CNI.'

'I don't understand why you're resurrecting the Calderón case,' said Elvira, his discomfiture making him testy. 'Is it because of your ex-wife?'

'It seems,' said Lobo, irritated by Elvira's departure from the script, 'that it's not just the CNI who are concerned about your mental state. I had a call from the Juez Decano complaining about your interruption of a press conference in the Andalucían parliament in order to question his son about how exactly he introduced Marisa Moreno to Esteban Calderón. He seems to think, and I agree, that it was unnecessary harassment.'

'My methods have been questioned before,' said Falcón, 'but never the results.'

'We think you're doing too much, Javier,' said Elvira.

'Two comments about your mental state from different sources on the same day,' said Lobo. 'That rings alarm bells with us, Javier.'

'Given your history,' added Elvira.

'What you mean is that the Juez Decano – who, by the way, I did not see – was persuaded by his son that my behaviour was unstable,' said Falcón. 'Do I appear mad to you? Have any members of my squad, who are the people closest to me and most able to observe any changes, expressed concern about my behaviour?'

'Even *I* can see you're tired,' said Elvira. 'Exhausted.'

'We're not taking any chances with you, Javier.'

'So what's the deal?'

'The deal?' said Lobo.

'Any further comment about concerns for your mental state and you'll be suspended from duty,' said Elvira.

'And for my part,' said Falcón, 'I promise not to talk to Alejandro Spinola on any matter relating to Marisa Moreno or Esteban Calderón.'

The two men looked at him, eyebrows arched.

'Wasn't that the purpose of this meeting?' asked Falcón.

*   *   *

It was early evening and the temperature had just dropped below 40°C for the first time since 11 a.m. Inspector Jefe Tirado sat in Consuelo's living room, preparing to give her a short report on the developments in her son's kidnapping. He was disconcerted by her poise. Most women who'd been made to sweat for more than forty-eight hours without hearing a word from the kidnappers would be on the verge of a breakdown by now. Most mothers he'd dealt with had been reduced to a state of tearful exhaustion by the constant oscillation between hope and despair within the first twelve hours. They'd look at him with begging eyes, pleading with every cell in their bodies for the thinnest sliver of good news. Consuelo Jiménez sat before him dressed and made up, even with her toes and fingernails painted with red varnish. He had never encountered a woman under these circumstances who'd shown such total composure, even refusing support from family members. She made him nervous.

He talked her through the interview with Carlos Puerta, her stalker back in June.

'He said that?' said Consuelo, outraged but remembering her instability at that time. 'He put his hands up my skirt, stole the money from my handbag and then kicked it down the street. At the very least it was a mugging.'

'I found a shot of this man. I've been around the neighbourhood here, and nobody has seen him in Santa Clara, certainly not recently,' said Tirado. 'The Narcotics guys down in Las Tres Mil say he's been a permanent fixture down there for the last two months.'

'So you don't think he's involved in Darío's kidnapping?'

'He was also in very poor condition,' said Tirado, flipping through his notes. 'I understand from the sound engineer that there have been no communications here.' Consuelo shook her head. The strain of keeping what she knew from Tirado was making her absurdly conscious of the functioning vertebrae in her neck. She realized, in that instant, that the phone call she'd made to the kidnappers had transformed Tirado into someone she could no longer trust.

Tirado looked up when he heard no reply.

'No,' she said. 'Nothing.'

'I've also been to Darío's school,' said Tirado, 'and conducted a number of interviews with the teachers and children. I'm afraid I have nothing to report from there, although they asked me to give you this.'

He handed over an envelope. She opened it and drew out the handmade card. The drawing on the front in coloured crayons showed a boy with standing-up hair in the sunshine, with trees and a river behind. Inside it said: *Darío is all right. We know he will come home again soon.* It was signed by everyone in his class.

Only then did Tirado discover what was going on underneath. Consuelo closed her eyes, her mouth crumpled, and two silvery rivulets crept hesitatingly down her face.

17

La Galería Zoca was owned by a venerable old gentleman for whom the word *señorial* had been invented. He had impeccable manners, superb conversational skills, perfect tailoring, precision coiffure and gold-rimmed half-moon spectacles which hung from his neck by a cord. You would be in no doubt, just from the look of him, that this man came from lengthy and outstanding lineage, but that he would be the last person in the world to tell you anything of the sort.

Although Falcón had known José Manuel Domecq for many years, he had not seen him this century. They sat in an office at the back of the gallery, where Domecq had led him after a genuinely warm welcome. Two small coffees were brought in. Domecq shook the sugar sachet empty over his and stirred it in for a length of time for which only an old man would have the patience.

'I know you don't have anything left of your father's to sell, Javier,' he said. 'I heard you burnt it all.'

'Under his orders.'

'Yes, yes, yes,' he said sadly. 'A travesty and a tragedy. So what brings you here?'

'I just wanted to know if you've ever seen this woman,' said Falcón, handing Domecq a photograph he'd printed off his computer after his meeting with Lobo and Elvira.

Domecq settled his specs on his nose and leaned forward to inspect.

'She's very lovely, Marisa, isn't she?' he said.

'Did you know her well?'

'She came in here asking me to represent her once, but, you know, wood carving, ethnic stuff, it's not really my thing,' he said. 'But she was very attractive so I asked her to some openings, and sometimes she came and lent a somewhat exotic atmosphere to the proceedings. A mango amongst the oranges, or rather, a leopard amongst the ... er ... reptiles might be a more accurate description of some of my collectors. They liked her, found her rather interesting.'

'About what?' asked Falcón, thinking some of those words and phrases had sounded very familiar.

'The work,' said Domecq. 'Although I didn't like her stuff, she knew how to talk about art.'

'When did you last see her?'

'Not for a while at an opening,' said Domecq. 'But she didn't live far from here, so she'd drop in every so often to say hello. I probably saw her three or four months ago.'

'That's very good, José Manuel. Thank you for that,' said Falcón, taking the photograph back.

Some minutes later Falcón walked back to the tree-lined, leafy square, got into his car and sat at the wheel with the photograph still in his hands. The Plaza Alfalfa was quiet, the heat too oppressive for anybody to be sitting outside the Bar Manolo. The captivating woman in the photo stared back at him with dark, wide eyes. Domecq was right, she was lovely; but it was a picture of the American actress Halle Berry he'd shown to the gallery owner, not Marisa Moreno.

It was clear that Alejandro Spinola had moved fast. First, getting his father to complain to Comisario Lobo, of all people.

Changing the story only a little so that it had come out as Falcón 'interrupting a press conference' just to talk about Calderón's old girlfriend. That could be construed as 'unstable behaviour'. And now, here he was, covering his tracks at La Galería Zoca. Domecq must have a need for Spinola's social and professional network to have to lie for him like that.

His mobile vibrated. Cristina Ferrera.

'*Diga*,' he said.

'My friend in the CGI just came back to me,' she said. 'I thought you might be interested to know that Charles Taggart is booked to fly into Madrid from Newark tonight. Antonio Ramos is flying in from Barcelona, also tonight. And, this is the interesting thing: I4IT has chartered a private jet to fly down to Seville tomorrow. The pilot has logged his flight plan with a take-off time of five p.m.'

'Are they staying the night or flying back?'

'The pilot's flight plan indicates a take-off time of eleven a.m. on Wednesday, 20th September, destination Málaga, which meant that my friend, being a very thorough person, checked all the upmarket hotels in and around Seville and found four suites booked in the company name of Horizonte at an exclusive country-house hotel called La Berenjena, which is just off the road to Huelva.'

'Four suites?'

'There must be someone else invited to the party.'

'That's a pretty good contact you've got at the CGI,' said Falcón. 'You might have to marry him for doing all that for you.'

'My friend is a "she",' said Ferrera. 'You don't think you'd get that kind of detail from a man, do you, Inspector Jefe?'

There were too many people for the meeting to take place in the judge's offices, so they'd had to wait half an hour for the conference room in the Edificio de los Juzgados to come available. At the end of the table sat the instructing judge,

Anibal Parrado. To his left were Sub-Inspector Emilio Pérez, Vicente Cortés and Martín Díaz. Opposite them sat Falcón and Ramírez. Falcón introduced Cortés and Díaz, whom the judge hadn't met before. He then gave an introduction to the three murders they were about to discuss and sat down. Anibal Parrado asked for an update on developments in the Marisa Moreno case. Ramírez described the sighting of three men down Calle Bustos Tavera by the young female witness. His description of the third man as a bodybuilder earned an interruption from Cortés.

'You mean a weightlifter,' he said.

'You know someone built like that?' asked Falcón. 'Because I have a witness from Las Tres Mil, Carlos Puerta, who gave a similar description of the possible shooter in El Pulmón's apartment.'

'Nikita Sokolov,' said Cortés. 'Just missed out on a bronze medal at the 1992 Barcelona Olympics, middleweight class, which means around seventy kilos, although he must be heavier than that by now, but certainly no taller, and he still trains. We haven't seen him in the Costa del Sol for a few months . . . not since May or June.'

'What did he do down there?'

'He was an enforcer. When the old Russian gang leader fled to Dubai after Operation Wasp, he carried on working for Leonid Revnik,' said Cortés. 'His job was to make people pay or perform and, if they didn't want to do either, he'd kill them. I'll get back to you with more information on him.'

'A photo would help,' said Juez Parrado. 'Only one witness in the Marisa Moreno investigation, Inspector Ramírez?'

'There's not much residential around there. The courtyard was closed off from the street. The chain saw was electric and therefore quiet. It was pure luck that we found this witness.'

'Forensic information?'

'We found two paper suits in some rubbish bins around

the corner, just off Calle Gerona. They were in a bin liner, which is what our witness described seeing in the hands of one of the three men she saw in Calle Bustos Tavera. The blood on the suits was matched to Marisa Moreno and some DNA has been derived from hairs found on the inside of one and from a semen deposit in the other. The data has been passed to CICO headquarters in Madrid to see if they can find a match on their database.'

'That could take some time,' said Díaz. 'Computer matches have to be confirmed by human inspection these days. We'll be lucky to have anything on that by tomorrow, *if* they exist in our database. If they don't, we have to pass the samples over to Interpol and that might take weeks.'

'So we have a sighting of three men, but DNA from only two,' said Parrado.

'Nikita Sokolov wouldn't do dirty work like that,' said Cortés. 'He'd shoot a guy, but he wouldn't get actively involved in cutting up a woman. He wouldn't lower himself to that.'

'Lower himself?' asked Parrado.

'These guys keep male company. Women, to them, are a lower form of life. They're good for preparing food, sex and beating. Sokolov is a real *vor-v-zakone*, which means "a thief with a code of honour". When he came back from the Olympics he served time in jail for murder. Most of the Russian mafia guys on the Costa del Sol these days have just bought the right to be *vory-v-zakone*, but Sokolov actually earned it in jail. He would have overseen Marisa's killing, but he wouldn't have done the work.'

'Do we have Sokolov's DNA on file?' asked Juez Parrado.

'That's what I'm not sure about,' said Cortés. 'I wasn't involved in the case, but I think Sokolov and this guy who was killed on the motorway, Vasili Lukyanov, were friends and they were both being processed as a result of an assault on a local girl. Blood samples would have been taken for DNA purposes, prior to the girl dropping the charges and the men being released. I'll check with the Sex Crimes squad in Málaga to see if they've still got them.'

'That was a rape charge,' said Falcón. 'I remember Comisario Elvira mentioning it when I gave him my first report on Vasili Lukyanov's accident.'

'So Sokolov *was* into sexually assaulting women on that occasion?' said Ramírez.

'I think he was more interested in *violence* against women,' said Cortés. 'I'll check the case history and get back to you.'

'Well, that's progress on Marisa Moreno,' said Parrado. '*If* we can match the DNA and find the suspects.'

'We've done some limited work on that,' said Ramírez. 'Before the incident in Las Tres Mil occurred, our two detectives, Serrano and Baena, were in Seville Este, trying to find out where one of these Russian groups are holed up.'

'Why Seville Este?'

'We believe that Vasili Lukyanov was defecting from Leonid Revnik to join a renegade gang run by Yuri Donstov. The GPS in Lukyanov's Range Rover had an address in Calle Garlopa in Seville Este.'

'Any sightings of Yuri Donstov?' asked Falcón. 'Or any Russians?'

'There are a lot of apartment blocks on Calle Garlopa and, so far, no Russians and no reports of having seen any.'

'It was probably just a meeting point,' said Cortés. 'I can't see him putting an address into his GPS. They've been more careful since Operation Wasp.'

'I have a source who tells me that Yuri Donstov could be in the Polígono San Pablo,' said Falcón.

'They don't advertise their whereabouts,' said Díaz.

'Let's move on to the two murders in Las Tres Mil,' said Parrado. 'Sub-Inspector Emilio Pérez is the investigating officer, I believe.'

'I'm not in possession of a fully confirmed ballistics report yet,' said Pérez, starting off in his characteristic fashion.

'But you have what we need to know, Emilio, so tell us that,' said Ramírez.

'Oh, right, Inspector. The autopsy revealed that the two dead bodies were killed by nine-millimetre rounds, which we assume were fired from the same gun, but this has not been confirmed yet.'

Ramírez tried to speed him up with quick turns of his fingers.

'The weapon found at the scene was a Beretta 84FS Cheetah. This is a .380-calibre weapon and only one round had been fired, which was found embedded in the living-room wall opposite the window. I have the plan here.'

'Keep going, Emilio,' said Ramírez.

'It is believed that this round wounded the assailant holding the nine-millimetre weapon. Preliminary findings from the autopsy reveal that the trajectory of the bullets entering Miguel Estévez, the Cuban victim, meant that the gun was fired from the floor, which encourages us to believe that the shooter has been injured. The first bullet smashed Estévez's spinal column at the sixth vertebra, the second hit his fourth rib and penetrated his heart.'

'Blood?' said Ramírez.

'Three blood samples were recovered from the apartment. One belongs to Miguel Estévez, the second to Julia Valdés, who was El Pulmón's girlfriend, and the third is unknown, but corresponds to the samples found on the floor and wall of the living room where the .380 round was found, the threshold of the door to the bedroom from where Julia Valdés was shot, the stairs up to the apartment block and the pavement outside. They're working on generating the DNA now. We have not had time to derive El Pulmón's DNA from hair and bristles found in his bathroom, but we believe that . . .'

'He wouldn't shoot his own girlfriend,' said Ramírez. 'What about the Beretta?'

'Ballistics say that it was fired lying flat on the table with the screw within the trigger guard. There were other screws holding the barrel in place. They think it was covered by the magazine. The recoil had sent the gun back to the window.'

'The knife?'

'The hunting knife had Estévez's fingerprints on the handle. The knife which stabbed him was not found.'

'Conclusion?'

'The first shot from the Beretta injured the shooter. Estévez tried to stab El Pulmón, who in turn stabbed him and then turned the Cuban so that he was between El Pulmón and the injured man on the floor. The shooter hit Estévez twice. Powder burns on the shirt suggest that the second shot was fired as Estévez was pushed back on to the shooter. El Pulmón escaped. The shooter then killed Julia Valdés and left the apartment himself.'

'Good,' said Ramírez. 'Any witnesses?'

'Just the one,' said Pérez. 'Carlos Puerta, one of El Pulmón's clients, who the Inspector Jefe mentioned earlier.'

'Four gunshots go off in an apartment in the middle of the *barrio* and we have only one witness?' said Juez Parrado.

'It's Las Tres Mil,' said Pérez, hopelessly. 'The only person who was prepared to say anything was the tenant above El Pulmón, who told us he'd heard the gunshots at about one p.m. When it comes to seeing people running around with blood all over them, especially when drugs are involved, then everybody is suddenly deaf and blind in Las Tres Mil.'

'So what did Carlos Puerta see?'

'He saw two men pull up in a dark blue car. He didn't notice the model or the number plate. They went into the building. One fits the description of the Cuban, Miguel Estévez, and the other this person we now know is the Russian weightlifter, Nikita Sokolov,' said Pérez. 'He heard three shots. Puerta saw El Pulmón run out wearing a T-shirt covered in blood and heard a fourth gunshot. Then the weightlifter came out, got into the car and drove off.'

'And Carlos Puerta didn't report the shooting?' asked Parrado.

'He's a junkie,' said Pérez, by way of explanation.

'What about El Pulmón?' asked Falcón. 'He being our most valuable witness of all.'

'I spoke to Serrano and Baena before I came here and they've come up against the same brick wall,' said Pérez. 'El Pulmón was late with his product, so there would have been plenty of his clients out on the street. He'd also have been running *and* with Estévez's blood down his front. There must have been fifty people who saw him. Only Carlos Puerta has come forward.'

'So why was Puerta prepared to talk?' asked Parrado.

'He said he was a friend of El Pulmón,' said Falcón. 'He was very upset about the girl, Julia Valdés, getting killed. There's more to his story than he's prepared to admit, but getting it out of him is a different matter.'

'I'll go back to him later this evening or tomorrow with the Narcs,' said Pérez.

'So, Puerta is unreliable, which means we have to find El Pulmón,' said Parrado.

'If I was El Pulmón, I would go to ground as far away from my regular haunts as possible,' said Ramírez.

'We do know he owned a car,' said Pérez, 'but it's not in Las Tres Mil any more. Traffic are looking for it.'

'In that case he could be out of Seville by now,' said Ramírez.

'He used to be a *novillero*,' said Falcón. 'Find the name of his sponsor and see if he has any old friends in that community.'

'He hasn't been in the bullfight game for years,' said Pérez.

'Work back, Emilio,' said Falcón. 'He's not going to go anywhere near his drug contacts. Family is equally unlikely. So it's old friends, and the ones from the bullfight game are the most likely to stick by him in his hour of need.'

'Especially if they've got gypsy blood as well,' said Ramírez.

'I'd like the DNA from the blood samples belonging to the nine-millimetre shooter,' said Cortés. 'If, as I'm hoping, we've still got Sokolov's DNA on file and we can get a match, that would put him at the crime scene in Las Tres Mil and then the girl who saw him in Calle Bustos Tavera would put him at the Marisa Moreno scene, too.'

'I'm not sure the witness we've got, who saw him and his two "comrades" in Calle Bustos Tavera, is reliable enough for court,' said Ramírez.

'Why not?' asked Parrado.

'Saturday night – she'd been using drugs.'

'If we can put Sokolov there, it will at least inform us,' said Cortés.

'Both Marisa and El Pulmón had direct contact with Russians. We believe that Marisa had been coerced, through threats to her sister who was working for the Russians as a prostitute, to start a relationship with Esteban Calderón and fulfil certain tasks related to the 6th June bomb conspiracy,' said Falcón.

'And El Pulmón?'

'I don't think there's a connection between him and the 6th June conspiracy,' said Falcón. 'This was just business. But it looks as if Nikita Sokolov, the weightlifter, was involved in clearing up the loose end of Marisa Moreno, and he's now made a mistake in failing to kill El Pulmón. If we can find El Pulmón, we can use him to locate Nikita Sokolov, and if we can charge Sokolov with the two killings in Las Tres Mil, that will give us some leverage in the case of Marisa Moreno.'

'Matching DNA from the paper suits to unknowns on a database is going to take longer than seeing if we have a DNA sample for Sokolov and matching the samples from El Pulmón's apartment,' said Parrado. 'So let's do that first.'

'We've still got the problem of finding either of them,' said Ramírez.

'Nikita Sokolov will be very keen to find El Pulmón. He's

the only credible witness we might get who'd be willing to place him in his apartment as the shooter,' said Falcón. 'I'll talk to my brother, Paco, as well. After his own accident in the ring he's always tried to help injured *toreros*.'

The meeting broke up while Parrado was called out for an urgent consultation on another case. Everybody turned on their mobiles, went to the windows to make calls.

Falcón called his bull-breeding brother, worked through the excuses for not having gone out to the farm for months.

'Paco, a question for you on your specialist subject,' said Falcón, hurrying things along. 'Do you remember a *novillero* called El Pulmón?'

'Roque Barba, you mean. El Pulmón was the name they gave him *after* his accident,' said Paco. 'I remember it. Got a horn in the chest. When they moved him back to Seville after his initial surgery, I went to see him. I told him if he needed any help to call me. That was three years ago. I saw him a few times in the months after he first came out of hospital. I tried to persuade him to come up to the farm to work. Then we lost touch.'

'A lot has happened since then, Paco, and not much of it good,' said Falcón. 'He became a heroin dealer in Las Tres Mil.'

'A dealer? Shit, that's bad.'

'The thing is, we need to find him.'

'This sounds like trouble.'

'He *is* in a lot of trouble, but not from us,' said Falcón. 'He's gone into hiding after a Russian gangster tried to kill him.'

'I've just seen something on Canal Sur about a shooting in Las Tres Mil. Two people dead,' said Paco.

'That was the incident. And now we need to find him before the Russian gangster does.'

'Well, he's not here, if that's what you're asking.'

'I want you to use your contacts to find out if he still has any friends from his *novillero* days. Somewhere he could hole

229

up and get watered and fed,' said Falcón. 'That's all I want you to do. I don't want you to talk to him, Paco. That's important. I just want some ideas about where he might be, and we'll do the rest.'

'He didn't kill either of those people in his apartment, did he?'

'No,' said Falcón. 'The gangster did that.'

'What's the worst that can happen to him?'

'That the gangster finds him first.'

'And from your side?'

'We want to protect him because we want him to testify against the gangster. The worst charge against him will be possession of an illegal firearm.'

'I'll see what I can do.'

Falcón went back to the table. The others finished their calls. Parrado came back into the room. The meeting resumed.

'Anything else we should talk about now?' asked Parrado.

'I've just heard that the hair and semen deposit from the paper suits does not match any of the Russian DNA we have on our CICO database,' said Díaz.

'That was quicker than you thought,' said Parrado.

'The database is smaller than I thought,' said Díaz.

'I spoke to the Sex Crimes squad in Málaga and Nikita Sokolov was definitely Vasili Lukyanov's partner in the assault on that local girl. He beat her up and held her down, but insisted he did not have sex with her,' said Cortés. 'The good news is that they do have a sample of Nikita Sokolov's DNA.'

'Felipe in Forensics has confirmed that he'll have the DNA from the blood samples of the unknown in El Pulmón's apartment generated by eleven p.m. tonight,' said Pérez.

'Good. Get that together with Cortés,' said Parrado. 'Now we know the direction we're heading in, let's find Nikita Sokolov and El Pulmón before they find each other.'

18

Santa María La Blanca, Seville – Monday, 18th September 2006, 20.15 hrs

They were sitting outside in the square in front of the church of Santa María La Blanca, which had just turned golden in the late evening light. Jackets were on the back of their chairs, top buttons undone, ties loosened. Beers stood in frosted glasses in front of them and a girl offloaded plates of *jamón*, fried anchovies, *patatas bravas* in a piquant tomato sauce, and some bread and olives. The talk was of Nikita Sokolov, but it was vague, amused, slightly fatigued after a working weekend and a long Monday.

'OK, so let's think about this scientifically,' said Ramírez. 'How tall do you think Sokolov is?'

'He's small – one metre sixty-six,' said Cortés. 'The closer you are to the ground, the less distance you have to lift the weights. And he's probably at least ten kilos heavier than he was in his Olympic days. I'd say closer to ninety kilos. I think a .38 is the bare minimum you'd need to knock someone like that over.'

'How high is the table in El Pulmón's apartment, Emilio?'

'Seventy-five centimetres.'

'Add two for the gun, that's seventy-seven,' said Ramírez. 'Where would a bullet have hit a guy one metre sixty-six tall?'

'In the leg or hip, if you're normal,' said Falcón. 'But Carlos Puerta didn't describe Sokolov as limping when he got into his car after the shooting.'

'Puerta's not reliable.'

'He could have been hit on the hand or wrist,' said Falcón.

'But would a hand or wrist injury have knocked him over?' asked Cortés.

'He might have dropped to the floor as a reflex action to the shock of the noise,' said Falcón. 'It was hot, no air-con in the apartment; El Pulmón would have been in a shirt, nowhere to pack his gun, so he hid it under the magazine. All he wanted was a bang to distract everybody in the room and make his move. Sokolov hit the deck as an evasive action.'

'But he *was* hit,' said Ramírez. 'A wrist or a hand shot is a better explanation of the dripping blood. Bleeding from the leg would get soaked into the trousers, the drips wouldn't be so consistent in the room or going down the stairs.'

'All the drips were on the right-hand side of the stairs going down,' said Emilio.

'OK, right hand or wrist, maybe right leg or hip,' said Ramírez. 'The next question is: who is Nikita Sokolov working for?'

'If he's a friend of Vasili Lukyanov, and we think Lukyanov was defecting from Leonid Revnik to Yuri Donstov, then . . .' said Falcón.

'And we haven't seen Sokolov on the Costa del Sol for a while.'

'My intelligence source told me that Yuri Donstov had set up a heroin-smuggling route from Uzbekistan to Europe and chose Seville as his centre of operations,' said Falcón. 'El Pulmón was a heroin dealer. The Narcs say that the heroin coming into Las Tres Mil always used to be Italian product, then things started changing. It looks to me as if Nikita Sokolov was trying to create an exclusive market for Donstov's product in Las Tres Mil and, for one reason or another, El Pulmón was not in agreement.'

They worked on the tapas for a few minutes, drank beer. Ramírez ordered more.

'Do you think it was Revnik or Donstov who was involved in the 6th June bombing?' asked Cortés.

'CICO in Madrid think Yuri Donstov has been operating since September 2005, which is about nine months before the 6th June bombing,' said Falcón. 'I'm not sure that's long enough to develop a conspiracy of that complexity.'

'All they had to do was plant a small bomb,' said Pérez.

'But a lot had to be put in place beforehand. Think about the political element: the Fuerza Andalucía party, the creation of their new leader,' said Falcón. 'I don't think a businessman like Lucrecio Arenas would have allowed anybody into the conspiracy who he hadn't been doing business with for quite some time. I always thought that he was dealing with people whose money he'd moved around the world while he was working at the Banco Omni, but maybe I'm wrong.'

'So you favour Leonid Revnik as the perpetrator?' asked Díaz. 'Except that he'd only been in place since his predecessor fled to Dubai in June 2005.'

'I suppose I do. There's no reason why Revnik and his predecessor shouldn't have been in contact with each other,' said Falcón. 'But having just learnt about Yuri Donstov, I'm beginning to think *he* might have found a role for himself in a new conspiracy that has its roots in the 6th June bombing. That was an attempt to gain political power in the whole of Andalucía. Now I think the sights have been lowered. Donstov seems to be shaping up to run a major criminal enterprise. The delivery of the disks by Vasili

Lukyanov was a crucial element, not just in the enterprise, but in a more localized project. The disks are going to give him leverage, especially with I4IT and Horizonte, whose executives had been filmed in compromising situations.'

'What is this project?' asked Díaz.

'I don't know,' said Falcón. 'But I think this time it's not about political power but more about money.'

'We didn't talk about the money,' said Ramírez. 'I forgot to mention that this afternoon Prosegur took away the money found in the boot of Vasili Lukyanov's Range Rover. It's in the Banco de Bilbao now.'

'How much?' asked Díaz.

'Seven million, seven hundred and forty-eight thousand two hundred euros,' said Ramírez. 'I was there when Elvira signed it off.'

'You know, Javier, if you're looking to nail the Russians for the June 6th bombing I doubt you're going to be able to do it through Nikita Sokolov,' said Cortés. 'I don't think he's the sort of guy who's going to talk. You might be able to stick him with the murders in Las Tres Mil, but that's not going to help you. He's a *vor-v-zakone*, and their code, like the Sicilian mafia's *omerta*, is silence.'

'And the big names we're talking about, they're invisible men,' said Díaz. 'We only got a photograph of Revnik's predecessor at the beginning of 2005. We have no shot of Leonid Revnik and only the old gulag shot of Yuri Donstov. All these guys could walk past us in the street and we wouldn't know.'

'And not one of the current charges against Revnik's predecessor is murder,' said Cortés. 'He was arrested for money-laundering, falsifying documents, fraudulent bankruptcies and being a member of a criminal organization. No drugs. No people-trafficking. No extortion. No murder.'

A mobile vibrated. Pérez took the call.

'Do you have anybody on the inside of Revnik's gang?' said Falcón, looking at Cortés and Díaz.

'We have informers,' said Díaz.

'How high up the ladder?' said Falcón. 'All these gangster-owned businesses must be run by local people.'

'But none of them get anywhere near Revnik,' said Cortés.

Díaz exchanged a look with Cortés, whose shake of the head was barely perceptible in the dying light in the square.

'That was Traffic,' said Pérez. 'They've found El Pulmón's car in Calle Hernán Ruiz. There's a bloodstained T-shirt on the back seat. I'd better get down there.'

'Take Felipe from Forensics with you,' said Ramírez, sighing. 'I'll come too; it's on my way.'

Falcón paid the bill, exchanged phone numbers with Cortés and Díaz, who were still finishing their beers. He headed back to the Palacio de Justicia to pick up his car.

They caught up with him in the Murillo Gardens.

'Sorry about that, Javier,' said Cortés. 'We just had to get clearance before we talked to you about our informers and we didn't want to do it in company.'

'We *have* just developed an informer close to Leonid Revnik,' said Díaz. 'She's a twenty-five-year-old woman from Málaga . . .'

'Who is completely fucking gorgeous,' said Cortés. 'She could be having the time of her life with any footballer or film star you'd care to name, but *she*, the poor stupid bitch, has chosen a gangster by the name of Viktor Belenki.'

'I've heard that name before,' said Falcón, remembering Pablo from the CNI mentioning him. 'He's Revnik's right-hand man and runs all his construction companies in the Costa del Sol. So, why does the girl inform on him?'

'We're still right at the beginning of developing her,' said Cortés. 'Last month we found her brother on a yacht with some of his stupid friends and seven hundred kilos of hashish, and he's not the sort of kid who'd last very long in a high-security prison.'

'Does she have a name?'

'At the moment we're calling her Carmen,' said Díaz.

The light was out over the doorway to Falcón's house on Calle Bailén. He reversed up and left the car on the cobbles between the orange trees. As he went up to the door he stumbled and a streak of fear flashed through his guts as someone came from the shadows and caught him by the arm.

'Steady on, Javier,' said Mark Flowers. 'Been drinking?'

'I've had a couple of beers, but not nearly enough,' said Falcón. 'I was wondering when you'd come . . .'

'Crawling out of the woodwork?'

'To see me.'

'Well, here I am,' said Flowers. 'Shall we go in?'

Falcón never knew where he stood with Mark Flowers, but then, that was the way Flowers liked it. He wanted to be unreadable. What was the point of being a Communications Officer in the American Consulate in Seville if the whole world could tell that you were really a CIA operative reporting to Madrid?

Flowers was a handsome fifty-four-year-old, much married and divorced. His hair had thinned dramatically over the last couple of years so that he'd had to resort to the comb-over. The hair should have been grey, too, but he dyed it. And Falcón suspected that, during a long vacation in the United States, Flowers had resorted to some plastic surgery around his eyes and neck.

'Are you in mourning, Mark?' asked Falcón, now realizing the reason why he hadn't been able to see Flowers outside was that he was dressed completely in black.

'It makes me look slim,' said Flowers, shaking the loose short-sleeved shirt out over his thickened stomach. 'You get to my age and weight and you need all the help you can get.'

They came into the patio of the house, the bronze boy was running across the fountain, the water was as flat as a mirror.

'Shall we sit out?' said Falcón. 'You'll want a whisky. I suppose you've already eaten.'

'You know me, Javier. I'm all done by six thirty.'

'Glenlivet?'

'That's a nice change from the usual peat bog you serve.'

'As you know, I went to London,' said Falcón. 'And I'm always thinking of you.'

'Ice, no water,' said Flowers.

Falcón went to the kitchen, came back with the drinks. A cold beer for himself. Some olives. A bowl of crisps.

'I've had some long days recently,' said Falcón, handing him the tumbler of whisky. 'Lost track of where I am. What time is it?'

Flowers was just about to look at his watch. Remembered.

'You're not going to catch me out that easily, Javier.'

It was their little joke since Falcón had noticed Flowers looking ostentatiously at his watch one day – a Patek Philippe. At the time it had meant nothing to Falcón, until he saw in an in-flight magazine that it retailed for €19,500. He'd brought this up with Flowers, who'd said: 'You never actually own a Patek Philippe, Javier. You merely look after it for the next generation.' Later Falcón had found out that Flowers had quoted him the strap line from the Patek Philippe advertisement, and he'd started teasing him. One of the reasons Falcón did this was to feel more relaxed in the company of a man he did not entirely trust.

'Long days,' said Flowers, setting his tumbler down on the table, 'in London.'

'And here.'

'What's happening here?'

'Consuelo's youngest child was kidnapped on Saturday while I was in London.'

Flowers nodded. He knew that. Which meant that he'd spoken to the CNI.

'I'm sorry,' he said. 'That's a big pressure. What the fuck is that all about, Javier?'

Falcón recited the litany about Marisa Moreno and the threatening phone calls from the Russians. Flowers wanted to know how the Russians got into the mix and Falcón began at the beginning with Lukyanov's car accident, the money, the disks and Ferrera making the link to Marisa's sister, Margarita.

'That is some heavy police work, Javier.'

'I've got a very good squad. They're all prepared to do that little bit extra, and that's where you get your breaks,' said Falcón. 'You might be interested in the identity of one of the guys we saw on the disks.'

'Don't tell me it was somebody in the American Consulate – I have to look them in the eye every day.'

'A guy called Juan Valverde.'

Flowers didn't react.

'Should I have heard of him?' asked Flowers. 'If he's a soccer player, I'm lost, Javier.'

'You remember that company I asked you to investigate for me back in June?'

'I4IT, owned by Cortland Fallenbach and Morgan Havilland.'

'Juan Valverde is their Chief Executive Officer in Europe,' said Falcón. 'Do you know if they have any investment plans for Seville, or in southern Spain?'

'I just got the information you asked for back in June,' said Flowers. 'I'm not following their stock, Javier.'

'There's another guy on those disks you *will* have heard of.'

'Try me.'

'Charles Taggart.'

'The fallen preacher?'

'He's a consultant for I4IT.'

'On what?' asked Flowers brutally.

'Religious matters?' said Falcón, and they both laughed. 'I thought you were supposed to be a *reformed* sinner to be a part of I4IT.'

'Once a sinner, always a sinner,' said Flowers. 'I don't believe in this redemption shit: confess your sins, clean your slate, get out there and commit some more. Just keeps the Church in work.'

'What do you do with *your* sins, Mark?'

'Keep them to myself,' said Flowers. 'If I confessed them all, I'd age a priest, and myself, by a hundred years.'

'What was your line, Mark?' said Falcón. 'It takes a profound moral certitude to behave immorally.'

'In the spy game, Javier,' said Flowers.

They drank. Flowers breathed in the heavy night air and crunched ice with his teeth.

'London,' said Flowers. 'You know how it happened? I got a call from my station head in Madrid telling me that you're running a rogue agent and the Brits are . . . what was that expression they use? Hopping mad. I like that. I said: "How can he be running a rogue agent? If an agent's gone rogue, nobody's running him." So what the fuck are you doing, Javier?'

'I have an agent . . .'

'Let's call him Yacoub, so we don't get confused,' said Flowers. 'He is your *only* agent.'

'Yacoub is under extraordinary pressure.'

'What did he expect, going into this business?' said Flowers. 'Pressure's what we've lived on since the beginning of time, since we've felt the need for our genes to survive, since the first cavewoman saw her man asleep on the floor and thought he should be out hunting. Pressure is a constant. It's like gravity, without it we'd drift aimlessly.'

'I know what pressure is, Mark,' said Falcón. 'If your station head is talking to the British then you'll know that the GICM have recruited Yacoub's son, Abdullah, as a mujahideen.'

'That's almost standard procedure for an agent like Yacoub,' said Flowers. 'A group like that won't expose themselves to an outsider with questionable friends and lifestyle without getting some insurance.'

'I didn't see it.'

'That's because you're an amateur,' said Flowers. 'A raw recruit, who was doing the recruiting. The senior CNI guy, Juan, he would have seen it even if Pablo didn't. They just wouldn't have told you about it. Didn't want to confuse your mind.'

'You mean they didn't want me to fail in my recruiting mission.'

Flowers shrugged, throwing up his hands, as if it was all so obvious it wasn't worth talking about.

'This is the problem I've got with Yacoub,' said Falcón. 'He doesn't trust anybody any more. He describes himself as being in the goldfish bowl, with all these agencies and his enemies looking on.'

'Maybe more like a murky aquarium,' said Flowers. 'I hear he's good at keeping himself out of sight when he wants to.'

'Wouldn't you?'

'I've got nothing to hide.'

'You still hide it.'

'Look, Javier, Yacoub is a valuable asset. He's the perfect agent, who has got to the heart of the enemy. We all have a vested interest in keeping him and his son alive and happy. We want the sort of intelligence he can give us,' said Flowers. 'We, more than anybody else, understand what he's going through. There's no reason for him – or you – to stop talking to us. It's the only way we can help.'

'When I was about to recruit Yacoub, you told me that he didn't like Americans. That's why he wouldn't work for you.'

'And what's so different about you and the CNI?'

'He won't talk to the CNI, he'll only talk to me, because he trusts me.'

'Does he?' said Flowers, fixing him with a look across the table. 'Why didn't he tell you that he'd already been trained?'

'Probably the same reason that Juan and Pablo didn't warn me about the sort of tricks the GICM would play on Yacoub. Not distrust, just omission,' said Falcón. 'And, anyway, this previous training was limited to making sure he wasn't being followed and losing a tail if he was. Not full spy craft.'

'How would you describe Yacoub's state of mind since you met him in Madrid?'

'The fact that you know we met in Madrid supports the goldfish-bowl theory,' said Falcón. 'You're all looking at him and you don't trust what you see.'

'This is the War on Terror, Javier. It's called pooling resources.'

'He was distraught in Madrid. Nervous. Desperate. Evasive. He alarmed me. He'd thought he'd "lost" his son and it had made him, in my estimation, unreliable.'

'So how did he get to be so much more persuasive in London?'

'He'd come to terms with his situation. It had made him calmer.'

'He lied to you in Madrid.'

'Not so much lying as the paranoia giving him the inclination to mislead.'

'What happened to *you* between Madrid and London?' said Flowers, keeping the questions coming thick and fast. 'One moment you're nervous enough to seek advice from Pablo, the next you're so relaxed you're going it alone and giving Yacoub a free rein.'

'But I *had* told Pablo.'

'A limited amount.'

'Only what I knew, but I *had* told him,' said Falcón. 'That was already a betrayal of Yacoub's trust but, given his volatile state and my inexperience, I felt it was a necessary step.'

'So telling Pablo gave you some comfort. I can understand that,' said Flowers. 'But why wouldn't you let the Brits listen in on your conversation with Yacoub in Brown's Hotel?'

'I wanted to re-establish trust. I couldn't do that with MI5 listening in.'

'And how did Yacoub persuade you that he was still trustworthy?'

'Instinct.'

'You know, there are a lot of people out there who can make you believe that they love you,' said Flowers. 'Especially when it's so important to them that they believe it themselves.'

'What can you do about it?'

'Let other people take a look,' said Flowers. 'People who are capable of total objectivity.'

'But not people who are paid and sworn in by a government which has interests.'

'So Yacoub is protecting his son,' said Flowers, changing tack, 'and how many others?'

'Just one other person.'

'Is that person a lover?'

'You're not going to wring it out of me, Mark,' said Falcón. 'I know you're clever. Yacoub does, too. You've carefully reminded me that Yacoub has lied to me, that I've already betrayed him because I needed the support of the CNI. So what's one more little betrayal? And the answer is: possible death. Yacoub will lose control, because all the intelligence agencies will set about protecting their interests and that will create more unknowns. A decision could easily be taken that, despite Yacoub's intelligence coups, he is expendable.'

'You're making this sound very serious,' said Flowers, 'as

if there could be grave geopolitical consequences. You're making it sound like something we really have to know.'

'But not yet.'

'We talked about pressure earlier,' said Flowers. 'The one thing I can tell you, Javier, is that I know about pressure. I am an expert in pressure . . . exerting it, I mean.'

'The thing about pressure, Mark, is that it's always exerted in order to cause pain. The GICM keep Yacoub under control by embracing his son. The Russians want to stop me from investigating their role in the 6th June Seville bombing, so they kidnap Consuelo's youngest child. Even we do it in the police force. We encourage a woman to inform on her criminal lover by threatening her brother with a heavy jail term.'

'That's right, Javier. We're all in the same business. The good guys and the bad guys. So what's your point?'

'Try offering solutions instead of threats,' said Falcón.

'What could I do for you that would make you feel sufficiently indebted to me that you would tell me what Yacoub is up to?'

'If you could get Consuelo's son back for me,' said Falcón. 'That would engender an enormous sense of gratitude in me.'

Flowers nodded, the light in the patio meant that only half his face was visible, the other half was completely opaque. The one seemed to inform the other, thought Falcón. Threats were always a lot easier to pull off than solutions.

19

It seemed later than it was. Flowers had only just left. Falcón sat in the patio, slumped in his chair, feet spread wide. He had been exhausted by the day and its lack of progress and, followed by the relentlessness of the CIA man's questions, he'd felt his lids growing heavier and his shoulder blades tightening. Now he felt as empty as that husk of a plant hiding in the corner of the patio but, with Darío in the centre of his consciousness, his mind was alive with the horror of the boy's situation and his helplessness beside it.

He began to wonder whether it was his particular fate to be haunted by abused, traumatized or persecuted children. Ever since he'd discovered how ruthlessly his father, Francisco Falcón, had exploited him as a small boy, he seemed to have become a magnet for these most vulnerable members of society. It did not escape him either, the appalling irony of his compulsion to discover what had happened to Raúl Jiménez's missing son, Arturo. Then, having found that he'd been brought up in Morocco as

244

Yacoub Diouri, to exploit him by making him an agent of Spanish intelligence, the CNI.

The patio was dark. He'd turned off the light. Wooden beams groaned somewhere far off in the large old house. He leaned forward, pinched the skin between his eyes, trying to tear out this ghastly nexus, but all that came to him were images in the chain of events of the last few years. An orphaned child being carried away by his aunt, two teenagers used as sex slaves buried in a shallow grave, four dead children covered by their pinafores after the 6th June bombing had destroyed their pre-school. He slapped his legs, stood up, cleared away the empty glasses and remains of crisps and olives, took them back to the kitchen. He hoped this mild activity would stop the fever in his brain. This is the blight of modern mankind, he thought, a world so full of accessible information, lives so crammed with work and relationships, people so constantly connectable that we've all developed what Alicia Aguado would probably call tachy-rumination. Nothing meditative about it, just a feverish mental grazing.

A bell rang, followed by three blunt thuds on the huge wooden door. Mark Flowers coming back with more questions. The afterthoughts. He made his way back through the house, under the gallery, around the patio. More thuds on the door, like a dull ache, followed by a sharper tapping. He slapped on the lights, opened the smaller door within the massive oak gates. Consuelo was standing there on one leg with her shoe in her hand.

'I couldn't seem to make any impression with my fist,' she said, slipping her shoe back on. 'You should get the bell fixed, or have a knocker fitted.'

'The bell works fine,' said Falcón, 'it just takes time to get from one end of the house to the other.'

'Are you going to invite me in?'

'Please,' he said.

245

They kissed formally on both cheeks, manoeuvred around each other awkwardly, and headed for the patio. She settled herself at the table. He offered her a drink. She'd take a small manzanilla sherry. He brought two and some olives. They sat in silence staring at the same point, exquisitely aware of each other's presence, but behaving as if there was some performance going on in which they could take no interest because of the vastness of what had come between them.

'I'm surprised to see you here after what happened the other night,' said Falcón.

'I didn't expect to have to come and see you,' she said.

'To *have* to come and see me?'

'We've been thrown together, Javier. It seems we cannot avoid each other,' she said. 'It's the only explanation I've got for what is happening. When we first met I was your suspect. Then I became your lover.'

'Then you left me,' he said.

'But I came back, Javier,' she said. 'Thanks to Alicia, I came back a different person.'

'And now?' said Falcón. 'Do we have Alicia to thank for you coming here this evening?'

'Not this time,' she said. 'I spoke to her. She listened. It's made me feel stronger.'

'And that didn't . . . No, I forgot, you *had* to come back,' said Falcón. 'I know *why* you're here, because I can't stop thinking about Darío myself, but who or what particularly has thrown us together this time?'

'This time, Javier, it's our enemies.'

They looked each other directly in the eye for the first time since she'd appeared at the door.

'Does that mean you've heard from the Russians?'

She nodded.

'But I told Inspector Jefe Tirado to call me if there were any developments,' said Falcón. 'He assured me nothing had happened. No phone calls . . .'

'*I* called *them*.'

Falcón blinked. She told him about the email and the call she'd made from the bottom of next-door's garden.

'And we have no record of this conversation,' said Falcón.

She handed him two sheets of A4 with the transcript of the dialogue as best she could remember it.

'I was not calm when I made that call,' she said. 'I realize now that I was stupid. I reacted in a state of excitement and panic, which was how they expected me to react.'

Falcón nodded, read the transcript several times.

'Talk to me, Javier,' she said, unable to bear the silence any longer. 'Tell me what you make of it. Ask me questions. Every detail, from the top.'

'When did this happen?' he asked.

'The email was timed two p.m., but I didn't see it until after four, then I had to charge the phone and open an account. I made the call at around five.'

'Five hours ago,' he said.

'I didn't want to call you. You can see how complicated it is,' she said. 'I only wanted to do this face to face. I've been waiting outside for the American to leave.'

'Tell me about the voice,' said Falcón. 'Was there only one voice?'

'The first voice was foreign. I don't know what Spanish sounds like spoken by a Russian, but I'm certain it was a foreigner. All he said was *Diga* and *Momentito*, but I could tell.'

'So the second voice was the one you had this conversation with, and he was Spanish.'

'Yes, definitely Spanish-speaking, but not from Spain. I'd say South American.'

'Or Cuban?' said Falcón. 'A lot of Cubans still speak Russian.'

'That must be it. I wasn't listening to the finer points of accent. I was concentrating on what he was saying and his

247

tone. He was quite gentle with me. The second time he asked whether I knew why Darío had been kidnapped, he put it a different way.'

'He said: "Do you understand why your son has been taken from you?"' said Falcón.

'He said it like a doctor who wanted to explain the necessity of Darío's quarantine. As if he had a contagious disease and it was better for him. It made me very emotional.'

'The next bit about . . .'

'That's about you, isn't it?' she said. 'I was angry and, I can't deny it, Javier, I still am.'

'Just remember, Consuelo, that I am your friend,' said Falcón. 'Whatever this has done to us, I am still your friend. I want to get Darío back as much as you do. *I* did not kidnap him and it's not *me* threatening him with harm, and I will do everything I can to bring him back safely.'

'That's why I said, it's our enemies who've brought us together this time,' said Consuelo. 'I only understood that by working on the transcript.'

'They are trying to do something very tricky here. They want to remind you that I am responsible for all this – not them,' said Falcón. 'But they also need me to be your friend because they know that what you're asking of me is very difficult.'

'I realize that they want me to corrupt you,' said Consuelo. 'They believe that by holding my son they will have reduced me to their own moral level and that I will make you my friend, or even my lover, in order to corrupt you for my own purposes.'

'You don't need to talk me through this, Consuelo.'

'I do. I need you to understand that I know exactly what they're doing,' said Consuelo. 'They're making me a whore, in the hope that I will entice you to corrupt yourself, and I hate them for it. I could kill them for that, let alone taking Darío.'

And in that moment he fell for her all over again. If he'd thought that he loved her in the airport on Saturday he'd been mistaken, because what filled him now was an admiration so complete that he wanted to kiss those lips that had spoken such words.

He knew then that he would do anything for her.

'The one thing that is not established here, and given the stress of the call you were unlikely to think of it, is whether they have Darío or not,' said Falcón.

'You mean I didn't ask for some proof that he was alive?'

'Not exactly. I'm sure that Darío is being held by Russians; we're just not sure which group,' said Falcón.

He explained how Leonid Revnik had taken over the Russian mafia on the Costa del Sol after his predecessor had fled to Dubai and how Yuri Donstov had arrived in Seville. He also laid out his theory of Russian mafia involvement in the Seville bombing.

'But why would the Russians involve themselves in something like that?' asked Consuelo.

'Because they were invited to do so by the conspirators,' said Falcón. 'Lucrecio Arenas and César Benito didn't know how to plant a bomb, they needed men of violence to do it for them. They had access to these people presumably because they were doing some money-laundering for them. The idea was that the Russians would be rewarded in the political fallout after the bombing. It didn't happen. And not only that, their whole criminal organization was put at risk. The Russians did the only thing possible and assassinated the Catholic conspiracy's ringleaders before they could implicate them.'

'And this huge amount of money and the disks?'

'They represent a complication. They came into our hands because of a defection from Revnik to Donstov by a gangster called Vasili Lukyanov,' said Falcón. 'It means that men in both groups were possibly responsible for the Seville bomb and also that both groups will want to get their hands on those disks, because they will give them the leverage they need.'

'What exactly is on those disks?'

'They show powerful people having sex with prostitutes. The most important people on those disks, as far as my investigation is concerned, are the ones who are representatives of the two companies who I think originally initiated the Seville bombing: an American corporation, called I4IT, who own a Spanish holding company in Barcelona, called Horizonte.'

'And those companies are now *excluding* the Russians because they no longer need, or want, their brand of violence.'

'I have no proof of any of this,' said Falcón. 'All I know is that the original idea behind the Seville bomb was to take political control of the Andalucían state parliament and I can only assume that there would ultimately be economic rewards for those involved. What's happening now is smaller scale. It's just business. I'm not sure what the business is, but it's probably something to do with construction in or around Seville. I think the Russians got their foot in the door with Lucrecio Arenas and César Benito, and they still want their reward for the dirty work they've done.'

'So whichever mafia group holds the disks can exert pressure on I4IT and Horizonte.'

'My guess is that Darío is being held by Yuri Donstov, who was expecting delivery of the disks from Vasili Lukyanov when the car accident put his whole strategy in jeopardy.'

'Does Leonid Revnik know that Lukyanov has disappeared with the disks?'

'We assume so, because Lukyanov's best friend was found shot dead in the woods behind Estepona.'

'So it could just as easily be Revnik holding Darío, trying to get back in the game?'

'If Lukyanov had the foresight to ensure that he had the originals and there were no copies, then yes,' said Falcón.

'If I was him, I'd have made sure of that,' said Consuelo. 'That money and the disks were probably in the same safe and he stole both.'

'Lukyanov ran *puti clubs*. He controlled the girls. So he was probably responsible for the secret filming of what they did with these men,' said Falcón, tapping the transcript.

'And the money?'

'I'm thinking about that,' said Falcón. 'They're asking for the return of €8.2 million, but Ramírez told me there was only €7.75 million accounted for.'

'Light-fingered Guardia Civil on the motorway?' said Consuelo.

'Or the Russians are lying.'

'Or they don't know. They're guessing.'

Falcón paced slowly around the patio.

'You're very calm,' he said, suddenly. 'I don't know how . . .'

'Because in making me their agent they've given me power,' said Consuelo. 'I know nothing will happen to Darío while I can still do things for them.'

'A further complication,' said Falcón, ideas occurring to him all the time. 'The reason we need proof that whoever we're talking to *is* holding Darío, is that they could *both* say that they're holding him.'

'So far I've only been contacted by one group,' said Consuelo. 'And they used an email address that is strictly for friends and family.'

'You think only Darío could have given them that address?' asked Falcón. 'Do you have any protection on that computer? It's a family PC. You probably don't even need a password to use it. Anybody could have found that out.'

'All right,' said Consuelo, thinking desperately. 'There's

251

been no media coverage yet, so only the group that's performed the abduction will know about it.'

'That's in the perfect world,' said Falcón, 'but these mafia groups have connections everywhere. The corruption is deep. They've penetrated the Guardia Civil and it wouldn't surprise me if they had someone in the Jefatura.'

'So they would know if you called on other resources, too,' said Consuelo, alarmed.

Falcón nodded, feeling the box they were in getting tighter and darker.

'What . . . what about their demands?' said Consuelo, the earlier calm beginning to dissipate now that she could sense their isolation.

'The first obstacle is the money,' said Falcón. 'We can't get our hands on the cash. It's already in the Banco de Bilbao and I have no authority over it. That lies with Comisario Elvira, and we don't want him involved in any of this.'

'The Russians probably know that, or have guessed it,' said Consuelo hopefully. 'They probably felt they had to ask for the money, especially that *amount* of money, or they'd have made the disks look too important. They'll be understanding about the money.'

'They'll have to be,' said Falcón. 'It's not a possibility.'

'If the Russians have their people in the Jefatura, why don't they just lift the disks themselves?'

'No, that's true, we're not exactly a high-security institution,' said Falcón, 'the disks are in a safe in the evidence room, which during office hours is heavily used and manned, especially as the money was kept there until it was moved this afternoon. Only two people have the key and the combination of that safe: Elvira and myself.'

'And there are only the originals in existence?'

'No, there are copies of parts of the disks on the Homicide squad's computer and to access it you'd need not only the passwords to the system, but also the encryption software to unscramble the shots.'

They fell silent again. Falcón focused on the problem. If, as Consuelo's business brain had intuited, I4IT/Horizonte were excluding the Russians from whatever this new deal was, then it could be crucial for the Russians to know that Juan Valverde, Antonio Ramos and Charles Taggart were going to be in Seville tomorrow evening and night.

'You've gone quiet on me again, Javier.'

Falcón reached for his mobile, called Ramírez.

'How did you know that the money from the Lukyanov accident had left the Jefatura?' he asked him.

'Because you'd signed the money into the Jefatura it was technically Homicide squad evidence, so I had to accompany Comisario Elvira to the evidence room and sign it over to him, so that he could sign it over to Prosegur for delivery to the bank,' said Ramírez.

'Was the money in the safe?'

'As much as they could fit in,' said Ramírez. 'There was still one block in the Prosegur box.'

'Did you see inside the safe when Elvira opened it?'

'Sure. We took the money out together.'

'What was left in there?'

'The disks from the car accident.'

'Did you see the safe locked afterwards?'

'Elvira locked it.'

'No other copies of those disks were made?'

'The guy from the Jefatura's IT department came to our office. He took one, sometimes two, images from each piece of footage, which best showed the faces of the participants, and that's all we have on the Homicide computer.'

'What about the images you sent to me which I emailed to the CNI?'

'They were cropped faces only. No visible fucking. If somebody could access your computer, those shots wouldn't

253

be much use to them,' said Ramírez. 'What's bothering you?'

'Just making sure,' said Falcón. 'How did you and Pérez get on with El Pulmón's car?'

'His bloody fingerprints were all over it and there was a bloody T-shirt on the back seat. All blood samples in the car correspond to the Cuban, Miguel Estévez,' said Ramírez. 'That was as far as we got on site. The vehicle's been taken down to the Jefatura so that the forensics can go over it tomorrow.'

Consuelo's mobile, the one she'd used to call the Russians, rang. Falcón glanced at her. She looked at the screen.

'The restaurant,' she said, and took the call.

'Did anybody see El Pulmón leaving the vehicle?' asked Falcón.

'Not leaving the vehicle, but we've found an old guy who saw a man stripped to the waist, with a red stain over his chest and a dark stain on the front of his trousers, running down Calle Héroes de Toledo towards the centre of town.'

'Work on it, José Luis,' said Falcón. 'We need El Pulmón.'

'I've got Serrano and Baena on it. They were getting nowhere with the Narcs. I think this is a better bet. They'll be at it tomorrow morning, first thing.'

Falcón hung up. Consuelo finished her call.

'That's not the mobile that Inspector Jefe Tirado is supposed to be recording?'

'It's the one I used to call the Russians.'

'Was that them?'

'I gave the number to my restaurant manager before I came out.'

'Haven't you got your regular mobile with you?'

'The Russians aren't going to call me on that one. I left it at home.'

'Who knows you're here?'

'Nobody.'

'What about the people in your house?'

'They think I'm in bed,' said Consuelo. 'I went into my neighbour's garden, out through the front and took a cab here.'

'You don't trust the good guys any more?'

'I can't,' she said, looking desperate.

'All right,' said Falcón, holding his hands up to keep her calm. 'What did your restaurant manager want?'

'Somebody came in off the street a few minutes ago, gave one of the waiters an envelope and said he was to make sure that it was given to me tonight.'

20

The envelope lay on Consuelo's desk. She locked the door to her office and booted up the computer while Falcón put on latex gloves. The envelope was a jiffy bag with SRA JIMÉNEZ written on it in black felt-tip pen. Inside was a white envelope with the flap folded in, not stuck down. On a piece of white card was written: TO SPEAK TO DARÍO CALL 655926109. He held it up to Consuelo, who had now accessed her home email account and opened the single message in the inbox.

'This is timed at 22.20, about an hour after I left home,' she said. 'It says: "Our patience is not infinite. Call: 619238741."'

'So, both players at the table now,' said Falcón. 'One bluffing.'

'We'll call the new people first,' said Consuelo. 'See what they want and how they ask for it. We might get an idea which group they're from.'

'Make a demand,' said Falcón. 'You should ask to speak to Darío first. That's what they've offered, but they probably won't allow it. They won't want to give away too much too early. In a kidnapping such as this information will be released by degrees. "Do this and we'll tell you something

256

about him, do the next thing and we'll let you hear his voice . . ." Then they'll send a photo and finally they'll let you speak to him. We want to establish who is holding him, so we must ask for reasonable proof. Is there something about Darío that no ordinary person would know?'

'He has a red birthmark on the underside of his left arm near the armpit. We call it his strawberry,' she said.

'Tell them to ask Darío about his mark and what he calls it,' said Falcón. 'Have you got a dictaphone?'

She dug out a small digital dictaphone. They tested it. She turned it on, wiped her damp palms with tissues, picked up the phone, switched on the loudspeaker, dialled the number. She took a deep breath, summoned the performance of her life.

'*Diga*,' said a voice.

'My name is Consuelo Jiménez and I want to speak to Darío.'

'Wait.'

The phone changed hands.

'Señora Jiménez . . .'

'I received a message telling me to call this number if I wanted to speak to my son, Darío. Would you put him on the line, please.'

'There are some things we have to discuss first,' said the voice, in perfect Castilian Spanish.

'What things? You have my son. I have nothing of yours. There are no "things" to discuss apart from the return of my son, and that can be done after I've spoken to him.'

'Listen to me, Señora Jiménez. I can understand that you are very anxious about your son. You would like to speak to him, that is natural, but there are certain things we must establish first.'

'You are absolutely right –'

'May I say, Señora Jiménez, that I admire your calmness in this situation. Most mothers I know would be incapable of speaking to me like this on the phone.'

'I *would* cry, beat my breast and vomit with grief, if I thought that for one moment it would make any impression on you,' said Consuelo. 'But if you think I'm made of strong stuff, I *know* you're made of crueller stuff, and so human emotion is unlikely to move you to return my son. So this is what you get. Now, let's establish something before we go any further: I want to talk to my son.'

'That is not possible at the moment.'

'You see, you are already going back on your word,' said Consuelo. 'Your message is clear. It says –'

'I know what the message says, Señora Jiménez,' said the voice, with a bit of steel in it now. 'I wrote it. But you must be patient.'

'Don't talk to me about being patient. You will never comprehend the *im*patience of a mother who has had her child taken from her. So don't use that word again,' said Consuelo. 'If you won't let me speak to my son, which I regard as the ultimate proof that he is safe and well, then you must go to Darío and ask him about his mark and tell me what he says.'

'His mark?'

'Ask Darío, he will tell you all you need to know to convince me.'

'One moment, please.'

A long silence.

'Is there anybody there?' she asked, after some minutes.

'Please hold the line for a moment longer, Señora Jiménez,' said the voice. 'This is something for which permission is required.'

'Permission?'

'There is a higher authority in this matter. We are in contact with them now.'

More silence. After five long minutes the voice returned.

'Señora Jiménez, do you understand the nature of the people you are dealing with here?'

'If you mean: do I know you are members of a Russian

mafia group, then the answer is yes. Which group, I don't know.'

'Perhaps your friend Inspector Jefe Javier Falcón knows,' said the voice. 'Yes, we know you're there, Inspector Jefe, we saw you enter the restaurant together.'

'Are you associated with Leonid Revnik?' asked Falcón.

'That is correct,' said the voice. 'Señor Revnik has been away in Moscow. Since he took over the operations in the Costa del Sol some structural problems have developed in our organization in the Iberian Peninsula.'

'You mean Yuri Donstov has assumed control of certain pieces of business in Seville and had poached Vasili Lukyanov.'

'Señor Revnik was in Moscow for a meeting of the Supreme Council of the five most powerful Russian brigades with soldiers on the ground in Spain,' said the voice. 'They found that Yuri Donstov was responsible for the murders of two senior members of one of the brigades and has moved into trades where we have agreements with our Italian and Turkish friends about how certain things should be done. We cannot allow that. It was the unanimous decision of the Supreme Council that Yuri Donstov's operations be stopped and his group disbanded.'

'This is all very interesting,' said Consuelo, 'but what about my son?'

'You have to understand the geopolitical situation before we can get down to the discussion of the detail,' said the voice. 'And there is also the question of the Seville bombing.'

Silence.

'I'm listening,' said Falcón, and he was, with every cell in his body.

'We are holding the men responsible for the making of that bomb and the positioning of it in the mosque.'

Falcón's heart rate doubled, he could feel it ticking in his throat. Something like greed came over him and he had to stop himself from snatching at what the voice was holding

259

out to him. He reminded himself that everything is calcu-lated, nothing comes free. This was just bait.

'And why would you be holding those men?'

'You are the police, Inspector Jefe,' said the voice. 'You operate from the outside, trying to find your way in. We are on the inside where everything is much clearer.'

'You're implying that Donstov was responsible for planting the bomb and that you disapproved of it.'

'For an operation which would change the political land-scape and destabilize a region, which has been a safe haven for a number of organizations for many years, Donstov would have needed the full backing of the Supreme Council. He did not have it. It was something done to his personal advantage.'

'And Señora Jiménez's son, Darío?' said Falcón. 'Where is the boy in all this? What is your purpose in holding him?'

'I think there's been a misunderstanding here, Inspector Jefe,' said the voice. 'We are not holding the boy. We vehe-mently disapprove of the involvement of civilians in our foreign operations. It brings unwelcome publicity and unnecessary attention from the police.'

'You're *not* holding Darío!' said Consuelo, unable to dampen the shriek in that negative. 'So why are we talking to you?'

'Certain things had to be established before we could proceed to look at the situation with your son,' said the voice.

'You said I could speak to him if I called this number.'

'One of the most important things to establish is the nature of the people you are dealing with,' said the voice. 'Señor Revnik has rules, Señora Jiménez. He has a code of honour. It may not be the same as yours, or the Inspector Jefe's, but it is the reason why he is such a respected man in the world of *vory-v-zakone*. Yuri Donstov has no respect for these rules. He is an outsider. He does things which are only to his advantage. He is the sort of person who gives no thought to the nature of a man such as Vasili Lukyanov.'

'But Lukyanov used to work for Señor Revnik,' said Falcón.

'Perhaps you are not aware of the extent of the disagreements between Señor Revnik and Vasili Lukyanov,' said the voice. 'Giving a man a beating when he is unable to repay a debt is permissible, but we draw the line at raping and beating a man's daughter. It proved very costly for Señor Revnik to extricate Lukyanov and his friend from that situation. Señor Revnik is even more furious now that he has returned from Moscow to find more than eight million euros and other property missing. You may not know this, Inspector Jefe, but nobody steals from a *vor-v-zakone*. There is only one punishment for that, which in this case has been carried out by the Ultimate Power.'

'This is all very well,' said Consuelo, who could feel herself being sidelined, 'but if you're *not* holding my son then I am unclear as to what you are proposing.'

'We *do* have a proposal,' said the voice firmly. 'The most important part of this proposal from your point of view is that you do not enter into negotiations with Yuri Donstov. He is probably offering to return the boy if the Inspector Jefe can get his hands on the money and some disks which were stolen by Lukyanov.'

'The money is impossible. It's already been banked,' said Falcón. 'We know what's on the disks.'

'They will be happy with the disks. They contain substantial bargaining power. Extortion is a core business,' said the voice.

There was an omission there that Falcón did not miss: the disks were a lot more than just an ordinary business tool.

'As you know,' said Consuelo, 'I am a businesswoman. Normally in business I negotiate with someone who has something I want. I might use a broker if they bring specialist knowledge, but in our situation here, you are trying to *become* the broker when I am already in direct contact with the person who has what I want.'

'I don't think you've listened to me very carefully, Señora

261

Jiménez. Not only have I explained what sort of a person Yuri Donstov is – a man with no code of honour and no rules, who has turned his back on the very people who made him a *vor-v-zakone* – but also that he is running an operation which will very soon cease to exist. I doubt you are in the habit of doing business with bankrupts,' said the voice. 'The other advantage to you, Señora Jiménez, is that you don't have to do anything. We will get your son back for you. You just have to sit and wait.'

'But I still have to call Yuri Donstov. He has already sent me an email saying that *his* patience is not infinite – as if *mine* is.'

'You tell him that there are complications. First of all, you cannot get the money because it is in the bank, and secondly, you have been approached by another group who say that they are the ones holding your son. You no longer know who to believe, and he must give you incontrovertible proof of your son's wellbeing before you do anything. I'm sure, with your experience, that you are an expert at playing for time in a negotiation.'

'But *how* are you going to get my son back? You are *all* men of violence. If you're going to fight this out, killing each other, I do not want my son to be in the middle of a war.'

'Believe me, Señora Jiménez, this is not a unilateral action. Pressure can be applied in all sorts of ways –'

'That sounds like a slow process,' said Consuelo. 'I don't have that sort of time. My son is in the hands of a monster. I'm not going to wait while you gradually squeeze this . . . this infected boil out of your organization.'

'Do not expect me to be explicit, Señora Jiménez,' said the voice. 'The Inspector Jefe has a personal interest in all criminal activity, even if it is for the general good.'

'I don't know *what* to think any more.'

'We're going to hang up now,' said Falcón. 'We need some time to make a decision.'

'Promise me one thing, Inspector Jefe,' said the voice,

'that you will delay, in any way you can, your negotiations with Señor Donstov. If you are unsure of our capabilities in this matter, please come back to us so that we can take the opportunity to convince you.'

'One last thing,' said Consuelo. 'What do you want out of this?'

'A small reward,' said the voice, and cut the line.

Falcón leaned back in his chair. Consuelo stared into the desk.

'You did a brilliant job,' said Falcón.

'I don't know what to think any more,' said Consuelo, repeating herself, trying to force some logic past a gigantic emotional obstacle.

'Think about the two parties you've spoken to,' said Falcón. 'How do you feel about them?'

'At least these people didn't threaten me or threaten to harm Darío, but then again, they're not holding him. Maybe they'd be more unpleasant if they were,' said Consuelo.

'What did you think when they asked you to hold and started talking about getting permission from a higher authority?'

'They were discussing a change of approach,' said Consuelo. 'Initially they were going to play a game with us: pretending they had Darío, but when I asked for the simple proof they realized the hopelessness of their gambit. They are being persuasively reasonable because they are weak. We have access – or rather, *you* have access – to what they want, but they can't give us what *we* want. So they make us believe that we are dealing with a monster and offer to intervene and be strong on our behalf. The only problem for me is –'

'What they're planning to do.'

'By the sound of it, they're going to kill Yuri Donstov. He's muscling in on their territory, breaking all their codes of conduct and they will use guns and, I don't know, rocket-propelled grenades to take him out.'

'I'm beginning to think that Lukyanov was very important

to Donstov's organization,' said Falcón. 'The voice told us that Donstov's operation will "soon cease to exist", which probably means that Donstov's supply lines of heroin will be cut, or already have been.'

'That is if we believe everything the voice tells us,' said Consuelo.

'Lukyanov, with the eight million euros, was bringing cash flow to the game and his expertise in prostitution. And, because we're talking about girls rather than heroin, the supply can come from anywhere.'

'Then there are the disks that Lukyanov was supposed to deliver,' said Consuelo. 'But you don't know what they're planning to muscle in on.'

'One of the guys on the disks is a civil engineer who heads up the construction arm of Horizonte,' said Falcón. 'I also know that one of these Russian groups has their claws dug into the mayor's office and that a crucial meeting will take place in Seville very soon, probably between the I4IT/Horizonte consortium and the mayor and other relevant departments.'

'Is time becoming an important factor for them?'

'The meeting is due to take place within the next twenty-four hours.'

'Businessmen consorting with prostitutes? Is that such a terrible thing these days?' asked Consuelo, shrugging. 'Raúl went whoring. Some of the people I do business with, especially in property and construction, take cocaine, go to orgies. We're not mired in Catholicism any more.'

'But I4IT is an American corporation, owned by two reformed addicts who are born-again Christians. They'll take you in as a sinner, but you have to reform. They would not tolerate the sort of behaviour you're talking about by any executives in any of their companies. Those guys would be out of a job that probably pays more than a million euros a year and puts them in a position to make double that in the black economy.'

'In that case, the one thing the voice was not quite straight about,' said Consuelo, 'was the disks. They *are* very important to Leonid Revnik.'

'A further admission of weakness would not have looked good,' said Falcón. 'They'd be saying we don't have the boy *and* we're desperate for what you've got.'

'W*ould* you give them the disks, Javier?' asked Consuelo, that question burning inside her, too hot for her not to let it out.

'Darío is my responsibility . . .'

'Have you noticed that?' said Consuelo, cutting in, suddenly unable to bear hearing his response. 'Neither of the Russian groups has mentioned the original reason for abducting Darío, which was to get you to stop your investigations into the Seville bombing.'

'They've effectively done that by killing my best witness, Marisa Moreno,' said Falcón. 'And the voice *did* offer me the men who planted the bomb. He certainly knows what I want.'

They lapsed into silence, looking at each other. Too much going on in their heads. Falcón checked the time. Ten minutes past midnight. Nearly two hours since the email was sent from Donstov.

'You have to talk to the other side,' he said. 'Play for time.'

Consuelo looked suddenly exhausted. The years piled into her face. The muscles in her jaw tensed. She reached for the phone, this call more difficult now that she knew for certain they were holding Darío. She gritted her teeth and dialled the number.

'You know, Javier, don't you, that if anything happened to Darío, I wouldn't be able to live with it. Even after all Alicia's work, he still means too much to me. He's not just Darío, my baby, he's the two I lost as well. I think it might be the end of me . . . This is Consuelo Jiménez,' she said into the phone, 'and I'd like to speak to my son.'

'You've taken your time.'

'There've been complications.'

'All right, tell me your complications, Señora Jiménez, but don't let them be from the Inspector Jefe. He is the whole reason behind this. If he hadn't stuck his nose into our business, none of this would have happened.'

'The first is the money,' said Consuelo, hunched over the desk, her whole body tensed against the simmering violence coming down the line. 'The money has already been transferred from the Jefatura to the Banco de Bilbao. The Inspector Jefe has no authority over it. Only his commanding officer can get that money out.'

'That is very simple . . . not complicated at all,' said the voice, and Consuelo's shoulders relaxed a notch. 'You will raise the money yourself, Señora Jiménez.'

Silence.

'Do you seriously think I can lay my hands on eight million euros in the space of . . .?'

'Eight million two hundred thousand euros, Señora Jiménez,' said the voice. 'That shouldn't be a problem. I know two of your restaurants here in Seville are leased, but the other two you own outright. There's been a property boom. Those two buildings are easily worth three million euros now, so there's only a further five million to raise. Be creative. We know you're good at that.'

'I can't –'

'You can, Señora Jiménez. Eight million two hundred thousand for your child's safe return. I really don't think that's too much to ask.'

Consuelo blinked. This was not going according to plan. Her left hand started to tremble.

'It will take time,' she said.

'We're in no hurry. We can afford to keep your son alive for a week,' said the voice. 'Your friend, though, the Inspector Jefe, he will have to bring us the disks today. Yes, today. It is today already. He will bring us the original disks by midday today as a demonstration of good will.'

'The original disks? Why do you need the originals? Why not copies?'

'Because we want the originals,' said the voice. 'All understood. No more complications.'

'There is one more complication,' said Consuelo, dredging for all reserves of strength. 'I need proof that you are holding my son.'

'Proof!'

'I need you to ask him about his mark.'

'His mark!' roared the voice.

'Ask him about his mark. He will tell you everything you need to know to prove to me –'

'You want proof –' said the voice, total threat.

'We have been approached by another group who claim that they are the ones holding my son. I therefore need you to prove to me . . .'

'I'll prove to you, Señora Jiménez. Listen –'

A child's voice. Distant, but in the same room as the phone.

'*Mamá, Mamá, Mamá.*'

'Darío!' screamed Consuelo.

A blurt of foreign language.

'Listen, Señora Jiménez.'

'*Mamá, Mamá. No, no, no –*'

The voice was muffled. A hand placed over the mouth. There was an audible clipping noise like shears going through the bones of a roast chicken, and then screaming, piercing horror screams of a child not just in pain, but in terrible shock at what had just been done.

'That was the small toe, Señora Jiménez. We won't bother to send that to you. Only later . . . the bigger parts. If you decide to make that necessary.'

267

21

Consuelo fell off her chair, slid under the desk as if she'd
been dragged there by some unseen riptide. She hid in the
footwell, held on to her face, squeezed her eyes shut,
clenched her body. She strained against the pain until a
creaking sound developed in her throat, but however hard
she tried she could not get those horror screams out of her
head. They were in there now for eternity and they'd torn
something in her. That connective tissue, which holds us
together and binds us to others, had just been slashed at
with a hooligan's mindlessness.

Falcón crawled towards her.

'Don't touch me!' she screamed, kicking at him with her
heels. She didn't want loving. She didn't want tenderness or
pity. What she wanted was someone to string her up by her
ankles, slit her throat and bleed her into oblivion. She wanted
to take the violence meted out to her child on to herself.

An immense silence settled in the room. It was so quiet
that for the first time they heard diners off in the restaurant beyond the soundproofed door. Like faint choral singing.

They sat on the floor. The chair fallen on its side. Consuelo's hands clutched to her chest, knees up to her face. Falcón on the outside looking in. No tears from her. This was beyond tears. She stared into the wood grain for an age.

'The voice was right,' she said quietly. 'We have no idea who we're dealing with. No rules. No code. No reason. It's like trying to negotiate more time from Death.'

'And the voice wanted us to find that out for ourselves,' said Falcón.

'The voice is cruel,' she said, 'but not quite as cruel as the other voice.'

'The other voice is speaking from a position of weakness.'

'I'm talking about the voice inside my head,' said Consuelo. 'I am beyond reason, Javier. You cannot hear what we've just heard and stay reasonable. What chemicals those screams have released into my bloodstream, I do not know, but I am not the same. I have irrevocably changed in the space of quarter of an hour.'

'Don't let it make up your mind.'

'You're used to this, Javier.'

'Nobody gets used to this,' he said, thinking about Marisa Moreno, the grey foot in the black lake, the head on the wooden statue.

'The only way to deal with a monster like Donstov,' said Consuelo, fists clenched, knuckles white with rage, 'is to set the dogs on him.'

'And Darío?'

'I can't think that he'd be in any more danger than he is now.'

They stood. She brushed herself down, sat on the edge of the desk.

'I'll get hold of the disks,' said Falcón.

She could see the damage it was doing him to go against the grain, but that he was willing. From her side there wasn't a scintilla of doubt.

'You know that once we've taken this road there's no going back,' said Falcón. 'And there might be no *coming* back either. You've got two other sons to . . .'

'Do you want me to sign a release form?' she said, eyes locked on to his.

'I'm not going to fail you, Consuelo,' said Falcón. 'I would corrupt myself. I would even hand over the money, if I had it. I would ruin my career. I'd let them drum me out of the force to spend the rest of my days in jail and ignominy, if I could be certain that Darío would come out of this all right.'

She held his face, kissed him.

'So we call Revnik,' said Falcón, righting the chair, sitting her down.

'I'm sorry, Javier. I know what this is costing you,' she said, and dialled the number, put the phone on loudspeaker with the dictaphone running.

'*Diga*,' said the voice.

'We spoke to Yuri Donstov's people,' said Consuelo.

'And?'

'He said I would have to raise the money myself.'

'How long did he give you?'

'A week.'

'Interesting,' said the voice. 'He must be suffering. What about the disks?'

'He wants them by midday, and he insisted on the originals.'

'Of course, things can be cut out of copies,' said the voice. 'Did you speak to your son?'

'When I asked for proof of my son's welfare, he responded by cutting off his toe.'

'It was probably just a bit of theatre,' said the voice.

'You didn't hear the screams.'

'Does this mean you would like us to act for you in this business?'

'Some questions,' said Consuelo. 'Do you know where my son is being held?'

'Not yet, but we have our people on the inside.'

'And they don't know?'

'Donstov is being very careful about who knows what. All we know is that the boy is not being held in Donstov's headquarters in Seville. Once we get inside, we will find the answer.'

'What is the "small reward" you mentioned before?' asked Consuelo.

'The original disks.'

'Wait,' said Consuelo.

She put the call on hold, clicked off the loudspeaker, clenched her fists and rested her forehead on her wrists. The torment of impossible decisions.

'I know that I'm being given three options,' she said, before Falcón could get a word out. 'The monstrous Donstov, the impenetrable Revnik, or the slow, indecisive forces of law and order. The first one is unacceptable. The third is precluded by the first because we have been given less than twelve hours. That means we have to go with the second option with all its unpredictabilities. We can agonize but it won't change anything.'

They looked at the phone. She hit the hold and loud-speaker buttons.

'We'll bring the disks to you when you've made Darío safe,' said Consuelo.

'We would need the disks in advance,' said the voice.

'Unacceptable,' said Consuelo.

'Hold the line.'

The phone went dead.

'They'll need the disks featuring the I4IT and Horizonte people prior to six p.m.,' said Falcón. 'Without them they can't affect whatever the deal is between the consortium and the mayor's office. Offer them a random selection of half the disks. See what they say.'

The voice came back.

'Each disk is numbered in felt-tip pen from one to twenty-seven. We will accept half the disks, from one to eight and twenty-two to twenty-seven inclusive.'

'When do you plan to act?' asked Falcón.

'Call this number again in fifteen minutes.'

The line went dead. They sat back, exhausted.

'What's on the disks they've just asked for?'

Ramírez was in bed when Falcon called. He told him all he could remember was that the first unidentified guy was on the first disk and that the final two disks were 'locked', requiring a password and encryption software. The techies were working on it. He hung up.

Falcón and Consuelo mused about the nature of the valuable data locked up on the last two disks and lapsed into silence again – the tension so unbearable that talk was becoming an irritation. The restaurant noise reasserted itself like a subliminal tease, reminding them that this was the life they should be having.

Her mobile rang in her handbag.

'It must be Donstov's people,' she said, and took the call.

'Any progress, Señora Jiménez?'

'You'll have the disks by midday.'

'So you've already been in contact with Inspector Jefe Falcón?'

'He's here now.'

'Señor Donstov would like to give you an incentive to act quickly,' said the voice. 'If you can bring us the disks before dawn today, Señor Donstov will release your son on receipt of just four million euros and you still have a week to raise the money.'

'Will I be able to see my son?'

Falcón scribbled on the pad, shoved it in front of Consuelo.

'Yes,' said the voice.

'You have to understand, too, that at such short notice we might not be able to supply *all* the disks. The last two are in a different department, which the Inspector Jefe does not have access to.'

'Hold.'

Consuelo tugged a tissue from a box on the desk, wiped the sweat from her eyes and face.

'When can you get hold of the last two disks? Earliest time?' asked the voice.

Falcón wrote on the pad, underlined an earlier question she hadn't yet asked.

'Ten a.m.,' said Consuelo. 'And where shall we meet?'

'Hold.'

They held for what seemed like an interminable amount of time. They didn't speak. Life was suspended. Consuelo imagined herself as a foetus with no concept of time, waiting to be born without even understanding that this was what waiting was.

'Once you have the first twenty-five disks in your possession,' said the voice, 'you will make your way north of Seville on the road to Merida. There is a petrol station where the N433 branches off in the direction of the Sierra de Aracena and Portugal. You will wait for further instructions there.'

The car park was empty, the Jefatura dark and silent. The heat of the day still radiated from the tarmac as Falcón let himself into the back door of the building. He ran upstairs to his office, booted up all the computers, took the key to the evidence room and went back downstairs. He brought all the disks up to the Homicide squad's offices and started burning copies, five at a time, on all computers.

Reasoning that Donstov wouldn't know the difference between the original and a copy of any of the disks, he hunted down a black felt-tip pen. Time, having been unbearably stationary when he was with Consuelo, now raced past at an ungovernable speed. He found a pen in Elvira's secretary's office and sprinted back down to the Homicide department, nearly lost his footing on the stairs, slowed himself down, didn't want to end up with a cracked skull, lying on the landing for the cleaners to find in the morning.

Thirty-five minutes later and he was on the fourth set of copies. Why wasn't technology faster? He numbered the disks. Sweat poured off him. No air-con and the night-time temperatures still in the thirties. There came a point when all he could do was wait. He swore horribly at the unconcerned computers. He gripped the arms of his chair, wondered what had happened to him. One moment he was drinking beers in the square outside Santa María La Blanca and the next he was going against everything he stood for, but with no gunman holding a barrel to his temple, no lunatic with a knife to his ribs, no fanatic with a bomb strapped to his waist. And yet hell seemed to be imminent. His mobile vibrated.

'Where *are* you?' asked Consuelo.

'Nearly there.'

Final copies. He breathed down the stress. Got the numbers right with the felt-tip pen. Back down to the evidence room, put the originals back in the safe, locked it. Pocketed the evidence-room key. Ran out into the car park. Threw himself into the car, hands slick with sweat, slipping over the gear stick and steering wheel. He turned up the air-con. The cool blasted into his chest. He drove back into town, pulled up outside the restaurant. Consuelo tore open the door, got in. He pulled away.

'What?' he said to her questioning eyes.

'What *have* you been doing?' she asked. 'You're soaked to the skin.'

'There's a shirt in the back seat,' he said. 'Revnik. The voice. What did they tell us to do?'

'They came back with a different plan,' said Consuelo. 'Fortunately the same as ours. They wanted us to offer Donstov the disks early. I told them it had already been done. They took it well. They're on the move.'

Falcón drove alongside the river, with the old Expo '92 site on the Isla de la Cartuja just across the water.

'They *do* know that we've been sent to this petrol station precisely so that Donstov can make sure we're not being followed.'

'Revnik's voice told me that he has two ex-KGB men working for him,' said Consuelo. 'And four years ago the Russian Interior Ministry disbanded a group called the SOBR, a special rapid-reaction unit. All these highly trained guys were suddenly out of a job on a small pension. Revnik has three of them working for him now.'

'You had quite a conversation with the voice.'

'He opened up when I told him you'd left to get the disks,' said Consuelo. 'I got a guided tour of the Russian mafia. You know, it's not so different to Seville. If you have friends in the right places, it all works.'

'The town hall hasn't got round to killing people yet.'

'But most of the Marbella town council are in jail for corruption.'

'Did the voice tell you anything practical, like how they were going to follow us?'

'He said they had "listening equipment". With my mobile number they can pick up my signal and listen in,' said Consuelo. 'Doesn't it make you despair when you see such contempt for the forces of law and order?'

He didn't answer.

She squeezed his arm. Falcon turned left, crossed the river over Calatrava's harp bridge, headed away from the lights of the city, past the Olympic stadium and into the darkness.

Barely any traffic. The odd truck. The new motorway bypassing Las Pajanosas was smooth and empty. The lights studding the tarmac were an odd comfort, a show of someone's concern. Consuelo sat with her legs crossed at the ankle, hands in her lap playing with her rings. She had her head tilted back against the head-rest, eyes open, drinking in the illuminated road. Occasionally she took a deep, quivering breath.

'I can hear you thinking,' said Falcon.

'What is said and demanded in business negotiations is one thing,' said Consuelo. 'But there's always a subtext.'

'You mean, why did the brutal Donstov suddenly become a reasonable human being half an hour later?' asked Falcón.

'Is there any significance to him getting those disks seven or eight hours earlier than he originally asked?' said Consuelo. 'Why have they halved their demand to four million euros? Why is he being weak?'

'Maybe the money is much more important to Donstov than we realized,' said Falcón. 'Revnik's man thought so.'

'And it's much closer to the amount of money that he knows I can raise,' said Consuelo. 'Which is why I'm thinking: why did Donstov release the pressure on me?'

'This doesn't feel like a release to me. If anything, he's racked it up. He's making us act quicker. He's given us less time to plan.'

'What about this: when I told him that another group had claimed they were holding Darío, it made him suspect that we'd formed the sort of relationship we have.'

'So, he gets us to speed up,' said Falcón. 'And, at the same time, he confirms that we still believe him and haven't fallen for the other side's bluff.'

They arrived at the petrol station where they'd been told to wait, Falcon filled up and extracted a couple of *café solos* from the machine, took them back to the car. They parked in front of the neighbouring *hostal*. He changed his shirt. They stared out into the dark and sipped coffee.

'If we get through this I'm never going to the Costa del Sol ever again in my life,' said Consuelo.

'Nothing's changed in the Costa del Sol for the last forty years. Why withdraw your custom now?'

'Because it's only now that I've faced up to what these

people have being doing,' said Consuelo. 'Almost every apartment building, every development, every golf course, marina, fun park, casino – every source of recreation for visiting tourists is built on the profit from human misery. Hundreds of thousands of girls being forced to work in the *puti clubs*. Hundreds of thousands of addicts sticking themselves with needles. Hundreds of thousands of brainless, decadent fools snorting white powder up their noses so that they can dance and fuck all night long. And that's not counting any of the migrants, who are washed up dead on the glorious beaches. It makes me sick and I'm not going to do it any more. I'm not going to do it any fucking more.'

She jabbed her heel down in the footwell with each vehement syllable. Falcón reached out to calm her down and it was then that the mobile rang. She grabbed it off the dashboard. The irritating sound of an SMS arriving filled the car.

Donstov's man sending a text.

'They're telling us to go north, direction Mérida.'

Falcón pulled away from the *hostal* with a squeal from the tyres and crossed the hot road, turning left.

'Do you think our friends can "hear" a text?' asked Consuelo, nervous, sneaking a glance at Falcón's impassive face.

'Technology is not my strong point,' he said, suppressing a sense of the complete madness of what they were doing. 'We have to believe that they know their work.'

After ten kilometres they were told to leave the main road north and, following endless instructions from texts sent on the mobile, they drove down narrow rough roads with patched tarmac, through small villages with just a couple of street lights, up hills with deep blackness on either side while the smell of the rock rose, the stone pines cooling, the wild herbs and the dry earth wafted through the half-open windows. Consuelo writhed in her seat, staring out of the front and side, checking the rear-view mirror.

'If Revnik's men were following us and we could see

them, they'd be visible to Donstov's people, too,' said Falcón. 'So keep calm, Consuelo. Look ahead.'

'Where the hell are we?'

The tyres rumbled over the roads. A sign. Castelblanco de los Arroyos. Turn left. Darkness again.

'How long have we been driving?' she asked.

'Forty minutes.'

She rested a hand on his forearm.

'There's nothing out there. There's nobody with us. There can't be anybody in this blackness. They'd see any headlights coming from kilometres away,' she said, losing heart. 'We're going to have to prolong this thing as much as we can.'

'It'll take time for them to go through the disks,' said Falcón.

The mobile rang, this time it was a call. Donstov's man.

'You'll see a sign to the Embalse de la Cala on the left. Take it, and tell me when you get there.'

Four minutes.

'We're here.'

'Take the second track on the right.'

They came off the tarmac on to a dirt road.

'Hand-painted sign: *Granja de las Once Higeras*. Follow it.'

They followed the signs through the tall grasses and low, wide-spread holm oaks. It went on for kilometres until they came through an open gate to a single-storey house. The headlights brushed over the whitewashed walls, the shuttered and barred windows, the door with red paint peeling off it.

'Put the car in the barn,' said the voice. 'Leave the keys in the ignition. Come out with your hands up . . . hold the disks on your head. Stand in front of the garage, legs apart.'

In the barn was a yellow rusting digger. Consuelo felt the warmth of its engine radiating towards her.

She and Javier stood a few metres from the back of the car, hands on heads. Two men in baseball caps, indiscernible behind their torch beams, approached the car. They had kerchiefs pulled up over their faces. One went into the garage while the other gave Falcón a thorough pat-down, put a sleeping mask over his eyes. He heard the boot pop open and, a few seconds later, close. The man came out of the garage, closed the doors. The second man moved over to Consuelo, crouched down behind her. She should have worn trousers. He started at her ankles, pen torch in his mouth.

'You can see I'm not hiding anything down there,' she said.

No response. The hands went up her skirt. She gritted her teeth as fingers and thumbs reached up to her crotch, over her buttocks, came back down again. Small of the back, stomach, cupped her breasts, a little grunt at her shoulder. He slipped a sleeping mask over her eyes, too.

'Come with me,' he said, and took Consuelo's arm.

The other man took care of Falcón. They headed for the low farmhouse. Their heads were pushed down as they entered the low doorway.

'Sit.'

They were pressed down into chairs. The one doing the talking was the Cuban they'd spoken to on the phone. Falcón had the small box of disks on his lap now. He did not like the sleeping mask, had not been prepared for it.

'I don't know how I'm going to be able to see my son with this thing on,' said Consuelo, 'so I'm taking it off.'

'Wait!' said the Cuban.

'Careful, Consuelo,' said Falcón.

'I'm not doing this blindfolded,' she said and ripped off the mask.

Falcón removed his as well, just so that the men in the room had too much to do at once, made them indecisive. Two of the Russians already had kerchiefs over their faces, the other two pulled down balaclavas with eye and mouth holes. One of these men stepped forward with a handgun, which he put to Consuelo's forehead. His hand trembled slightly, but with rage rather than fear. He had his finger on the trigger and the safety was off. Consuelo's eyeballs shivered,

279

her neck tensed and ducked into her shoulder as she felt the barrel touch her skin. The Cuban spoke in Russian. There was a brutal exchange and the man stepped back.

'If you want to stay alive to see your son then you have to do as you're told,' said the Cuban. 'These men do not care one way or the other whether you survive this or not. To them, killing you would be no more trouble than lighting a cigarette.'

The Cuban came round to stand in front of them. He was the only one of the men in the room who was not physically intimidating. He had spectacles above his kerchief.

'Do not do anything of your own accord. If I ask you to do something, move slowly. Most important: keep calm.'

The four Russians ranged behind him were all heavily built and Falcón knew, just by looking at them, that his fist, even if delivered with maximum force, would make no impression. They had the solidity of labourers. There was nothing gym-built about their physiques, even though two of them were wearing track suits with no vests underneath so that chest hair sprouted out over the zips. Their muscle looked as if it had been generated over decades of not just giving, but also taking, punishment. They all wore heavy gold watches on thick wrists and had messily tattooed hands that looked hardened by the breaking of facial bones.

'Are we going to meet Señor Donstov?' asked Falcón.

'He will arrive in due course,' said the Cuban. 'First, we must take a look at the disks.'

'Before you do anything, I want to see my son.'

'You will see your son as soon as we have established that these disks are genuine,' said the Cuban. 'You can understand that.'

The Cuban pulled out one of the four raffia-seated chairs, sat at the table and opened a laptop. Falcón handed over the disks. There was a room behind where the Cuban was sitting, door closed, and another room behind the four Russians, who were all now smoking. There was no electricity. The room was lit by an assortment of gas and kerosene lamps, which gave off a harsh white and oily yellow light under the wooden roof. The floor was of unglazed clay tiles, some light and smooth, others dark and roughened from saltpetre coming through. The walls were thick and had not seen whitewash for a few years so that they were flaking and the tiles below were powdered white.

The Cuban worked his way through the twenty-five disks, making notes on a pad as he went. He had the volume turned down so there were no accompanying grunts and groans as he played through the footage, fast-forwarding, playing, fast-forwarding again.

'What's going to happen here?' asked Falcón, who'd taken in every detail of the Russians, including the fact that they kept themselves completely separate from their captives. He couldn't put his finger on the meaning of this distance, but he knew it made him feel uneasy.

'Patience, Inspector Jefe,' said the Cuban. 'All will be revealed in due course.'

'My son isn't here, is he?' said Consuelo, hysteria rising in her voice. 'There's something that's telling me he's not in this place. Where is he? What have you done with him?'

'Your maternal instinct is wrong. He is here,' said the Cuban, looking at the room beyond where the Russians were standing. 'He's under sedation. We had to give him a small injection. You can't keep a boy like that still or quiet.'

'Let me see him then. You've got what you want. You're going through all those disks but you know you've got it all.'

'I'm just doing what I've been told to do,' said the Cuban. 'If I deviate from my orders things will go wrong.'

'I'm going to see him,' said Consuelo, and she was up and off her chair and across the room.

The Russians threw down their cigarettes. The one closest to the door drew his gun from behind his back. Two closed in on her. She battered at them with her fists, kicked with

281

her feet. They were impervious, didn't even close their eyes to her swatting or so much as wince with annoyance. The Cuban spoke in Russian. They picked her up off the floor. Her legs flailed. They brought her back across the room, thumped her in the chair. One raised his terrible hand to her. The Cuban spoke again in Russian.

'I'm asking them to be gentle with you,' he said, in Spanish now. 'If he slapped you, I doubt you'd wake up before next week, or he might just accidentally break your neck. They don't know their own strength, these people.'

'I don't like this,' she said, fear in her eyes for the first time and not for her own skin. 'I don't like this at all.'

'The only reason you're upset is that you are trying to fight against it,' said the Cuban. 'I know it's difficult, but just relax.'

'Then tell us what's going to happen,' said Falcón. 'She'll calm down if you tell her how you're going to proceed.'

'I will check the disks. I'm more than halfway through them now,' said the Cuban. 'When I am satisfied, I will make a call and Señor Donstov will arrive to pick them up. At that moment you will be able to see your son before he is taken away by Señor Donstov. Your son will then remain with him until you comply with the rest of the agreement. Is that all right?'

Falcón and Consuelo exchanged a look. Her head, without the slightest shake, told him that it was *not* all right. That this was all very, very wrong. The Cuban glanced up from the screen. He knew what he had on his hands. He'd been in this situation before. He knew there was nothing a human being intuited better than the approach of their own demise. He knew how all the killing had been done in the world's civil wars; people from the same village killing each other, people who'd known each other and their families since birth killing each other. What they did was herd them together, stick them in pens and thereby diminish their humanity, so that they became nothing more than sheep to be slaughtered. The Cuban saw the same realization dawning on Falcón, who'd been looking at the Russians, trying to understand them, what they were doing over there. Now Falcón understood their separateness; the distance was so that the slaughtermen didn't smell the sweetness of their humanity and the animal caught no presentiment of the blade.

'Why are you doing this?' asked Falcón.

'What?'

'Don't make me say it.'

'Be calm, Inspector Jefe. All will be well,' said the Cuban, lazily, as if speaking from a hammock.

He made a call on his mobile, spoke in Russian.

'Did you know Marisa Moreno?' asked Falcón.

The Cuban shrugged. Closed down the phone. He nodded to the Russians, started boxing the disks, closing down the laptop. A hard day at the office and now the final unpleasantness.

'What about the money?' said Falcón. 'You don't want the money?'

'That's going to be too complicated now,' said the Cuban.

'And the locked disks with the encrypted data?' he asked, as they came for him.

'We don't have the means to crack that code,' said the Cuban.

Two Russians, one on either side, took Falcón out into the night. Consuelo ran at the door where they were holding Darío under sedation. One of the Russians caught her around the waist, lifted her bodily off the ground, whirled her round, brought her into his chest. The other grabbed her thrashing legs and they carried her out.

They walked around the house. Torches came out. There was no moon. The darkness had such a palpable thickness it surprised Falcón just by giving way to each of his faltering steps. There was the smell of water on the breeze. They were near the lake. The torch beams lit the ground and occasionally swept ahead over two mounds of freshly piled earth at the edge of the long grass. He couldn't quite believe that this was happening to him . . . to them. How could he, with all his experience, have allowed this madness to take place?

The pit was deep. The digger in the barn. It all made ludicrously cogent sense now. What do you do with this sort of brilliant hindsight? They stood him at the far edge, then turned him so that he had his back to the lake and was facing the low farmhouse. The other Russians arrived with Consuelo, now passive. They righted her and stood her next to him. He grabbed her hand, entwined it with his, kissed the back of it.

'I'm sorry, Consuelo,' he said, resigned now.

'I'm the one who should be sorry,' she said. 'I got too involved in the game.'

'I can't believe I let this happen.'

'And I didn't even get to see Darío,' she said, her distress weakening her. 'What will they do with him now? What have they done with my poor, sweet little boy?'

He kissed her, a fumbling, bumping kiss, but it planted his shape on her and hers on him. The Russians pulled them apart, pushed them to their knees at the edge of the pit. Their hands were still locked together. The two men who'd brought Consuelo to the pit were already back at the house. The remaining torch was dropped to the ground where its beam played over the pit, lighting up the dark soil, moist from the lake. The slides on the two handguns were racked. Heavy hands were placed on the crowns of their heads. They squeezed each other's hands until the bones cracked. An owl hooted. Its mate responded with a little titter. Was that the last sound of this life?

No, there was just one more.

22

Granja de las Once Higeras – Tuesday, 19th September 2006, 04.47 hrs

The shots, two dull thuds, simultaneous. First Consuelo, then Falcón fell forward, their positions on the edge of the hole too precarious to avoid it. Their reluctance gave them a slight advantage over the Russians, who had no choice. They fell like two beef carcasses, their knees knocking into the backs of their erstwhile victims, taking them to the grave. The torch beam still cast its light across the dark hole and lit up the black, gaping wounds in the back of the heads of the two men, who had landed face down in the pit. Consuelo, trapped under the legs of the inert Russian, was struggling and whimpering with panic. A man landed on his feet next to them. His face was covered in dark paint and his camouflage outfit was just visible in the torch beam. He heaved the slack limbs of the executioners away so that Falcón and Consuelo could roll out. The man put his fingers to the necks of the dead Russians.

'How many inside?' he asked, in heavily accented Spanish.

'Two Russians and a Cuban,' said Falcón.

'Stay here . . . in the hole,' he said, and scrambled out.

Other men rushed past. It was impossible to say how many. It was too dark. One of them kicked the torch into the pit. Falcón pulled Consuelo silently towards him. He sat with his back to the wall of the pit. She crouched between his legs, his arms encircling her. The smell of earth was as thick as chocolate, sweet as life. They heard nothing. They waited. The stars emitted their ancient, uncertain light. The smell of the lake filled the hole with the promise of further days. He kissed her hand, perfume and dirt. Her knuckles wriggled on his lips.

A loud bang. Consuelo started, dropped her head on to her raised knees. Muffled shots. Silence. After a while an engine started up. The digger in the barn. It reversed out. Headlights illuminated the night on the other side of the farmhouse. The digger's engine farted up and growled forward. It stopped for a minute or two and then continued slowly. The beams of light swung round, settled over the pit, crawled forward, narrowing. Falcón stood up. The silhouette of a man approached, walking in front of the digger.

'It's safe now,' said a voice.

A hand came down. Falcón lifted Consuelo towards it and she was hauled out. She started running immediately. The hand came down again. Falcón walked up the earth wall of the pit and out. He moved to one side as the digger came through. Consuelo had fallen down twenty metres away. The digger tipped its bucket and two bodies fell into the pit on top of the inert Russians. Consuelo scrambled to her feet and ran again. The man shouted an order in Russian. Two men came out from behind the farmhouse, caught hold of her, held her there. She struggled but didn't seem to have much left in her.

The man turned to him, his painted face unreal in the harsh light from the digger.

'The boy is there . . . room on right as you enter, but . . .'

'They said he was under sedation.'

'He's not breathing. Pillow on face. Maybe two hours ago,' said the man. 'Look before her. Not good.'

'They killed him?'

'You knew the boy?' asked the man, nodding.

'They *smothered* him with a pillow?' said Falcón, again, completely mystified.

'Hours ago. Before you here. Nothing you could do.'

'Why would they do that?' asked Falcón; the Inspector Jefe, who'd never seen the logic of murder, whose job it was to return sanity to the grossly illogical, was dumbfounded. 'They had no reason to do that.'

'These people not think like that,' said the man. 'Go now. She very unhappy.'

Consuelo was screaming herself helpless in the arms of the two men. She wasn't fighting them, all her fight had gone into hysterical, wounded animal screaming. He ran over to her. They laid her down on the ground. She stopped as if choked when Falcón's face came into her vision.

'What's happened?' she said, weakly. 'What have they done?'

'I'm going to go in there now to have a look at things,' said Falcón. 'When I'm ready, in a minute or two, then you come in. All right?'

She looked at him as if he was a doctor who'd just told her that she was going to die, but there was a good chance of it being peaceful.

'Tell me,' she said, too emotionally exhausted to speak properly.

'I'm going to take a look,' he said, stroking her face. 'I'll call for you. Two minutes. Count the seconds.'

He trotted over the rough ground to the farmhouse, ducked through the low front door. Off to the left, the laptop and disks still on the table, three chairs blown over, the remains of a stun grenade in the corner. Beyond the table, through the door, the Cuban, stripped naked, tied to a chair, arms hooked over the high back, ankles secured to the legs, thighs apart, genitals exposed, wild, animal fear in his eyes.

'Not for you,' said a heavily accented voice to his right. 'In here.'

He went to the door, wiped the sweat out of his eyes, tried to calm himself down. He searched for that professional distance. Nothing there. The door was hanging ajar. A beefy Russian, with painted face and a handgun, thick cylindrical silencer attached, beckoned him. He forced himself through it, found his throat clogging with grief which, only a moment before, had been breathing in the damp earth with relief. As he crossed the threshold, playing soccer in the garden with Darío flickered through the gate of his mind, and he wasn't sure whether he could cope with this.

The room was lit by a kerosene lamp. The light was a slow, fluid yellow. There was a single bed, metal frame, pushed up against the wall. The windows were shuttered and had a metal bar across them, padlocked. Darío was lying face up, head still under the smothering pillow, bare chest. His right arm lay by his side, his left arm formed a right-angle, fist closed by his head. A sheet lay over his torso, legs awry underneath, the feet sticking out. His right foot was bandaged. There was a dark stain on the sheet where the blood had soaked through.

'Skinny kid,' thought Falcón, pushing himself forward. 'Always on the move.'

Falcón felt for a wrist pulse, but he knew a dead body when he saw one. He set the legs straight, brought the arms down by the boy's side, reorganized the sheet over the body, and that was when he saw it. A large scar, as of a messy appendix operation. He checked under the armpit for the 'strawberry' that Consuelo had talked about, but the light was not good in the room. And for the first time he brought himself to look under the pillow. Even now he peeled it back slowly, flinchingly, as if he was going to see something he didn't want to. The face staring up at him, wide-eyed, purple-lipped was not Darío's.

'Bring me a torch,' he said.

The big Russian came in. Falcón pointed at his belt. He handed the torch over. Falcón shone it in the boy's face. Still not Darío.

'What?' asked the Russian.

'It's not the boy.'

'I don't understand.'

Falcón went out into the night. This time he was angry, almost insanely angry. He called for Consuelo and they released her, lifted her to her feet. She stumbled towards him over the uneven ground. He caught her.

'It's not Darío,' he said. 'Darío is not dead.'

'Who is it?' she asked, utterly confused.

'A dead boy,' said Falcón. 'A nameless, dead boy.'

They ducked in through the doorway, went into the room. Falcón shut the door behind him with his foot. It slammed to. Consuelo knelt by the bed, held on to the boy's arm and shook her head and sobbed as she stared into his inert face.

Falcón undid the bandage on the boy's foot.

'They cut off his toe,' he said, beside himself with rage. 'They cut off the poor boy's toe.'

Consuelo sat on the floor with her back to the bed and started crying, huge racking sobs came up as if from her pelvis, physically lifting her off the clay tiles. It lasted for a few minutes until she got a hold of herself.

'I can't take any of this in,' she said. 'You'll have to explain it to me.'

'They didn't have Darío,' he said. 'They never had Darío. They played a game to see if they could get what they wanted.'

'But Revnik doesn't have Darío either,' said Consuelo. 'We know that. He's told us.'

'That was why Donstov's man called us back,' said Falcón. 'You were right. He was nervous. You'd enraged him by telling him that Revnik claimed to have Darío, which was why he cut off this boy's toe. Then he calmed down. Came back with the incentive just in case you were bluffing him. He had nothing to lose by trying to *pretend* that he had Darío, and it worked. He brought everything forward, made everybody work under pressure. And there is, of course, the possibility that he still has a friend in Revnik's group.'

'But *who's* got Darío?' said Consuelo.

'I don't know.'

The sound of a muffled scream came from the other room.

'Take me away from this place,' she said. 'These are hell's people in here.'

They went out into the main room. The Spanish speaker was back.

'What is the problem?' he asked.

'The boy is not her son,' said Falcón. 'We don't **know** who he is.'

'He must be,' he said, looking at the door.

'I know my own son,' said Consuelo.

'Stay there. Don't move.'

The Spanish speaker went into the room where **they** were interrogating the Cuban, who was still tied to the chair, but face down on the floor and bloody with a wad of cloth in his mouth. The door shut. Questions in Russian. Muffled screams of pain. Then a dry indiscernible whisper. The door opened.

'He says they never had the boy, they cheat you,' said the Spanish speaker. 'I'm not sure I believe him. Anyway, we work on it. You go now. Wait.'

He reached into his combat trousers, pulled out two disks in their sleeves.

'These are exact replicas of the locked disks numbers

26 and 27, but with different encrypted data. Change these for the originals. They require the same password and encryption software to unlock and unscramble them as the ones you've got in the Jefatura. Bring those originals to us. Now *you* go. She stays.'

'What?'

'She stays as security,' he said, shrugging. 'We don't have the boy any more.'

'No,' said Falcón. 'I'm not leaving her here. She stays, I stay. You won't get your disks.'

'Wait.'

'You don't need her as security,' said Falcón. 'You know where to find us.'

The Russian went out of the farmhouse. Three minutes. The Cuban's punishment continued. Consuelo had to put her hands over her ears. The front door opened again. The Russian beckoned them out.

'Señor Revnik agrees. Less complicated for us.'

He walked them to the car. The digger worked away in the distance. Consuelo got in the passenger side. The Russian took out a pen torch, slid under the boot of the car, came back out with a small black box in his hand.

'Nearly forgot,' he said. 'Tracking device.'

'You took your time,' said Falcón.

'We had to cover the last three kilometres on foot,' he said. 'But our timing was perfect, no? Not too early so we get nervous and not too late so that you . . .'

He left it unfinished, said *adiós*, went back to the farmhouse. Falcón joined Consuelo in the lit cockpit of the car. They set off down the track, on to the rough road. They passed a car parked in the long grass, headlights masked with black tape so that only slits were visible. They thumped back up on to the tarmac. Falcón drove hunched over the wheel. He stopped in Castelblanco de los Arroyos, took his police mobile out and ran through the numbers.

'It's a bit too late for the police,' said Consuelo.

'I can't blame you for forgetting that *I* am supposed to be the police,' said Falcón, still in a rage. 'I've nearly wiped it from my own mind.'

'Who are you calling now?'

'The head of the IT department. He's got to crack the encryption code on those two disks as quickly as possible.'

'Leave it, Javier. It's six in the morning,' said Consuelo. 'You're going to have to do a lot of ugly explaining to some guy you've just woken up and, I can assure you, you'll come out of it badly. Sort it out when you get into the office.'

'What about Revnik? Do you want him after you?'

'I don't care. Let's just go. Revnik will have to learn to be patient. You can delay him somehow. With the disks in police possession, you're in control,' she said. 'I know you want to do something positive after all that horror, but my advice to you now is not to call anybody, because the repercussions will be serious.'

Back in the car, driving through the night. After the tension, a colossal tiredness. He drove with one hand, his arm around Consuelo, her head in his chest. She changed the gears when he needed it. They were silent for some time.

'I know you're angry,' she said.

'I'm angry with myself.'

'I feel as if I've ruined you,' she said.

'I'm not ruined,' he replied, but he thought he probably was.

'I know what that cost you, having to walk away from the dead boy,' she said. 'Because it's cost me, too. They'll bury him in that pit with those people. They'll bury him like a bird that's broken its neck flying into a window. And his mother will never know.'

'I'll face that in the morning,' he said. 'I need the light of day and a mirror for that.'

'I want to come home with you,' she said. 'I don't want to be alone tonight, not even for a few hours.'

He held her tight to his chest.

But he couldn't stop his brain from picking over the mangled wreckage of events. Where had he gone wrong? From the moment he'd started working on Marisa Moreno the Russians had been on to him with their telephone threats. Then they'd contacted Consuelo, and that had confirmed it. But he'd done what Mark Flowers had warned him never to do: put uncorroborated bits of information together to make the picture fit the one he had in his head. He was going to have to remember those phone calls, what time they'd happened, what had occurred before and in between each one, and what was said. What *exactly* had been said.

'You're thinking,' said Consuelo. 'This is no time for thinking, Javier. You said it yourself. Wait for the light of day. Things will be clearer then.'

He parked outside his house in Calle Bailén. Still not light, time closing in on seven o'clock. They went straight upstairs, stripped off and got into the shower. They washed the filth off each other. The water disappeared black and grey down the drain. She washed her hair. He soaped her shoulders, kneaded the muscles back into life. They sat on the floor of the shower, she between his legs, his arms wrapped around her. The water cascaded down. He kissed the back of her neck.

They got up wordlessly, turned off the water, dried themselves with towels in the dark bedroom, lit only by an oblong of light from the empty bathroom door. She threw the towel away, his dropped to the floor. After the night they'd been through he had no idea why his cock should be so massively swollen. She didn't understand why she felt a desire for him so strong it made her feel twenty all over again. The whole night had been illogical. They came together like fighters, wrestling for position. She bit his shoulder so hard he gasped. He rammed into her with a shuddering vehemence that riveted her to the bed. Their skin slapped together with each questing thrust. She dug her nails into his back, spurred him on with her heels in his buttocks. He couldn't seem to get deep enough inside her. It maddened him so that he quickened his pace and she sensed a great trembling inside her as his heart thumped wildly in his throat and she clung on with the thrill welling in her body and he reached a shuddering collapse and she lay underneath him, crying and beating the mattress with the flat of her hands.

He rolled to the side, drew a sheet up over them, gathered her quivering back to his chest where she fluttered against him like a rescued bird. They slept, still as stone effigies on an ancient sarcophagus in a moonlit chapel.

23

Outside, the world broke about them as Falcón and Consuelo slept on. Only at midday did a call on Falcón's mobile crack open their sedation. He came to as if from some coma life where fantastic goings on were now reduced to the dullness of reality.

'Late night?' asked Ramírez.

'You could say that,' said Falcón, panting into the phone, his heart walloping in his chest. 'What's going on?'

'I got a call from Pérez about ten thirty. He was in Las Tres Mil with one of the Narcotics guys, following up on Carlos Puerta. They found him in an empty basement, still with the needle in his arm. Overdose. I told him not to disturb you and to handle it himself.'

Falcón ran his hand down his face, tried to rub some feeling of reality into it.

'He just called me again about ten minutes ago,' said Ramírez. 'He's been doing some hunting around, talking to people with the Narc. Remember Julia Valdés, El Pulmón's girlfriend, who was shot yesterday in his apartment? She used

295

to be Carlos Puerta's girlfriend. They worked together. She was a flamenco dancer, he sang. They bust up in June and she started going with his dealer. Closer to the source, I suppose.'

'Are we looking at a suicide?' asked Falcón, still not quite with it. 'Had Puerta taken the bust-up badly?'

'Very badly. He went downhill fast,' said Ramírez. 'His junkie friends said he got some royalties from a recording contract and put the whole lot up his arm. By the time you interviewed him with Tirado he was at the end of a three-month binge.'

'How much money did he get?' asked Falcón. 'Three months is a long binge.'

'Good point,' said Ramírez. 'For some reason I don't think we've quite got the full story on Puerta.'

Falcón nodded, said he would get into the office as soon as he could. They hung up. Consuelo called her sister, spoke to her sons Ricardo and Matías, told them she'd be with them in an hour. No news.

Breakfast was a stunned affair, conducted by automatons in wordless understanding. She wore a shirt of his and a pair of boxer shorts. The toast soaked up the green olive oil, the fresh red tomato pulp, the thinly sliced *jamón*. They ate and drank small cups of bitumen coffee. The sun was bright in the patio, the water in the fountain flat as glass, birds swooped between the pillars. They could not eat slowly enough for this to last longer than twenty minutes.

The car's windscreen framed their view of the city, a documentary so dull, of people going about their business, that its audience could not believe that this was what it had all been about. There must be more to it than shopping, having your hair done and painting a door.

'Did it happen?' asked Consuelo.

'It happened,' he said, and held her hand.

'What now?'

'I have to think where I went wrong,' said Falcón. 'I have to retrace my thoughts to find the deviation point.'

'What do I tell Inspector Jefe Tirado?'

'Let him carry on,' said Falcón. 'He'll have his own way of doing things, and he's probably got as good a chance of success as we have.'

'He might be concentrating too much on the Russians.'

'I'll put him right about that.'

He came off Avenida Kansas City and went into Santa Clara, found her street.

'I can't stop thinking that I've ruined you,' she said.

'You said that last night, Consuelo, and I told you . . .'

'You corrupted yourself because of me,' she said. 'I forced you to join hands with gangsters and made you complicit in the kind of aberration you're paid to investigate, and I can't tell you how . . .'

'Francisco Falcón and I used to play chess together,' he said. 'I remember one time when he forced me into a position where the only move I could make would get me deeper into trouble, and, having made the move, his response meant that, again, I had to do something which made things even worse. And so it went on to the inevitable checkmate. That's what's been happening here. Once I'd made the mistake of believing that the Russians had taken Darío, I drew us both into a series of inexorable moves. *You* didn't ruin me. I ruined myself with a blinkered approach. I panicked because . . .'

'Because Darío means almost as much to you as he does to me,' said Consuelo. 'And I think it brought back the horror of what happened to Raúl's child, Arturo, too. That was the first time I fell for you, four years ago, when we asked each other: What happened to that little boy? And that's partly why you did it: all that terrible stuff came back to you.'

Falcón put his foot on the brake. The car eased to a halt

297

in the middle of the road. He stared vacantly down the shaded street. The street where Consuelo lived.

'How could I forget it?' he said to himself. 'How could I possibly have forgotten that?'

A car pulled up behind them and, when its driver saw that nobody was going to get out, honked its horn. Falcón pulled over.

'It happened in the Plaza San Lorenzo,' he said. 'I got the call just before we met at the Bar La Eslava. The voice said: "Something will happen. When it does, you will know that you are to blame because you will recognize it. But there'll be no discussion and no negotiation because you'll never hear from us again."'

'You'll *recognize* it?' she repeated. 'And what did you think they meant by that at the time?'

'I don't know that I did think about it that much,' said Falcón. 'It was just another threatening phone call. I'd had several.'

'You'd been somewhere that night.'

'Madrid. On the train. I had a call on the AVE telling me to keep my nose out of other people's business.'

'What was the business you were going to do in Madrid?'

'Yes,' he said slowly. 'Police business and . . . other business.'

'The same business you were on when you went to London and Darío was abducted?'

'Exactly that,' said Falcón. 'I thought the call I received on the AVE was because I was pushing Marisa Moreno to talk to me. So when I got back to Seville I went to see her again before I went to meet you, just so that she knew I wasn't scared by the calls. I even told her I'd be waiting for a call from her people. So when I got that call just as I came into the Plaza San Lorenzo I didn't think about it. My brain made the automatic connection back to Marisa.'

'But they weren't Marisa's people.'

'And by going to London I disobeyed their instructions to keep my nose out of their business.'

298

'And who are *they*?'

'I'm not quite sure,' said Falcón. 'Let me use your mobile.'

'But do you know *why* Darío was taken?'

'I think,' said Falcón, punching out a text to Yacoub, 'that it was done so that my attention would be diverted elsewhere.'

'You're saying things without saying anything, Javier.'

'Because I can't,' he said and sent the text.

Need to talk. Call me. J.

'But you *think* you know who took Darío?' asked Consuelo.

'I'm not precisely sure who would have done the job, but I know the group who ordered it.'

'And they are?' said Consuelo, grabbing his head, turning it towards her. 'You don't want to tell me, do you, Javier? What could be worse than the Russian mafia?'

'This time I'm going to get my intelligence right,' said Falcón. 'I'm not making the same mistake twice.'

Crawling along Avenida Kansas City looking for a public phone. The heat oppressive. Falcón alone now. The text back from Yacoub had told him that he was in a hotel in Marbella and gave the telephone number of a Spanish mobile to use. Falcón gave up looking, went to the railway station.

'What are you doing in Marbella?' asked Falcón.

'Business. I mean, clothes,' said Yacoub. 'It's a small fashion show, but I always pick up a lot of work for the factory here.'

'Is Abdullah with you?'

'No, I left him in London. He's going back to Rabat,' said Yacoub. 'Why all the questions?'

'There's been a development. We need to talk face to face.'

'I don't know whether I can get all the way to Seville,' said Yacoub. 'That's three hours in the car.'

'How about half way?'

'I'm on the road to Málaga now.'

'Could you get to Osuna?' asked Falcón. 'That's about a hundred and fifty kilometres from Málaga.'

'When?'

'I'll call you with a time. I haven't been into the office yet.'

As he was leaving the station he picked up a message from Mark Flowers asking for a meeting in the usual place. Falcón was desperate to get to the office, but the river was on the way.

Ten minutes later he parked by the bullring, crossed the Paseo Cristóbal Colón and trotted down the steps to their bench. Flowers was waiting.

'I haven't got much time,' said Falcón.

'Nor have I,' said Flowers. 'These Russians holding the boy . . .'

'What are you looking at them for?'

'I thought you wanted to find Consuelo's kid?'

'Right,' said Falcón, needing to think about Flowers's relationship to this before he told him anything important. 'A lot on my plate, Mark. Long nights.'

'I need some help.'

'Does that mean you've been given permission to help me?'

'I don't always need permission,' said Flowers.

Falcón briefed him on the power struggle between Leonid Revnik and Yuri Donstov, only giving him as much detail as Pablo of the CNI had told him and not touching on any of the developments of last night. He couldn't afford to have that knowledge swimming around in Flowers's head.

'And you don't know which group has the boy?'

'Either or neither,' said Falcón.

'But the threatening phone calls were about what exactly?'

'Initially they wanted me to stop investigating Marisa

300

Moreno and thereby make a connection through her to them and the Seville bombing,' said Falcón. 'But then they identified me at the scene of Vasili Lukyanov's accident and saw an opportunity to get their disks back.'

'Which would allow them to pressurize I4IT and Horizonte in whatever business they're doing,' said Flowers. 'So why neither? You said: "Either or neither".'

'The threatening phone calls are unidentifiable. I've been guessing that it's the Russians, but it could just as easily be something to do with . . . other things.'

'Yacoub, you mean?' said Flowers immediately. 'And you've heard nothing since the kidnap?'

'One of the calls said I would never hear from them again.'

'Can you get me copies of these disks?'

'What for?'

'*You*, as an inspector jefe, can't be seen to be negotiating with criminal gangs, but there's nothing to stop me in my line of work.'

'Is this your profound moral certitude coming out again?' asked Falcón.

'I wish I'd never said that.'

'The disks are evidence.'

'Just copies, Javier. Copies.'

'You want me to start making copies of certified evidence in a busy Jefatura?'

'It's dead in there at lunchtime,' said Flowers. 'If you want me to find the boy, you've got to give me the tools.'

'I'll see what I can do,' said Javier, who was feeling a strong desire to get away from Flowers, something smelling very bad about his request.

It was 1.30 p.m. by the time he got to the Jefatura. Cristina Ferrera was alone in the office. He told her he'd heard from Ramírez about Carlos Puerta and asked if there'd been any developments on the various murders.

'We picked up some further sightings of El Pulmón after he left his vehicle yesterday afternoon,' said Ferrera. 'He bought a bottle of water on Avenida Ramón y Cajal and was seen washing himself off in the street. He was spotted again, still stripped to the waist, running down Calle Enramadilla. The last sighting was in the bus station in the Plaza San Sebastián.'

'That sounds as if he was getting out of town.'

'They're still working the bus station, but at some point he must have got a T-shirt because we're not picking up any more sightings of someone stripped to the waist.'

He got her to check the arrival time of the I4IT private jet in Seville and went down to the computer room. No natural light. Banks of computers. Young faces lit by grey light coming from the screens. The Inspector Jefe told him that they'd been working on the disks since eight thirty that morning. At eleven thirty they'd brought in a couple of mathematicians from the university. By midday they were in touch with Interpol to see if they'd cracked any Russian mafia codes recently. They hadn't heard anything back.

'How urgent is this?' asked the IT chief.

'There's a late afternoon meeting between a Spanish business consortium and the town hall, which we believe the Russian mafia are trying to influence,' said Falcón. 'We assume this because some of the participants in that meeting feature in the sex footage on the disks. We think that the two encrypted disks you're working on contain "associated material" and we'd like to know what it is before the meeting takes place.'

Back up to his office. Ferrera with news of a revised flight plan logged by the pilot of the private jet. It was now due to arrive at Seville airport at 19.00 this evening. Falcón's mobile vibrated. His brother, Paco.

'El Pulmón,' he said. 'Are you still interested in finding him?'

'You've had a tip-off?'

'Not exactly,' said Paco. 'But I've managed to find out that the only guy he's kept in touch with in the bullfight business is another gypsy, a brilliant horseman, who looks after the animals on a finca in the Serranía de Ronda.'

Falcón took down the address, hung up, began to plan his afternoon.

'Where's Ramírez?' he asked.

'Lunch with Serrano and Baena,' said Ferrera.

'Ask them to come back here as soon as they can. We might have a lead on El Pulmón.'

The mobile vibrated again; he put it to his ear without checking the screen.

'I hope you haven't forgotten about us,' said the voice.

'You said you'd call. I've been waiting,' said Falcón, going into his office, closing the door.

'You've got the disks?'

'No, they're in use. They're being examined. I don't have access to them.'

'You'll never crack that code,' said the voice. 'We have the resources to pay for the best minds in the business. You'll be doing better than MI6 if you crack it . . . and they've been working on it for three years.'

'The process is not in my hands,' said Falcón. 'And even if it was and I could access those disks I'd still be waiting for you to deliver on your promise.'

'Our promise?'

'I delivered those disks, but you haven't kept up your end of the deal.'

'But there *was* no boy,' said the voice. 'And we saved your lives.'

'If you wanted to get your hands on those disks you were always going to have to do that,' said Falcón. 'Now you have what *you* want and I have nothing.'

'You're negotiating with us?' asked the voice, perplexed.

'You want those two remaining disks,' said Falcón. 'I want the Seville bombers. That means: the two men who masqueraded as building inspectors and the three electricians who planted the device. I also want to know where I can find Nikita Sokolov.'

'You're being very demanding, Inspector Jefe.'

'*And* I want the person who murdered Esteban Calderón's wife in her apartment early in the morning of 8th June this year.'

'The judge murdered her himself,' said the voice. 'He's confessed.'

'I don't know where you heard that from,' said Falcón. 'Maybe your source in the Jefatura is not so reliable. That was the prime reason why Marisa Moreno was murdered, wasn't it?'

'Why do you think *we* had anything to do with that?'

'Nikita Sokolov,' said Falcón, and left it at that, hoped that would be enough to persuade the voice that he knew more than he did.

'Sokolov is not one of ours.'

'But he was.'

'I'll have to get back to you.'

'And before you deliver on Sokolov, you can ask him where his two friends are, the ones he used to cut up Marisa Moreno with a chain saw.'

'This is a lot of people,' said the voice. 'This is . . . two, five, six, seven – nine people you want in return for the two disks. I'll have to come back to you, but I can assure you that Señor Revnik will not be happy about this.'

'There's no rush.'

'I don't follow you.'

'If, as you say, we'll never crack the code on those two disks, then we have all the time in the world.'

24

On the road to the Serranía de Ronda – Tuesday, 19th September 2006, 14.30 hours

They took two cars. Falcón, Ramírez and Ferrera in the lead car, Serrano and Baena behind. Only Pérez was left in Seville, still working on the murders in Las Tres Mil and Carlos Puerta's suicide. Falcón was anxious about taking all his men off their various cases, but El Pulmón was an important witness and the intelligence they'd had from the local Guardia Civil, who they were going to meet in Cuevas del Becerro, about twenty kilometres north-east of Ronda, had been promising. He needed all this manpower because the farm was in an area protected by high mountains to the north. There were a lot of horses on the farm and if the two gypsies got wind of their approach they could ride into the *sierra* in minutes and, once up there, they'd never find them.

Falcón had arranged to meet Yacoub in Osuna at as close to five o'clock as possible. Just as he was leaving the Jefatura he'd bumped into Inspector Jefe Tirado of GRUME, but hadn't been able to think his way round all the complications of warning him off the Russians. He'd just told him what he'd mentioned to Flowers – either or neither – and to keep an open mind. Tirado didn't think that was helpful. His investigation was stalled. He was doing a lot of work around the Nervión Plaza for nearly no return.

The heat was more brutal out in the open country, where the bleached sky and the bare, chalky brown earth seemed drained of all vascular circulation. The ridge of mountains they had to cross to get to the village where they were meeting the Guardia Civil was lost in the afternoon haze. The endless hectares of olive trees, ranked like ancient armies ready for battle on some vast uncontested plain, were the only evidence of civilization in this arid, deserted landscape.

On the way he briefed Ramírez and Ferrera on the situation with Alejandro Spinola, his involvement with the mayor's office and his relationship with Marisa Moreno and therefore, very possibly, the Russians. He also told them what had happened when he went to see Comisarios Elvira and Lobo.

'So, what are we going to do about Spinola?'

'When we finish this business, you two are going to the airport to see who comes out of the I4IT chartered jet and follow the car to wherever it takes them. Serrano and Baena are going to track Spinola.'

'But they're all going to end up in that fancy hotel, La Berenjena,' said Ferrera. 'Why don't we just go straight there?'

'It looks like the Russians want to influence the outcome of whatever this deal is between the mayor's office and the I4IT/Horizonte consortium,' said Falcón. 'We just don't know how or when they're going to do it.'

'And we can't touch Spinola because of Lobo and Elvira,' said Ramírez.

'And we can't mount an official operation at La Berenjena either,' said Falcón. 'Who knows, it might turn out to be a completely legitimate deal, with no mafia involvement, and we can all go home and sleep easy. On the other hand, with the intelligence we've gathered, I think we have to be available in case things go wrong.'

'Can we at least do some preparation work?' said Ferrera. 'Like get a list of the other guests, warn the manager that we're coming and get some idea of the security set-up at the hotel.'

'What do you know about this place?' asked Ramírez.

'The website says that it's an exclusive celebrity hangout, that royalty has stayed there, and that it's not just an ordinary country-house hotel. They have a head of security and the management is willing to consult on additional security arrangements.'

'It's important that Elvira doesn't hear about any of this,' said Falcón. 'So if it can be achieved in total secrecy, then go ahead.'

'We might need some help in identifying the players we don't know,' said Ferrera. 'There are four suites booked at La Berenjena, so who is this extra person on the I4IT/Horizonte team, and how do we recognize the mafia men?'

'There are no existing shots of Leonid Revnik and only an old gulag shot of Yuri Donstov,' said Falcón. 'The rest should be on the CICO database.'

'We'll have to take shots of them when they arrive and send them to Vicente Cortés and Martin Díaz for identification,' said Ramírez.

'I'll bring a laptop,' said Ferrera.

'You'd better brief Cortés and Díaz,' said Falcón. 'And I'll talk to the CNI.'

They crossed the main road, climbed the ridge and dropped down to where the Guardia Civil were waiting for them on the outskirts of Cuevas del Becerro. They had a large-scale map of the area and some further intelligence. El Pulmón's gypsy friend had been seen in Ronda buying clothes and shotgun shells. The owner of the farm was touring up in the north and the place was being run by a manager, who had gone down to the coast with his family. There was a stable for twenty horses and the gypsy lived in a small cottage adjoining it. His job was to look after the animals.

He was well known in the area and he knew the country like the back of his hand.

'Where do you think they're most likely to be at this time of day?' asked Ramírez.

'With any luck they'll be having a siesta,' said the Guardia. 'But they could be . . . that's a point – at the back of the stables there's a practice bullring for training the horses with bulls.'

'Is that what the horses are used for?' asked Baena.

'Yes. He's one of the best *rejoneadors* in the business. Fantastic horses. He goes all over Spain and Portugal with them,' said the Guardia.

'They won't be out in the fields, not at this time of day in this heat,' said the other Guardia.

'Those horses are going to be pretty valuable,' said Baena.

'So,' said Serrano, taking out his revolver, checking that it was fully loaded, 'we'd better not shoot any of them by accident.'

'Fuck, no,' said the Guardia. 'You do that and you'll have to find at least a hundred thousand euros per animal.'

'And the rest,' said Baena.

'Do you know the practice ring?' asked Falcón. 'How many ways in or out?'

The Guardia shrugged. Falcón decided they'd go in their two unmarked cars and not risk taking the Guardia in their green-and-white Nissan Patrols with them.

'When we get there,' said Falcón, 'Serrano and **Baena** will go into the stables and check them out. Ramírez and I will search the cottage. Ferrera will stay outside and keep watch. If there's no sign of them, we'll move to the practice bullring. The three of you will man the entry points and Ramírez and I will go into the ring.'

'*Toro!*' said one of the Guardia, and they all laughed.

The Guardia led them out into the country and pointed out the entrance to the Finca de la Luna Llena. The farm buildings were not visible from the road. There was a long two-kilometre slope up from the entrance gates and the main building could be seen at the top of the rise.

'If they're out and about, they're going to see us coming over this rise,' said Ramírez.

'That's if they're looking out for us,' said Falcón. 'El Pulmón isn't expecting anybody to find him out here.'

'Shotgun shells?' said Ramírez.

'That's the minimum he'd need to take on Nikita Sokolov,' said Ferrera.

The two cars coasted down the track, engines idling, into the farm buildings. The stables were behind the main house and the cars came to a halt in front. Silence. No movement. Too early in the afternoon even for cicadas. They got out, guns ready. Nobody slammed the car doors. Baena trotted up to the far end of the stable block, checked round the back, held up his thumb, went into the building at the far end. Serrano took the door next to the cottage. Ferrera moved silently between the buildings, listening for voices and movement.

The cottage was open. Ramírez took a quick look around, just three rooms. Empty. Falcón pointed to the ceiling. Went upstairs. Nothing there. Outside, Ferrera was waiting, told them she'd heard voices in the practice ring. Serrano came out of the stables and the four of them headed for the practice ring, guns out.

Falcón stood in the middle of the main entrance to the practice ring. There was a stone staircase on the outside wall of the ring where spectators could go up to watch from a roofed seating area above the main gates. Ramírez went right, Serrano left.

Two minutes. Ramírez came back at a trot.

'Serrano's positioned at the entrance for the animals, just in case; there's a small bull in there,' he said. 'The only other way out would be to run up the seating in the ring and then down the stone staircase here.'

An animal snort came from inside the ring.

'There's at least one horse in there,' said Falcón.

'Let's take a look,' said Ramírez.

Ramírez went up the staircase, crawled the last five steps, came back down.

'Two guys, both gypsy-looking, one horse. The horse is tied up. It's got padding around it. One guy, who looks like El Pulmón, has a cape. The other guy is holding a mock-up of some bull's horns.'

'El Pulmón practising his old moves.'

'There's a lance leaning up against the wall of the ring and there's a shotgun next to it.'

'This is the only way out on a horse, isn't it?' said Falcón.

'There's no way to manoeuvre a horse in the bullock pen.'

'All right,' said Falcón. 'Cristina, you go up to the seating area above and cover us. Fifteen seconds and we go in.'

Ferrera crept up the steps. Falcón nodded to Ramírez, who opened the door. They slipped in, closed the door behind them. The two men were facing away from them. The horse seemed to acknowledge their entrance with a nod of the head and a snort.

'Roque Barba!' shouted Falcón, gun out, pointing directly at the man with the cape. 'Police!'

It happened at lightning speed. The gypsy dropped the practice horns and in one leap was on the back of the horse. El Pulmón threw his cape up in the air and it came spinning towards Ramírez.

'Freeze!' shouted Ferrera, from above.

The gypsy slapped a button on the barrier and the main door to the practice ring sprung open. He slipped the rein and picked up the picador's lance. The shotgun was too low down for him. El Pulmón hesitated, thinking about reaching for it. The gypsy put the horse between El Pulmón and Falcón, dropped his head low to the horse's neck, tucked the lance under his arm. El Pulmón grabbed the padding at the side of the horse and kicked his feet up in the air. With a jab of the gypsy's heels the horse took off out of the open door. Falcón and Ramírez scrambled to one side; the steel tip of the picador's lance flashed past at face height. Ferrera let off a shot over their heads. It didn't stop them. In the space of twenty metres El Pulmón got his leg up over the rear of the horse. The gypsy chucked the lance and hauled his friend up behind the saddle. El Pulmón grabbed hold of his waist. The horse galloped the length of the stable block. Falcón and Ramírez ran out of the practice ring in time to see the horse getting into its full stride, kicking up dust and heading for the fields above the farm.

'What a fuck-up,' said Ramírez.

'I didn't want to risk shooting the horse,' said Ferrera, from above.

They were all watching the galloping horse when from the far side of the stable block came another rider on a black stallion. The gypsy's horse was badly encumbered by its protective padding, and the black stallion, which was a beautiful beast, had no difficulty in catching up.

'Fuck me,' said Ramírez. 'That's Baena.'

Baena was ducked low by the horse's neck, arse up in the air, looking every bit the professional rider. He reached out and grabbed El Pulmón's fluttering shirt and yanked it hard. El Pulmón had no stirrups and came straight off the back of the horse. Baena pulled up and was on him, gun in his face, his other hand hanging on to the stallion's rein. El Pulmón had landed on his back and was badly winded, rolling around and cycling his legs in the dust, trying to get some air into his remaining lung. The gypsy reined in the padded horse, which came up on his hind legs, while its rider stood up in the stirrups and did three or four complete turns as he looked back. Ferrera ran for the car, picked up Falcón and Ramírez and they joined the gasping El Pulmón. Baena calmed the stallion, which had been alarmed by the rush of the arriving car.

'I didn't know you could ride, Julio,' said Falcón.

'I went to riding school for years when I was younger,' he

said. 'I fancied myself as a *rejoneador* but, you know what happens. Not many people make it. I did a couple of years in the mounted police, but it was too boring. I tell you, when I saw that stallion already saddled up I thought, I've got to have a go. That's a quarter-million euros' worth of horse there.'

They lifted El Pulmón into the back seat of the car, cuffed him face down. The gypsy on the padded horse was still there, pacing his animal to and fro.

'What about him?' asked Ramírez. 'He came at us with a lance.'

'We haven't got time for that,' said Falcón. 'We've still got a long day ahead of us. Take that horse back to the stables and let's get on with what we came here for.'

They drove back to the farm buildings while Serrano and Baena walked the stallion to the stable block. Ramírez righted El Pulmón, sat him up in the middle of the back seat. Falcón got in the other side.

'I'm not talking to you,' said El Pulmón. 'Fucking Narcs.'

'You don't have to talk to us,' said Ramírez. 'We're taking you back to Seville and throwing you to the Russian bears. You'll talk to them. Your old friends. They're the ones who supply you with dope, let you make a lot of money, and kill your girlfriend.'

'What?'

'You didn't hear about that?' said Falcón.

'They killed her?' said El Pulmón.

'We're homicide cops,' said Ramírez.

'We're looking for the guy who shot the Cuban, Miguel Estévez,' said Falcón. 'He's the same guy who went into your bedroom and, for no reason at all, shot Julia Valdés.'

'In the face,' said Ramírez.

'His name is Nikita Sokolov,' said Falcón. 'He used to be a weightlifter. Stocky guy. Very muscular legs. Remember him?'

'You'll be glad to know, Roque, that you winged him,' said Ramírez. 'With that shot from your Beretta, you drew blood.'

'I used to get my product from the Italians,' said El Pulmón. 'At least I knew where I was with those guys. They spoke my language. Then back in March this stocky Russian turned up and started giving me different stuff, very pure. The Cuban, Miguel, came along to translate.'

'So why did they come to see you yesterday?' asked Falcón.

'I was due a delivery.'

'What about the gun? Your Beretta?' asked Ramírez.

'I was still selling Italian product. I didn't want to drop my old suppliers because I didn't know how long the Russian stuff was going to last. The Russian wanted me to sell his gear exclusively. A few weeks ago the big guy hung me out of the window to make his point, warned me that he would install his own dealer if I didn't stop selling the Italian shit. So I got myself prepared.'

'Didn't clear your girlfriend out, though, did you?' said Ramírez.

'I didn't think they'd come to *kill* me,' said El Pulmón. 'It was just a delivery, but I was nervous enough to take precautions. And, fuck, I wish I had got Julia out of there.'

'So what happened?'

'One of my clients ratted on me,' said El Pulmón. 'Told the Russian I was still selling Italian product.'

'Aha!' said Ramírez. '*Now* we get the full story. Was Carlos Puerta the rat?'

'How do you know that?'

'We picked him up on some associated business,' said Falcón. 'He described the Russian for us. He saw the whole thing from outside your apartment block.'

'That fucker. He's still crazy about Julia. And then he got himself badly strung out. Needed more dope and his money ran dry.'

'And the Russian stepped in with a little bribe,' said Ramírez. 'Puerta's dead. Committed suicide this morning. Happy?'

'*Joder,*' said El Pulmón, head bowed.

'We need to find Nikita Sokolov,' said Falcón. 'How did you make contact with him?'

'I called Miguel, the Cuban. That was my only way in.'

'You know how to catch a Russian bear?' said Ramírez.

El Pulmón shook his head.

'Honey,' said Ramírez. 'We're going to cover you in honey and tether you out in the sun and wait for Nikita to turn up.'

El Pulmón looked from Ramírez to Falcón to see if he was going to be more friendly.

'When we bring Sokolov in,' said Falcón, more reasonably, 'you're going to identify him.'

'You're fucking kidding.'

'It's either that or the honey treatment,' said Ramírez.

'And you'd like to get the guy who shot Julia, wouldn't you?' said Falcón.

El Pulmón's shoulders dropped. He stared into the footwell and nodded.

A quarter to five and Falcón was making his way up to the main square in Osuna. A strange town, which looked unassuming from the outside, but the low, tiled, whitewashed houses gave way to opulent sixteenth-century mansions from the time when New World wealth had found its way into deepest Andalucía.

The Plaza Mayor had colossal palm trees which shaded the few bars, the 1920s casino and the empty square. Yacoub was early and Falcón watched him sitting alone in the heat at a table on the pavement. He had a *café solo* and a glass of water beside him. He was smoking and looking remarkably unperturbed, compared to their last two meetings.

Pleasantries over, Falcón sat at the small, round metal table and ordered a plate of squid and a beer, with a coffee to follow.

'You're looking more relaxed,' said Falcón.

'I've passed another loyalty test,' said Yacoub. 'The GICM

say Abdullah isn't ready yet. They put him through his paces in training and his platoon commander says he needs to toughen up mentally. They don't want to lose someone of his intelligence and potential through poor preparation. They wouldn't think of giving him any sort of mission for at least another six months.'

'Your strategy worked then.'

'That's how you have to be with radicals. If you don't show the same fervour as they do, you're suspect.'

'Will they involve you with the mission when he *is* ready?'

'I don't know. I've been told I will be involved, but who knows with these people?' said Yacoub. 'Whatever . . . it doesn't *solve* my problem. I've still lost a son to radical Islam, I'm just in a slightly better position to stop him getting killed.'

'We've got time now,' said Falcón.

'And what is time going to do for us? You think I'm going to be able to change his mind? And, even if that were possible, then what? Hide him for the rest of his life? Hide myself?' said Yacoub. 'No, Javier, you're not thinking straight. What I've come to terms with over the last week is that this is a lifelong commitment. That's why I suffered so much. I've been thinking short term. I couldn't see beyond the horror of Abdullah being drawn into this organization. Because I have the mentality **of** a dabbler, I was kidding myself that there was still a way out. Now I know there isn't, and I've started to think much longer term. Not years, but decades. My Western mentality has always tempted me into the belief that there was a "quick fix", as the Americans like to call it. And, of course, there is one, but it always breaks. So now I've gone back to my Arab way of thinking and I've re-taught myself the art of patience. My purpose is different now. I will crush them, but . . . in the end.'

'What about the immediate problem you had with your Saudi friend, Faisal?'

'Yes, I wanted to thank you for being so discreet with the British,' said Yacoub.

'They put me under a lot of pressure,' said Falcón. 'They've even brought in Mark Flowers.'

'Don't go near him,' said Yacoub. 'He has the smell of rot about him.'

'Tell me how things went with Faisal.'

'That was part of the test. That was why the GICM sent me to London. They want to see where my loyalties lie,' said Yacoub. 'One of the things they feel sure about the Western mind is that it has grown soft.'

'Soft as in sentimental?'

'They believe that Westerners no longer have the necessary endurance for duty. They attribute it to a decadent culture in which love, money, family – all the things that a Westerner would betray for – now have greater value than political, patriotic, religious and moral beliefs. The Westerner has become a victim of the importance of self in their minds. And so they wanted to see where on my integral scale did my son and lover appear, compared to what they consider to be more manly beliefs.'

'Were there any surprises?' said Falcón.

'They've forced me to think,' said Yacoub. 'It's been humiliating and exhilarating.'

The food arrived. The waiter set down the plate of squid, some chips and salad, bread and a glass of beer.

'You're looking stricken, Javier,' said Yacoub. 'Is what I'm saying bothering you?'

'If we've gone soft and, as you say, lost sight of our beliefs, why are you fighting for us? What are you fighting for?'

'That's a good question. Any soldier needs to know what he's fighting for,' said Yacoub. 'Before I went into this, I thought I knew. It's only having been on the inside, by concentrating on what I'm fighting against, that I've understood. And it's not Saddam Hussein and Osama bin Laden. They're like phantoms now. But is it what Bush tried to replace those ogres with: that ultimate Western ideology?

So while I watched young men blowing themselves up, killing their fellow Muslims because of an intense religious belief, I asked myself: Am I fighting for freedom and democracy?'

'Isn't that part of it?'

'You know who soldiers fight for?' said Yacoub. 'Each other. The guys in their platoon. They don't crawl out to a wounded comrade for democracy. They don't mount an assault on an enemy position because of freedom of speech.'

'And you?' asked Falcón. 'You don't have a platoon.'

'I only have those closest to me. And I realize that in this respect I am a Westerner. Ideology breeds fanatics, and fanatics compete with each other to be more fanatical, until all the original clarity of their ideology has gone,' said Yacoub. 'The fanatics have damaged me by taking away what is dear to me, and I will hold them to account for it. I know my enemy now. I've lived with the narrowness of their minds, seen their vision of the future, heard their uncompromising views. I've had to absorb their ruthlessness, too, and now I'm beginning to make it my own.'

Falcón finished the food, downed the beer. Yacoub made his every action seem banal. The waiter came over with the *café solo* and a glass of water, took away the detritus of the meal.

'You've changed,' said Falcón.

'As I said, you can intellectualize as much as you like when you're on the outside, but I only found out the emotional truth by being on the inside,' said Yacoub. 'This feeling of purpose I have is from knowing that I'm fighting for those I love.'

'Not revenge?'

'Revenge too, but it's not the only driver,' said Yacoub. 'The disturbing and unsettling reality is that *love* is the other driver. I'm not sure that love and revenge aren't inextricably entwined. But what about you, Javier? What are you doing here? You didn't bring me here to talk about this.'

'Maybe the GICM are right and we Westerners have gone

317

soft,' said Javier. 'Last night I turned my back on all my principles. I negotiated with criminals, stole evidence, allowed myself to be corrupted and, finally, I walked away from murder.'

'Why?'

'Not revenge,' said Falcón. 'Just love.'

'Whose love?'

'Consuelo's. And because I love her son, Darío.'

'And what has the boy got to do with any of this?'

'He's been kidnapped.'

Yacoub stiffened on the other side of the table and leaned slowly across to look at Falcón, who told him everything down to the whole horror of the previous night, which came back to him with surreal intensity.

'So if the Russians haven't got the boy, who has?' asked Yacoub.

'I think he's in Morocco.'

'Why?'

'Because one of those threatening calls I took, after seeing you in Madrid, told me that something would happen and when it did I would understand my responsibility for it and that I would "recognize" it. And now I do recognize it. Don't you . . . Arturo?' asked Falcón, using Yacoub's long-forgotten Spanish name.

'When did they take him?'

'When I was with you in London,' said Falcón. 'They took him from a football club shop in the Sevilla FC stadium while his mother was on her mobile phone.'

The two men were staring at each other, alive as hunting hawks, not daring to blink.

'And you think the GICM are responsible?' asked Yacoub.

'I don't know. They could be.'

'What would they gain from it?'

'To mess up my head. To put me under pressure. To make sure that my attention was diverted elsewhere,' said Falcón, 'so that they could achieve what they wanted with their new recruit.'

'And . . .? Go on. Say it.'

'To screw up my relationship with you,' said Falcón. 'Because I would know that the only reason it had happened was because of our involvement with each other.'

'So they're testing *your* resolve, too,' said Yacoub. 'And what have they found?'

'That while love and family ties can be considered soft and sentimental,' said Falcón, 'they have also, throughout history, driven us to as savage a ruthlessness as any ideology or religious fanaticism.'

'Listen to me, Javier,' said Yacoub, fixing him from across the table with his dark eyes. 'You must not reveal, under any circumstances, what I told you in London. It is vitally important. If you do, I can guarantee that you will never see Darío again.'

'What the hell does that mean?' said Falcón. 'I thought your strategy had worked and this Saudi thing was over.'

'It is over, for the time being, but the intelligence services still want to know what happened,' said Yacoub. 'And believe me, they will set everyone on you to find out what I've told you. But you must *not* tell them.'

'So you know where Darío is?'

'No, I don't. But I think I know what this is about, and I will find out where he is,' said Yacoub, standing up. They embraced at the table. Yacoub kissed him on the cheek.

'One thing I don't understand,' said Falcón, 'is why you told me all that stuff in London when you knew it could be so dangerous to you.'

'First of all, you are my only true friend,' said Yacoub. 'And, strange to say, there are some things that can only be safe in the hands of a good friend. Secondly, it was imperative to me that you would be the one person who would know and understand the whole truth.'

319

25

Driving back to Seville, Falcón talking on the mobile to Ramírez, the sun low in the sky, the glare so penetrating that it hurt even through sunglasses – or was it something else twitching in the back of his mind, alongside Darío, making him uneasy?

'Where are you, José Luis?'

'I'm in the control tower at the airport. The private jet hired by I4IT/Horizonte is due in around five past seven,' said Ramírez. 'The flight plan out has just been logged for tomorrow. They're going to Málaga, taking off at midday.'

'El Pulmón?'

'In the cells.'

'Detectives Serrano and Baena?'

'They're parked outside the Andalucían parliament building, waiting for Alejandro Spinola to come out,' said Ramírez. 'Sub-Inspector Pérez is in a car outside the town planning office on the Isla de la Cartuja, because one of my contacts in the town hall told me that the mayor has a meeting there at seven thirty.'

'And you've been in touch with the manager of the hotel?'

'One minor development there. Horizonte called earlier today and dropped one of the ordinary suites and booked the presidential suite instead. Yours for two thousand five hundred euros a night,' said Ramírez.

'That's got to be for someone important,' said Falcón.

'There's a dinner booked for eleven o'clock – ten people in a private room, again under the name Horizonte.'

'What about the other guests?'

'There's an American couple under the name of Zimbrick, a German couple under the name of Nadermann, and three booked in Spanish names: Sanchéz, Ortega and Cano,' said Ramírez. 'Two of those have already notified them of a late arrival.'

'Who's made a booking in the last forty-eight hours?'

'Sanchéz and Ortega,' said Ramírez. 'And Horizonte made that alteration.'

'Anything else I should know?'

'Horizonte have also reserved the conference room and cinema before dinner for one hour and asked for DVD projection facilities to be available.'

'So, it looks as if we're right about it being a big new construction project,' said Falcón. 'First they'll have the site inspection, then the video of what it's going to look like, followed by the celebratory dinner and maybe even the signing ceremony.'

'Horizonte have specifically asked that six bottles of Cristal vintage champagne be made available after the dinner.'

'This isn't just another stepping stone in the negotiating process,' said Falcón. 'This is the big moment, and it's why the contents of Vasili Lukyanov's briefcase were so crucial.'

'But without the disks what can the Russians do?' asked Ramírez.

Falcón winced behind his sunglasses. Was he going to start lying to his right-hand man? This was what he told suspects: the first lie begets a hundred others and nothing sticks in your mind like the truth.

'The meeting I've just been to in Osuna was about the abduction of Darío,' he said. 'I don't think the Russians have him. I'm nearly certain that he's in Morocco.'

'CNI business?' said Ramírez. 'Inspector Jefe Tirado of the GRUME told me there's still been no contact from the abductors, and if the Russians were trying to influence the outcome of this meeting with the mayor tonight they'd need those disks, which are still in our safe.'

'Which could mean that at least one of the mafia groups has copies,' said Falcón. 'So we have to assume that is the case.'

He was appalled at the smoothness with which he'd plastered over that little crack.

'If the Russians are going to muscle in on this deal,' said Falcón, 'they're not going to do it in the business park on the Isla de la Cartuja with all its security. If it happens it'll be in the hotel.'

'Maybe we should get back-up,' said Ramírez. 'Fuck Comisario Elvira, we can't put our own people –'

'Back-up will involve Elvira, and we'll still be briefing him by the time the meeting takes place in a couple of hours' time,' said Falcón. 'And besides, the Russians aren't going to go in there guns blazing. This isn't gang warfare. They're going to put pressure on the Horizonte/I4IT consortium. These are civilized people who scare very easily. We also have to keep our strategy quiet, because if the Russians have informers in the Guardia Civil, I'm sure they have them in the Jefatura as well.'

'I was thinking more in terms of securing the hotel so that the mayor can have his meeting and sign the deal in peace,' said Ramírez. 'The mafia don't get a look in. None of our people have to take any risks.'

'Perfect, as long as the deal is totally legitimate,' said

Falcón. 'Alejandro Spinola has created a question mark over that.'

'How do you think Comisarios Lobo and Elvira are going to take it when a corruption scandal of this magnitude hits the press?'

'Badly,' said Falcón. 'But the attraction of this scenario to me is that it's likely that the extortion will be done by senior mafia group members: Viktor Belenki and possibly even Leonid Revnik himself. For once we might actually catch some major players committing serious crimes, rather than picking them up for money-laundering or running illegal businesses,' said Falcón. 'And in the fallout, I think we're going to find answers to the Seville bombing, too.'

'Right. I forgot. It's all connected,' said Ramírez. 'Where are you now?'

'On the outskirts of Seville. I'm going into the Jefatura. Just keep me informed of any developments.'

He hung up, continued driving into the sun. Something about his conversation with Yacoub still bothered him, but there was too much going on for him to pick it out of his memory. And anyway, it was less to do with words and more to do with a feeling about Yacoub.

There was a lot of traffic on the ring road taking him from east to west Seville. He suddenly had to concentrate, and it was at this moment that 'the voice' chose to call.

'How are you getting on with our last two disks?'

'I'm just heading over to the Jefatura to see what progress the IT department are making on them. They might be available now.'

'We've been able to comply with all your requests,' said the voice.

'What? Round up all the perpetrators of the Seville bombing? Including Nikita Sokolov and his two friends?' said Falcón, incredulous. 'I find that hard to believe.'

'As we told you, Yuri Donstov's operation was in the process of being closed down.'

'And what's happened to Yuri Donstov himself?'

'He has disappeared.'

'Are you sure you don't mean terminated?' said Falcón. 'Remember, I had a very special insight into the workings of your organization.'

'Yuri Donstov saw the way things were going and decided that disappearing was more advisable than the alternative. Although the alternative is only a question of time.'

'We're going to have to interview all these people you've brought together for me.'

'Interview them? Why? They'll be arriving with signed confessions.'

'We have to establish that you're sending us the right people,' said Falcón. 'Their confessions have to satisfy a court of law.'

'You're not just being demanding now, Inspector Jefe,' said the voice. 'You're being impossible.'

'The Jefatura's IT department have been hard at work, deciphering those disks. They've brought in some mathematics professors and Interpol, and it won't be long before they'll be approaching the intelligence community . . .'

Back at the Jefatura he went straight to the IT room. The two disks were still in use. So far they'd made no significant progress. They'd contacted the CNI, who were sending someone down to take a look. He went upstairs to his office, sat at his desk. The wall chart – my God, he was looking forward to tearing that down. It depressed him. That's what Alicia Aguado had said in his later sessions with her: contemplation of the past induces depression, but who are you without a past? Falcón had always thought that, if you had a past full of joy you wouldn't mind contemplating it. Aguado countered: If you only had joy to contemplate you'd learn nothing, until you reached the point where you questioned your relative happiness. He'd thrown up his hands. 'The unexamined life is not worth living,' she quoted.

'Is this the philosophical Inspector Jefe?' said Pablo, leaning against the door jamb of his office.

'I was wondering what had happened to you,' said Falcón.

'I've been spending too much time on the AVE. I came down from Madrid with our software-encryption specialist,' said Pablo. 'You don't call us any more, Javier, so I have to seek you out and force you into face-to-face meetings.'

'I'm not avoiding you,' said Falcón. 'I'm just busy.'

'Not helped by having to drive out to Osuna this afternoon.'

'Are you following him or me?'

'Him, of course,' said Pablo. '*You* don't represent a threat.'

'Nor does Yacoub,' said Falcón, who briefed Pablo on his 'rogue' agent's mental state and his resignation to a future of long-term dissimulation.

'Agents like Yacoub have to go through this phase,' said Pablo. 'We're trained for it in the service and plenty of people fall at that fence. This isn't a game that you pack up and put away. It's not suspended reality, like a good novel or a great film. It's a whole life to lead in a certain way and very few people are suited to it. And even those who are suited to it necessarily go through this . . . well, it's almost a grieving process, I suppose. Saying farewell to the simple life involves anger, despair, sorrow, anxiety, depression . . . all those emotions that we associate with the loss of something or someone important to us. And the only way out of it is to replace it with something that gives us purpose.'

'And what happens to people like Yacoub when this purpose he's so carefully cultivated disappears?'

'Do you mean . . . been accomplished?'

'That's the easier question to answer,' said Falcón. 'What I mean is that *now* he is setting out with this new resolve, but he is just one man, surrounded by numerous enemies. He will be constantly tested. He's already resigned himself to the loss of his family. Now all he has is his purpose, which, given the need for constant pretence and lying, must inevitably get whittled away.'

'Inevitably?'

'Because we're not talking about a job, Pablo. This isn't professionalism, acumen, or managerial skill. This is about who you are.'

'Soul, you mean?' said Pablo, smiling.

'Yes, that probably is what I mean . . . if I could be certain what "soul" was. But whatever it is, it needs nourishment, and that normally comes from the people around you, who you love, and who love you. That's finished for Yacoub. So it's a question of how long his "soul" can last on a nourishment of, say, revenge.'

'A long time.'

'Until you go mad,' said Falcón, falling back in his chair, suddenly tired of all this dialogue. Where did it get him? Words and language had such constraints, as their use of the word 'soul' had just demonstrated.

'Do you know where his son is?' asked Falcón.

'He's still in London.'

'What's he doing there?'

'What you'd expect any kid of his age to be doing,' said Pablo. 'Eating out. Bars. Night clubs. MI5 even sent some of their girls to talk to him. They danced all night, had a great time.'

'Not exactly Islamic behaviour from Abdullah.'

'He has his cover,' said Pablo. 'Even the 9/11 terrorists went to bars, drank beers and talked to girls.'

'Is that all he's doing? No other . . . activity?'

'Six months is the minimum we'd expect for an agent of his age to become active,' said Pablo. 'It would make MI5's job a lot easier if they knew Abdullah's proposed target.'

326

'There *is* no target any more,' said Falcón. 'This was all a test of Yacoub's loyalty to the cause.'

'Once a target, always a target,' said Pablo. 'If Yacoub and his target are out of danger, you shouldn't mind telling us.'

'We didn't discuss that.'

'What *did* you discuss?'

'He said he was going to help me find Consuelo's son.'

'How can he help you with that?'

'Because I think the GICM have got him,' said Falcón, and regretted saying it instantly.

'They would only kidnap Darío to put pressure on you,' said Pablo, coming fully into the office for the first time, his curiosity piqued. 'Why would they want to do that?'

'The kidnapper said I would "recognize" it,' said Falcón. 'In other words, I would see the similarity between Darío, a son of Raúl Jiménez, being abducted, and Arturo, another son – now known as Yacoub – also having been kidnapped thirty years ago when he was a similar age. The caller said we would never hear from them again, which was something that happened in the original Arturo case, too.'

'That's in your personal context,' said Pablo. 'I'm interested in what it means in *our* context.'

'That's the point, though: it's meant to be personal.'

'But why? I don't understand why, even on a personal level,' said Pablo. 'What is the point? You're not even sure yourself, are you? I mean, I can see the similarities between Arturo/Yacoub and Darío, in that they share the same father, but I don't see the motive.'

'Apart from putting pressure on my relationship with Yacoub?' said Falcón.

'That hasn't worked. You seemed to be closer than ever in Osuna, according to our surveillance.'

'What about: he's punishing Yacoub by recruiting his son, and he's punishing me by taking Darío, the closest I've ever come to having a son?'

'"He"? Who is "he"?'

'I mean the GICM.'

'Do you know "him"?' asked Pablo, suddenly suspicious. 'The person who is doing this?'

'No. How could I?'

'*He* knows *you*,' said Pablo. 'But the fact is, you are not concentrating on Yacoub. Your attention has been diverted. Am I right? I think I am.'

Since London, last Saturday, the only time he'd thought about Yacoub was as he drove Consuelo back to her house early this afternoon, when it finally occurred to him what the phrase 'you will recognize it' might mean. In the landscape of his mind over the last seventy-two hours the foreground had changed but the background had been constant. Whenever the foreground lapsed, Darío sprang immediately to mind.

'You're right,' said Falcón. 'And now it's changed. The pressure is off Yacoub.'

'Is it?' said Pablo, to himself again. 'Has it changed?'

'Abdullah is in London having a great time. Yacoub is at a fashion show in Marbella.'

'He was calm, you said.'

'Completely.'

'Why do people who've been very anxious suddenly become calm?'

'Because what was making Yacoub anxious is no longer imminent,' said Falcón.

'But it also happens to people when they've been decisive,' said Pablo. 'When they've finally made up their mind.'

Falcón's mobile vibrated on the desktop, creeping towards him with each ring tone. He took the call.

'There were only two men on the private jet which just landed,' said Ramírez. 'Our old friends from the disks: Juan Valverde and Antonio Ramos. But no sign of the American consultant, Charles Taggart. We're following their Mercedes back into town now.'

'Any movement on Alejandro Spinola?'

'He's already arrived at the town planning office,' said Ramírez. 'And I presume that's where we're heading.'

'I'll be there in ten minutes,' said Falcón, and hung up.

Pablo had lapsed into silence and was hunched over, thinking with a frightening intensity.

'I've got to go, Pablo,' said Falcón, 'but I need some help from you.'

'What help?'

'I might want to send some shots through of people we need to identify.'

Pablo scribbled an email address on a scrap of paper.

'I'll call them, make sure it's OK.'

'Thanks, I'll see you later,' said Falcón.

'It's not finished, Javier. I know it's not finished. You have to tell me.'

Falcón came right up to the brink and got into a struggle with his old self: the conservative, duty-bound, by-the-book Inspector Jefe. All he had to do was say the word 'Saudi' and it would all be over. He knew who would win. There had never been any doubt in his mind. It was just a small test he'd set himself.

'There's nothing to tell,' he said, and left the office.

26

The large black Mercedes containing the men identified by Ramírez as Juan Valverde, boss of I4IT Europe, and Antonio Ramos, the Chief Engineer of Horizonte, drove directly from the airport to the Isla de la Cartuja. Lying across the river from the old city, this was where the Expo '92 had taken place. It had now been transformed into an area of prime commercial real estate. The car waited at the heliport, where it was joined by another Mercedes. The two drivers got out, smoked and chatted. Four minutes later a helicopter's faint rhythmical beating could be heard coming from the south. The clatter of blades grew louder and the drivers turned their faces as the helicopter swept in, dipped momentarily and, amid a violent thrashing and rucking up of dust, settled its runners delicately on the painted yellow H.

As the blades came to rest, an employee from the heliport trotted up and opened the door to the helicopter. Two men got out: one was a corporate Spaniard in a light grey suit, white shirt, blue tie; the other clearly American in jeans, a blue button-down shirt with a light sports jacket folded over his arm. In the thirty-metre walk to the cars,

Ramírez got four good close-ups of both men with his digital camera.

The two men got out of the Mercedes, shook hands with the new arrivals, who had an air of seniority about them. They accompanied them to the second Mercedes. The heliport employee handed over a couple of suit carriers and two small cabin cases to the driver, who had the door to the car already open. The two men got in. Juan Valverde and Antonio Ramos returned to their Mercedes. The drivers got behind their steering wheels. The cars took off.

While Ramírez drove, Ferrera sat in the back and downloaded the images from the camera on to her laptop. The men's faces meant nothing to her. When they came into the wi-fi area near the town-planning management offices she sent the shots and her mobile number to the email address that Falcón had phoned through some minutes ago. Ramírez pulled up outside the town planning office on Avenida Carlos III, just next to the heliport, picked up Falcón, who got into the passenger seat. Ferrera handed him the laptop with an image of the two men. He shook his head.

They looked out at the two Mercedes. Nobody moved until the double doors of the town planning office opened and Alejandro Spinola led three people out. The first was the mayor, who was followed by a man and a woman.

'She's the head of Agesa, the company responsible for the Isla de la Cartuja,' said Ferrera. 'He's the head of town planning.'

Everybody got out of their cars. There were warm, insincere greetings all round. The unknown American smiled with perfect teeth and treasured any hand offered to him in both of his. He didn't seem to have any trouble speaking Spanish. After a few minutes they dispersed to their cars and the mayor's Mercedes joined the convoy which headed down Calle Francisco de Montesinos.

The cars pulled up at the Spanish Discoveries Pavilion

from the Expo '92 site. The group gathered in front of the building, walked around it, and then down to the river, going as far as the Puente de la Cartuja. The cars met them again outside the Monasterio de Santa María de las Cuevas, picked them all up and drove into the secure, fenced-off area of the business park. They arrived at a vacant lot in a prime location. Again the group gathered and walked around.

'What do you think they're doing?' asked Ferrera. 'There's nothing to see. It's like some Papal delegation come to bless the site.'

'More like corporate jackals come to spray their territory,' said Ramírez.

'I've read something about the pavilion, that they want to convert it into a museum and build apartments down by the river,' said Falcón. 'And my sister, who knows everything there is to know about property in Seville, told me that the site we're looking at now is the prime piece of real estate on the Isla de la Cartuja and is reserved for a bank to build a twenty-storey office building on it.'

The cars left the secure business park and crossed the Camino de los Descubrimientos and pulled up next to the Pavilion of the Future. The delegation got out and walked the full length of the pavilion, heading away from the Isla Mágica amusement park towards the Auditorium. On the way back they cut through into some parkland on the other side. At this point there was much arm-spreading and genuine excitement at the prospect of superb views of the river.

'This is where they're going to make a lot of money,' said Ramírez.

'All this belongs to the Isla Mágica amusement park, but they don't use it,' said Falcón. 'There's been talk for years of making this into an area for offices, shops and hotels.'

'Well, they've just given us a tour of the biggest building

project to happen in Seville in the last fifteen years,' said Ramírez.

The sun had set by the time the delegation went back to their cars. Detective Serrano followed Spinola and the mayor. Ramírez stuck with the two Mercedes containing the members of the I4IT/Horizonte consortium. Within minutes the two Mercedes had crossed the flood plain heading out of Seville and were on the road towards Huelva. Ferrera took a call on her mobile.

'Serrano says the mayor's delegation has split up back at the town planning office.'

'He should stick with Spinola and he can tell Pérez to go home.'

Twenty minutes later the two Mercedes pulled up at the gate to the Hotel La Berenjena, whose emerald, sprinkler-kissed lawns stuck out in the brown, sunburnt countryside. Ramírez glided past, turned round in a petrol station a hundred metres further on.

'Give them a quarter of an hour to settle and we'll go and introduce ourselves to the manager,' said Falcón.

Another call for Ferrera. She listened, jotted things down, hung up.

'That was the CNI. They've confirmed the ID of the heli-copter occupants. The Spanish businessman in the grey suit is Alfredo Manzanares, the new Chief Executive Officer of the Banco Omni. The American is Cortland Fallenbach, one of the co-owners of I4IT in the USA. They also thought we'd like to know that it was announced just an hour ago that the Banco Omni have acquired a controlling stake in the Banco Mediterraneo, which has five million customers and will be transferring its headquarters to a site in Seville in 2009.'

'Fucking hell,' said Ramírez. 'This really is coming together. When Lucrecio Arenas and César Benito were alive they must have promised the Russians a slice of this construction project in return for their dirty work on the Seville bombing.'

'That was probably just part of it,' said Falcón. 'Yuri Donstov was gearing up: Lukyanov was being brought in to run the girls, another guy to run casinos, while Donstov himself already controlled the drugs. And Sokolov would be running the protection rackets for the shops and restaurants. They were preparing to claim the Russians' reward for providing the violence in the Seville bombing which was a large slice of the income from tourists' "recreational activity". And if the right political party had taken power, it probably wouldn't just be Seville but the whole of Andalucía. Can you imagine how much money would be involved in running gambling, prostitution, drugs and protection throughout the whole of the Andalucían tourist industry?'

'So the Russians are very disappointed that their partners are *not* in control of the Andalucían state parliament,' said Ramírez. 'But what are they hoping to get out of this situation here? Lucrecio Arenas and César Benito, the people they had agreements with, are dead, and we reckon the Russians themselves were their executioners. Now we've seen the projects that the Banco Omni and Horizonte have got on the Isla de la Cartuja, we know they're legitimate. They have to be. The press will be all over them. After the public relations disaster that Lucrecio Arenas dragged them through, Banco Omni are going to make sure everything is whiter than white. Horizonte might have had to pay some backhanders to get the work, but that's no different to anywhere in the world. How are these Russians hoping to fit themselves in?'

'Blackmail. I think that's a fairly standard mafia ploy,' said Falcón. 'Here we are, a few hours before the signing ceremony, and some big guys pay you a visit in your hotel room, show you a DVD of yourself having sex and taking drugs, and say: "This is the subcontracting agreement you're going to sign or we'll spoil your show, maybe worse."'

'How do you think Alejandro Spinola is involved?' asked Ferrera.

'I know he introduced Marisa Moreno to Esteban Calderón and that connection was an important element in the Seville bombing conspiracy,' said Falcón. 'I'm sure he was put up to that by the Russians. As far as this building project goes, he's in a unique position, working for the mayor, to be able to give the Russians or Horizonte valuable inside information.'

'We don't have any proof that Spinola was a friend of Arenas and Benito,' said Ramírez, 'but he clearly knows Juan Valverde and Antonio Ramos.'

'Hopefully tonight we'll prove that he's the link between the Russians and the I4IT/Horizonte consortium,' said Falcón. 'But you'll notice that there are two important people missing from all this dodgy dealing.'

'Alfredo Manzanares from Banco Omni and Cortland Fallenbach, the owner of I4IT,' said Ferrera.

'And one of the projects in the contract is the construction of Banco Omni's high-rise – presumably with Banco Omni's money,' said Ramírez.

'Manzanares will want everything above board,' said Falcón. 'Which is where it will probably all go wrong for Spinola, and therefore the Russians, which could result in violence.'

'Or spoiling the show,' said Ferrera.

'I don't want to repeat myself,' said Ramírez, worried, 'but we could really use some back-up for this operation.'

'Let's look at the security arrangements when we get there,' said Falcón. 'And we have to remember, José Luis, it's quite possible that nothing will happen at all.'

They checked their watches. Ramírez pulled out of the petrol station and drove back to the hotel entrance. Falcón phoned ahead. The gates opened as they arrived and they drove up to a large señorial house. A bell boy told them where they could park the car out of sight. They got out, stretched their legs. Expensive cooking smells wafted out of the kitchens. The bell boy took them through the kitchens and into the manager's office behind the reception area.

The hotel manager was with his head of security. They laid out a plan of the hotel. The main building had a large patio in its centre around which was the reception area, a restaurant with three private dining rooms, a set of toilets, a conference room, a cinema with another set of toilets, two shops, one for perfume, the other for jewellery, an art gallery with a further set of toilets and the main security office. In the grounds were the nine suites and the presidential suite. Each suite was a flat-roofed bungalow with a large bedroom and bathroom, a living room with dining facilities, a sauna and mini-gym. Outside each suite was a car port, a private terrace and a small swimming pool. There was another larger swimming pool in the *palmerie*, which was the centrepiece of the garden. On the other side of that was the presidential suite, which was a two-bedroomed house with bathrooms, dining room, living room, kitchen and full staff. Outside it had its own gym, sauna, hot tub, swimming pool, terrace and bar.

'This is where the King and Queen stay when they come,' said the manager.

The head of security showed them the extent of the perimeter fence, which consisted of five-centimetre-thick steel bars two and a half metres high, topped with razor wire. There was a three-metre-wide dog run on the other side and a further fence. Every metre of the perimeter fence was filmed by CCTV cameras, which were under constant supervision in the screen room of the main security office.

'We provide the minimum requirement,' said the head of security, 'but if we have ministers or heads of state they will usually bring their own people.'

'Have this Horizonte/I4IT group brought any of their own people with them, or made any special security requests?'

The security man shook his head.

'If you want to move around the hotel without drawing attention to yourselves you should wear the staff uniform,' said the manager. 'Black trousers, white shirt, black waistcoat for men and a black belted dress for women.'

'Do you know what the mayor's delegation are doing after the event?' asked Ramírez.

'They're all going back to the city. The car bringing them will wait.'

'How many security guards patrol the grounds?'

'Four in the grounds, two in the main building, one of whom looks after the CCTV screens,' said the head of security. 'All armed.'

'What could go wrong?' asked Ramírez, cheerfully.

The manager looked at him nervously. They shook hands and the head of security took them on a tour of the main building. He described what the mayor's group would be doing, where and when. Drinks and canapés at ten o'clock in the conference room. A half-hour show in the cinema at ten thirty, followed by dinner in a private dining room at eleven. They inspected the projection room at the back of the theatre and were introduced to the technician, who had just been briefed by Antonio Ramos, the chief engineer of Horizonte, as to what was required and been given the necessary DVD showing the proposed construction project. They'd completed the sound-system test and were ready to go.

Outside in the lush gardens, privacy was the theme of the nine suites. Once inside, or out on the terrace, there was no sense of there being a neighbour. A good thirty metres separated each suite. At night security guards were told not to walk in the lit areas but to keep to the dark.

'There's camera entry to each suite,' said the head of

security, 'and light sensors if you approach the front door or terrace.'

Falcón's team went back to the security office and changed into their staff uniforms in the toilets. The only problem was for Ferrera, who had nowhere to put her gun in the simple black dress. Falcón and Ramírez tucked theirs down the backs of the trousers and covered them with the waistcoats. Ferrera left her revolver in the security office, went to reception to check on the changes in the reservations, saw Taggart's cancellation and Fallenbach's booking of the presidential suite. On the way back she took a call on her mobile.

'Alejandro Spinola has just left home in a taxi,' said Ferrera, coming into the security office. 'He's heading out of the city on the Huelva road. Looks as if he's coming early. Detective Serrano wants instructions.'

'I don't want any more people in here, or it'll look too crowded,' said Falcón. 'They should wait down the road in that petrol station we were in.'

They went into the CCTV-screens room with the head of security.

'Why are all these screens on the right dark?' asked Ramírez.

'They only light up if the sensor on the terrace of any of the suites is triggered,' said the screen supervisor. 'Nobody's sitting out at this time of night so they're all dark.'

'How does it work with guests arriving?' asked Ramírez.

'When they make the booking they give their car registration, model and colour and the number of people who will be staying. When a car arrives at the gate we check it against our list and, if it complies, let it in. If we have VIPs staying and they bring in other guests, we'll ask them to roll down the window and identify themselves to the camera. Our guest list today have not asked for anything unusual so we'll admit everybody on the vehicle registration. Of course,

338

we have another opportunity to check the people in the car when they arrive at reception. In fact, here's a car arriving now.'

A dark BMW had pulled up at the gates. The guard at the screens checked it against his list, let it in.

'This is the guest party registered as Sanchéz,' he said.

The car came up the drive, parked in front of the main building. A young woman got out of the passenger side of the car. She was tall, with extraordinary long legs, and was wearing four-inch heels. Her hair bounced on her shoulders as she made her way to the reception.

'No secret cameras in the bedrooms?' asked Ramírez. Ferrera hit him on the arm.

'Names?' asked Falcón.

'Isabel Sanchéz and Stanislav Jankovic. She's Spanish, he's a Serb,' said the guard.

The woman appeared on the screen at reception, handed over her ID and her partner's passport.

'Can we isolate her face?' asked Falcón. 'Download it and send it back to our organized crime experts, Cortés and Díaz in the Jefatura.'

'Who do you think it is?'

'On the basis of Cortés's description of Viktor Belenki's girlfriend as "fucking gorgeous" I thought she might be worth checking out,' said Falcón.

Ferrera went to take her laptop out. The guard at the screens told her not to bother. He downloaded the image, pasted it into an email and sent it off to Díaz. Thirty seconds later Díaz was on the line, confirming Isabel Sanchéz as their informer known as Carmen.

'So this Serb, Stanislav Jankovic, is in fact Viktor Belenki, right-hand man to Leonid Revnik,' said Ramírez. 'Do you have any cameras outside the front doors to the suites so we can pick up his face?'

'Once inside the car port they have total privacy,' said the

head of security, 'but, of course, they can check the identity of someone coming to their door with the camera entry
system.'

'This must be Alejandro Spinola's taxi arriving at the main
gate,' said Ferrera.

'What do you do in this scenario?' asked Ramírez.

'He has to identify himself and state his business,' said
the head of security.

Alejandro Spinola got out of the cab and pressed the
buzzer, identified himself to the camera. He was told to go
to reception. They opened the gates.

Isabel Sanchéz had her room key by now, went back to
the car which moved off to her suite and reversed, out of
sight, into the car port. Alejandro Spinola arrived in reception. The cab returned to the front gate.

'We can do voice in reception as well,' said the guard.
'That being where we're most likely to have conflict.'

The guard at the screens flipped a switch. They heard
Spinola ask to speak to Antonio Ramos. The receptionist
put a call through. Spinola spoke to Ramos inaudibly. The
receptionist summoned a bell boy.

'Any ideas what this is about?' asked Ramírez.

'I should think it means that the Russians have got their
hooks into Spinola, possibly some time ago,' said Falcón.
'They've told him who appears on the disks and he's going
to use that information to the best of his ability.'

'To blackmail the I4IT/Horizonte consortium round to the
Russian way of thinking?' said Ramírez. 'He's leaving it late
in the day.'

'Nothing like an imminent contract-signing to speed up
the process,' said Falcón. 'He's giving them forty-five minutes
to agree to the Russians' demands, with Fallenbach breathing
down their necks. I think you could call that brinkman-
ship.'

The bell boy appeared, leading Spinola down the path.

Viktor Belenki came out of his suite and lit a cigarette, got Spinola's attention, nodded.

'Go in close on Belenki,' said Falcón. 'Send a shot of him back to Díaz, just to check.'

Even in black and white Belenki was impressive, with blond hair and high cheekbones, and an animal muscularity under a white shirt and black trousers. He paced in leisurely fashion up and down outside his suite, smoking all the while, taking the night air. Spinola went into Ramos's suite. Several minutes eased past. Díaz called to confirm that the so-called Serb, Jankovic, was Viktor Belenki.

'Look at the state of Valverde,' said Ramírez.

Juan Valverde, the I4IT Europe boss, came out of his suite, fists rammed into the pockets of his towelling robe which gaped to show a pair of brief swimming trunks. His jaw was set and he looked thunderous under knitted eyebrows. He walked across to Antonio Ramos's suite.

'He's had at least some of the bad news,' said Ramírez.

Viktor Belenki started on his third cigarette. Suddenly he stood still. A development. Juan Valverde came out, his towelling robe now done up tight, looking less ominous, more scared. Antonio Ramos followed him, staring into the path as if he couldn't quite believe this was happening to him. They walked quickly over to Alfredo Manzanares's suite.

'I wouldn't involve the banker at this stage, would you?' asked Ramírez.

'We don't know how Spinola has put the Russian's proposal to them,' said Falcón. 'Valverde and Ramos must have a good relationship with their bankers, if not Manzanares personally. They're either going to try talking him round, or invoke the earlier agreement, whatever that was, between his predecessor, Lucrecio Arenas and the Russians.'

Viktor Belenki seemed content with the way things were

going. He dropped his cigarette, crushed it underfoot and, hands in pockets, kicked it on to the grass.

'Are you seriously expecting violence here?' asked the head of security, reacting to the tension in the room.

'By all accounts, we're dealing with some very unpredictable people,' said Falcón.

'But he's just one guy, isn't he?'

'We don't know,' said Falcón. 'There is no existing photograph of Leonid Revnik and only a gulag shot of Yuri Donstov, although he does have extensive tattoos – if we can get that close. The only instantly recognizable mafia man we can identify is Nikita Sokolov, an ex-weightlifter.'

'Another party at the gate,' said the guard at the screens. 'This is the Ortega couple.'

The car came through the gates and up to the main building. A man and a woman got out, went into reception. They were both in their late forties, obviously Spanish. Señora Ortega had an extensive list of demands, which she elaborated during the check-in process.

'You can't invent a woman like that,' said Ramírez. 'So, only the Cano party still to arrive and Alejandro Spinola's dinner companions, the mayor's delegation.'

'Did you see the Zimbricks or the Nadermanns when they came in?' asked Falcón.

'Sure,' said the man at the screens. 'They looked like tourists.'

'Do you have copies of their passports?'

'On the screen over here,' said the head of security.

Falcón clicked through the Nadermanns, but his hand faltered at the second American passport, belonging to a Nathan Zimbrick. Staring out of the screen was Mark Flowers.

'Have you got anywhere on the property which would do as a lock-up?' asked Falcón, clearing the screen, unable to compute what the CIA agent's presence meant.

'We've got some staff buildings down by the perimeter fence, where drivers can sleep,' said the head of security. 'There's a room there we could use to keep people until the Guardia Civil can come and take them away.'

Fifteen minutes passed. Viktor Belenki went inside, came back out in an expensive-looking suit and tie. Valverde and Ramos left Manzanares's suite on their own, hunched, not talking, body language declaring their complete failure. They headed off to the presidential suite.

'So Alfredo Manzanares told them to fuck off,' said Ramírez, 'and then called their boss to tell him his senior executives have been compromised.'

'Cortland Fallenbach knew about this,' said Falcón. 'I'm sure of it.'

'He was only booked in when Charles Taggart's suite was cancelled,' said Ferrera. 'I don't think this evening was originally a part of his schedule.'

'Valverde and Ramos have been the main contacts for the mayor and the town planning office for a long time, so Fallenbach probably sees the value in keeping them in place until the deal is signed,' said Falcón. 'Then they're out of their jobs.'

Ten more minutes. They stared at the entrance to the presidential suite where they'd seen the two men disappear. Nothing.

'Look at Belenki,' said Ramírez.

The Russian was leaning slightly forward and staring into the night as if he was beginning to suspect they'd all somehow escaped over the perimeter fence. He turned and went into the car port. At that moment Alejandro Spinola came out of Ramos's suite at a sprint. He'd obviously been waiting for Belenki to disappear and, as Ramos's suite was the furthest bungalow from the main building, he had a good hundred metres to cover.

'Spinola's realized or been told that Manzanares has

rejected the deal and he doesn't want to get caught in the open,' said Falcón. 'He wants to be safe in a public space to give the Russians the bad news.'

Belenki came out of the car port, crossed the path and headed across the grass to cut Spinola off.

'Let's go,' said Ramírez.

'Wait,' said Falcón. 'Let's see where they end up. No sense in running around the hotel when we can see it all here.'

The cameras showed two men crossing the patio. Belenki had his arm around Spinola, hugging him tight. Spinola was terrified. They went into the toilets by the art gallery.

'No cameras in the toilets,' said the head of security.

'Cristina, go and stand outside Belenki's suite with your weapon,' said Falcón. 'I don't want him to have a chance of getting back in there. Ramírez and I will go to the toilets. Can you back us up?'

The head of security nodded. They left the room. The shops and art gallery were empty apart from an assistant. Ramírez told her to go and wait in reception for a **few** minutes. They took out their weapons. Falcón eased open the door to the toilets. Ramírez closed it silently behind them. No sign of Belenki or Spinola. A harsh, guttural voice speaking good Spanish came from the last cubicle. It **was** the wide-doored disabled toilet.

'I don't know how to impress upon you the importance of this, you little piece of shit,' said Belenki. 'Did you tell them that this is the deal, or there *is* no deal and they get *this*?'

No answer, apart from a kind of grunting noise.

They moved towards the cubicle. Falcón stood poised, gun at shoulder height in both hands. Ramírez readied himself.

'What?' said Belenki.

A spitting, gagging sound from Spinola.

'What we're both going to do now is pay a visit to Alfredo Manzanares and explain to him the nature of our earlier agreement,' said Belenki.

'Alfredo Manzanares is not the only problem,' said Spinola, gasping for air. 'Cortland Fallenbach, the owner of I4IT, is here. He's the one who has to be persuaded.'

'Is he?' said Belenki. 'Do you think he could be persuaded like this?'

More grunting, heavy nasal breathing.

Falcón nodded. Ramírez took four steps and kicked the door with such a savage blow that it cracked back into the tiled wall with the sound of a rifle shot. Belenki, a hank of blond hair over his forehead, was in the middle of the floor, he had Spinola's tie wrapped around his fist and the man was dangling, his knees just brushing the tiles. Belenki's gun, a thick silencer attached, was forced hard into Spinola's mouth so that his Adam's apple jumped.

Belenki dropped Spinola, who fell to his side, as if the noise he'd heard was the shot that had gone down his throat. Because his tie was still wrapped around Belenki's fist, his head hung about a half-metre from the floor.

'Police! Drop the fucking gun,' said Ramírez, his weapon pointed at Belenki's chest.

With intense, ice-blue eyes Belenki looked from Ramírez to Falcón, weighing up all the violent possibilities. He let Spinola's tie slip slowly from his grip as if preparing himself to move.

'You want to lose an arm, Viktor?' asked Falcón.

Silence and then the gun clattered to the floor. The room seemed to exhale.

'Come here,' said Falcón, beckoning to Belenki. 'Face down on the floor, hands behind your head.'

Belenki got down. Ramírez frisked him thoroughly, found a small firearm in an ankle holster.

'Hands behind your back,' said Ramírez, and handcuffed him, hauled him to his feet.

They called in the head of security. Falcón checked Belenki's pockets for disks. Nothing.

'Who's with you, Viktor, apart from Isabel?' asked Falcón.

No answer.

'You didn't come alone, did you?'

No answer.

'Is Leonid Revnik with you?'

No answer, but a slight widening of the eyes.

'Take him down to the lock-up,' said Falcón. 'Start questioning him, José Luis. See if you can get anywhere. I'll look after this one.'

27

Alejandro Spinola was still lying on his side in the disabled toilet, shaking, the image of the accomplished networker from the mayor's office gone for good. His mouth was connected to the tiled floor by strings of bloody saliva. He was dry-retching and crying. Falcón knelt beside him, patted him on the shoulder.

'All right, Alejandro?' asked Falcón. 'Glad to see me this time?'

A nod, his fists jammed between his thighs, like a little boy who'd taken his first bullying on the playground.

'Good,' said Falcón. 'Let's get you cleaned up.'

Spinola stood at the sink, looked at himself in the mirror. His lips were cut up and swollen, and he'd lost one of his front teeth, an incisor. He buried his face in his arms and sobbed.

'Wash your face, Alejandro. Pull yourself together. We have to talk before this little event gets under way.'

Falcón helped Spinola out of his jacket. The shirt underneath was so drenched in sweat that the cotton was transparent. While he washed his face, Falcón asked the receptionist to bring a white shirt. Spinola lifted the tie over his head and unpicked the dense knot. He straightened the material with trembling fingers. A girl arrived with a shirt. He put it on, reconstructed the tie around his neck, combed his hair back into place and, staring into the mirror, touched his tender lips with the tips of his fingers.

'I'm finished,' he said, and his stomach started juddering with emotion.

'You're alive and Viktor Belenki is out of the game,' said Falcón, patting him on the shoulder. 'When did he first talk to you about his plans for Russian involvement in the Isla de la Cartuja construction projects?'

'In August,' said Spinola, thighs shivering uncontrollably. 'We met in Marbella.'

'What did he tell you?'

'That he had Valverde, Ramos and the American, Taggart, on film fucking whores and taking drugs,' said Spinola. 'All I had to do was line up the I4IT/Horizonte consortium to make sure it tendered the best possible bid, and he would sort out the rest.'

'Which meant that you leaked information about the other bids to whom?'

'Antonio Ramos, Horizonte's head of construction. He was the guy who was putting the building project together.'

'Couldn't they have sorted all this out before today?'

'Alfredo Manzanares has only been in charge of the bank for a fortnight. The whole financing of the Horizonte deal was being discussed with other parties from Dubai. Then the big boss in the US, Cortland Fallenbach, stepped in and said he wasn't going to have a project of this magnitude being financed, well, he said by the Middle East, but we all know he meant Muslims. You know how they feel about non-Christian religions in I4IT. He told Antonio Ramos that he was going to have to use the Banco Omni.'

'When was this?'

348

'The beginning of this month.'

'Were the Russians involved in the financing from Dubai?'

'I think they must have been, but I don't know,' said Spinola. 'They were furious when it was taken away from Dubai.'

'So the Russians lost their way into the building project through the financing, laundering their money in the process, and had to try a different tactic.'

'Alfredo Manzanares, as the financier, wanted all contractors on the job to have pristine track records. He's hardline Opus Dei and after the Seville bombing, with all its associations with Lucrecio Arenas and the Catholic Kings shit, he wasn't going to allow anything that had the faintest stink about it. So telling him he had to use Viktor Belenki's construction companies was never going to work. I don't know how Valverde and Ramos put it to him, but that, in effect, is what they would have been asking him to accept this evening.'

'All right, that gives us some vital background detail on tonight's event,' said Falcón. 'Now, I just want to clarify why you introduced Marisa Moreno to your cousin, Esteban Calderón, last year.'

'I was told to,' said Spinola. 'I didn't understand what it was all about at the time. I couldn't have known the implications.'

'Except that you knew you'd been asked by members of a criminal organization to introduce a woman to the leading instructing judge in Seville,' said Falcón. 'You might not have known about the intended bombing or Inés's murder, but you knew you were giving gangsters access to a very important person in the justice system. Why did you do it? Did they have you on film with your pants down? A single guy? No, I don't think so.'

He shook his head, sniffed. Falcón rummaged through Spinola's jacket, rammed his hands into his trouser pockets.

Spinola put up no resistance. Found it. A sachet of white powder.

'Coke?'

Spinola nodded.

'Is that it?' said Falcón. 'You did all this for some coke?'

Spinola stared into the sink, choked up again. He blurted out a few more sobs as the sudden vision of his collapsed career and spoiled life came to him again.

'I don't get paid very much,' he said. 'What little I make, I gamble. You know what gambling is like, Inspector Jefe.'

'Anything else?' asked Falcón, sensing there was more. 'How do you feel about your cousin? The brilliant lawyer.'

Spinola doubled over as if in agony, rested his head on the edge of the sink.

'I've lived in that fucker's shadow all my life,' he said. 'Do you have any idea what it's like to have your father holding up this guy all the time as someone to aspire to, when you know that he's been a first-class bastard all his life?'

'OK,' said Falcón, calming him down. 'Let's think about tonight. You've done something illegal: leaking information on the construction tenders to the I4IT/Horizonte consortium is a criminal offence, and you're going to have to explain that to the mayor – unless he was in on this?'

'*No, no, no, que no,*' said Spinola emphatically. 'He knows nothing, nor do Agesa or the town planning office.'

'Right,' said Falcón. 'I'm going to take you to the security office, where you'll wait for a guard to take you to the mayor as soon as he arrives. Tonight's event cannot continue under these circumstances, and you've got to do the right thing.'

They looked at each other via the mirror. Spinola nodded. They went back to the office together. Falcón asked the screen supervisor if the mayor's delegation had arrived. No sign. Running late. Falcón needed to get into the Sanchéz/Belenki suite and the head of security might be required for that. He got the screen supervisor to call him up and get another guard to take care of Spinola.

'Anybody else arrived yet?'

'Señor and Señora Cano.'

'Regular types?'

'A Spanish couple in their sixties.'

The head of security came back, they went to the Sanchéz/Belenki suite, picked up Ferrera standing guard outside on the way. Falcón pressed the buzzer. No answer. Pressed it again. Nothing. The head of security opened the door.

As soon as the air in the room touched Falcón's face he knew they were in trouble. Blood does something to an atmosphere: electrifies it, so that other humans know to tread with care.

The living room was unlit and empty. The terrace doors were open. The night had moved in, moths fluttered and batted against the bedroom door, which showed a crack of low light. The television was on in the next room. Falcón drew his gun, took four paces across the floor, nudged the door open with his foot. A reading lamp was casting light on to Isabel Sanchéz's body from the chest down. She was wearing bra and panties only. Perfect figure. Legs so long and slim they reminded him of a foal's. Her head was in darkness. He stepped fully into the room. She didn't move. He turned on the light. That was what was wrong. The vision of beauty they'd seen on the CCTV screens had gone. A hideous black hole where her nose and mouth should have been.

The light was on in the bathroom, too. The sound of the shower. Falcón stepped to his left, leaned in. There was a hole in the glass panel of the shower cabinet, which had several long hairline cracks in it. Beyond was a man slumped against the marble-tiled wall, blood still oozing from a hole in the

351

back of his grey head. The water from the shower cleaned and re-cleaned the constant rivulets of blood that ran down his back.

'Who the fuck is that?' asked the head of security, on his shoulder.

'This is probably Leonid Revnik,' said Falcón.

'He must have been hidden in the back seat, or the boot, when they came in,' said the head of security.

'Cristina, ask one of the security guards to take you down to the lock-up and get Viktor Belenki to confirm who this is in his suite. Be careful. Have your weapon at the ready. There's a killer out there and, given the way he's shot Isabel Sanchéz, I think it's Nikita Sokolov. Bring Ramírez back with you. Meet in the security office.'

The head of security sent out an alert to all guards in the grounds. Falcón gave him a one-line description of Nikita Sokolov. Using some toilet paper, he turned off the shower over Revnik's inert body.

'He came in from the back terrace,' said the head of security, 'but can't have triggered the light sensor.'

Back in the security office they went straight into the screen room. The screens on the right were all dark. The supervisor had seen nothing.

'If you hug tight to the side of the building it's possible you wouldn't trigger the light sensor,' he said.

'Run the footage on suite number six,' said the head of security.

The supervisor took it back ten minutes. The outside light hadn't come on. They looked closely and could see only a vague dark movement, nothing more.

'Has the mayor's delegation arrived?' asked Falcón.

'Yes, they went straight into the cinema,' said the guard.

'What do you mean? Spinola was supposed to talk to the mayor as soon as he arrived,' said Falcón. 'And what's happened to the guard looking after him?'

'I don't know. I've been watching the screens,' said the supervisor. 'I can't . . .'

The head of security held up his hand, radioed the guard, asked the question, listened.

'He never showed up. He thought responding to my alert about the weightlifter was more important, and he's out in the grounds looking for him.'

'Find Spinola, you must have him on those screens somewhere. I can't believe you didn't see him leave this office,' said Falcón. 'Why didn't the mayor have drinks and canapés before the viewing?'

'They were running late,' said the supervisor. 'There's a dinner afterwards. All I know is that they were met in the reception area by the guests from the Horizonte/I4IT consortium and they went straight into the cinema.'

Ramírez and Ferrera came in panting and sweating.

'Belenki's confirmed it's Leonid Revnik,' said Ramírez.

'Is Belenki secure?' asked Falcón.

'I've handcuffed him to the bed, and the door to the staff quarters is locked. There's not much else I could do,' said Ramírez.

'We're going to the cinema now,' said Falcón. 'Tell us when you find Spinola.'

The cinema doors were shut. The faint sound of the film presentation came through the wooden soundproofed doors. The head of security tapped Falcón on the shoulder, pointed at the projection room. The lock had been shot out. They all took out their guns. Ramírez shoved against the door. It wouldn't open. There was something jammed up against it on the other side. Between them they forced it open. Apart from a dead body on the floor there was another man, sitting quite calmly with his legs crossed, by the projection equipment.

'Mark,' said Falcón, nodding.

Flowers said nothing, looked tired, bags heavy under his

eyes. The dead man had fallen on his side, face turned to the corner of the room.

'Who's this?' asked Falcón.

'I don't know,' said Flowers, sighing, as if this killing had taken something out of him. Falcón knelt over the dead man, who had taken a bullet to the temple. Falcón fingered his hair, felt it was false. He eased up the hair piece, saw that the man had a head shaved down to the skin.

'What happened here, Mark?'

'The projectionist set the film running and I told her to get out. I locked the door after her. A couple of minutes later someone tried the door. There's no peep-hole, so I couldn't check who it was. I stood behind the door. He shot out the lock. The first thing that came in the room was a gun. I recognized it as a nine-millimetre Makarov. Given that sequence of events, I didn't bother to ask questions. As soon as his head appeared I shot him.'

Falcón pulled up the man's jacket, yanked his shirt out of his trousers and revealed his naked back, which was covered in tattoos: some Russian lettering, a crucifix and angel wings.

'This must be Yuri Donstov, also known as the Monk, judging by these tattoos,' said Falcón, checking the man's pockets, which were empty, not even a set of keys.

'I assumed from his weapon that he was Russian,' said Flowers, his exhaustion making him preternaturally calm. 'Those tattoos must make him mafia.'

'You're going to have to give me your gun, Mark,' said Falcón.

Flowers reached across to a low shelf under the projection equipment and handed over his silenced gun.

'Stand up,' said Falcón, handing the gun to Ferrera.

He searched Flowers, found a disk.

'Where did this come from?'

'I found it on our Russian friend,' said Flowers.

354

'You know what's on it?'

'I think it contains the material we talked about the other night.'

Falcón turned to the people behind him.

'Mount a guard on Viktor Belenki. Look out for the weightlifter, Nikita Sokolov. Find Spinola. Cristina, get some handcuffs and come back here. I'll talk to the mayor when we're ready.'

Everybody left. Falcón nudged the projection-room door to, moved in front of Flowers.

'What time is it, Mark?'

'You got me there, Javier.'

'You don't wear the Patek Philippe when you're working?'

'Breitling for ops,' said Flowers.

'And that was how you got paid by Cortland Fallenbach?'

'It was an opportunity,' said Flowers, shrugging. 'You know, we're public servants. We don't get paid very much and I have a number of ex-wives. I think I've spoken to you about them. American ex-wives are more demanding than European ones. And then there's the kids. That's a lot of outgoings. Why do you think I came out of retirement? You don't think I prefer fucking around with these shits to lying on a boat in the Florida Keys, do you, Javier?'

'What about Mrs Zimbrick?'

'I'm treating my girlfriend. There's no need to get ugly with her. She's a civilian. An English teacher.'

'This is hardly what you'd call soldiering, is it, Mark?'

'What can I say but, needs must, Javier?'

'You're here at Cortland Fallenbach's invitation?'

'I'm his security consultant. We got together after you asked me to research I4IT in June. I told him he was going to need help and he agreed.'

'What happened tonight?'

'He told me that under no circumstances was anybody to interrupt the showing of the I4IT/Horizonte presentation movie,' said Flowers. 'But he gave me no indication that it was going to come to this.'

'You *were* armed.'

'People calm down when you point a gun at them,' said Flowers. 'And if they've got one themselves, you're even.'

'We're going to have to put you in the cells until we can speak to the American consul.'

A knock on the door. Cristina came in, handcuffed Flowers to the projection equipment stand.

'Time for an announcement,' said Falcón.

'You must be a nice guy, Javier,' said Flowers. 'If it was me I'd play the DVD and listen to the bastards howl.'

Time had flown by and the film at that moment ended. Falcón raised the lights and shut Flowers in the projection room. The double doors to the cinema opened and the group filed out, led by the mayor, who was talking to the banker, Alfredo Manzanares. Falcón showed him his police ID card, tried to usher him into the conference room where they were supposed to have had their drinks earlier. Valverde and Ramos intervened, blocked the doorway, started some vociferous protesting.

'Open the projection-room door, Cristina,' said Falcón.

The woman from Agesa screamed at the sight of the dead body. Cortland Fallenbach saw Mark Flowers, turned to stone.

'I think you'll agree that this needs some explanation,' said Falcón. 'Close the door, Cristina. Take these people to the private room where they were supposed to be having dinner. Nobody is to leave that room under any circumstances. As you can see, there is a killer on the loose. Detective Ferrera is armed.'

The sight of a dead body had subdued the group completely and they went into the private room like a flock of sheep into a slaughterhouse holding pen.

Falcón took the mayor aside into the conference room

and had just embarked on his devastating introduction to the evening's events when his mobile went off.

'Belenki's been shot,' said Ramírez. 'Shot dead.'

There was a hammering on the door. A security guard said he was needed up in the main office. Falcón took the mayor to join the others in the private room where Ferrera was standing guard.

'Lock the door. Let nobody in or out,' he said, and left.

In the security office the supervisor was tapping one of the screens showing the thick-set, stocky weightlifter, Nikita Sokolov, gun in hand, striding up to the main building.

'He doesn't care now,' said the supervisor. 'He's not hiding from the cameras any more.'

'He's heading towards the main building, so he's not bothered about getting away just yet,' said Falcón. 'He must have come back to meet up with his boss, Yuri Donstov. Keep the other guests in the restaurant, clear the reception area, turn the lights off inside, keep them on outside. Whatever happens, I do not want this man shot unless it's absolutely unavoidable. Where's Spinola?'

'He got out over the main gates,' said the supervisor. 'He's on the run and we don't have the manpower to go after him.'

Falcón called Detective Serrano, who was still waiting with Baena in the car in the petrol station nearby. He told him to find Spinola, who would be out on the main road somewhere.

'Be careful with him. He's in a state. You have to make sure he survives. No accidents.'

By the time Falcón got to the reception area the lights were out in the patio. The shops and art gallery were in darkness. Between him and the main door were two thick marble supporting pillars. Beyond the pillars were four panels of plate glass, two of which were double doors. The mayor's delegation Mercedes was parked outside. No driver. Falcón hid behind one of the pillars. He didn't have to wait long.

Nikita Sokolov came out of the night, his colossal

quadriceps straining against the material of his trousers, biceps with a thick cord of vein bursting out of his polo shirt, which flapped at his waist. He had a thick, white bandage around his right forearm where El Pulmón's bullet had grazed him. The gun, silencer attached, was in that hand. He tried the door to the Mercedes. Locked. He looked through the driver's window, swapped his weapon to his left hand and dealt the glass a savage blow with the butt of his gun. It bounced off. Now that his work was done, Revnik and Belenki shot dead, his mission completed, he was thinking about escape. He checked the unlit main building. Didn't like it. He jogged off to his left. Disappeared back into the darkness.

Falcón told the head of security to stay in the reception area while he sprinted across the patio, down a corridor to the kitchens, which were totally silent on the outside and a cacophony of brutal swearing, hollered orders, clattering pans and sizzling fat on the inside. He ran down the corridors of stainless-steel work surfaces. Diminutive sous chefs with large knives, flaming pans, blow torches and cleavers, glanced over their shoulders as he tore past them. He asked after the mayor's driver, nobody answered. He found a *plongeur*, asked if there was a staff dining room. The man walked him past boiling cauldrons and flat metal griddles crackling and spitting with hot oil. He pointed him to a door with a porthole window at the end of a short corridor, said there was an outside entrance as well.

'What's out there?'

'The bins.'

Falcón looked through the porthole. The mayor's driver was sitting at the table in the empty room, eating. There was a window, barred on the outside, and a door, both to the driver's right. Falcón knelt down, crawled into the room. The driver's food stopped on its way to his mouth.

'Police,' said Falcón. 'Carry on eating. Don't look at me.'

He crawled under the window, was just about to get to

his feet when the door out to the bins burst open and Sokolov came in. Blue polo shirt, hairy arm outstretched, white bandage, gun, safety off, finger on the trigger.

'Keys!' he roared.

He'd seen the driver on his own, eating. Wasn't prepared for Falcón coming up on his right side, who chopped down with his revolver on Sokolov's bandaged arm. A shot, a dull thud and a crack as the bullet went through the wooden table, before the silenced gun dropped from Sokolov's deadened hand. Falcón lost grip of his own weapon, which scuttled off into the corner. The Russian turned and crouched and Falcón found himself precisely where he didn't want to be: facing off against the former Olympic weightlifter.

Sokolov charged him, caught Falcón in the midriff with his shoulder, wrapped a steel-reinforced arm around his back and lifted him up as if he was nothing more than a cardboard cut-out.

'Hit him over the head, hard,' Falcón yelled at the driver.

Sokolov hefted him to shoulder height and slammed him down on the wooden table.

The mayor's driver jettisoned himself out of his seat, reached behind him, picked up the metal chair and brought it down so that the edge of the seat made horrific contact with the back of Sokolov's head. The noise it made was violently musical, a pianist's mad discord. Sokolov turned and the driver thought for a moment that he'd made a terrible mistake, but the light went out of the Russian's eyes and he crumpled to the tiled floor. Falcón, too, was on the floor, staring bug-eyed at the unconscious Russian, trying to remember how to breathe.

The porthole door opened and the *plongeur* charged in with a shining stainless-steel cleaver in one hand and a rolling pin in the other.

'Damn!' he said, as if he'd just missed out on the ultimate culinary experience.

*   *   *

Alejandro Spinola was out on the Huelva road, running towards Seville, the velvet night air on his sweaty skin, the smell of hot, dry grasses in his nostrils. Occasionally he looked behind him, but each time he found he was only running away from the dark. He wasn't moving very quickly because he was in no condition to. His head was full of the junk of his life, the wreckage of tonight's events.

He couldn't have faced the mayor. He couldn't have faced approaching the mayor and the people from Agesa and the town planning office with his bruised lips and missing tooth, saying that he had to speak privately to the boss. He couldn't bear even the thought of the mayor's disappointment in him. Then there was his father. He'd have to face him, too. The whole messy business was going to come out, right down to what he'd done to his cousin, Esteban Calderón. It was going to be intolerable and he wasn't going to face it. He was going to run. He was going to run and run and not stop until . . .

Headlights came up slowly behind him, stopped. He looked back, couldn't see anything behind the blinding lights until a man stepped out from behind them, running after him. Who the fuck? He tried a sprint, but he had nothing in the tank, and slowed to a lolloping jog. The car started up again, pulled alongside him, the window down.

'Alejandro, we're the police,' said the driver. 'Come on now. Just stop and get in the car. No sense in this.'

He could hear the other man's footsteps behind him, it gave him a surge of panic. He saw headlights coming the other way. Something shrill and exciting rose in his throat. He thumped his foot down, stopped, turned back, ducked under the arms of the policeman following him, shoved past him, slipped round the back of the car and stood up straight between the oncoming headlights. The truck's horn blew the night open for three seconds, a white light covered Spinola from head to toe, and the black grille with thirty-five tons behind it gathered him in with a sickening crunch.

28

Hotel Vista del Mar, Marbella – Wednesday, 20th September 2006,
01.00 hrs

Lying on his back on the firm, expensive bed, pillow supporting his neck, phone to his ear, Yacoub Diouri was talking to his sixteen-year-old daughter Leila. They had always got on so well. She loved him in the uncomplicated way that a daughter loves her protective father. Leila and her mother was a different story, that was to do with her age, but she'd always been able to make her father happy. And Yacoub was laughing, but tears were also leaking out of the corners of his eyes, trickling down the sides of his face and coiling around the curlicued passages of his ears.

He'd already spoken to Abdullah in London, who'd been annoyed because he'd never been so popular with the girls before and he'd had to stand outside a club in the dark and cold, listening to his father prattling on about matters that could easily wait for when they were back in Rabat, but he indulged him. Yacoub was sorry for this, not because he would have liked a better conversation, but because he knew that Abdullah would always remember his irritation and

361

exasperation as the prevailing sentiment of this particular conversation with his father.

Leila said good night, passed the phone to her mother.

'What's going on?' asked Yousra. 'It's not like you to be calling home while you're away, and you'll be back here on Thursday.'

'I know. It's just that I missed you all. You know what it's like. Business. Madrid one day, London the next, Marbella the day after. The endless talk. I just wanted to hear your voices. Talk about nothing. How's it been without me?'

'Quiet. Mustafa left last night. He's gone back to Fès. He managed to get his consignment of carpets out of customs in Casablanca and he's got to go to Germany at the weekend. So it's just been Leila and me.'

They talked about nothing and everything. He could hear her moving around in her private living room, which she'd decorated in her own taste, where she received her woman friends.

'What's it like outside?' he asked.

'It's dark, Yacoub. It's eleven o'clock.'

'But what's it like? Is it warm?'

'It can't be much different to Marbella.'

'Just go outside and tell me what it's like.'

'You're in a funny mood tonight,' she said, stepping out of the french windows on to the terrace. 'It's warm, maybe twenty-six degrees.'

'What does it smell of?'

'The boys have been doing the watering so it smells of earth and the lavender you planted last year is very strong,' she said. 'Yacoub?'

'Yes?'

'Are you sure you're all right?'

'I'm fine now,' he said. 'I really am. It's been wonderful to talk to you. I'd better go to sleep now. Long day tomorrow. A very long day tomorrow. I mean today. We're two hours ahead here, of course, so it's today already. Goodbye, Yousra. Give a kiss to Leila from me . . . and take care of yourself.'

'You'll be all right in the morning,' she said, but she was talking to no one. He'd gone. She went back inside and, before she closed the doors, took one last breath of the lavender-infused night air.

Yacoub swivelled his legs off the bed, sat on the edge and buried his face in his hands. The tears ran down his palms. He wiped them on his bare legs. He breathed deeply, got his head back together. He put on a pair of black stretch-cotton jeans, a black long-sleeved T-shirt, black socks and a pair of black trainers. He wrapped a black sweater around his shoulders.

He lit a cigarette, looked at his watch: 01.12. He turned his bedside light off, let his eyes get used to the dark. He rested the cigarette on the ashtray, went to the window, slipped out on to the balcony and looked down into the street. The car, which had been there for days, was still there, the driver still awake. He shrugged, went back in. He checked his pockets. Nothing but the photograph. From the side pocket of his suitcase he removed a single ring with four keys. He looked around him, knowing there was nothing else he needed now. Took one last drag of the cigarette, stubbed it out and left the room. He had a powerful sense of relief as he closed the door.

The corridor was empty. He took the stairs down to the ground floor, came out into the hotel and immediately went through the door marked 'Staff Only'. It was quiet. He walked past the laundry and down a small flight of stairs to the kitchens. Voices. They were wrapping up the dinner service. He waited, gauging the different sounds, then stepped into the corridor, ducked underneath the portholes of the double doors and went out into the night and the stink of the rubbish bins. He climbed up the metal bin closest to the wall and checked over the top.

A complication had arisen here. On his return from his meeting with Falcón in Osuna, he'd been told that the CNI had put a car in the street at the back of the hotel as well as the front. The car was there now and almost directly opposite the rear exit of the hotel. He was going to have to drop over the wall into the street at the side of the hotel, and this involved a leap of some two and a half metres.

He made the jump, hit the wall messily, smacked his chin, but clung on to the top of it with his arms and shoulders cracking under the strain. He swung his leg up, lay flat on the top, gasped, looked down. Empty. As he lowered himself the strength drained from his arms and he dropped heavily into the narrow alleyway, went over on his ankle and limped to the corner. He checked out the car: only a driver with his head resting against the window. No movement. Yacoub looked left and right. Nobody around. He ducked and ran along the line of cars, found a gap, squeezed into it, held on to his ankle and waited. Blood trickled down his chin. A car turned into the street, headlights swept the tarmac. As it passed, he crossed the street running low and went straight up the narrow alley opposite. He hopped to the next street.

The Vespa and the helmet were locked to a lamp post. He used one of the four keys to unlock the heavy padlock and unthreaded the chain from the wheel and helmet. He used the second key to start the Vespa. He wiped out the helmet with his hand, put it on. It was sticky with the hair gel of the kid who'd left it there.

There was little traffic in the town. He set out west, heading for a small bay along the coast, which was protected from the sea and had shallow waters. On the other side of Estepona he turned towards the sea. He hid the Vespa and helmet by the side of the road and limped two hundred metres down to the water's edge where the boat was waiting for him. The only light came from the tower blocks of tourism set back from the road above.

Nobody could accuse the GICM high command of having no sense of humour. The power boat they'd bought for this mission was called the *35 Executioner*. It was dark blue, ten metres long and had twin Mercury 425-horsepower engines, capable of speeds in excess of 130 kilometres per hour. It looked sleek, almost flashy, as it rocked gently against the small wooden jetty where it was moored.

He unclipped the awning over the rear of the boat and dropped himself into the cockpit. He inserted the third and fourth keys in the ignition panel on the right-hand side of the dashboard, but did not turn them on. He threw the sweater off his shoulders into the passenger seat. He opened the hatch, leading to the cabin, which had been stripped out and a false wall installed. Yacoub felt his way around to the side, peeled back the edge of the carpet. He ran his fingers over the wood until he felt the metal ring inset and lifted out a thirty-centimetre square of wood. He found the pen torch first, turned it on, put it in his mouth. Blood on his hands from his chin. He lifted out a compass and a mobile phone, which he turned on, and a pair of binoculars. All that was left was a switch mechanism from which two copper cables emerged. He could now see the five jerry cans of fuel strapped to the bulkhead, two five-litre flagons of water and a tupperware box of food.

The phone was ready. One message. He opened it, nodded, turned off the phone and threw it in the cache. He checked his ankle, fat and soft as a ripe mango.

Back outside he rolled up the awning, threw it in the cabin, checked the stern lockers, more jerry cans of fuel. He opened up the two engine hatches. He stood in front of the driver's seat and familiarized himself with the gauges, switches and controls. In the middle of the dashboard was the SatNav screen, which he would not deploy until he was outside Spanish territorial waters. He turned on the battery switches and flipped on the blowers. He gave them five minutes, checked that the shift handles were in neutral and the throttles down all the way. He armed the safety switch. He turned the ignition keys one click clockwise. Indicator lights and audible alarms came on for a moment. He turned them on to the start position and released. The engines came alive with what seemed like a colossal noise in the silent bay.

The pressure gauge told him that the water flow through the engine was normal and he glanced over the side at the exhaust tips. While the engines warmed up he checked the bilge and engine compartments, made sure there were no leaks or weird noises. He closed the engine hatches. He raised the throttles slightly to check response. Good. Checked shifters. He slipped the moorings, pushed himself away from the jetty. He put the shifter into forward gear and, at very low throttle, moved out into the open sea, which was almost as flat as the cove's protected waters.

It was warm but he continued sweating, even with the gentle cooling breeze. The first part of this mission had its difficulties. He had no SatNav and no moon. He had to find a bearing out to sea and get himself out of Spanish territorial waters. The compass could be illuminated by pressing a button and he did this once a minute to check his course. There were a few lights out on the water – fishing boats, which he had to avoid. He, himself, was unlit. He maintained low revs. The coastline of the Costa del Sol gradually revealed itself. The lights of Estepona appeared to the west.

It took him more than an hour to get three kilometres from the shore and only then did he open up the throttles a little, feeling the eagerness of the two big engines beneath him. He scoured the blackness for fishing boats, checked his bearing, looked back to the east at the lights of Fuengirola, Torremolinos and Málaga.

The danger was different now. He wasn't so scared of

being picked up by the coastguard, but he was entering one of the busiest shipping lanes in the world. Colossal container ships, which could rise forty or fifty metres above the sea, coming in from the Atlantic, or massive Liquefied Natural Gas carriers sailing from Algeria to Sines on the Portuguese coast. If they hit him they wouldn't know it. He listened and searched the darkness.

Thirty kilometres out he switched on the SatNav to see where he was. He was supposed to be heading for a point forty-five kilometres south-east of Estepona and about the same distance north-east of the Monte Hacho, just outside the Spanish enclave of Ceuta on the north-east tip of Morocco. He was further east than he'd anticipated, the current much stronger than he'd allowed for. He was more than fifty kilometres from his rendezvous point with around two and a half hours to go before first light.

He had to have faith in his instruments. There was no longer any coastline to guide him. He turned the vessel direction south-west and gave it few more revs. He checked all the gauges, was puzzled to see the fuel had dropped to three-quarters. He'd been told the tank had a capacity of six hundred litres, that the extra jerry cans strapped to the cabin bulkhead and in the stern lockers were just for emergency. As he fussed over this new problem a cliff of black metal loomed out of the darkness and he heard the rhythmic thump of massive engines. He swung the wheel to his right, opened up the throttles, put a hundred metres between himself and the towering hull of a dry cargo ship. Eased back. Shaken. He didn't feel competent in this situation, had no real knowledge of the sea or boats, couldn't even name things properly. What was a cleat? He calmed himself, desperate for a smoke. His ankle throbbed. Panic rose again as he battled disorientation, a sudden queasiness and a tremendous desire not to be out in the middle of a black ocean on what seemed to be a matchstick, surrounded by mobile skyscrapers. His boat canted and rolled as the vast, unseen wake of the ship passed beneath him. Get the breathing going again. Don't hyperventilate. Look at your instruments. Get back on course. Proceed.

As he increased power he winced at every slight modulation of noise coming to his ear, every variation in tone of the blackness coming towards him. His nerve trailed behind him like a frothy, bubbling wake. He tightened his grip on the wheel, forced himself into a routine. He stared at the fuel gauge. Below three-quarters now. This boat went through 150 litres an hour at a cruise speed of 100 kilometres per hour. He doubted he'd been over fifty kilometres per hour the entire trip, so how had he gone through a hundred and fifty litres? He looked at his watch. He'd been on the water just over two hours. Maybe that consumption was normal. Ignore it. Don't get obsessive. He checked his course, raised the throttles. The boat surged. The darkness parted before him. The thought occurred to him that he didn't want to be on a boat with a dead engine and an LPG tanker bearing down. Panic quivered below his diaphragm. He should have worn a nicotine patch, couldn't remember when he'd last been six hours without a cigarette.

Don't look at the fuel gauge.

The fuel gauge was at the halfway mark. He rapped it with a knuckle. There was a problem. Three hundred and fifty litres in three hours at the speed he was going? He pulled back the throttles, centred the shift, turned off the engines and the battery switches. Silence. The waves slapped at the sides of the boat, which lolloped on the water. He got down on his hands and knees and sniffed. He plugged the torch in his mouth and opened up the engine hatches, sniffed. Was he seriously going to be able to fix a fuel leak? He didn't even know if there were tools on board. He checked the bilge for the smell of fuel until he wasn't sure what he was smelling any more.

This had not been part of his training. Refuelling the boat in mid ocean. He turned off the fuel valves, closed the engine hatches. Found the funnel in the stern lockers, heaved out a jerry can, located the fuel fills on the right of the cockpit. Slow down. Think. What was he going to gain by this? Was he just going to pour fuel into the ocean? He checked his watch. Plenty of time. The boat rose and fell. Let's do it. He jammed the funnel in, fitted a nozzle to the jerry can, poured the fuel in, looking about himself crazily for approaching walls of metal, listening, trying to hear above his tinnitus for the distant thump of marine engines. He'd never felt such physical vulnerability. As the fuel chugged into the tank he began to think that what was happening to him now was just a physical expression of his mental condition over the last three months. The sense of powerful forces ranged against him, happy to crush him without a second thought, yet he was unable to see them, just living inside his head, his tiny inner world, desperately clinging to the bits and pieces of his life that made him feel human. He changed jerry cans. A larger wave jogged the boat, fuel cascaded down his leg. Damn. This was dangerous. He reconcentrated his efforts. Poured the last of the second jerry can into the tank. That'll do. At least he would be able to see if this had made an impression on the fuel gauge. He took off his soaked trousers, threw them overboard. He hosed down the deck, reasoned that mid ocean would have aired the cockpit of fumes. He washed his hands. Heart in his mouth, he turned on the battery switches. He didn't burst into flames. He let the blowers run.

Again he looked around. Spooked himself. Leapt for the ignition, started the engines. Nothing. Shit. He *had* just poured fuel into the ocean. Wait. Calm down. Open the fuel valves.

The engine started. He couldn't see with the light of the pen torch still burning faulty images on to his retina.

He switched it off, jammed it in his underpants. Looked at the fuel gauge. Had it gone up? He checked the SatNav. He'd drifted off course again. The currents so strong out here. Filling up with fuel had cost him nearly two kilometres. Should he put another two jerry cans in? He listened again, stared hard into the grainy darkness which, rather than remaining stationary, seemed to be approaching him. How had he talked himself into this insane plan?

Turned off the ignition. Back to the jerry cans. Pen torch back in the mouth. Where was the funnel? He'd left it sticking out of the tank. It must have gone overboard. His eyes roved the side where the fuel fills were and it was then that he saw the words 'saddle tank' and 'main tank'. He nearly burst into tears with gratitude as he remembered something from his training. He knelt down, crawled back to the rear bench seats, switched the fuel from main tank to saddle tanks.

Engines sounded off to his right. He nearly coughed out the pen torch until he saw the container ship pass four hundred metres away. He envied those men high up, standing in the green light of the bridge, having a smoke and a coffee while their radar told them everything. Back to the SatNav. He was going south-east fast.

He started up the engines, wheeled the boat round, opened the throttles. Making headway towards the Straits of Gibraltar, he glanced at his watch. First light must be coming soon; he was desperate for an end to this blindness, this sense of impending steel hulls.

The current must be immensely strong. They'd told him it was what did for most small boats full of African immigrants. He'd seen the bodies once, lined up on a beach outside Tarifa, the Guardia Civil standing back from the stink. He gripped his forehead, banished these morbid thoughts. The current. He'd have to overshoot the target by a couple of kilometres and drift back into position.

He reined in his galloping mind. First light would come and all would be well. He looked behind him for a glimmer. Still uniformly black. He breathed back another rush of what he thought was panic, but then he was laughing, giggling uncontrollably as if he'd smoked some weed and suddenly seen the hidden absurdity of everyday life. He sat back in his seat, the hysteria trembled inside him, his thoughts quivered on the margins of sanity.

And with that came an extraordinary calm. His trepidation vanished. It was as his father-in-law had told him before undergoing his heart op in Paris: 'You push your fear like a rock up a mountain in the days beforehand and then, suddenly, they come for you and you deliver yourself into their hands and hope that Allah is with them. It is the calmest you will ever feel in this life.'

And it happened just when he hadn't been looking for it. First light. The miracle of the planets. The glow spread along the seam of the world. Ships revealed themselves against the gathering light. He would have loved to see land; even after a few hours he missed it enormously. He couldn't imagine how those lone yachtsmen who circumnavigate the globe could bear the solitude with the endless great unknown beneath them.

More light; 07.50 – twenty minutes to sunrise. His fear long gone, torn away from him and replaced by the confidence of illumination. The target should have left Tangier nearly two hours ago. He smiled to himself. This was going to work. The horizon blushed magenta, crimson, pink and violet, glowing yellow and white before creeping into blue, which became anil and made his chest ache at the thought of what he would miss. A thin streak of grey cloud, parallel to the perfect line of the horizon, like a stiletto piercing the flesh of a blood orange, made his jaw tremble with emotion.

08.07. He was at the rendezvous point. He dug out the binoculars, surveyed the sea. Five ships, now, to the west;

a tanker to the east. A splashing sound ahead caught his attention and he lowered the binoculars. A school of dolphin within ten metres of the boat. Diving and surfacing, leaping and plunging. He shouted at them for joy.

The sun came up at 08.11. The horizon quivered as if a meniscus had to be broken for the red orb to push up into the sky. He spread his arms like a jubilant conductor before his orchestra and then turned his back on it, surveyed the Straits of Gibraltar again with the binoculars. He was looking for a boat, not a big ship, although this vessel was sizeable, given that it wasn't cargo-carrying. It was forty metres long, about twelve metres high, had a Moroccan flag and was called the *Princess Bouchra*. But he still wasn't sure of scale out here. Even a one-hundred-and-fifty-metre tanker looked like a toy on the water.

The boat had drifted. He manoeuvred her back into position, just seven hundred metres north-west. 08.27. He scanned the ocean once more. Seven ships now to the west, four to the east. The *Princess Bouchra* must be visible by now. They'd worked it out meticulously. He knew everything about that boat. She must have left Tangier late. He released the binoculars, held on to the windscreen of the cockpit, checked the SatNav, perfect position.

The sun was fully up and out of the water now, its heat on his back. He stripped off his shirt and threw it behind him. He closed his eyes for a moment, relaxed them; he'd worked them hard in the dark. He brought the binoculars up to his face, opened his eyes. One, two, three, four ships. Stopped, went back. Between three and four, a smaller vessel. He throttled up, moved forward a hundred metres, two hundred, picked up the Moroccan flag at the back, moved along to the hull. *Princess Bouchra*. He suddenly needed to piss.

He throttled back, went down into the cabin, lifted up the cache, turned the switch 180 degrees, a red light, then a faint wheezing sound came from the point of the hull and a click. The red light changed to green. Primed. Back in the cockpit, binoculars to his face. There she was. Five hundred metres away now. He rested the binoculars on his chest. Reached for the photograph in his back pocket, wanted to kiss the memory of Yousra, Abdullah and Leila. It was in his trousers, which he'd thrown overboard. No matter, he kissed them anyway. He opened the throttles gradually, taking the boat up to full speed. The power wanted to force him back into his seat but he remained standing, hanging on to the wheel. The *Princess Bouchra* was getting bigger, more to scale. Hundred metres to go now. Yacoub wasn't thinking any more. He was concentrating on nothing but the porthole in the middle of the starboard side of the boat, which he aimed to hit at one hundred and twenty-five kilometres per hour.

The sea beneath his hull seemed as hard as tarmac. The bow smacked the surface, juddering his organs. The vessel was huge in his vision. Its white superstructure towering above him. He smiled at the wind in his face, the thought of being on the other side, of going straight through to another dimension, shivering through the transparent wall that would make all his suffering appear suddenly absurd. His hull and the porthole met. He slipped through the fissure of time, while the *Princess Bouchra* broke in half with a sound that wasn't loud enough for him to hear.

29

There was something about the intensity of the two vibrating mobile phones on the marble top of his bedside table that seemed more alarming than usual. They kissed and came apart like molluscs engaged in some mating ritual. Falcón wiped his hand down his face, asked himself: *Was anyone completely innocent killed last night?* Isabel Sanchéz. He shook his head, levered himself up on an elbow, grabbed a phone and clamped it to his ear.

'*Diga.*'

'Finally,' said Pablo. 'Don't bother to pick up the other one, it's me as well.'

'I had a late night last night, with four murders and two arrests in the space of about one hour. And that doesn't include the suicide on the Huelva road. So I hope you're not going to ask anything complicated of me,' said Falcón. 'I've got a lot on my plate today, probably starting with a very ugly interview with Comisario Elvira.'

'There's no easy way to break this to you, Javier,' said Pablo, 'so I'll tell it to you straight. Yacoub Diouri drove a power boat packed with high explosives into the side of a Saudi royal family vessel called the *Princess Bouchra* at around eight forty this morning.'

Silence. Falcón blinked.

'The captain and crew abandoned ship and were picked up by a passing dry cargo vessel. The *Princess Bouchra* went straight to the bottom. We're not sure who was left on board.'

'Are you *sure* it was Yacoub?'

'We're absolutely positive,' said Pablo.

'How do you know?' asked Falcón. 'This happened less than an hour ago. How can you be so positive?'

'Listen to the news. I just wanted to warn you before you saw it. It's the only story on all channels,' said Pablo. 'We'll talk later when you're in the office.'

Falcón threw off the sheet, sprinted downstairs in his underpants, turned on the television, sat back in his chair.

'The captain and crew have been taken by helicopter to Algeciras where they have been admitted to hospital un-injured, but suffering from shock. The *Princess Bouchra* sank immediately. It is believed that four members of the Saudi royal family were on board, two with government portfolios and two provincial governors. We are still awaiting confir-mation of their names.'

Zap.

'The suicide bomber, who has been named as Yousef Daoudi, is believed to have set off from the coastal town of Mertil, about ten kilometres from the northern Moroccan town of Tetouan.'

Zap.

'The explosion was first reported by the captain of a gas tanker called the *Iñigo Tapias* at eight forty-two. The position was confirmed later by the coastguard just out of the Straits of Gibraltar, about forty-three kilometres due east of La Línea. It is believed that there were no survivors.'

Encarnación, his housekeeper, appeared at the door of his study.

'What's going on, Javier?'

'Just trying to get some news.'

'The ship that blew up off the Costa del Sol?' said Encarnación, crossing herself. 'They said on Ondacero that it was al-Qaeda.'

That gave him the idea to try the Al Jazeera channel. Encarnación handed him the post she'd picked up by the front door.

'A crew member of the dry cargo vessel, which picked up the survivors of the *Princess Bouchra*, said that he saw the power boat take aim at the luxury cruiser and hit her amidships. There was an explosion, a massive ball of flame and the *Princess Bouchra* broke in two and sank immediately. We are still trying to get confirmation who was aboard the vessel. It is believed that there were six members of the Saudi royal family, who were travelling from Tangier to Marbella. A Moroccan-based terrorist organization called the GICM – the Moroccan Islamic Combatant Group – have claimed responsibility. They have named the assassin as Yacoub Diouri, who we understand is owner and director of a clothes manufacturing company based in Salé, near Rabat in Morocco. And here to talk to us about these developments is –'

Falcón turned off the television, let the remote drop to the floor. The mail Encarnación had given him scattered across the tiles. He leaned forward, elbows on knees, head viced in his hands, trying to force some logic into his stunned brain cells. If last night had gone badly, this was disaster on an epic scale. He felt hollow, black and hideously cold inside.

Grief and the horrific repercussions of Yacoub's act fought for supremacy in his mind as he stared into the clay tiles and noticed a hotel envelope on the floor: the Vista del Mar in Marbella, with his address in Yacoub's handwriting. He picked it up, it was stamped with yesterday's date.

Marbella
19 September 2006
Dear Javier,
By the time you open this you will already have been told about what happened last night in the Straits of Gibraltar, or you will at least have seen it on the news. (Al Jazeera is my recommendation for this kind of thing.) Although, because it took place out at sea, there will inevitably be some confusion. The confusion is deliberate and an important part of the plan. But rather than starting with confusion, let me begin at the beginning and hopefully make everything clear for you.

First of all, I am sorry, Javier, that I have lied to you. Abdullah has not been, and now never will be, recruited by the GICM. You will remember what I told you in Madrid about their ruthlessness; I learned about it the hardest way – through practical experience. I also told you that they were nervous of my non-Moroccan half. That was quite true. They did not completely trust me, not from the very first moment. But they wanted access to Faisal. So the first thing that happened was that they declared their intention to recruit Abdullah to the cause. They said he would be proud to join his father in the jihad and they would train him up to be a great mujahideen fighter.

I was not acting when you saw me in Madrid. I was completely horrified at this prospect. It would, of course, have been impossible for me to prevent this from happening without revealing myself as an enemy to their cause. They, having proposed this idea, then did nothing about it, but rather started talking to me about Faisal. They approached the subject as if they already knew Faisal and that he was, if not an active supporter of their cause, then at least an ideological supporter. And to a certain extent that is true, except that Faisal has a much broader mind. Over the weeks this attitude gradually changed and they drew my attention to some of Faisal's less likeable traits as far as they were concerned. They also started to grill me about his security arrangements when he was travelling.

The threat of Abdullah's conversion was meticulously maintained by a person whose capability to successfully recruit him I did not doubt. The worst of it all was that they infected my mind. From the moment they first mentioned his recruitment I started watching Abdullah, looking for changes, checking his computer, his friends, where he went. They made me spy on my own son.

I had already told them that Faisal's security arrangements were impregnable. Nobody was allowed to see him without being searched. This was not quite true. I was never searched, but his security detail watched me, checked my movements, made sure I was clean even before I got to see him. But I didn't want the GICM to think that they had any chance of getting someone close to Faisal. That would be an unpredictable situation. This was when the marine navigation training started. They were clever. They trained three of us at the same time. None of us was given any clue of the mission.

I was getting increasingly nervous. The pressure on me has been enormous. I told Faisal everything. Sorry, Javier, but he was the target, after all, and, as you so rightly said, you had no experience in these matters. He could have saved himself a lot of trouble by just getting rid of me, but he feared for my safety and, of course, Abdullah's future. He was that sort of man. Our only resort was to counteract the GICM plan by hatching our own.

I told the GICM of Faisal's travel arrangements, which included his annual trip from Tangier to Marbella. They already knew about this, which was the reason for the marine navigation training. Then I struck the deal with my closest contact in the GICM. I volunteered to ram the Princess Bouchra and in return he would guarantee that Abdullah would never be recruited to the cause. I explained that it was not a life I wanted for him. It was quickly apparent that this had been their aim all along.

I won't bore you with all the details about how we planned to get Faisal and his fellow royals on to the boat and then off it again in Tangier. Suffice to say that the idea was to create a big confusion with lots of people and in the end the Princess Bouchra would set sail with the captain and a slightly larger crew of highly trained marines on board. The ship, by the way, was fifteen years old and in need of a complete refit. They were going to trade her in for a new one, but now the insurance will take care of that. The Saudis will delay their press release about those on board for at least twenty-four hours. You'll understand why later.

In the original plan I was going to jump from the boat before the fatal collision, but only James Bond can get away with that sort of thing and anyway I would have been condemned to a life without my family, living in secret in Saudi Arabia and, after my childhood, this was not what I wanted. The other alternative — to tell Abdullah everything — would have put an intolerable strain on the boy and, because of his close relationship to the GICM recruiter, would have left me constantly exposed. And I didn't want to be a spy any more, Javier. I found that out very quickly. The way I had imagined it contained nothing of the horror of the reality. Believe me when I tell you that I am completely at peace. My vision, which I told you about in Madrid, beneath the cotton shroud, is where I am.

Some final requests. You must show this letter to Abdullah, but it must not remain in his possession. It is, of course, vital that he does not see me as a martyr to any terrorist cause, which is why I have penned this in my own hand. You must do this as quickly as you can. He will be in Rabat on Thursday, but given the developments, possibly before.

I would also like you to go to Fès and find Mustafa Barakat. He should be there until Friday, when he is scheduled to fly to Germany. If the CNI are any good at their job, you should know more about him by now. There are very strong ties between the Diouris and the Barakats. He has been like a brother to me, and this is why I could never do what I am going to ask of you.

I want you to find Mustafa Barakat and kill him.

He has been my main contact with the GICM and is a very dangerous man. He recruited me specifically to carry out the assassination of Faisal and he is responsible for the abduction of Darío. He might argue that he did this to distract you, so that you would be less likely to discover 'his plan' to ram the Princess

Bouchra. However, I know that it was done as much out of spite as anything else, and this has made me very angry. He has also committed the unforgivable transgression of threatening a family member and for these reasons he must die. The Saudis will delay their press release until they hear from you.

I am sure you will find Darío in the Diouri family home in Fès. Be careful of the woman there, who lives apart from the rest and is probably the one holding the boy. She is Mustafa Barakat's mother and is both vicious and, in my opinion, clinically insane. If she hears that her son is dead, she will kill Darío immediately.

This is the challenge: you must kill Mustafa Barakat and rescue the boy straight away. Do not do this in a way that threatens your safety or your future. However, I do not want you to contact the Moroccan intelligence services through the CNI. They will have no compunction about torturing Mustafa Barakat, and it will be to the death because he will reveal nothing. I do not want that to happen. I am afraid that a conscience may come with me into the afterlife.

One final mystery for you, because I know that it is in your nature. You might be interested to check Mustafa Barakat's DNA; from that you will understand his story.

You are, no doubt, in a state of shock. I am sorry, my friend, to have done this to you. I was very touched by what you told me in Brown's on that grey afternoon in London. You must believe, Javier, that you will never be alone, you have far too great a heart for that.

I wish I could embrace you again. I was very glad to be able to say goodbye in Osuna that afternoon.

Do not be sad for me. I am free now.

Your friend,

Yacoub Diouri

Falcón folded the letter, put it back in its envelope. He called Consuelo and told her to pack and be ready to leave for Morocco before midday.

30

The square reinforced-glass window set in the door of interview room number four perfectly framed Nikita Sokolov, who was considered sufficiently dangerous to be held in handcuffs, hands behind his back. Ramírez was waiting for the translator and was dismayed, several minutes later, to be shaking hands with a small middle-aged Cuban woman.

'Have you done this before?' he asked.

'Translate?' she said, giving him the eyebrow.

'For us,' he said, 'with criminals.'

'What's he done?'

'He's a particularly nasty murderer and you're going to hear some ugly stuff . . . to do with women.'

She had to stand on tiptoe to see through the glass.

'Thanks very much for being so considerate, Inspector,' she said. 'But I used to live in Miami. There the ugly stuff happened in your living room.'

'Did they cut women up with a chain saw there, too?'

'Only if they were feeling kind,' she said.

* * *

381

'Guess what?' said Ferrera, appearing on Falcón's shoulder. 'Comisario Elvira wants to see you.'

'When?' asked Falcón.

'Probably since he got a call from the Juez Decano de Sevilla at around two o'clock this morning,' she said. 'Ramírez is about to give Sokolov his first interview.'

'Is Inspector Jefe Tirado from GRUME in the building?'

'I'll find out,' said Ferrera. 'By the way, last night Juan Valverde gave me the name and address of the *puti club* where they're holding Marisa Moreno's sister, Margarita, or at least where he had sex with her.'

'You'd better get out there then,' said Falcón. 'Contact the local Guardia Civil and take Sub-Inspector Pérez with you.'

'OK, Detectives Serrano and Baena are going through Alejandro Spinola's apartment looking for evidence of his involvement with the Russians and sending inside information to Horizonte.'

Falcón went up to Elvira's office. The secretary sent him through. Elvira looked barricaded behind his desk and didn't even let him sit down.

'I can't believe you mounted an operation like that without getting my approval.'

'Normally I would have done, but you told me I was not to have any contact with Alejandro Spinola on pain of being suspended,' said Falcón. 'Not only did I realize that Spinola himself was in danger, but I could also see that he was potentially drawing other people into a dangerous situation in the Hotel La Berenjena. I therefore had to act without your approval of the plan.'

'The plan?'

'The improvisation,' said Falcón, correcting himself. 'There hasn't been much time for planning.'

'Do you know what the Juez Decano told me last night?' said Elvira. 'That you'd hounded his son to his death.'

'His suicide, you mean,' said Falcón. 'Remember, Detectives Serrano and Baena were present and the truck driver was emphatic.'

'We'll see.'

'Alejandro Spinola told me he was into Belenki and Revnik for gambling debts and cocaine and that he'd leaked confidential information about competitors' bids for the Isla de la Cartuja development to Antonio Ramos, Horizonte's chief construction engineer. He'd also betrayed his own cousin by introducing him to Marisa Moreno, who was being coerced by the Russians,' said Falcón. 'That was a guy I didn't hound nearly enough.'

'I can only hope that with Belenki, Revnik and Marisa Moreno dead and Antonio Ramos keeping his mouth firmly shut, we can gather enough evidence to prove you right,' said Elvira, who looked at his watch. 'As it is, Inspector Jefe Falcón, I am going to have to suspend you from duty with immediate effect, pending a full inquiry. Inspector Ramírez will run the investigation from now on. You will leave the building by eleven o'clock. That is all.'

Falcón left the Comisario's office, went down to his own, where Inspector Jefe Tirado was waiting for him, chatting to Ferrera. Falcón told him the latest intelligence about Darío being held in Morocco and that it would probably be a matter for the CNI, working with the Moroccan authorities. He also told him about his own suspension from duty and that he would ensure that the CNI contacted Comisario Elvira with news of Darío. Tirado left. Ferrera looked at Falcón, shook her head in dismay. He went into his office, closed the door and called Pablo, who'd just arrived in the Jefatura and was on his way up the stairs to his office. He took out Yacoub's letter, reread it. This was going to be a hard sell.

Ferrera let Pablo in, said she was leaving for the Costa del Sol, pulled the door shut. Pablo put his briefcase down, sat. He was angry. Falcón decided to let him start.

'We've just heard from Saudi intelligence,' said Pablo. 'They've been in touch with the British, too, confirming that no members of the Saudi royal family were on board that vessel and there will be no press release for at least twenty-four hours on the matter. How much did you know?'

'Pretty well nothing, except that there was a Saudi connection. Yacoub didn't even tell me his real name.'

'That was a very dangerous game you were playing there, Javier,' said Pablo. 'He was an assistant to the Saudi Minister of Defence.'

'Think how you and the British would have behaved if you'd known that last week,' said Falcón. 'And if the Americans had been informed?'

'I'm not sure that blowing a ship up on the high seas is what I would call a contained intelligence operation,' said Pablo.

'Did Saudi intelligence come directly to you, or higher?'

'What do you think?' said Pablo. 'I've been made to look an arsehole on my own territory. As soon as Yacoub got off the plane in Málaga I had a man on his tail. After you met him in Osuna I had two agents, front and back of the hotel. And still a GICM logistics cell can put a power boat, packed with high explosives, at the disposal of an amateur, to complete a fucking impossible mission. We were nowhere . . .'

'How could I have helped you?' said Falcón. 'I didn't know about the power boat or the *Princess Bouchra*.'

Pablo grunted, looked out the window into the hot car park.

'I've got a problem,' said Falcón, 'and I'm going to need your help.'

'I don't know why. It seems that amateurs have just as good a chance as the professionals,' said Pablo. 'Is this about Darío?'

'Partly,' said Falcón. 'But in order to get to Darío I have to kill someone first.'

Silence. Pablo's brain ticked over.

'The problem is,' said Falcón, continuing, 'this person is someone that both you and the Moroccans would very much like to interrogate, but Yacoub's last request was that, while he wants this person killed, he does not want him tortured to death.'

'This isn't what you talked about in Osuna,' said Pablo. 'It couldn't have been. He'd have had to tell you he was going to die. So, somehow you've heard from Yacoub, but not by email. Did he write you a letter?'

'You can read it in a minute.'

'In the meantime, you want me to agree to facilitating a mission in a foreign country in which you assassinate an anonymous but valuable intelligence source,' said Pablo. 'Fuck off, Javier. That's all I can say.'

'I thought that might be your attitude.'

'You're in no position,' said Pablo. 'Let me read the letter.'

Falcón handed over the letter, sat back while Pablo read it.

'I want a copy of this and I'm going to have to make a call,' said Pablo. 'Would you mind waiting in the outer office?'

Falcón left the room. Ten minutes later Pablo called him back in.

'It seems that assurances were given to the Saudis from higher up,' said Pablo. 'Ministers of Defence and those close to them are very powerful people, especially when they buy military equipment. I have been instructed to make the necessary arrangements for you. But are *you*, the Inspector Jefe del Grupo de Homicidios, really going to do this?'

'Not that it makes any difference, but I've been suspended from duty, pending an inquiry into the events of last night.'

'I won't ask.'

'I have to admit it's not my preferred method of meting out justice, but not only is it my friend's last request, it's

385

also the only way to rescue Darío. With Barakat alive on the outside we wouldn't get near the boy,' said Falcón. 'And I know you used to run agents in Morocco before you were given the Madrid job and you can help me.'

'I can arrange a firearm for you, give you some men on the ground, and I can clear it with the Moroccans after the event,' said Pablo. 'Or I can get a professional to do it.'

'As you can tell from the letter, there's something personal about this. I have no idea what it is, but I don't think Yacoub would ask me to do it unless he had good reason.'

'And what about the boy?'

'First of all, you have to contact Comisario Elvira and tell him that you believe Darío is in Morocco and he will relieve Inspector Jefe Tirado from the search for him here,' said Falcón. 'As soon as I've dealt with Barakat your men have to seal off the information that he's dead until I've rescued Darío. I'm not sure how I'm going to get into the house in Fès unless Yousra, Yacoub's wife, or Abdullah maybe, could help me get in there.'

'How are you going to get to Fès?'

'Drive to Algeciras. Ferry to Ceuta. I could be in Fès by this evening.'

'We'll book you a room in the Hotel du Commerce. It's quiet, out of the way, and you won't draw attention to yourself as you would if you were in the Palais Jamai or the Dar Batha. It's still in the old town, but in Fès El Djedid, rather than Fès El Bali, where Barakat has his shop and the Diouris have their house,' said Pablo. 'What about Yousra?'

'I'll call her. She'll meet me in Fès.'

'Leave your car in Meknes, meet her there. The Hotel Bab Mansour has a garage. We'll organize a room for you. Take a taxi from there,' said Pablo. 'Don't turn up in a Spanish-registered vehicle; Barakat will have his informers in Fès.'

'Consuelo will be coming with me.'

'Really?'

'There's no question of her staying here.'

'Why tell her?'

'I already have.'

'Call me from Ceuta,' said Pablo. 'Go to the Hotel Puerta de Africa and ask for Alfonso. Tell him you're a great admirer of Pablo Neruda and he'll look after your border crossing.'

Falcón went down to the forensics lab, picked up some DNA swabs and continued to the observation room to see Ramírez's first interview with Nikita Sokolov. He was waiting for the right moment to interrupt, but was also fascinated to see how Ramírez would play the Russian. They were still working their way through the preliminaries. The translator sat well back from the table between the two men. Sokolov leaned forward, a large white bandage around his head. His huge bulk made him look like a figure from a cartoon. His face bent down was oddly sad, as if remorse could potentially take up residence. Occasionally, when he'd become a little stiff, he'd hook his arms over the back of the seat and sit up straight, then his face would lose that look of sadness and become devoid of any recognizable human emotion.

'I'm just going to summarize that for you,' said Ramírez, concluding a fairly long opening statement. 'There are five murders that we can charge you with today. There are no questions about any of them. We have witnesses and we have your weapon with your fingerprints on it. And in the case of the first two murders we also have your blood at the scene. These killings are: Miguel Estévez and Julia Valdés in the apartment of Roque Barba in Las Tres Mil Viviendas on Monday, 18th September. And Leonid Revnik . . .'

Ramírez paused as Sokolov spat a contemptuous globule of sputum at the floor.

'Leonid Revnik,' continued Ramírez, 'Isabel Sanchéz and Viktor Belenki in the Hotel La Berenjena on Tuesday, 19th

September. You will be charged with all these murders later this morning. Do you understand?'

The translator did her work. Sokolov turned his mouth down and nodded as if this was a reasonable summary of a couple of days' work. He did not look at the Cuban woman as she spoke. His eyes were fixed on Ramírez's forehead, as if this was where he was planning his first assault on his way out of the room. Ramírez was extraordinarily calm. His interview style normally tended towards the aggressive, but he'd decided on a different approach with Sokolov, although the Russian did look impervious to aggression.

'Given that these five murders will put you behind bars for the rest of your life, I was wondering if there were any other killings you'd like us to take into consideration at the same time?'

Sokolov's response was very surprising.

'I would like to help you, Inspector,' he said, 'but you must understand that this is my job. I was an "enforcer" for a number of years on the Costa del Sol with Leonid Revnik and his predecessor before I joined Yuri Donstov in the same capacity. I was given the names of people I was required to kill, but I did not always remember them. It was just business. If you can be specific and remind me of the circumstances, I might be able to help.'

Ramírez was momentarily wrong-footed by the tone of this reply. He'd been expecting a belligerent silence. It made him concentrate on his adversary. Falcón began to think that inside Sokolov's brutal frame there must be a young man with a briefcase, a set of pens and an eagerness to please. Then it occurred to him that the last thing this sort of work needed was craziness. What it demanded was discipline, calmness, attention to detail and a clear uncomplicated mind. Maybe weightlifting wasn't such bad training for the work.

'I was thinking of Marisa Moreno,' said Ramírez, jogging himself back into the interview. 'You knew her, of course.'

'Yes, I did.'

'She was cut up with a chain saw.'

'As you've probably already gathered, that is not my method,' said Sokolov. 'Sometimes I have to satisfy the needs of others. The two who did that were animals, but they were brought up on brutality. They know nothing else.'

'Where are they now?'

'They are dead. They were captured by Revnik's men on Monday night and taken away to be . . . processed.'

'Was that why you and Yuri Donstov were in the Hotel La Berenjena last night?' asked Ramírez. 'Was that just revenge?'

'I will tell you things, Inspector, but I would like you to guarantee me one thing.'

'I'm not sure I can offer you any guarantees.'

'Just this one,' said Sokolov. 'I want everything I tell you to come out in court.'

'Any reason?'

'There are people in Moscow who should know the sort of a man Leonid Revnik was.'

'I think that can be arranged.'

'Leonid Revnik had the backing of the Supreme Council of *vory-v-zakone* in Moscow to terminate Yuri Donstov's operations in Seville. He was given this because he'd told them that Donstov had killed two directors on the Costa del Sol. This was not true. Revnik had executed them himself. You do not kill a *vor-v-zakone* without repercussions,' said Sokolov. 'Very quickly our supply lines of heroin from Uzbekistan were cut. Then Vasili Lukyanov died in a car accident last Thursday on his way to Seville.'

'So, it *was* revenge in the Hotel La Berenjena last night?'

'I did you a favour, killing Revnik.'

'Why's that?'

'He had agreements with people. Politicians,' said Sokolov.

389

'He'd keep Seville clean in return for big favours on the Costa del Sol.'

'Why did you have to kill Marisa Moreno?'

'She was at breaking point. She could not be relied upon to keep her mouth shut.'

'What did she know?'

'She knew people by face and name. If she found out that I was not working for Revnik any more, she might have felt that her sister was safe enough and would start talking to you,' said Sokolov. 'She would also reveal that she'd been forced to have a relationship with the judge.'

'Esteban Calderón?'

'Him.'

'Why did she have to do that?'

'Information.'

'I thought it was so that she could provide you with a key to the judge's apartment.'

'You might be right.'

'*Did* she supply you with the key?'

'Yes.'

'What was done with that key on the night of June 7th/June 8th this year?'

'It was used to get into the judge's apartment.'

'But the judge wasn't there, was he?'

Sokolov glanced over at the observation panel.

'His wife was there,' he said.

'Were you the person who gained access to the judge's apartment that night?'

'Yes.'

'Did you murder the judge's wife, Inés Conde de Tejada?'

'If that was her name, yes.'

'Why did you do that?'

'Because I was instructed to do so by Leonid Revnik.'

'Did you know why you were instructed to kill her?'

'Of course. I had to make it look as if the judge had

murdered his wife, so that he would be removed from the investigation of the Seville bombing,' said Sokolov. 'One thing we didn't expect was for him to try to get rid of the body. Fortunately, I'd left a man watching the apartment and he was able to report the judge to the police . . . otherwise he might have got away with it. And that would not have been fair, would it, Inspector?'

Ramírez and Sokolov looked at each other across the table. The translator stared, mesmerized.

'No, that wouldn't have been fair,' said Ramírez, and his next question came out with his heart in his throat. 'Do you know who was responsible for placing the bomb in the mosque on Calle Romeros, in the barrio of El Cerezo, in Seville on 5th June 2006, which exploded the following morning?'

'I know that it was organized by Leonid Revnik, but I don't know who put the bomb there.'

'What about the building inspectors?'

'I don't know anything about that,' said Sokolov. 'That was not my work.'

'What about the murders of Lucrecio Arenas and César Benito?'

'I killed César Benito in the Holiday Inn, near the Real Madrid football stadium,' said Sokolov. 'Another of Revnik's men shot Lucrecio Arenas at his home in Marbella.'

'Name and where can we find him?'

'I don't know who did it, but you'll probably find him in the *puti club* near Estepona, which was run by Vasili Lukyanov,' said Sokolov.

'You were a friend of Vasili Lukyanov,' said Ramírez. 'He was coming to join Donstov when he was involved in an accident. He had money and some disks with him . . .'

'It was all stolen from Revnik,' said Sokolov. 'We were having cash-flow problems, so the money was to get us through the next few months. The disks: Vasili thought we could use them to get involved in the building project here in Seville.'

'Was that all?' asked Ramírez. 'There were a lot of people on those disks, more than sixty. There were also a couple of encrypted disks, which we haven't been able to unlock.'

'With the disks that Vasili was bringing, Yuri said we'd be able to force Revnik out into the open so that we could kill him. I don't know the people who were filmed,' said Sokolov. 'The encrypted disks contain the real accounts of all Revnik's businesses on the Costa del Sol. They were very important to him. That was valuable information for the tax authorities.'

'I'd like to thank you for being so co-operative in our first interview,' said Ramírez.

'As you say, Inspector, it's all over for me now.'

'But normally you people don't talk to the police.'

'Those two directors that Revnik shot were *vory-v-zakone*. They should have been paid off, not killed. Once Revnik had done that, and put the blame on Yuri Donstov, in my eyes he forfeited the right to the terms of *vory-v-zakone*. I will tell you anything you need to know about him.'

Falcón left the observation room and knocked on the door of the interview room. Ramírez came out with the translator, who excused herself.

'Great interview, José Luis,' said Falcón. 'Not your usual style.'

'Pure luck, Javier. I was going to go in hard about cutting women up with chain saws and shooting them in the face but, you know, the translator. So . . . I was gentle.'

'He could have been mistaken for civilized, if he hadn't confessed to seven murders,' said Falcón.

'What else do we want from him?' said Ramírez. 'He seems keen to talk.'

'Don't look at me, this is your investigation now, José Luis. I have to be out of the building in three minutes,' said

Falcón, telling him about his suspension. 'What you should do is go through all those faces on Vasili Lukyanov's disks with Cortés and Díaz and get them to identify all the building inspectors. Then look into the backgrounds of all the other men and see if any of them were trained electricians, possibly even army trained. Interview them and see if they crack. I think that was one of the things Lukyanov was bringing with those disks. The answers to the Seville bombing conspiracy.'

They shook hands, clapped each other on the shoulder. Falcón went to the bottom of the staircase.

'And one other thing, José Luis: Ferrera and Pérez are on their way to Lukyanov's *puti club* to pick up Marisa Moreno's sister,' he said. 'From what Sokolov's just said, they're dangerous people out there. They should have full back-up before they go in.'

'You'll be reinstated, Javier,' said Ramírez. 'They're not going to be able to –'

'Not this time, José Luis,' said Falcón, and with a quick salute he went up the stairs.

31

The Hotel Puerta de Africa was a new four-star hotel in the Gran Via of the Spanish enclave of Ceuta, a short taxi ride from the ferry terminal. Under a later instruction from Pablo, Falcón had left his car in Algeciras on the Spanish mainland, which meant they could take the quickest hydrofoil across the Straits of Gibraltar. On the way over he had told Consuelo almost everything of the contents of Yacoub's letter, but had not let her read it. There were things that weren't for her eyes. He left her in the taxi and went into the gleaming white hotel atrium, which looked as far from Africa as you could get. He asked for Alfonso and was pointed across the marble floor to the concierge's desk. He hit the bell. A man in his forties with a heavy moustache and matching eyebrows came out. Falcón told him he was a great admirer of Pablo Neruda and was taken into his office.

'You didn't bring your car?' said Alfonso, making a call.

'We're in a cab.'

'Good. It's less complicated. I'll get you through the border in a few minutes. There'll be a car waiting for you on the other side. Don't worry. They'll find you. There's another cab outside. Transfer your bags and get going.'

That was it. There was a five-minute drive to the Moroccan border. The cab went straight through to the Moroccan side without stopping. The driver took their passports, got them stamped, came back and told them to go to the Customs guy with their bags. At Customs they were taken to a Peugeot 307 and given the keys. Not a word was spoken. They got in, eased through the crowds and drove along the coast to Tetuan. He called Yousra from there, and asked her to meet him in the Hotel Bab Mansour in Meknes. Abdullah had already flown in from London. He would drive her there.

Through the Rif mountains was a beautiful drive but exhausting, so Falcón took the route via Larache and Sidi-Kacem. It took three and a half hours, but they gained a couple of hours in time difference so it was just 5 p.m. when they parked up in the garage of the Hotel Bab Mansour in Meknes. Yousra, Leila and Abdullah were waiting in the bar area, drinking Coke. The women were dressed in black, Abdullah in charcoal grey. Yousra looked composed until she saw Falcón. He went over, hugged the three of them to him. He introduced Consuelo, told Yousra he needed to speak to Abdullah alone for a while.

In the bland businessman's hotel room Falcón handed over Yacoub's last letter, which Abdullah read sitting on the edge of the bed. Until now Abdullah had been holding it together, playing the man of the family. The letter destroyed him. He went into the reading experience as an eighteen-year-old boy and its initial effect was to reduce him to a child. He lay on his side on the bed and bawled silently, with the face of a starving baby. Then he sat himself up, wiped his tears from his eyes and rebuilt himself into a twenty-five-year-old man there and then. Falcón burnt the letter in the hotel waste bin.

'We won't talk about that letter now,' said Falcón. 'Just let it sink in.'

'When I heard his name on the news in London, I couldn't believe it,' said Abdullah. 'I could not believe he'd done that. So that letter was terrible, but it was a relief, too.'

Abdullah stood up and embraced Falcón.

'You've been a good friend, Javier. My father would not have entrusted these things to you if you had been anything less,' he said. 'If ever you need me, you can count on me – and I mean that. Even in the same way as my father.'

'Don't even think about it, Abdullah.'

'That's not something I need to think about,' he said. 'I know. You can count on me.'

'I *do* need your help now,' said Falcón. 'Has your mother ever been to the Diouri house in Fès?'

'Of course. She goes there every month. She saw that as one of her duties as my father's wife,' said Abdullah. 'She mustn't know what you are going to do, though. She is very fond of Mustafa. As my father said, Mustafa was like a brother to him, and that was how she treated him.'

'And he was an uncle to you,' said Falcón.

'But an impostor,' said Abdullah, looking Falcón in the eye. 'What my father didn't tell you in the letter is that Mustafa is very charismatic. Apart from anything else, he sells a lot of carpets. The tourists love him even as he despises them. My advice to you is not to engage.'

'I need Yousra to get me into the Diouri house afterwards.'

'That is perfectly possible. It will be quite natural for her, under these circumstances, to go to Fès and mourn with the other women there. They will expect it of her,' said Abdullah. 'The woman with you, Consuelo, is this boy her son?'

Falcón nodded, stunned by the transformation of Abdullah from the slack-limbed teenager he'd known on the family holiday a month ago, to this focused young man he'd become in the last half-hour.

'It's better that neither my mother nor Leila are told about the boy. These women in the Diouri house know each other very well and my mother is not an actress,' said Abdullah. 'She will have an audience with Mustafa's mother as soon as she arrives, and that woman is frightening. She might be mad, but she doesn't miss anything.'

'All right, so how will I get into the house?'

'I will be accompanying her, but I will not be party to their conversation. I will stay downstairs and let you in.'

'Do you know the house?'

'I know everything about that house. When Leila and I were children we were left to play – and you know what children are like. We discovered everything. All the secret passages and back staircases. Don't worry, Javier. Everything will be fine. I think it's best we go our separate ways now. We will arrive in Fès as the grieving family,' said Abdullah, writing down his mobile number. 'Call me when you are ready and I'll make sure everything goes smoothly in the house in Fès.'

They embraced again. Abdullah went to the **door**, fitted his feet into his barbouches. Falcón could see his mind still working.

'Nothing will change my **mind**, Javier,' he said.

'But remember, Abdullah: your father sacrificed his life so that you would not suffer what he went through,' said Falcón. 'You've just read his letter. He did not want to be a spy, and he did not want that life **for you either**.'

As they set off for Fès the clouds in the western sky were aflame, with the reddening sun already low on the horizon. Falcón drove in silence.

'I can nearly hear what's going on in your head, but not quite,' said Consuelo, after half an hour.

'The usual problem,' said Falcón. 'Trust. I don't know whether I've just made a big mistake in assuming that Abdullah is as his father believed.'

'A "friend"?'

Falcón nodded, turned on the headlights as the sun disappeared behind them. The light in the car was strange, with the flamingo sky behind, dark night ahead, and the dashboard glowing in his face.

'I just witnessed an extraordinary transformation from a boy into a man in the space of fifteen minutes,' said Falcón. 'This is what intelligence work does to you. You question everybody's loyalty. Abdullah's response to that letter, it just . . .'

'Didn't quite ring true?'

'It did and it didn't,' said Falcón. 'That's what you could hear going on in my head. For us to gain access to the Diouri house in Fès I must rely on him. I had to tell him everything. I've made myself vulnerable to him.'

'Was there an alternative?'

'Originally I was going to ask Yousra to let me in. Abdullah advised against it for perfectly plausible reasons. But when things matter so much, there's always a question.'

'You're not giving me the full story, Javier. I can tell.'

He should have known.

'In order to make Darío safe, I have to kill a man first. Abdullah's uncle.'

She looked at him, his profile, the jawline, the cheekbone, the ear, the eye. What had she done to this man?

'No, Javier. You can't do that. I can't let you do that.'

'It has to be done.'

'Have you ever killed a man before?'

'Twice.'

'But you've never assassinated someone,' she said, 'in cold blood.'

'There's no other way, Consuelo. I'm doing it for Yacoub as much as anyone else. It will happen,' said Falcón firmly.

'Abdullah knows this,' said Consuelo. 'And if he's not a friend, when you go to kill this man you might be walking to your death.'

'We need an alternative plan in case I've been wrong about Abdullah.'

The Hotel du Commerce was on the Place des Alaouites. They parked nearby and went up to their room. It wasn't a class of hotel that Consuelo was used to staying in, but it was right in front of the golden doors of the royal palace.

They had a shower, changed clothes. Neither of them was hungry. They lay on the bed, Consuelo with her head on his chest. Falcón stared at the ceiling. There was a knock at the door.

One of Pablo's agents identified himself, looked nervously at Consuelo.

'It's all right,' said Falcón, introducing her. 'She had to know.'

The agent took out a light brown burnous from the small cabin bag he was carrying.

'Put this on,' he said. 'It has a hood to cover your face.'

Falcón wrestled into the long, ankle-length cloak, put the hood over his head, checked himself in the mirror. The pockets of the burnous went straight through to his trousers. The agent screwed a silencer on to a nine-millimetre Glock handgun, gave it to Falcón. He showed him that it was fully loaded, with one in the chamber, and where the safety catch was. Falcón put it in the waistband of his trousers. The agent laid out a large-scale map of the medina of Fès El Bali on the bed. Showed him the gate where he would come in, where the shop was and the best route from the shop to the Diouri house. He gave him a recent photo of Barakat, let him look at it for a minute, took it back.

'You will go into Mustafa Barakat's shop at eight thirty,' said the agent. 'There will be one other person in the shop, a Spanish tourist. As you enter, another agent will man the door from the outside. He will be Moroccan. You will shoot Mustafa Barakat, hand the gun to the Spanish tourist and leave the premises. Do not look back. The Moroccan will close the shop behind you.'

'I'll need a gun for when I go into the Diouri house,' said Falcón.

'We will make sure you have one,' said the agent. 'It's just a precaution that after the killing you walk away from the shop unarmed.'

'I want you to show Consuelo where the Diouri house is,' said Falcón. 'She's never been to Fès before and the medina can be confusing. I want her to see it for real and memorize a route. If anything happens to me and I do not show at the gates of the house, you must knock at the door and ask for Yousra.'

'And what will Consuelo do?' asked the agent.

'You will give her the weapon intended for me. She will ask Yousra to take her to Barakat's mother.'

'What do you think might happen to you?' asked the agent.

'I have had to inform Abdullah Diouri of this plan.'

'That was not what we were told,' said the agent.

'It was unavoidable.'

The agent looked at his watch.

'I have to take up my position now,' he said. 'I will talk to Pablo. If we are to abort the mission, you will get a one-word text on your mobile telling you just that.'

Consuelo and the agent left.

Falcón looked at his watch, still some time to go. He remembered the DNA swabs, put a couple in his pocket. He took the gun out, put it on the bed, paced the room. He lay down with the gun on his chest, had to get up again. Too hot, stripped off the burnous. Time got stuck, wouldn't move on.

Forty minutes later Consuelo returned. He locked the door behind her and went back to pacing the room.

'You saw the house?' he asked.

'It's not far,' she said. 'You're tense, Javier. You're still thinking about Abdullah. We've got to clear your mind. Tell me everything that worries you about him.'

'Was the transformation too quick? Was it too complete? Did it feel rehearsed? Was there something playing behind his eyes when he said the words: "You can count on me"? Why did he offer his services when his father had just sacrificed his life for him? Did he pledge his loyalty a little too quickly and too hard? Is he acting?'

'You're too wired for this.'

'It's just the paranoia talking. I'll be all right once I'm moving.'

'Your shirt is soaked through. Take it off. Put this on.'

He looked at his watch for the hundredth time. Not quite 20.05. He peeled off the shirt. She rubbed him down with a towel. He put on a T-shirt, got back into the burnous. He checked the gun, slipped it into the burnous and down the waistband of his trousers. He walked around. Comfortable.

'It's time,' he said.

She gripped his shoulders, slipped her arms around his neck, kissed his face. He held her, almost delicately, feeling the individual ribs with the tips of his fingers.

'This isn't it, Javier. This isn't the end, I know it. This is the new beginning. Believe me,' she said, and squeezed him hard. 'Do you believe me?'

'I do,' he said, but his eyes said something different over her shoulder.

They parted. He held her hands, looked into her eyes.

'When you came to see me that night, before the negotiations with the Russians, you could have lied to me. You could have easily drawn me into their corruption. That you didn't, that you were so furious at what they were trying to do, even at the risk of your own child, was magnificent, and I fell for you all over again,' he said, and let her hands

401

fall from his. 'Whatever happens, I want you to know that I do not regret any of this.'

'It's taken me all my life to find you, Javier,' she said. 'And I know you'll be coming back.'

Falcón pulled the burnous hood with its elfin point over his head. The door closed after him and she immediately wanted him back, didn't believe her own words now that he was gone. She wondered what she would do with herself if this was to be the last time she saw him. She went to the window. He came out of the building beneath her, walked towards the royal palace, turned at the end of the street, raised his hand and was gone.

Falcón walked swiftly. Now that he was on the move his mind was clear. He felt a tremendous solidity in his torso, as if he was wearing an armour of clean and shining steel as light as his own skin. He called Abdullah on his mobile and told him he was on his way. He passed through various gates, the Bab Semarine, up Grand Rue des Merenids to the Bab Dakakan. It was only a matter of taking a right at the Bab Es Seba and a long walk by the Boujeloud Gardens and he was in Fès El Bali. He was in his stride now, walking towards the Bab Boujeloud. More activity here, more tourists. Full of hustlers. The burnous did its job. Nobody came near him. He went through the gate into the medina.

The tourist traffic became more intense. The shops were heaving with people. Brass trays glowed in the yellow light, next to mother-of-pearl inlaid furniture, camel-bone framed mirrors, silver jewellery, colourful scarves. His hood trapped the cinnamon smell from the *pastilla* food stalls. He dodged some mule droppings. The streets were clogging up with slow-moving gaggles of tourists. He tried not to look at his watch. Not a Moroccan thing, to be too concerned about time. He would get there. The timing would be perfect. Wood smoke shunted out the food smells. The stink of curing leather. Old men sitting out drinking tea, fingering their worry beads. A boy crouched, sweating as he fanned the flames of the fires beneath the massive blackened boilers of the hammam. The hiss of steam. The ponderous clopping of a donkey's hooves on cobbles. He turned left at the Cherabliyin mosque. The streets were darker and emptier here. He joined up with another main thoroughfare. The carpet shops. He saw his destination. His hand gripped the butt of the gun.

He stopped, took a deep breath, glanced at his watch for the first time: 20.29. Do not think. Do not engage. Two shots would be enough. He crossed the street, heading for the door to the shop, pulled the gun out of his waistband, thumbed off the safety catch under his burnous. Just as he reached the doorway a figure in a pale blue jellabah flitted in front of him, slipped over the threshold, so that they were in the shop together. What the fuck? Too late, he was committed now. The Spanish tourist was coming up off his cushion. Mustafa Barakat was standing and spreading his arms wide. He was smiling even as Falcón pulled out the gun. He was going to embrace the figure in the pale blue jellabah. Then he was not. His eyes widened over the pale blue cotton shoulders of the man, whose right arm punched in, once, twice, three times. Barakat fell back on a pile of carpets. The word on his lips never made it into the air. The killer put his foot on to the pile of carpets next to Barakat's face and drew the knife across the dying man's throat. He said something in Arabic and stood back. Barakat's white jellabah was already blossoming with a vast, shining bloom of blood. His throat gaped and gargled, blood leaked on to the carpets, the arterial pressure already gone from the ferocious stabs to the heart. Abdullah turned to Falcón, held out the knife in his bloody hand. Despite his closeness to Barakat in his death throes, his pale blue jellabah had only a small smear of blood across the arm. The CNI agent playing

403

the tourist was in a state of shock at this development. Falcón spoke to him quickly in Spanish as he knelt down and dipped a DNA swab into Barakat's blood.

'Take the knife. Carry on as planned. Any water?'

The agent took the knife, handed over a bottle of water he'd been carrying. Falcón put the gun back in his waistband, washed Abdullah's hand. Threw the bottle to the agent and left the shop. The metal blind rolled down behind them. Abdullah led the way off the street and down into the alleyways of the medina. He was crying. His shoulders were shaking, abdomen trembling.

'Why did you do that?' asked Falcón.

Abdullah stopped, threw his back against a whitewashed wall. Tears streaked his face.

'I've loved that man all my life,' he said. 'Since I can remember, Mustafa has been a part of our family. I used to fall asleep on his chest in the back of the car. He rescued me when I nearly drowned in the sea at Asilah. He took me to Marrakech for my sixteenth birthday. He is my *uncle*.'

'But you knew I would kill him. You didn't have to do that.'

'He has betrayed us all. I can hardly bear to speak his name. He has disgraced us. I don't care if I go to jail for the rest of my life,' said Abdullah. 'At least I have restored some of our family honour.'

Falcón grabbed him by the arm, told him they had to keep moving, the news of Barakat's death might leak out. They jogged through the empty streets. It was no more than a few hundred metres to the house. The door was open a crack. Abdullah went in. Consuelo appeared out of the darkness wearing a headscarf, startled him.

'Is it done?' she asked.

Falcón nodded.

They left Consuelo by the main door. Abdullah led Falcón across the first patio of the house. Women's voices came from one of the upstairs rooms. In the second patio Abdullah ducked into a doorway and went down a long unlit passage to a stone spiral staircase at the end. It was only just big enough for a single person to pass.

'There's no electricity in this part of the house,' said Abdullah. 'When we get to the door at the top I will go through and leave the door ajar. You must stay behind. Nobody comes to this part of the house without being invited first.'

'Think about what you're going to say to her.'

'I'm not going to take any nonsense,' said Abdullah, determined. 'She'll know I mean business just by the fact I'm in her quarters without her invitation.'

'You mustn't give her the slightest chance.'

'There's nothing she can do, Javier.'

'Are you sure?' said Falcón. 'After all this, I don't want anything to happen to the boy.'

'She'll be on her own up here. The boy will be kept elsewhere. I'll ask her where she's keeping him and, if she doesn't tell me, I'll beat her until she does.'

Abdullah took off his shoes. They crawled up two floors in the narrow staircase. At one point the women's voices in the patio were as clear as if they were next door. Abdullah reached the door at the top. It did not appear to have a handle or a lock but he felt up and down the stone wall near the door jamb and pressed. The door sprung open silently. The room had a floor of heavy wooden planking covered with carpets. The windows had broken latticework over them and the smell of jasmine from the garden below had come in with the warm night air. A floorboard creaked as Abdullah went in. A woman's voice in Arabic asked:

'Who's there?'

'It is me, Abdullah, my great aunt,' he said, approaching her. 'I'm sorry to come here without your invitation, but I wanted to talk to you about my father's death.'

'I have already spoken to your mother,' she said.

'I was sure that you had been told, but I would like to talk to you about it as well,' said Abdullah. 'You know that your son, my uncle, and my father were very close.'

'My son?' she said.

'Mustafa and my father, they were like brothers.'

'Come here,' she said. 'Step into the light where I can see you. Why are you wearing these clothes? These are not mourning clothes. And what is that mark –?'

There was a sharp intake of breath. The silence of shock before the comprehension of pain. Falcón opened the door. The woman was dressed completely in black, which made the curved blade of the knife stand out in the oily yellow light. The sight of Falcón distracted her from Abdullah, who was holding his right arm, with blood oozing through his fingers. He grunted with pain. The woman tipped a lamp on to the wooden floor. The oil spilled, caught fire immediately and flames spread across the carpets and floorboards. The hem of Abdullah's jellabah was alight as he staggered backwards. The woman opened the door and disappeared into the darkness.

Falcón used a small rug from the floor to slap out the flames climbing up Abdullah's legs. He used one of the other larger carpets to smother the fire creeping across the floor. He ran to the door. She'd locked it. He kicked at it, once, twice, on the third savage blow it came open. No light. His sight still a wavering green from the flames. His hands found a door across the landing, a top stair to his right. The rest of the stairs could have been a lift shaft for all he could see. He went down the stairs, right hand on the wall. A landing. No door. More stairs. Another landing. Two doors. A window. Faint light coming from outside. He listened at one door. Then the other. Went back to the other door, tried it. It opened on to an empty room. He turned, ran at the other door, and shouldered through it into the room, crashing into some furniture and landing on his front. The door kicked back against the wall and slammed shut again behind him. Still no light. Movement in the darkness. A faint whimpering sound of a small animal, cowering in a dark corner. He got up on to his knees, no higher than that, he was aware of the window behind him. Didn't want to stand out. Something flew over his head with a swish, like a low flying bird. He rolled to one side. Feet in light slippers padded across the floor. Falcón crawled deeper into the room, turned, lay on his back. He could just make out some of the broken latticework across the window. His eyes searched for a silhouette. Somebody was coming down the stairs. Abdullah recovered, or the woman getting away. His eyes improving all the time. He lay still. By the door he was aware of a denser mass. There was a twitch of silver. He felt around him. A small table came to hand. He sat up, brought his knees to his chin, rocked forward and in one movement came to his feet and ran full tilt, table out in front of him, at the black mass. There was a collision. The woman cannoned backwards and hit the window frame. The rotten latticework did not hold, the window frame cut her mid-thigh, her centre of gravity toppled and she was out **and** into the night before Falcón could grab at anything. A shout, more of surprise, followed by a compact thud and a **crack**. Then silence. A long silence, which was broken by that whimpering in the room.

'Abdullah?' said Falcón.

'I'm here,' he said. 'On the landing. She cut me with a knife. I can't let go of it, I'm bleeding too much.'

'Where's the light?'

'You'll have to find a candle or a lamp.'

Women's voices raised down below. They'd found the body. Abdullah yelled some Arabic out of the window. Uncertain light and footsteps came up the stairs. A lamp came into the room. Falcón turned to look at the corner

407

where the whimpering was coming from. There was a child's cot with bars around it. Behind the bars he could see a child's back completely still. Falcón stumbled through the furniture in the room. At the foot of the cot, curled in a tight ball was a small, black, trembling dog. Next to it was Darío, inanimate. There was a strong smell of faeces and urine. The boy was naked. In the hopeless light he could not tell whether the mad crone had killed the boy out of spite, as Yacoub said she might. After that night with the Russians outside Seville, he could barely bring himself to do it, but he reached out a hand, touched the small naked shoulder, let his hand slip into the crook of the neck and felt the pulse ticking under the warm skin.

32

There was no lingering on that hot night in Fès.

The women in the Diouri household did not seem unduly troubled by the death of Barakat's mother, they were far more concerned about the injury to Abdullah and confounded by the presence of a child and a small dog in the house. When Abdullah told them he'd been knifed by the mad woman, and they found the bloody blade still in the woman's hand, they were appalled. Falcón looked at the wound. It was a deep cut in the shoulder muscle and, although bloody, the blade had not severed anything serious. The women brought alcohol and bandages. He dressed the wound, but said it would need stitches. Given the circumstances, he told Abdullah, this would best be done in Ceuta. Yousra and Leila would stay in Fès.

They were led to the car through the back streets of the medina. Consuelo would not let Falcón carry the boy. She was frightened by Darío's total lack of animation, but encouraged by the steadiness of his pulse. They left for Ceuta at 9.30 p.m. On the way Falcón called Alfonso, the concierge, at the Hotel Puerta de Africa and told him they would be arriving at about 1 a.m. Moroccan time at the border and would need help to get through. Abdullah had changed out

409

of his bloody clothes and back into mourning. He had his ID card, but had left his passport in Rabat. Consuelo had had the foresight to bring Darío's documents. Falcón also told Alfonso they'd need a doctor on arrival at the hotel and a couple of rooms for what was left of the night.

At the border they were walked through to the Spanish side, with no official inspection. A taxi was waiting. Darío had still not stirred. He had the distressing feel of a large ragdoll. The doctor was waiting at the hotel and they went straight up to the room. Abdullah insisted that Darío was seen to first. The doctor lifted Darío's eyelids, shone his torch into the pupils. He listened to the heart and lungs. He minutely inspected the boy's body and found needle punctures in the crooks of his elbows. He declared there was nothing wrong with him apart from having been heavily sedated.

He took one look at Abdullah's wound and said he'd have to come with him to his surgery and have it properly cleaned and stitched. Falcón and Consuelo washed Darío in the bath and put him to bed. They slept with the boy in between them and were woken just before midday by his crying. He had no recollection of what had happened to him. Although he vaguely remembered being taken away from the Sevilla FC shop, he could not recollect how it had happened or who had done it.

It was decided that Abdullah would travel with them and stay in Seville with Falcón until the Barakat murder and the death of the mother had been dealt with by the authorities. They took a cab to the hydrofoil and were across the straits by 3.30 p.m. They drove back to Seville, where Falcón left Consuelo and Darío in Santa Clara with her sister and the boys, Ricardo and Matías. He and Abdullah went to the Jefatura, where he gave Barakat's DNA swab to Jorge in the forensics lab and asked him to check it against samples on the Jefatura's database.

'You know Comisario Elvira is looking for you,' said Jorge.

'He's always looking for me. I'm going home to bed,' said Falcón. 'You haven't seen me.'

He and Abdullah went home. Encarnación fed them. Falcón turned off all his mobiles and disconnected his phone. He slept the rest of the afternoon and whole night without waking.

In the morning he inspected Abdullah's wound and redressed it. He took a slow breakfast out in the patio, staring at the marble flagstones. At midday he called Jorge and asked if he'd run the DNA test.

'There was a match to Raúl Jiménez,' said Jorge. 'The DNA you gave me would probably have belonged to his son. Does that help you?'

'Interesting.'

'You might also be interested to know that your squad are on a high. Last night they arrested two building inspectors in Torremolinos, who they'd identified from those Lukyanov disks. They've already charged them with conspiring to cause an explosion,' said Jorge. 'This morning they picked up the owner of a small hotel in Almería, who also happened to be an electrician and was trained by the army in the use of explosives. He'll be arriving in Seville this afternoon. Ramírez has been trying to call you and Comisario Elvira is still very eager to know where you are. I've said nothing.'

Falcón hung up, called Consuelo. Darío was playing with his brothers and some friends in the pool.

'He seems untouched by it all,' she said, amazed. 'I was going to get Alicia to talk to him, but I'm not sure whether it will just make him unhappy.'

'See what Alicia says. You don't have to rush,' said Falcón.

He told her about the DNA match from Barakat to Raúl. Consuelo couldn't understand how Raúl Jiménez, her ex-husband, came to be Mustafa Barakat's father.

'The reason Raúl suddenly had to leave Morocco back in the fifties was because he'd made the twelve-year-old daughter of Abdullah Diouri Senior pregnant. Diouri Senior had demanded that Raúl marry the girl to preserve the family honour. Raúl couldn't because he was already married, so he fled. Diouri took revenge by kidnapping Raúl's youngest son, Arturo. And for whatever reason – guilt, or because he loved him – Diouri gave Arturo the same status as his own sons with his family name. So Arturo Jiménez became Yacoub Diouri.

'But because Diouri's twelve-year-old daughter had brought shame on to the family, *her* son by Raúl was not allowed to bear the family name. However Diouri Senior didn't totally reject him. The close ties between the Diouris and the Barakats meant that the boy was introduced into that family to become Mustafa Barakat.'

'That sort of knowledge in the wrong mind could breed a special kind of hatred,' said Consuelo.

'And how do you think Mustafa Barakat would feel about Yacoub Diouri?'

'Imagine the bitterness that poor girl must have felt at her own rejection for being defiled by Raúl, only to have to witness Yacoub's smooth integration into the Diouri family while her own son is kicked out.'

'Profile of a terrorist?'

Consuelo invited Javier to dinner that night, asked him to bring Abdullah.

Falcón drove out to the prison in Alcalá de Guadaira. He'd called ahead so Calderón was already waiting for him in a visiting room. He wasn't smoking. He had his hands clasped in front of him on the table to stop them from fidgeting. He still looked haggard, but not as reduced as he had been when Falcón had last seen him. The supreme self-confidence had not been recovered, but he seemed more solid.

'You've heard,' said Falcón.

'My lawyer came to see me yesterday,' said Calderón, nodding. 'I'm still going to face assault charges, but . . .'

He trailed off, looked up at the high barred window.

'You're going to get your life back.'

'In the end,' he said. 'But it'll be a different one. I'm going to see to that.'

'How's it been going with Alicia Aguado?'

'Hard,' said Calderón, leaning back, hooking his hands around his knee. 'I spend a lot of my day thinking about myself, and not much of it is good. You know, Alicia told me in our last session that it was rare for a male patient to turn on himself as comprehensively as I'd done. I told her: "This last week has been the longest sustained period of facing the truth that I've ever been through in my life." A lawyer speaks, Javier.'

They grunted laughter at each other.

'I also spend a lot of my time thinking about you. I feel I owe you an explanation.'

'It's not necessary, Esteban.'

'I know, but you started me on this journey with Alicia, and we have this curious relationship that's entwined with both Inés and Marisa. So I want to clarify a few things, if you can bear to listen to me. It's not going to make me look very pretty, but then you're getting used to that.'

They sat in silence for a moment while Calderón prepared himself.

'As you know, four years ago I nearly lost my career. I needed all my family connections, and Inés's, to maintain a foothold in the Edificio de los Juzgados. Inés was fantastic throughout. She was strong. I was weak. And, as you know from your murder cases, Javier, the weak man is full of self-hatred and develops a bottomless pit of savagery, which by rights he should unleash against himself, but inevitably he turns on the person closest to him.'

413

'Is that when it started?'

'The beatings? No. The hatred, yes. When Inés became my wife and the balance of power shifted in my favour, I started breaking her down with my extravagant philandering,' said Calderón. 'By the time that bomb went off on 6th June we were both primed for violence. By that I mean: I was ready to give it and she was ready to receive it. I was feeling sufficiently strong and angry, and she was sufficiently fragile and humiliated. I'm not sure there wasn't something sadomasochistic in the state of our relationship. When I came back from Marisa's that morning we could have had just another row, but this time she wanted it to be taken further. She goaded me, and I, inexcusably, complied.'

'*She* was goading *you* to violence?'

'It probably wasn't as clear as that in her mind; we'd shouted and screamed, thrown things at each other, and I suppose it was the only possible next step. You know how important Inés's public image was to her, she couldn't walk away from a second failed marriage. And I would have found it hard to split from her. What she wanted was for me to hit her, then for me to be filled with remorse, and in that softening she would bring us back together. I surprised her and myself. I didn't know I had that pent-up rage inside me.'

'Did you feel any remorse?'

'At the time, no. I realize this sounds pathetic, but I felt immensely powerful,' said Calderón. 'To have beaten a fifty-kilo woman into terrified submission should have appalled me, but it didn't. Then, later, after Marisa told me about her confrontation with Inés in the Murillo Gardens, I became incensed once again and gave Inés an even worse beating. Still no remorse. Just madness and rage.'

'What happened after that beating?'

'I walked the streets telling myself it was all over. There could be no going back.'

414

'But you already knew how difficult it would be for you to split from Inés,' said Falcón. 'So did it occur to you then . . . that little joke you had with Marisa about the "bourgeois solution" to complicated divorce?'

'Yes, it did. Not quite in that way. I was in a rage. I just wanted to get rid of Inés.'

'And what? Fall into the arms of Marisa?'

'No,' he said, shaking his head.

'Why did you give Inés the most savage beating of all for badmouthing a woman you didn't care about?'

'In calling Marisa the whore with the cigar, Inés had pointed out to me what I thought of her,' said Calderón. 'Marisa was an artist, but that never interested me. Throughout our relationship I treated her like a whore. Much of our sex was like that. And Marisa despised me. In fact, looking back on it, she hated me. And, I have to admit, my behaviour was loathsome.'

'So, what are you saying about Inés and Marisa now?'

'You know when you came to see me last I told you that Alicia had accused me of hating women. Me? Esteban Calderón. The greatest lover of women in the Edificio de los Juzgados? Yes, well, that's what I found out: I treated Marisa like a whore and Ines worse than a dog. And that's what I've been finding hard to face up to.'

Falcón nodded, stared at the floor.

'The first real glimmer of the truth that I could remember, one that really shook me to the core, was when I regained consciousness after my faint to find Inés dead in the kitchen. That was when I saw the damage from my earlier beatings and it was what made me panic, because I knew my evident abuse of her would make me the prime suspect in her murder,' said Calderón. 'Whenever I'd recalled that night I'd always concentrated on my lack of intent to murder her.'

'Because that would be your defence in court,' said Falcón.

'Exactly, but what came back to me during my sessions with Alicia was, having come into the apartment, seen the light on in the kitchen and been annoyed at the possibility of another confrontation and wished her gone from my life, I then saw her lying there in that vast pool of her own blood. That was when it came to me that *I might as well have killed her*. To see her there, in such hideously bright light, was like being confronted with the image of my own guilt. I fainted at the thought and sight of it.'

In the early evening Falcón went to the Jefatura. The whole squad was in the office. The atmosphere was upbeat. They'd had two very successful days. Serrano put a cold beer in his hand.

'Guess what?' said Ramírez. 'Elvira wants to see you.'

'You'd think this guy doesn't have my phone number,' said Falcón.

'He's going to reinstate you.'

'I doubt it.'

'First of all, Spinola,' said Ramírez. 'Tell him, Emilio.'

'We went through his apartment and found seventy-eight grams of cocaine, forty grams of heroin and a hundred and fifty grams of cannabis resin,' said Pérez.

'So he's a drug user,' said Falcón, shrugging.

'*And* . . . copies of all the rival bids in the Isla de la Cartuja development.'

'Which have also been found in the possession of Antonio Ramos, Horizonte's head of construction,' finished Ramírez.

'That was lucky,' said Falcón, nodding, taking a pull of the beer.

'The Juez Decano appointed the instructing judge, who was present throughout the search of the apartment, and he's totally accepted our findings.'

'What about Margarita?' Falcón asked Ferrera.

'She's in hospital in Málaga,' she said. 'She'd been given

416

a very severe beating by one of Leonid Revnik's men when they found that Vasili Lukyanov had gone to Seville.'

'Was she his girlfriend?'

'Not exactly. She was special to him, that's all she would admit, but she was in very bad shape. They're going to call me when she's recovered enough to talk properly. Broken jaw, left arm and two cracked ribs.'

'El Pulmón?'

'He's identified Sokolov. We're in discussion over the knifing and the illegal firearm.'

'And what are they going to do to Mark Flowers?'

'They're not going to press charges for killing Yuri Donstov, but he's finished here in Seville,' said Ramírez. 'They're putting him on a plane back to the States, and he'll face a disciplinary hearing there.'

'And the big question for me,' said Falcón. 'What about Cortland Fallenbach? Was he involved in the original conspiracy?'

'They've taken away his passport,' said Ramírez, 'and he's got a team of lawyers fighting to get it back. I don't know. Without Lucrecio Arenas and César Benito around, that might be a difficult thing to prove.'

The phone rang. Baena took it, held the phone to his chest.

'Guess what?'

'All right,' said Falcón. 'I'm going up there. Tell him I just wanted to see the most important people first. Great work everybody.'

Comisario Elvira didn't keep him waiting. His secretary offered him coffee. This almost never happened.

'I'm writing the press release,' said Elvira.

'What's that for?'

'The final charges have been made relating to the planting of the Seville bomb.'

'The *final* charges?'

417

'All right, the people who planted the device have been apprehended and they're going to face justice.'

'What about the chain of command from the suspects we've had in custody since June, through to Horizonte and I4IT?'

'We can't make any announcements relating to that.'

'Are you going to work on it?'

'We'll have to take a view on that,' said Elvira. 'Anyway, this evening there's going to be a televised press conference. The mayor and Comisario Lobo want you to be there to read out the statement that I'm preparing for you.'

'I'm suspended from duty pending a full inquiry,' said Falcón.

'You were reinstated last night when we determined Alejandro Spinola's involvement in leaking information about the Isla de la Cartuja development project.'

'What about my unapproved improvisation in the Hotel La Berenjena?'

'Look, Javier, I've really got to get down to these press releases and statements,' said Elvira. 'I'd like you to join me in my car in an hour's time to go to the state parliament.'

Falcón nodded, left the room. The secretary brought the coffee. He drank it standing in front of her. He went back down to the Homicide office.

'There's going to be a press conference in the state parliament in about an hour and a half's time,' said Falcón. 'I'd like you all to listen to that.'

He went into his office and was about to close the door when he saw the wall chart. He lifted it off its hook and took it back into the outer office.

'You can strip this down and file it,' he said. 'We're finished with it now.'

The phone rang. It was the scrambled line used by the CNI. He went into his office, closed the door, answered it

'I got a full report from my agents in Fès,' said Pablo.

418

'And Alfonso has briefed me on the aftermath. You got the boy.'

'He's in good shape, considering. Doesn't remember a thing about it . . . for the moment,' said Falcón. 'How have the Moroccans taken it?'

'They got a call from the Saudis as well, so . . . they're philosophical. Oil has a very loud voice,' said Pablo. 'Still, all is not lost. The Germans have uncovered a network related to Barakat's export business there. The Moroccans are pursuing two very strong leads into the GICM from other connections they've made to Barakat. There was also an Algerian link. And MI5 are working on that cell the French told them about, which, it seems, was connected to Barakat's carpet business in London. So, although we didn't get the man . . .'

'What about you?' asked Falcón. 'Did you get anything out of it?'

'Yacoub had left all the details of the GICM logistics cell he was using on the Costa del Sol with the Saudis,' said Pablo. 'And two more he'd heard about in Madrid and Barcelona. We're all happy.'

'I'm glad.'

'I wanted to ask you about Abdullah,' said Pablo.

'He had to have twelve stitches in his shoulder . . .'

'Would he be interested in helping us?'

'You? How could he help you? He's been exposed.'

'Maybe and maybe not,' said Pablo. 'I just wanted to know how he'd feel about, you know, playing the game.'

'That letter has left him a lot to think about,' said Falcón.

'And you, Javier?'

'Me?' said Falcón. 'The amateur?'

'Think about it,' said Pablo, and hung up.

Falcón went to the window, looked out over the car park in the late evening light. House martins were ducking and diving, weaving in and out, scribbling the air with their antics. He felt empty and immensely lonely. Police work did this to him. When it was all over there was nothing left but disappointment. Mystery gone, quest terminated. All that remained was an overwhelming sense of loss and pointlessness.

As he stared into the inane ranks of cars, each within their neat lines of demarcation, he found himself searching for a reason. And what came to him was an image that had first come to him as he'd driven back from Fès: Yacoub in the middle of the ocean on a small boat in complete darkness, with the power of sacrifice in his hands to rescue his son from fanatics and, in doing so, restore some nobility to the human race.

He sat and let the world grow dark around him until Ferrera knocked, leaned in and told him that Elvira's car was ready. He went down, got into the back seat with the Comisario, who handed him the press release and his statement. He read them and looked out at the lights of the city and the faceless people going about their business.

The press conference was packed. It hadn't heaved like this since the day Comisario Lobo had announced that Calderón had been found trying to dispose of his wife's body in the Guadalquivir river and was being replaced as the instructing judge in the Seville bombing.

The long tedious process started. Everybody had to have their say and bask a little in the afterglow of success: Lobo, Elvira, the mayor. Normally, the Juez Decano Spinola would have been there, but, given the circumstances, that did not seem appropriate. Falcón tuned out of the proceedings, looked back at the avid faces staring up at him, blinked at the flash photography. His turn came. It was the last word, but in this case, the least important. He read Elvira's prepared statement and then added his own:

'Nobody in this room should forget that everything that has been said here today could only come about as a result

420

of some extraordinary and, in many cases, unpaid dedication, from people who are unknown, never seen and rarely heard. They work tirelessly, under dangerous circumstances, to keep the people of Seville safe, removing murderers and gangsters from the streets so that men, women and children can live in this city without fear. For once, I think, their names should be heard. They are: Inspector José Luis Ramírez, Sub-Inspector Emilio Pérez, Detective Julio Baena, Detective Carlos Serrano and Detective Cristina Ferrera. And I'd like to thank them all.'

He sat down. Comisario Elvira was annoyed at the departure from the script. A couple of journalists clapped, four more joined in and then the room rose as one and applauded the unseen and the unheard. Elvira smiled and basked in some partially deserved adulation.

As they filed into the mayor's private rooms where drinks were being served, Falcón asked for a quick word with Comisario Elvira. It lasted a matter of two minutes, they parted and rejoined the gathering. A dinner had been planned afterwards and Falcón was duly invited, but he politely declined. The powers that be were quite glad about that. The presence of the taciturn Inspector Jefe seemed to imply some unspoken criticism.

Falcón went home. He showered and changed. Abdullah declined Consuelo's dinner invitation. It would be a celebration and he was still in mourning. Falcón drove out to Santa Clara, where they had a family dinner. Consuelo's sister's family were there as well. It was a welcome home for Darío. Consuelo had baked him a cake. It felt like his birthday. They ate and drank. People left. Others went to bed.

At a little after one in the morning Consuelo and Falcón lay naked in each other's arms, their contours smoothed out by a light sheet.

'I want you to come and live with me, Javier,' said Consuelo.

'I will,' said Falcón. 'But it might have to be somewhere different.'

'What's wrong with here?'

'Nothing,' he said. 'It's just that tonight I resigned as Inspector Jefe del Grupo de Homocidios de Sevilla.'

'Did you jump or were you pushed?'

'I jumped,' he said.

'That's a big jump. When did you decide?'

'It first occurred to me when we drove back after that night with the Russians. Then, when I went out to kill Mustafa Barakat, I realized how much I'd changed and that I couldn't do the work any more,' he said. 'You should be happy. I know you never liked it.'

'I can't pretend I'm sad,' she said. 'What are you going to do with yourself?'

'I haven't got that far.'

'Sell your house. Live on the proceeds. Paint?'

'Maybe I'll learn how to sail a yacht,' he said, squeezing her shoulder, '. . . so you'll still have me.'

'We could live by the sea in Valencia,' she said. 'The estate agent called again today.'

'I can already smell the paella on the beach.'

And, rather than thoughts of the future, he remembered what he'd done before coming out that night. He'd found that dried husk of a plant skulking in its dark corner under the gallery, taken it by the scruff of the neck and marched it to the bin.